Praise for *Red Mountain*

In *Red Mountain,* Charles Entrekin writes with an unflinching yet poetic eye, exploring the parallel courses of a nation and a young man forced into maturity. As America's South is plunged into racial insanity, Eddie Anderson must grow beyond the confines of his narrow upbringing; his coming of age includes the tragic descent into madness of his beloved wife. A gripping and enlightening read from someone who lived and breathed and wrote his way through one of America's most tumultuous times.

Sands Hall, *Catching Heaven*

Charles Entrekin, in *Red Mountain,* rediscovers an important and brave time in recent history, but in a neglected territory; that is, the early 1960s in a backward Birmingham, Alabama (and later in the more familiar terrain of a bohemian New York City). He describes not only the racism and meanness of the old South, and the squalor and the intoxicating intellectual excitement of New York City; but also, throughout, the recklessness that was so essential to this time of innocence. Every detail is so right, this must have been lived experience. If this wasn't lived experience, it is certainly rendered with a quiet artistic ferocity that makes it seem too real to be made-up.

The central story is a love story, of a young man's stalwart fidelity to a young woman, the sort of young woman described in sentimental novels as the "doomed girl living under the curse of a forbidden love." But there's no artificial sentimentality in this story, where the young woman's love truly is of a forbidden sort, and where she is genuinely doomed. Entrekin's narrator practices a restraint—a restraint of judgment, as well as a restraint in prose style—that provides an extraordinary, tender clarity and a wisdom for the illumination of events that, in their time, had little of clarity or wisdom. *Red Mountain* shows how we're all capable of transcendence and self-transcendence, even in the worst circumstances and among our most hectic mistakes.

Louis B. Jones, *California's Over*

Red Mountain

Birmingham, Alabama, 1965

Red Mountain

Birmingham, Alabama, 1965

a novel

Charles Entrekin

EL LEÓN LITERARY ARTS

Berkeley, California

*Author's note: The characters in this book, their
motivations, and their interactions are the work of my
imagination, though the historical events in this book
did, in fact, take place.*

El León Literary Arts is a nonprofit public benefit
corporation established to extend the array of voices
essential to a democracy's arts and education.

El León Literary Arts is distributed
by Small Press Distribution, Inc.,
800-869-7553; www.spdbooks.org.
orders@spd.org

El León books are available on Amazon.com
El León web site: www.elleonliteraryarts.org

Publisher: Thomas Farber
Managing editor: Kit Duane
Cover photograph: Heather Sharit
Cover design: Brook Design Group
Text design: Sara Glaser

ISBN 978-0-9795285-0-7

Library of Congress Number 2007938395

For my children,
Demian, Caleb, Benjamin, Nathan, and Katherine

Part One

*Very few people are capable of being
independent; it is a privilege of the
strong. And whoever tries it, however
justified, without having to, proves that
he is probably not only strong but bold
to the point of complete recklessness. For
he walks into a labyrinth; he increases
a thousandfold the dangers which are
inherent in life anyway. And not the
smallest of his dangers is that no one can
witness how and where he loses his way,
falls into solitude, or is torn to pieces by
some troglodytic minotaur of conscience.*

F. NIETZSCHE, *Beyond Good and Evil*

Prologue

That night outside Memphis
the Mississippi mosquitoes bid you goodbye
as you turn in your mind the meaning of escape,
almost, you wanted to lie, you're innocent
if you don't go back. The child asleep,
your red car packed, you douse the fire
and drive out fast.[1]

Looking back, I now can see that when I graduated from Woodside High School in Birmingham, Alabama, in 1959, I believed in the South, in my family, in my culture, and in Plato's faith that God is truth, and that truth is divine. In the fall of 1966, seven years later, my faith shaken, I bid good-bye to Birmingham. I stuffed everything I owned (typewriter, pots, pans, dishes—all carefully interleaved between bedding and blankets) into a large cardboard box, strapped it to the top of my maroon Corvair, and left for California with my one-year-old daughter, never to return.

Remembering those years in Birmingham, I think of the smog from the steel mills and how every downtown building was coated in its oily, dirty, brown residue, and I think of the history of this town that calls itself the "Pittsburgh of the South," the "Magic City" because it "grew up overnight" to support the war effort with its steel mills. I think of the infamy of the city that bred the bigots that bombed a church and murdered four black children. I think of how we lived our young lives in the midst of all the infamy surrounding us and how we breathed it in and accepted it like it was a kind of weather, not realizing what impact such weather would have on us all.

But in the end I think of Vulcan, a statue erected as a tribute to the steel industry. Cast in solid iron, he holds in his right hand an electric torch to announce the city's traffic fatalities, red for death, and green for life. Vulcan, rising high above Red Mountain, the second largest statue in the United States, painted silver against the elements, stands somehow inextricably for what Birmingham fails to understand about itself. The city fathers must not have researched just who this Vulcan was. Would they have accepted his statue if they had known that Vulcan was the Roman god of cuckolds? Yes, he was the smithy of the gods, just as the steel barons were told, but he was also a lame god who, according to the Gnostics, was a forebear of the Christian concept of the devil.

In the Birmingham where I was born, on the eastern side of town, under the shadow of Vulcan's Red Mountain, in the summer when one of those heavy, near-tropical storms would arrive bringing us relief from the heat, it would, at first, rain big heavy drops that would splash down on our sidewalk, rising back up as steam. Then, after a while, with a crack of thunder, it would begin to pour down in buckets. And after that, the churning red water would come charging unchecked down the mountain, carrying iron rust and mud from the abandoned mines, and it would create an instant swirling pond around the gutter that sat at the foot of our driveway on Ninth Avenue South.

Sometimes, when those heavy rains arrived, my brother Bobby and I would rush to the big picture window at the front of our house and look out over the back of my mother's flowery, plastic-covered couch, staring out at the downpour, watching as the deluge overwhelmed the storm drain at the bottom of our hill. Then, as soon as our street corner was flooded, Bobby and I would take off our clothes and run with barefooted joy across the lawn, out into the street. And then, the heavy rain plastering our hair to our heads, we would march naked up the black-topped street in the downpour. Up to the top of the hill. And shout "Geronimo." And leap into the rushing, red current overflowing the gutters. And we would be caught up in the torrent, swept away, our skinny little bodies flying down the hill's slippery slope, turning and tumbling all the way to the bottom, crash-landing in the warm water that was backing up from the drain at the foot of our driveway.

This was a part of the Birmingham of my youth, circa 1950. This was the white, working-class side of town. This was a place and a time when naked children could play in the gutters in the rain. People got along. Neighbors looked after each other. There were few pretensions. In this neighborhood, just south of East Lake, our house, like most of the other houses, was a one-story, boxed-in rectangle. Ours was covered in dark-green shingles.

As you climbed up from the valley floor toward the hills you could find the beginning of a new wave of more expensive houses. These had larger yards, and they sat back from the road with a rich, sub-urban primness, Middle American ranch style. These homes had neatly trimmed yards and white picket fences, but there was still that ambient feeling of poverty lurking nearby, of the possibility that just over the next ridge you could stumble across a shantytown, with abandoned, broken-down pickups rusting in somebody's front yard, or illegal whiskey stills hidden back along dirt roads, or that some-where deep in the woods, across a slow gurgling creek, there would be a black family's unpainted, wooden house perched up on the top of corner-brick legs, with mangy dogs under the front porch, asleep, keeping out of the heat.

In this Birmingham of my childhood, in my family, and in those families around us, there were a few things that everyone could agree on: *If you don't have anything nice to say, don't say anything at all.* Civil Rights could not be discussed in public. And neither could such topics as premarital sex, atheism, divorce, or homosexuality, which was considered a perversion beyond redemption. But times were changing and by the end of 1959 anyone who was willing to look could see that life-altering changes were coming. It was just that we didn't talk about them. We breathed in the news about the attacks on segregation and the perversions of Northern outside agitators; we attended church; we listened to our ministers; and we went about our business. Some of us understood what was happening better than others, like the Reverend Martin Luther King, who told the first black student to integrate the University of Alabama, "Thank God there are some people who can rise above the old and broken-down thoughts of their parents, who can rise above their background and their heritage." He was talking about Autherine Lucy. Surrounded by troops, with Governor George Wallace standing in the doorway to stop her, she walked right past him into the history books, a brave young woman determined to get an education.

It was during the spring of 1960 that I met Chrissy Lee Williams. Nineteen years old, I had just completed my obligatory six months' active duty at Fort Jackson, South Carolina, with the U.S. Army, for the Alabama National Guard, and I had made my first life-changing decision. I had decided to do what no one in my family had ever done before—go to college. I made that decision because of what I saw in the army. The college-student draftees were different from all the rest of us. They seemed, well, sophisticated, as if they knew something the rest of us didn't. They knew how not to be taken advantage of, how not to become a victim of the army's system. For my entire six months of service I struggled to get along. I tried to be invisible, to blend in, to avoid anyone even learning my name. Because I had seen what could happen. I had watched while other uneducated eighteen-year-olds had tried to buck the system. They failed to understand what could happen. Some went crazy from the harassment or ended up in jail for drunken indiscretions. And a few committed suicide, two in our barracks. One hanged himself from a crossbeam a few rows down from my bunk. We were told that these were accidents, and we were warned not to talk about them. For my part, I chose to hide by bunking with the Puerto Ricans. They barely spoke English, and I had studied Spanish in high school. So they tolerated my living with them in exchange for my willingness to help them understand what the drill instructor was always shouting about.

So, after my six months' active duty, I hitchhiked back to Alabama and began to plan for my college career. And that's when I met her. It happened on a visit to my high school to talk to an administrator about applying to college. There a friend set up a blind date for me with a graduating senior. I was to meet her after the last night of the high-school production of the musical, *Oklahoma!* Her name was Chrissy Lee Williams, and she had the part of Ado Annie, "a gal who cain't say no."

The evening of the performance, I sat in the audience, enchanted. Whenever Chrissy was on stage I watched only her, her every movement. She stayed completely in her cowgirl character, whirling excitedly through her numbers. I sat in the back of the dark auditorium, an anonymous admirer, hoping that my application of Clearasil cream was sufficiently obscuring a new outbreak of acne on my face. But as the music, the story line, the sheer energy washed over me, I forgot about how my big ears stood out, exposed by my U.S. Army buzz haircut, and I forgot about how out of place I felt surrounded by the cheering parents and screaming students in my old high school. And I began to put behind me the anger, the loneliness, and the frustrations that had been my life for the past six months: a life of being told when to sleep, when to eat, when to speak; a life of mastering only those things the army had to teach: how to kill without thinking about it, with guns, with bayonets, with bare hands.

After the play was over, after introductions, Chrissy and I left the auditorium and walked across the lawn under the big American flag waving in a spotlight, arm-in-arm, to my just-washed-and-polished 1947, blue-gray, four-door Plymouth. As we pulled out of the high-school parking lot onto First Avenue South, Chrissy, still flushed with the breathlessness of post-performance energy, bounced her way across the front seat and settled in right next to me.

"Well, did you like it?" she asked.

"You were terrific," I congratulated her, and pointed the car toward the Atlanta Highway and one of the local hangouts, an A&W Root Beer drive-in.

After we parked under a green and white striped awning and ordered, she placed her hand on my shoulder and grinned. Her touch was electric. I was stunned by her star energy, and I found I could not stop looking at her: flushed red cheeks, soft brown hair, and bright eyes brimming over with excitement. Her smile seemed to light up the inside of my car. And for a long moment I sat there, awkwardly not talking. But then the moment passed, and, without waiting for an invitation, this smiling, brown-eyed girl with perfect pitch moved into my life and took charge.

"Well, Eddie Andersen, Mister Blue-eyed Man, so you're just out of the military, aren't you? How long were you in for? What're you doing now?"

"Six months. It was awful. I'm planning to apply to college. Mrs. Johnston at the high school said my grades were good enough to get in most anywhere. So now I'm looking for a college and a summer job."

"You mean you haven't applied yet?"

"No."

"And you don't know where you want to go?"

"No."

"Okay, so let's consider your options…"

She had already applied to college. Her plans were set. After she talked about the whole process for a while, I thought, *Okay, I like her; maybe I'll just follow her lead…*

My plan had been an unformed, amorphous idea in my head. Now as I leaned back and listened, I knew suddenly that I was really going to do it. Chrissy knew just what steps I needed to take to make it happen. I was going to go to college. And the more we talked, the more I could barely contain my excitement.

"Where have you been all my life?" I asked.

She leaned back in a staged look of surprise, then grinned, and, mockingly batted her eyelashes at me.

"That's for me to know, and for you to find out," she said.

She felt dangerous and challenging, and real.

Earlier I had watched her be a cowgirl, sing and dance across the stage. Now she seemed to be an entirely different person, talking meticulously about different colleges and their entrance requirements. She spoke in rapid-fire bursts as she reached out and touched my hand to make a point. Dazzled, barely listening, I smiled and nodded in agreement. Then she reached over me, picked up one of my French fries off the tray, our heads almost touching, and began explaining confidently why I should apply to Crestview College, her choice. But abruptly, right in the middle of her sentence, she stopped. Leaned back casually as if she were reconsidering. And then, taking on the voice of her character, Ado Annie, she said, "So, before we go any further Mister-New-Man-in-My-Life, I need to know—do you believe in God or don't you?"

That challenging question took me by surprise, and I don't remember what I said in response. I just remember feeling that whatever I was about to say was going to be inadequate. I thought about what I'd seen during my stint in the U.S. Army, about the lies and the suicides, and I thought about my doubts about what I had been told in Sunday school, about some unknowable, vengeful, invisible, omniscient being called "God," but I also wanted to impress her. So I stammered around a bit and then finally told her about my doubts, and that, as it turned out, was what impressed her.

[1]

In 1959, the Methodist Laymen's Union met
in Birmingham and resolved that integration
was "a betrayal of unborn generations and
a monstrous crime against civilization." [2]

In the fall of 1960 a young man I never met was sitting in on an organizational meeting of the Methodist Laymen's Union in Birmingham. In my imagination I can see how a sudden, new feeling of discomfort was building in him. Sweat must have trickled down the back of his neck as he twisted his hands nervously, pocketed his asthma inhaler, and took out his handkerchief. Then, pulling his coat down to get rid of the wrinkles, he straightened his tie, removed his glasses and stood up. For a long time no one noticed him. He coughed and patiently waited.

Until this day in history Thomas C. Reeves had been pretty much invisible. He had always followed a set path and done the right thing. He was a Phi Beta Kappa honors student at Crestview College, a small liberal arts teachers' college perched on a sweeping green hillside, and he paid for his education by serving as a lay minister for a nearby Methodist church. But on this day Tommy changed his life forever. He raised his hand and waved it. A rivulet of sweat ran down his side. His hand-held handkerchief fluttered like a small white bird in the stiflingly hot room. He had never felt quite so alone.

In due course, smiling across the assembly at the tall anxious young man before him, the elderly president of the Laymen's Union held up one hand and called on the members for quiet. Attending this meeting were many of the power people of the city: judges, church ministers, city council members, real-estate brokers, and especially one man everyone knew as Sheriff Bull Connor. The proposed topic of conversation before them was how to handle the racial unrest and the problem situations brought about by the political activists and outside agitators who were involved with "illegal activities." The majority had seemed to be in agreement. They would resist this assault by every legal means possible.

The president asked Tommy if he had something to say, and the members all twisted in their seats and faced to the rear. But then, in a ripple of discord across the still surface of an ordinary afternoon, as everyone turned to look at him, one could sense that here was the beginning of some small trouble surfacing. Tommy nodded, yes; he did have something to say. He stepped into the aisle to gather himself, then politely thanked the president for recognizing him, thanked everyone for giving him a chance to speak, and then he began to talk, very quietly, slowly, confidently. And as he gathered volume he became taller as once again he understood what he was, a practicing preacher. And Thomas C. Reeves, a twenty-year-old bespectacled student, pulled himself into his most powerful self and told the assembled members that what they were planning was wrong, that it was un-Christian, that Christianity did not allow for slavery, and that they should all abandon these plans and unite together to say that Christians stood for love and compassion, not for hate and the inequities of segregation. At the end of his speech, he spread out his arms to the assembly and waited, confident he would be heard and understood.

At first there was silence, then chaos erupted as the anger in the room exploded in a cacophony of raised voices, until finally, like distinct raindrops heard in the midst of a downpour, isolated threats pierced Thomas's consciousness, and, for the first time, he realized that he might be in grave danger.

"Who does he think he is?"

"Outside agitator!"

"Communist!"

"Traitor to his race!"

"Get his name!"

The temperature in the room increased dramatically as everyone seemed to be speaking at once. The echo from the president's gavel sounded like rifle shots. Then a few burly sheriffs' deputies signaled to each other and started threading their way through the unruly crowd toward him.

Thomas saw them coming and fled down the aisle.

After he jumped into his car and drove off, his pulse slowed, and for a short while he thought it was over. Maybe he was imagining the whole thing. Maybe he should go back and talk with them. But then he discovered several cars cutting across traffic and rapidly closing in behind him. So he stepped on the gas and took the next turn at real speed. Luck stayed with him after that, and he made it back to campus. He drove straight up the hill, through the gates onto Campus Drive, and parked in front of the home of Henry King Stanford, the president of his college, the only man he felt he could trust.

Together, they stood in his arched entrance way and faced the accumulating crowd of police officers and strangers. A number of unmarked cars mixed in with police cruisers filled the circular driveway. Finally a heavyset man in a suit that would not quite close over his belly stepped forward. He argued that Tommy was wanted for questioning concerning his involvement with outside agitators. Dr. Stanford stepped forward, pushed Tommy somewhat behind him, and asked to see the warrants. There weren't any.

The detective took out his badge, showed it, and reached toward Tommy's arm, claiming the department only wanted to talk to him. Dr. Stanford stepped between them again and spoke calmly, quietly, saying that without a warrant for his arrest Tommy remained the college's responsibility, and he could not in good conscience release him into their care without consulting Tommy's parents and the college. He then turned his back on the detective and ushered Tommy into his home and closed the door.

That day the police left empty-handed and, for a time, there was a sense of relief and even joy. Courage and faith and friendship had prevailed. But there was a strong wind blowing. Meetings were being held. Anger was rising. Within a week's time Thomas lost his job as minister of the small Methodist Church, and approximately a year later Dr. Stanford was no longer president of the college.

But on that day, because of Thomas Reeves, Crestview College achieved a notoriety it did not want. And it was on that same day that Chrissy and I came to visit the college. We toured the campus, the bookstore and cafeteria, and visited the neo-classical buildings that formed the Quadrangle. Afterwards, we sat on a grassy knoll overlooking the president's home, and it was from this vantage point that we watched the sudden arrival of police cars, the strange but obvious confrontation, and finally the slamming of car doors and the speedy, tire-screeching departures. We looked at each other and wondered what the ruckus was about. We didn't know Thomas C. Reeves. We were unaware of the events that were unfolding around us. We knew only that the sun was shining, the campus was beautiful, and that we wanted to begin our college careers here. Together.

[2]

My father and mother grew up during the Depression in large families: nine children in my father's, eleven in my mother's. At seventeen, my mother escaped the tyrannical rule of her Methodist father by running away with the most dangerous, good-looking boy she could find. Neither of them finished high school. They had me and then World War II intervened. Over the next few years my Dad would return home from the war, I'd get kicked out of my mother's bed, and then he'd go away again, and before long I'd have another sibling. After the war, I used to plead with my mother to send him away again, but she never did. The deal my mother and father made was: he made the money; she provided meals, childcare, and sex. So we were stuck with him, my mother and I, and eventually my five brothers and sisters.

My early childhood summers were spent out-of-doors in the woods surrounding our backyard until one summer the construction of a new highway started at the end of our street. And that was when we discovered there were colored children nearby. That summer, when they made the initial cuts through our hillside hideouts, they sliced right through our forest, our street, and our imaginations. The woods we had played in were gone. Instead of a tangled brown and green forest, our neighborhood playground became the construction zone of the new Atlanta Highway, complete with tractors, caterpillars, earthmovers, and the steep banks of raw red earth that framed the freshly cut bed for the new highway. In the daytime the giant yellow machines belonged to the workers, but after the workers went home, in the sweltering heat of early evenings, amidst the smoke pots with thick black wicks, they belonged to us, to our neighborhood. Or so we thought. Until one evening we discovered there were other kids we'd never seen before, colored kids from a suddenly revealed neighborhood across from us.

Colored kids were different from us somehow, but we didn't know what that difference was supposed to be. No one had ever said. We didn't know if we were supposed to play with them or not.

So we did.

We threw mud balls at them.

They threw mud balls at us.

We reorganized our games around a new principle: them against us.

Each evening we became neighborhood armies with reconnaissance teams, supply lines for making mud balls, and then we made forays into each other's territory in surprise attacks.

This went on for weeks.

We began to know each other's names, laugh and wave before going home to our mothers and dinner.

But then World War II ended and Dad returned home to stay, and we moved away to a new neighborhood, to an all-white neighborhood on the eastern side of town, to Ninth Avenue South, just below a fire tower at the foot of Red Mountain. And then everything changed, and our family, year by year, was gradually forced to adjust to having a father around all the time. At first we thought it would be great, that we would get used to him, but we hadn't counted on Dad's ongoing fits of rage and violence. Like the time when my younger brother, Bobby, without understanding the consequences, left school without permission. He and a few friends, during his lunch period, had an idea. They would go over to East Lake and collect baby turtles for their classroom's empty aquarium. When Bobby and his friends showed up missing, the principal called our home, and Dad, home for lunch, answered the phone. Bobby was suspended, and that evening after work, Dad, convinced that Bobby had been "up to no good," refused to listen to his explanations and beat him so severely with a belt that he was unable to go back to school for a week.

But we learned how to avoid our father. For years, as young children, if we heard him in the house during his lunch hour—he had taken a job as a cable repairman for Southern Bell Telephone Company—we hid in closets, whispering to each other, and listened in the dark until we heard the closing of the back door and the starting up of his big, green telephone truck. If we were alone and couldn't avoid him, we tried to remain silent until Mother showed up. She always seemed able to handle him.

And so it went until one day Mother returned home from the hospital and went into her bedroom and began crying. Dad followed in behind her, shut the front door, walked into the kitchen, poured himself a cup of black coffee, and stood stock still, not drinking it, but staring blankly outwards at the big oak tree in our backyard. Our mother almost never cried. Troubles seemed not to affect her; she'd always quietly taken charge and managed the situation without any fanfare, leaving my father standing around looking confused, his hands stuffed deep in his pockets. We were all shocked. But we didn't ask questions, and it was not until many months later that we learned that she had been diagnosed with tic douloureux (an extremely painful, uncontrollable throbbing next to her right temple caused by an exposed, damaged nerve circuit) and Parkinson's disease. For years, we didn't understand any of that medical explanation. All we really understood was that Dad was getting meaner, that Mom was getting quieter, and that our house, usually the chaotic hub of our family's comings and goings, had suddenly become a no-play zone. And Mom, never complaining, still trying bravely to manage her situation, her shaking fingers caressing the right side of her face, sometimes didn't come out of her bedroom. And we could hear her moving about in that darkened room in her dressing gown, the soft sound of her collapsed bedroom slippers shuffling back and forth over the hardwood floor.

But time passed, and suddenly I had graduated from high school, served six months active duty with the U.S. Army, and decided I wanted to go to college. My life seemed filled with opportunity. I had met a girl I really liked, and I had landed a part-time job at a bookstore, Smith & Hardwick, in downtown Birmingham.

I felt my future like a downstream current, and I was ready to flow with it.

So the afternoon after Smith & Hardwick had hired me, with my letter of acceptance from Crestview College in my pocket, I returned home and found Dad's big, green Southern Bell truck blocking our driveway. I parked in the street, dashed into the house, and blurted out that I had been accepted at Crestview College.

Mother, her face thin, her cheekbones visible, her hair now cut short and going completely gray, with hands shaking as she held her trembling fingertips up to her right temple, smiled distractedly, worriedly, and spoke softly as she leaned against the kitchen bar for support.

"Well, Eddie, if that's what you want to do."

Dad, in his work clothes, wearing a fat leather belt of telephone tools around his growing beer belly, still as handsome as he was dangerous, with straight black hair slicked back with strong smelling hair tonic, turned suddenly with that scary look of his, that tight-jawed containment of his rage.

"Why you want to go to college?"

Having been unexpectedly hit too many times as a child, I always stood a little distance from him, but, even so, I found myself taking a step backwards.

"Because...I...want to be a teacher."

"Why don't you get a real job?" he snapped. "You know I could get you on with the phone company. You could be making real money."

I spoke slowly, choosing my words carefully.

"I don't want to work for the phone company, Dad. That's your thing. I want to get a college degree. I want to make something of myself."

"Bullshit." He looked at me disgustedly.

Mother, in her nightgown and slippers, softly countered, "Now, Charlie, don't talk like that."

He glared at her a moment, then turned back to me.

"The communists are in charge. They're the ones who run all these colleges. All they want to do is teach you to love faggots and niggers and Jews and hate your own people! Besides, the only reason you want to go to college is because you're lazy and you don't want to work."

We stared at each other for a long moment until finally, looking like he had decided to dump the whole matter in a garbage can, he stood up and said, "I've got to go back to work."

"Dad, I've made up my mind."

He waited impatiently.

"I'm going to go to college."

Turning away, his hands swinging beside him like a gunslinger's, he pushed open the screen door and shouted back over his shoulder, "Fine, do what you want, but don't expect any help from me!"

The screen door slammed shut behind him.

"Don't worry," I said quietly to his retreating form, "I'm not planning to ask you for anything."

Standing alone in the wake of his leaving, Mom and I listened as the truck roared into life. Together we watched him back out of the driveway: a green Southern Bell bucket truck, heavy, ponderous, mechanical, the big white lift bucket swaying as he rounded the corner and passed out of sight.

[3]

My freshman year, I paid for my college tuition in part by selling all the fishing and hunting gear I had accumulated throughout my life. My shotguns and shells, a twelve gauge and a sixteen; my rifles, a twenty-two with telescopic sight and a .30-30; my tackle box with everything including weights and lures; my spinning reels and rods; my boots and waders. I didn't know it then, but I was leaving one kind of life for another. I was ready for the future, and I didn't care to look back.

College was not like high school. For me Woodside High had been about football and cheerleaders and avoiding the gangs that patrolled the hallways; the High Toppers, the Deuces Wild. No one ever spoke about going to college. The teachers were occupied with crowd control: the students were busy discovering their place in the social order of things, locating the safety net of belonging to cliques, or gangs, and making out with the opposite sex. As an introverted, skinny, high-school freshman (and winner of the public library's award for reading the most books over summer vacation), I thought, when an English teacher gave our class the option of writing either a critical essay or an original poem: *Hey, a no-brainer, a poem will be everybody's choice.* But, as it turned out, I was the only one to make that choice. So I was asked to read it before every English class in the school. At first I was excited and pleased, but very quickly I discovered my mistake. My reputation was ruined. Poetry and homosexuality were somehow considered synonymous, and I soon found that coming to school, never much fun in the first place, had become an ongoing bad dream. For weeks afterwards there were whispered comments about my sexuality; my books were knocked from my hands in the crowded hallways; and anonymous, murmured threats and laughter followed me into the classroom.

College was completely different. I couldn't wait to get to school each day. Each morning I left home before anyone in my house was awake, and I drove for more than an hour across town so that I could be there early enough to park my old gray Plymouth, find an empty cafeteria table amongst the early-rising, sleepy students, have a cup of coffee, toast, and a bowl of hot oatmeal with brown sugar, and jot down notes and questions about the day's assignments. I sat in the front row in each of my classes. I was amazed at the casual grace of my teachers as they dispensed their knowledge about the age of the earth, the etymology of the English language, about so many things I was aching to know about. I hated to leave school at the end of the day. And then I began to make friends.

I first saw Doug Lasler standing in line in a phys-ed class with about twenty other freshmen, all wearing shorts and tennis shoes. It was an eight o'clock class, all of us nervous, half-asleep, not sure of anything, when suddenly the whole class became fixated on watching Doug struggle and fail to complete a single chin-up. Doug was known by all to have the highest I.Q. ever recorded in the state of Alabama, but he could not do a single chin-up. In wrinkled gym clothes, clearly not an athlete, he stood under the bar, a bit pudgy, with a big butt and close-combed blonde hair that sprouted up at the crown of his head in a short rooster's tail. He seemed downcast, his skinny arms drooping at his sides in defeat, when somebody behind me in our line giggled. Doug, straightening his shoulders and raising himself up to his full height, suddenly turned around and his eyes lit up, hawk-like, pointing his sharp beak of a nose directly at us in defiance. He said nothing, but I could see grim determination taking him over as he turned back to the bar and tried again. But it was obvious almost at once that he could barely support his own weight and that he could not possibly complete a chin-up. I watched as he strained to lift himself. His entire body shook, but it did not rise. Then his grip failed, and he fell to the floor, arms flailing, in a jumble of confusion. Red-faced, he pushed himself to his feet, wiped his hands on his shorts, and walked stiffly toward the locker room.

"I guess the genius can't do it!" someone remarked at his retreating form.

Doug did not look back, but Tim Baker, curly, dark hair, pale white skin, and flushed red cheeks, broke out of line, walked over to the student who'd spoken up, and said, just loud enough for everyone to hear, "Shut your mouth, smartass! You aren't even qualified to carry his books." Then he broke into a run to catch up with Doug. Tim was an athlete. He had done fifteen chin-ups his first try.

Soon Doug, the genius, and Tim, the athlete, freshmen friends, showed up each morning before classes and entered the cafeteria like royalty to hold court as groups of students, including seniors, gathered around them to hear and participate in their conversations. They talked about Nietzsche, Shakespeare, Sartre, Coleridge, and Keats. Here, over coffee, toast, scrambled eggs, and sweet rolls, our classroom subjects suddenly came alive and real to those of us who were looking for something more. In these wide-ranging conversations, ideas—like those miraculous African frogs that hibernate in the dust until revived by the rain—rose up and took form in our minds because Doug and Tim took up where the professors left off. They picked up class material like it was alive; they explored the backdrop of history and argued the context of interpretation and meaning as if they were building a fresh, new understanding of the continuity of human consciousness. I was thrilled, so excited I could barely sleep at night.

Suddenly education made sense. With Doug around, with that blonde rooster tail of hair sticking up at the back of his head, with that large pointy nose of his aimed straight at us and speaking to us in that uniquely nasal and yet controlling, high-pitched voice that carried confidence and certainty, I found myself caught up in the excitement of this huge mind at work, in the way he could make everything make sense. He could pick up a subject, instantly organize the available information, and take all of the confusion out of it.

And because he could see how to make sense of a problem, because he could find his way to the solution in the very definition of the problem, we could see it too. And we weren't simply memorizing and regurgitating what he showed us; we were becoming dangerous. We were learning how to think for ourselves. Classes became more than lectures. With Doug in the room, the professors had to be on their toes because he asked the challenging questions and would not back down. So we went beyond the textbook, read secondary sources; we read critiques from the library that were not on the reading list. Doug organized discussions before exams. He explored the ramifications of Immanuel Kant's *Critique of Pure Reason* against the backdrop of David Hume's attack on the concept of cause and effect. He challenged the teacher's opinions, quoted external authorities, brought back the reason for these issues into our daily lives. The word would go out about which subjects and teachers Doug was signing up to take, and, voila, those automatically became the most sought-after classes. The other really bright students, like James McPherson with his photographic memory, vied to get in. Some of the professors seemed to rise to the occasion, realizing that these classes were almost certainly unique, not likely ever to be repeated, and prepared for class discussions with excitement and enthusiasm. But some, threatened, became openly hostile, created a battleground atmosphere, and defended their egos in hopeless, losing struggles against their own students.

One professor, a dapper Coleridge scholar who always wore a tweed suit and who seemed particularly unwilling to listen to student ideas about scholarly matters, after handing back an exam, found himself under attack for not crediting an answer we had discussed in the cafeteria: Where does the phrase "All the world's a stage" come from? And some of us knew, because Doug had found in a recent article in *New American Review* that Shakespeare had perhaps first found it, in a language older than English, on the walls of the Globe Theatre, *Totus mundus facit histrionem*. And so we all answered the question accordingly. The day he handed back our exams, we came to class with excitement, prepared with our outside sources, knowing he would have marked it wrong and believing we had him, but also wanting to force our own larger discussion of how theatre worked as a social construct that forced us to come to understand ourselves in new and different ways.

But it didn't work.

Doug raised his hand to beg to differ about that answer on the exam. But before he could even begin to explain, the professor shut him down saying, "I am not interested in why several students failed to perceive the intent of this question and incorrectly offered an answer to some imagined question."

Then Tim Baker, his athletic body tense, his ruddy complexion lit up with excitement, rose to defend his friend and chimed in defiantly, "Are you telling us you're not interested in the opinions of other scholars like Eric Bentley or Lionel Trilling?"

And the chaos began.

We tried to force him into a discussion about how social ambience is the necessary breeding ground for ideas, but he would not join in. Finally, he stood up, gathered his briefcase to his chest, and announced that since we were clearly not prepared for today's assignments, class was dismissed. When he walked out, we couldn't believe it. We were stunned. Tim jumped up, ran to the front of the class, looked out the door and down the hall, then turned back to us, pumped his fist in the air, and gave out a loud Rebel yell, "Whooo— ey! Who—ey! Whooo—ey!"

[4]

A glimpse of Mystery: that you are there and
I am here and we are not separate...
From the diary of Chrissy Andersen

"Well, Eddie, I do think it's about time."

Mother and I were sitting side by side in white wicker rockers drinking iced tea on our screened-in back porch, humidity about eighty-five percent. Mother, who had her good days and her bad days, was having a good day. The backyard was lined with beds of roses. Mother's gloves rested beneath her pruning shears on the glass tabletop. I was staring out at our tree swing hanging from the giant red oak that graced the backyard. The heavy hemp rope seemed to be pulling away from the inner tube we had wrapped around the big limb it was attached to. I was considering climbing the tree to see if I could remedy the situation when Mother interrupted my thoughts.

"Time for what?" I asked.

"Time for you to get married," she laughed. "You are old enough, and you and Chrissy have been spending a lot of time together."

I laughed uncomfortably. Chrissy and I had been parking under Vulcan's shadow, kissing, touching, and almost going too far, but I hadn't thought about marrying, hadn't expected my mother to suggest it.

"You don't think we're too young?"

She grinned as if she knew some secret that I didn't.

"Well, when your father and I were married he was seventeen and I was sixteen. But times change, and you two are old enough to know your own mind."

She stood up, a little unsteady, the Parkinson's becoming more and more evident, and put her hand on my face in a shaky caress. "I guess I'd better start supper," she concluded, and went back inside.

The kitchen door banged shut behind her.

I looked out at the big red oak and our tree swing, sipped my iced tea, and wondered if maybe Mom thought we were having sex. Then it occurred to me that maybe we *should* get married. I was twenty, but if Chrissy and I decided to get married, and maybe that was a good idea, what about school? What about enough money to live on? But then again, what if Chrissy didn't want to get married? What if she said no?

I put down my tea, ran out, leaped and caught hold of the swing, began pumping it to go higher.

Then a scarier thought occurred to me as I gathered speed and twisted in the air: What if she said yes?

Except for occasional visits with her father, a sales executive in Atlanta, Chrissy lived with Evelyn, her mother, and Mama, her grandmother, in a small white clapboard house with a tiny manicured yard, fenced in with waist-high hedges and a wooden gate. Three generations of single females in one small house. The grandmother, always in slippers because of her swollen feet, was cheerful as a child, but she weighed over two hundred pounds, dipped snuff, and lived in the back of the house in self-imposed isolation. As a poverty-stricken, fifteen-year-old farm girl she had gotten married, dropped out of school, become pregnant, and had her baby. Divorced a year later, she never tried to be anything other than a mother, a mama. Mama was now her daughter's dependent.

Evelyn, a slender, green-eyed beauty, was the breadwinner and the head of the household for the three of them. She, like her mama before her, had married early, just out of high school, but couldn't live with the man. She seemed always to be calculating her chances for a better life—if only she could find the right man. But she never seemed to find the right one. Each time a new man entered the picture, she would let him come into her bedroom and lock the door, but afterwards she made him go away. Evelyn had divorced Chrissy's father after three years, as she put it, "because of his miseries, misunderstandings, and misfortunes with money." When I think of Evelyn, I think of her sitting up late into the night, alone, sipping her gin and vermouth with toothpicked olive, lighting one lipstick-stained cigarette from another, and trying once again to refigure which bills had to be paid and which ones could be stiffed for an extra month.

It was on a January evening in Evelyn's house that I proposed.

Chrissy and I had just come in and settled down on the couch, sinking in close to each other because of the fallen springs, when Evelyn, like a character out of a Tennessee Williams play, came in from the kitchen on her way to the bedroom, tipsy, wearing high-heeled slippers and a revealing nightgown. She stopped, unsteadily holding her martini out in front of her, and provocatively leaned back against the white mantelpiece, one elbow keeping her upright, one bare leg thrust forward.

I stared, unprepared for this strange vision before me.

Chrissy looked down at her hands and whispered under her breath, "Please...go away."

Evelyn inclined her head in my direction and winked knowingly. But then she seemed to take in her daughter's disapproval, took a long breathy hit from her cigarette, and said, "Now y'all be good." And laughed, throwing her head back before swishing her way into her bedroom.

Earlier that evening Chrissy and I had gone to the symphony in Birmingham. We had served as ushers. On our way home we had taken the scenic route, crossing town by following the roads along the top of Red Mountain. Vulcan's light had been green—no traffic fatalities—and the air had been crisp and clean, and the city lights had sparkled below. Chrissy had gotten her hair done up in a French twist. I liked it better down, but I didn't tell her. After her mother had disappeared, closing her bedroom door behind her, Chrissy pulled me over onto her in a full-bodied, all-embracing kiss. Then I nuzzled her neck before pulling back a bit, my heart pounding, and asked her if she would take her hair down.

She replied, "Well, my blue-eyed man, since I had it done up just for you, you may take it down."

As I reached over and began taking out hairpins, I felt overwhelmed by the honor and the present she had made of herself. Suddenly I heard myself saying, "My mother says she thinks we should marry."

Chrissy turned, and my hands awkwardly let go of her still-tangled hair. She stared directly into my eyes. "What about you?"

Suddenly, I realized that this smart, dark-haired beauty was choosing me. Me, with acne on my face, with my big ears and my limp blonde hair that wouldn't stay combed, me who hadn't even figured out how to get into college. Her large brown eyes locked on mine, she took hold of my hands and looked up at me invitingly. Waiting, vulnerable. And I said, "Yes. I want to. Oh yes."

Our marriage that following June was a traditional Methodist ceremony. I remember very little, just the sight of her mother in high heels, bright red lipstick, veil; her grandmother in a shapeless print dress down to her ankles; my father and mother standing together, dressed up and looking strangely pleased. The reception took place at Evelyn's house. I cut the cake, and then we were off. We had very little money to spare so we planned to drive the few hours to Montgomery, the capital of Alabama, the seat of the Confederacy, to see the home of Jefferson Davis. It was all so formal, like being in a play, each of us acting out our parts. But suddenly we were on our honeymoon, and we didn't have a script, and we didn't know what to say.

Chrissy and I had not yet had sex. We had necked, kissed, touched, but always she had pulled back. Now, alone in the car, family and friends behind us, our wedding night before us, we suddenly became shy with one another. Now, as we drove down the Montgomery highway, I looked to see her face out of the corner of my eye. She was still wearing her Jackie Kennedy pillbox hat, her ornamental veil obscuring part of her face. She sat looking straight ahead, hands folded in her lap, her cream-colored suit buttoned up, still wearing her long, off-white gloves. I looked down at my olive-green, two-button suit, my first, and felt inadequate to carry on a conversation.

In silence we drove through the rural countryside.

Small plots of cornfields and cotton rows slipped past the car window; shanty homes, rusted-out truck beds disintegrating in backyard clearings, dying pine forests obscured and suffocating under the rampant pale green of the ever-spreading kudzu, that rope-like vine that had been imported from Japan, already becoming an ecological disaster.

We were on our honeymoon. Our wedding night lay ahead of us. We would be free to do whatever we wanted to do. I offered Chrissy a quick grin. She grinned back but then looked away. We both started to speak at once, stopped, then looked away. We both grinned. Again. A wasp's nest of nervous energy spread out around me.

Finally, in Montgomery, after registering in our hotel in our new designation as Mr. and Mrs. Andersen, we carried our own bags, climbed the hotel's carpeted stairway under a lighted chandelier, and found our way to our room down a dim hallway decorated with small statues of black children carrying hobo sacks, Southern plantation style. Inside, our room held the odors of stale tobacco and an odd chemical-smelling lemon air freshener. We turned on the overhead fan, opened the windows, and left to find a restaurant.

Outside in the warmth of Montgomery's humidity we walked until we found a central area of town where the streets were lined with flowering purple jacaranda trees and chose a restaurant that advertised lobster bisque soup and fresh red snapper.

But we barely touched our food.

Conversation was at a standstill.

After an awkward meal of long silences, we walked back to our hotel, avoiding each other's eyes, not talking, not touching.

Returning to our one room—still muggy, the overhead fan barely stirring a breeze—we sat, still in our wedding clothes, across from each other as Chrissy unpinned her hat and pulled off her gloves and placed them on an end table. She sat primly perched on the edge of the bed; I sat at a small desk with a black telephone, a leather-bound Bible, and a dingy desk lamp. I could not think of a single thing to say that didn't sound stupid.

The silence was oppressive.

"I'm going to the bathroom," she announced without looking at me. She picked up her suitcase and left, closing the door behind her.

I stood up, looked out our open windows at pink mimosas and purple jacaranda. The night air was heavily scented with honeysuckle and jasmine.

I paced. I sat back down.

"Is everything all right?" I asked the closed door.

"Yes," she said, as she came out wearing a pink nightgown, fluffy and unrevealing under a frilly darker pink housecoat. She sat down on the edge of the bed and stared at her hands.

Not knowing what to do or say next, I offered, "I'll change in the bathroom," and in I went. But I didn't have anything to change into. I took off my suit, tie, and shirt and folded everything up on the toilet seat. I looked at myself standing there in boxer shorts, T-shirt, and black socks. I looked and felt skinny, un-sexy. Unprepared. I took out a Trojan rubber from my wallet and held it up to the light over the sink. It seemed okay. I could feel my supper rising with an unpleasant second taste of lobster bisque. When I opened the door and came out, I kept my clothes in my arms in front of me, providing me with a shield.

The room was dark. Chrissy had turned out the lights and was under the covers.

I dropped my clothes in a chair, took off my socks and my underwear, got in bed, and then discovered Chrissy was still wearing her fluffy pink, stiff nightgown.

"Don't you want to take this off?" I whispered, pulling at her gown.

"Not really," she whispered and became quiet.

I lay there with my rubber in my hand and tried to think of what to say next. I knew it was up to me to do something. I waited a long time then decided to say out loud everything I was about to do.

Softly, I said, "I'm going to take off your panties," and put my hand lightly on her hip, one finger under the elastic of her cotton underwear, and waited.

She was silent, acquiescent. Her body felt hot, heavy, unresponsive.

And nothing I said after that helped at all.

We couldn't have sex that night.

The more I tried, the more she cried out in pain. In the end we lay side by side, sore, and stared at the ceiling, awake until almost dawn and suffering with the inexplicable distance between us.

In the morning, after sharing the same toothbrush, we became friends again. We agreed we would drive back that afternoon. It would give us a few extra days to move our things into married student housing.

Later on we stood together, awkward and defeated in our new world, like wounded spirits, and visited the home of Jeff Davis, the elected president of the Confederate States of America. Like walking into a piece of the history of hoped-for elegance and glory, we stood beside the central spiral staircase and watched it rise gracefully to the upper story, a gleaming mahogany brown, as if a part of a dream. Without any support whatsoever beyond its circular structure, containing no nails, it climbed upwards, defying gravity, a still life balanced on an invisible spine.

On our guided tour through that dark museum of the past, with red carpets all around, we walked behind two blue-haired ladies in fancy dresses who whispered to each other in hushed tones about the glory of the Confederacy and the sheer meanness of Sherman's March to the Sea. But Chrissy and I grew bored, and somehow we automatically understood one another's mood. And we liked each other, once again. We had had a bad night, but that was behind us. There was still a future life that lay ahead. We felt out of place in

Jeff Davis's home, in that old world of failed fantasies. Dressed in tennis shoes and blue jeans, halfway through the tour, suddenly we grinned and held hands again. Then we turned and walked out the door into the sunshine where the jacaranda was in bloom, and the smell of jasmine was in the air.

We checked out of our hotel and left Montgomery. Then, in the car alone, just the two of us, we lost our good spirits. Conversation ebbed away, and the heat of the day remained oppressive as we drove back to Birmingham in near silence.

One afternoon, several days later, Chrissy surprised me. Returning from the grocery store with the requested French bread, I found her waiting in our bedroom, naked, and when I entered, she mutely lifted her arms invitingly.

I left a littered path of clothes on my rush to the bed.

She had gone to see a doctor in downtown Birmingham the day before.

In her diary, a notebook of poetic fragments and thoughts which I discovered years later, Chrissy wrote:

Friday. Saw Dr. Adams today. I bled for over four hours afterwards. He broke my hymen. Forced his way into me with his cold hands. He said, "Now go home, honey. Show that husband of yours you know how to make him a happy man."

It hurt.

[5]

From Red Mountain, where a cast-iron Vulcan
looks down 500 feet to the sprawling city,
Birmingham seems veiled in the poisonous
fumes of distant battles.

On a fine April day, however, it is only the
haze of acid fog belched from the stacks of the
Tennessee Coal and Iron Company's Fairfield
and Ensley works that lies over the city.

But more than a few citizens, both white and
Negro, harbor growing fear that the hour will
strike when the smoke of civil strife will mingle
with that of the hearths and forges...
New York Times, John Milner
April 12, 1960

We chose to move into a corner apartment on the second floor of married student housing: two-story, small red brick buildings with tile floors, pastel walls, and cheap modern furniture. Each apartment contained, as listed on the lease: one desk, one dining table with four chairs, one double bed, one couch, two armchairs, and two coffee tables—all contained in one kitchen, one bathroom, one bedroom, and one combination living and dining room. The best thing about these apartments was that they were on campus and were walking distance to the Quad, a grassy square with crisscrossing sidewalks surrounded by four multistoried, red brick buildings, each with a Greek facade of Corinthian pillars. The grounds were beautiful, maintained with great care. Huge weeping willows dripped slender branches to the ground; tall, arching limbs floated up over the campus paths in a canopy of interlacing red oaks, black oaks, and sweet gum. It was our safe place, and we often walked over to campus to read and hang out on our nearby grassy hillock, to feel the light breezes soften and dispel the heat of the apartment and the noise of nearby streets.

We moved into married student housing in August as sophomores and began planning. Chrissy had decided that she was going to major in French. I was still undecided. Maybe philosophy or English.

So it was on an early morning in September when, like the newly-weds we were, Chrissy and I walked over to campus hand-in-hand to buy some books and see what was going on. The campus was crowded and buzzing with incoming students. Chrissy was wearing her tan raincoat over gym shorts and tennis sneakers because she didn't want to change into a dress.

At the bookstore we ran into her old roommate, Anita Jewett, who was also wearing a tan raincoat. She said she was wearing her raincoat because she didn't feel like getting dressed. She showed us a bare leg and laughed. Anita was the president of the only liberal sorority on campus, and she had won the women's tennis tournament her freshman year. She had short black hair, flashing green eyes, and a heavy warm smile, the smile of a winner. She and Chrissy had roomed together their freshman year, but this year Anita had got-ten a private room in the girls' dormitory. So I didn't think anything about it when Chrissy wanted to go see her room, and the two of them walked off in their matching raincoats. Chrissy and I agreed we'd meet back at our apartment, and I continued looking for my textbooks.

Later, on my way home, I stopped off under a big weeping wil-low on the hillside just opposite our apartment to peruse my pur-chases: essays of John Locke, David Hume, and John Stuart Mill on self-determination, natural rights, and constitutional limits on government. I was pretty absorbed in looking through them when Chrissy appeared on the path before me. I started to shout when I saw her, but there was something strange in the way she held herself. I was sitting in shade, deep under the willow tree, concealed by its branches. She didn't see me. She stared straight ahead, a vacant look in her eyes. The sun cut through the trees along the path and cast an unkind glare across her face as she walked stiffly toward me down the path. She rubbed her eyes and wiped away the tears on her cheeks, smearing them with dark streaks of mascara. Her dank brown hair drooped heavily in clumps around her face. She did not toss her head or brush away her hair. Instead she absently tugged at the belt of her tan raincoat. It seemed suddenly too big for her. As she walked, she kept pulling at the belt encircling her waist. The coat ballooned out in an unflattering and careless way. This was not anyone I recognized. Passing almost directly in front of me, she paused, thrust her hands deep in the pockets of her coat, let out a forced guttural sigh of displeasure, stamped her foot, and strode firmly away from our apartment with a determined step. She was heading toward the drugstore off campus.

I stared after her in disbelief as she disappeared in the distance, and, in spite of the warm day, I felt a chill pass through me. When Chrissy and I had parted in the bookstore she had been light hearted, almost exaggeratedly happy. Her arm over Anita's shoulder, she had laughed and waved goodbye, a light skip to her step, blowing me kisses.

What did it mean? What had happened between Chrissy and Anita? They had been happily hugging each other... They must have had a fight. But where was she going? And why was she so upset?

Suddenly the afternoon sun penetrated my shade. I found I was unable to sit still. I struggled to my feet, stuffed my textbooks and notes into my book bag, and started following her down the path to the off-campus drugstore.

But when I arrived she was not there.

I ordered a Coke, sat in the cool air, stared at the "Request for Rides" board with hand-scribbled pieces of paper—"Seeking one-way ride to N.Y.C., will pay for gas, call Larry." Whatever it was, it seemed to have nothing to do with me. I felt strangely left out.

When Chrissy came home that afternoon, after she took a shower, she came into the room without a word, stared out the window onto the parking lot, and absent-mindedly combed her hair.

I watched her for a few minutes, her bone-white comb sliding down through her dark, wet hair, each stroke ending with beads of water shaken into the air, and then I closed my book, put away my new schedule of classes and work assignments, and asked, as casually as I could manage, the question uppermost on my mind.

"Did you have a disagreement with Anita today?"

With her back to me, her purple blouse now damp from her wet hair, she straightened up and replied without looking at me, "Oh, no, of course not. What makes you say that?"

"Oh, nothing, you just don't seem yourself, a little preoccupied I guess, since your visit with her."

"Oh, don't be ridiculous," she laughed as she turned around to face me, adding "Hey, you know what we should do? Let's get dressed up and go downtown for dinner."

So we went to Joy Young, the only Chinese restaurant in Birmingham, where she seemed to put aside her somber mood. She ordered her favorite dish, butterfly shrimp in bacon and onion sauce.

In order to maintain us in college I held two jobs, one at the bookstore from one o'clock till five, and one at Birmingham Public Library, from five till nine. The bookstore, Smith & Hardwick, was on Twentieth Street and Fifth Avenue, around the corner from the library at Sixth Avenue and Twenty-first Street. I walked from one job to the other. So I arranged to have all my classes between 7:30 a.m. and 12:30 p.m., and then I was off to work. I could usually grab a sandwich after I got there.

Smith & Hardwick was run by two elderly, hunch-backed ladies, Anna and Virginia Praytor, high-school Latin teachers, sisters, who always dressed in black and wore their long gray hair braided in coils on top of their heads. They cracked jokes with each other, whispered pieces of gossip, chortled, but became very formal once you were within hearing distance.

I enjoyed both of them, though Anna was my favorite.

Anna was the one who bestowed warmth on Smith & Hardwick. She worried that they weren't paying me enough, $1.25 an hour. She loved books and seemed always to have a smile and a whispered suggestion (so as not to distract me from whatever task they had set) as to what I should read next.

"This is a fine translation of Herman Hesse's *Siddhartha*. Have you read it? You really should, you know."

And then she'd grin, hand me the book to buy or to shelve, lower her spectacles on her nose, and go back to reading the invoice and unpacking the latest order of books. I had never heard of Herman Hesse, but after *Siddhartha* I read everything of his that was translated. His book *Demian* was about an impressionable young man in Germany, Sinclair, who was enthralled by an older man, Max Demian, who was helping him come to grips with prejudice and the dark forces at work in his culture, who was teaching him about the power of symbols in art and religion, and who was teaching him how to think for himself. That book left me disturbed and thrilled. Anna was seldom wrong in her recommendations.

Virginia, on the other hand, once a freckled redhead, was the penny-pinching, quick-tongued harridan of Smith & Hardwick. She did the hiring and firing and the accounting. She paid the bills. She signed my check. Virginia scared me. She would lift up her graying red head and bark out questions, random thoughts, instructions, as if she were talking to me by way of speaking to the ceiling.

"Where're the invoices from today's deliveries? Did you call this list of people and tell them their books are here? So many people dropping out of school... Do you know what Faulkner says, and he certainly does make a good case for it. Faulkner says that evil is not the work of the devil. No, evil is the result that we reap from the soil of ignorance! Where is that shipping list? Did you make sure we got what we ordered?"

I was always afraid Virginia would catch me in some mistake like misfiling a book or miscalculating taxes on book sales, and that she would fire me on the spot.

Virginia and Anna taught school during the week and would come by around four in the afternoon to relieve me at five. During the hour we overlapped, I would hand-deliver books or take the cash receipts to the bank.

Once I'd completed my day at the bookstore, I'd walk over to the library, where I would take over from Mrs. Humphries, the librarian responsible for the Art and Music Department on the fourth floor. Mrs. Humphries, a single mom, heavy-bodied and soft-hearted as a warm day in winter, always greeted me with hurried concerns about how much the Praytor sisters were paying me, about how much sleep I should be getting, and how she hoped my jobs weren't interfering with my classes. Then she would rush to the door with an oversized bag that displayed a large green frog holding out a handful of daisies, and shout, "Don't forget to lock up." Mrs. Humphries knew my schedule well enough so that around midterms or finals, I would arrive at the library and discover that there was very little work for me to do.

My library job consisted of re-shelving all the returned books and records that came in during the day and helping people find whatever they were looking for. At some point I was also assigned the task of coming up with an alphabetical way of filing the library's entire classical music section (symphonies, concertos, sonatas by composer). Therefore, I had to read the record jackets and listen to the albums while I worked at determining how much space had to be allowed for each composer.

These were weekday jobs, and I could usually sneak in some much-needed study time. My weekends were free to do the larger assignments and catch up on my classwork.

Often, after work on Friday nights, I would come home and find a party in full swing in our apartment. It was usually the same crowd: Doug Lasler, Tim Baker, Anita Jewett, Sarah Deason, and Allan Gregory, all brilliant students, all in love with Chrissy, and Chrissy with them.

But Anita was special.

In Chrissy's diary she wrote:

My dear friend Anita, I might address this letter to my alter ego; you are as well known as a part of myself and, at the same time, other-than and strange to me. I cannot say I miss you—I see you on the tennis courts, and in a group of the girls walking on Dormitory Hill, and sometimes in the balcony of the auditorium. I will not forget what happened, and I only hope that you will remember that there is always one who cares, who will never forget.

I suppose I should have been more curious, more concerned about Chrissy's mood swings, but so much was happening. In downtown Birmingham, good people were getting arrested by Sheriff Bull Connor's police for defending civil liberties. At school, though we lived in the protected bubble of academia, it felt like we were engaged in a critical exploration into the major truths of human consciousness. And though I found that I had no free time between reading assignments, daily homework, attending classes, and commuting between my two jobs and school, Chrissy and I both seemed to be happy, no, thrilled with our classes, our friends, and each other. She had joined the French Club, the Theater Club, and had a part-time job reading for a blind student. And while I seemed always to be rushing from one thing to the other, calculating and recalculating my time and my commitments (I cut my sleep hours down to six), I still somehow found time to join the Poetry Club, which met on weekends and on Tuesday evenings. The pace of my life made me feel like I had thrown myself into a rushing torrent that was sweeping me toward some unknown destination. But I was so excited, I didn't care where it might end. Nothing in my upbringing had prepared me for the life I was living.

But then things started to get confusing.

One Friday evening when I arrived home in the dark, fumbling for my keys, Anita opened the door for me, wearing a revealing blouse that left one shoulder bare. She leaned across the threshold, kissed me on the mouth, handed me a gin and tonic, and said, teasingly, "Welcome home, honey."

And I enjoyed it. I kissed her back.

It was a teasing game Anita occasionally played, sometimes with me, sometimes with Chrissy. Anita wanted to be an actress. She batted her eyes, pausing for effect, and leaned in close to whisper in my ear with an actor's exaggerated Southern drawl.

"You know, of course, that Chrissy is only attracted to you out of a need to save herself. She'd rather have me."

She winked mysteriously, keeping me standing in the doorway, keys, books, backpack, and gin and tonic in my hands, blocking my way into my apartment, a party continuing behind her.

I decided she was a little drunk.

"What are you talking about?" I laughed.

She pursed her lips, blew me a kiss mixed with perfume, alcohol, and cigarettes, and said, like a character out of Tennessee Williams's *A Streetcar Named Desire*, "She thinks of you as representing her *normal* side."

She nodded significantly.

I gave her a puzzled look.

Staying in character, she continued, "You know: family, kids, all that stuff. But there is another side to Chrissy that will never be satisfied with only that..." She hesitated as if considering an abstract problem, and then added "Just so you know." She turned away and walked back into the noise of the party.

Puzzled, I stood there trying to absorb her words while Doug and Tim raged back and forth in another corner of our living room. Doug's voice was loud, articulate, and strong.

"I wonder what it would be like if Nature, instead of staying on the sidelines and letting things simply fall out the way the circumstances dictate, suddenly rose up and became, like our Christian God, an interested party in human folly and began passing out rewards and punishments..."

As I passed into our bedroom and dropped my books and backpack on our bed, I wondered what Anita was up to, but Doug's argument pulled on me. Hands free, I sipped my drink and headed out to join the party.

Anita, like all the rest of our group of friends, had become an integral part of our lives, part of our newly formed extended family. Sarah Deason and Allan Gregory were two of our newest friends, who were suddenly at our house practically every night. Sarah had moved into married student housing a few doors down from us. She was a transfer student from Tulane, almost thirty years old, usually dressed as the Southern belle she truly was: soft accent, bare shoulders, ankle-length dresses. She was blonde, sensitive, blue-eyed, intelligent. A widow with two young children who were sometimes with her, sometimes back home with their grandmother, she had a sensuous, swaying gait to her walk that brought her unwanted attention wherever she went.

Sarah was looking for the man who could take control of her life and her children. She held herself aloof, yet she allowed Allan to dedicate himself to a pursuit of her favors. Allan Gregory, chess champion of the State of Alabama, was a music student with thick glasses and a long straggly beard, who seemed incapable of coping with ordinary living. He could play, and win, twelve games of chess simultaneously, but Allan was the outsider in any social situation that was made up of more than two people. He was soft spoken and round and dressed without regard to appearance, but he was a tyrant where questions of art and aesthetics were concerned.

Everyone knew that Allan Gregory desired Sarah with a passion, but they also knew that he would never win her. An older woman with a past and two children, Sarah would take no more chances. Her next man must have more than a strong aesthetic sensibility; he must either have a future or he must have money. The odd couple on campus, they traveled together, went to parties together, shared a love of Bach and T. S. Eliot, and leaned on each other for companionship.

Sarah and Allan moved into our lives almost at once.

◁▶

In her diary Chrissy wrote:

I have this problem: not to say, or try to say, too much. It was *a hurtful experience—contact, that touching of another's soul that sustains and drives me to death wishes. There is so much that can never be expressed. Yet I feel compelled, and just this side of able, to put forth my efforts, for I am persuaded **there is** something for me to affirm. This contact, an hour's conversation, was unique. Unique in the same way that others like it were, are, will be unique.*

Allan's small soft soul, as he calls it, is ever so large and gentle. He is neither male nor female to me. He is a person, a being in whom I can find father, mother, sibling, friend—or just a recognizable acquaintance. He invites me to crawl in and lie with him in cool green grass. If Bach had not already crept into his being, he would now. Allan Gregory has moved in as a part of me.

Sarah: sensuous body undulating in time with pulsing warm calls, invoking response, hiding and yet suffering from the grief that lives inside her. Sarah is distinctly female, as much as one can be in the male-female balance of an individual. She can be at times, and is, Mother, Sister, Friend, never just a recognizable acquaintance. She is loveliness. She is Love. And she invites me into another world, into the warmth of her touch, and into the special realm of a deep dark friendship.

Some evenings, when I came home from work I would find a note: "Gone out with Sarah, Anita, and Allan." There would be a plate of food waiting for me, and I would settle into studying and waiting. And then they would all come in the door singing, hug me, hand me a beer, and continue on with a discussion of a symphony that Allan was composing for Sarah. And we would all stay up way past midnight, hugging, touching, and talking.

Chrissy wrote in her diary:

Oh, the poetry of us, the lovely flowing lines of form flowing into formlessness, the small strong utterances birthing worldlessness... And the music of us, singing, oh so softly, straining round crescendos, hard and tempo-driven, tumbling into humming soundlessness... Oh, the painting sight of us, splashing reds and touching pinks onto the white, warm canvas, and oh, the dim dark brightness never before glimpsed until now through the eye of us. What will I do when my people go away? We have only this limited time together and then— Sarah to grad school and Allan to the West Coast. Anita says, "You'll find others," but I am afraid I will not.

[6]

[It was the middle of May, 1961]...*on a hot
afternoon, when a Greyhound bus rolled out of
the Anniston, Alabama, station carrying Freedom
Riders pursued by as many as fifty cars and trucks.
Five miles outside of town one of the slashed
tires finally blew and the bus hissed to a dusty
stop, the driver fleeing. Immediately the bus was
surrounded and a firebomb exploded through a
window. "Sieg heil!" someone shouted from the
angry crowd encircling the trapped riders, "Let's
roast 'em." But then suddenly, unexpectedly, gray-
haired Eli Cowling, a private investigator hired
by the governor of Alabama to keep tabs on these
outside agitators, could take no more. He pushed
open the door, stepped down from the burning bus
with drawn gun, and shouted down at the mob,
"Now you get back and let these people off, or some
of you are going to die."* [3]

"Do you want to go to the concert or don't you?" Tim, the athlete,
who was pushing Doug to improve his body, was now pushing him to
improve himself in another direction. He wanted Doug to shake off
his monastic, bookish lifestyle and join him in discovering what was
out there and happening in the real world. Tim aspired to Doug's
easy self-assurance about abstract matters. And Doug, the genius,
constantly amused by Tim's flamboyant ways, was happy to have

found in Tim's companionship his first real friend in the world.

Tim and Doug had just finished their weekend workout at the gym. Doug had been working hard, with Tim's coaching. He could now complete five chin-ups and run a mile in under ten minutes. They sat side by side on the steps of the library, a light coating of wet sweat glistening from their faces in the warm sun. It was early Saturday morning, and the Quad was nearly empty. The smell of coffee drifted behind two passing students as they ambled along the sidewalk that crisscrossed the green lawn occupying the center of the campus. In the distance the concrete facades of Corinthian columns stood two stories tall in front of the administration building. Perched on top of each of the column's concrete scrolls was a papier-mâché doll of a shapely colored girl: black face, big lips, large breasts, dressed as a cheerleader with a white sweater and purple shorts, and holding up a sign that boldly read, "Outside Agitator."

"Your parents are not poverty stricken," Tim said, standing up and beginning to stretch, sweat still beading up on his ruddy face, his dark, curly hair matted.

"I'm here because I've got a full scholarship. The Methodists are paying. My minister and my parents have it all worked out. But the strings are attached. You just can't see them," Doug's piercing blue eyes suddenly flashed angrily.

"No way," Tim said, jumping up and down, his legs like springs.

"Yeah," Doug said in that nasal, high-pitched certainty of his, looking up at the papier-mâché dolls, combing his straight blonde hair to one side, leaning back on one elbow, "they pay for everything. And what do you think they expect in return for their money? Something like: stay out of trouble? Like stay away from the sit-ins, and especially, stay away from all those outside agitators?" Doug grinned and pointed at the bold, black-faced dolls. "Like go to church and help spread the gospel, the good news? But guess what—can you keep a secret?"

Tim nodded, grinning in acknowledgement of the humor of the dolls. He began bending his athlete's body, first to one side then the other, stretching out his hamstrings.

"I'm an atheist. I shouldn't be taking their money," Doug said, his gray sweatshirt damp around his pudgy middle. He stood, pushing his lank, blonde hair away from his face, his nose still pointed up at the dolls.

Tim, stopped for a moment, and stared blankly. He looked around and then leaned over conspiratorially, "So what?"

"*So what?*" Doug wrinkled his nose at Tim.

But Tim, now dancing backwards on the top step, was not daunted. "Who cares? I mean, what they don't know won't hurt them."

"I care. I *am* taking their money..."

Doug paused, lifted his arms, straightened, waited for another student to pass, and continued in a lowered voice.

"Look, the Church doesn't sell dispensations anymore, no more tickets to heaven, but it still runs the same old scams. They created the concept of sin so that they could have the power to save us from Satan. If we do what they want, then they will save us. They will forgive us. See, it's all about who controls what we think. Now the Church and our Southern good old boys have something in common. Control! Today the worst 'sin' is to question authority. My God, my country, and my sheriff. Bull Connor, right or wrong."

Doug threw up his hands and laughed, mockingly, a kind of doomed, false humor in his voice.

"Oh, I don't really give a damn. The truth is I'm like everybody else. My biggest sin is: I don't want to take a stand. I've got a good ride here, and I don't want any trouble. I just want to get my degree and get out of here."

"Okay. I get it," Tim said, "No trouble! So, if this isn't your basic Students for a Democratic Society outsider-agitator creation, and you know it isn't, will you go to the Ray Charles, Lena Horne concert?"

He paused, looked around like he was looking for spies, and then took a more challenging tone.

"Or do you feel you can't because you might be seen? Doug, this is not a protest. No. And no one is ever going to know whether you go or not. Besides, they can't kick you out of school for going to a concert. And if we get enough fellow students to go with us it'll be a complete non-issue. Besides, don't you want to go? Just to spite 'em?"

Doug smiled wryly as they both started walking across the grass of the Quad, stretching arms and legs still tight from their earlier workout, close friends, laughing and talking like two Greek athletes passing beneath the Parthenon, shoulder to shoulder in the brilliant sunshine of their Saturday morning, at home in the good opinion that each held of the other.

Tim continued his argument as they walked.

"And maybe it's something we ought be doing anyway. Support the cause because it's the right thing to do. And have a good time doing it. Come on, what do you say?"

Outside, in the shade of the row of our married student apartments, Tim, wearing a gray sleeveless athletic shirt and P.E. shorts, jogged in place beside us. Doug and Tim had come over to convince us that we should go with them to the upcoming Ray Charles concert taking place on the nearby all black campus at Miles College.

"Come on, youse guys, it'll be a great concert, and besides don't we have some responsibility here…don't we?"

Chrissy, one arm around my waist, both of us in sandals and shorts, goosed me surreptitiously as Tim presented his arguments. We were just starting out on our way to the grocery store when they showed up. There was a warm breeze carrying the scent of honeysuckle and newly mown grass. A sprinkler went off in the distance. Doug sat down on the lawn under a pink-flowering mimosa tree and stretched. His hand shading his eyes from the glare of the sun off the sidewalk, he looked back and forth between Tim and Chrissy and me, a bemused expression on his face.

The summer workouts with Tim were making a difference. Doug's face was more angular, thinner, stronger looking. He no longer had that angry, defended look about him. In this light he suddenly looked more grown-up, more hawk-like with that sharply pointed nose of his, even handsome. No longer a pudgy youth, but a young man coming into his power. But, if you didn't look into those steely bright eyes, you might conclude from that unruly hair standing up on the crown of his head, and from that fresh baby face of his, that there was still a brilliant little boy trapped inside this young man's body.

Abstractedly, he commented musingly to no one in particular, "It all comes down to a variation on what William James said—that not making a choice when you have a choice is making a choice."

"Okay. Right on," Tim nodded, acknowledging Doug's comment. "But can you imagine what it's going to be like to have Ray Charles and Lena Horne on the same billing?"

Tim began lifting his knees as he bounced up and down like he was on springs, sweat glistening over his arms, his face, his chin, and he turned expectantly, first toward Chrissy, and then towards me.

"It'll be such a gas to be there! Come on, Eddie, commit. Or don't you think we should go? Come on, give us your reasons."

"I'm not sure. Do you think it'll be safe?" I asked, thinking, *if this turns into a protest demonstration and the police show up, we could all get thrown out of college or worse.* "I mean, how many other students do you think will be there?"

"You're a worrywart, Eddie." Tim stopped bouncing up and down, placed his hands on his hips, and exclaimed, "We've got to be there! I mean, think about it. It's on the radio: *Miles College invites all students at discount prices.* They're our neighbors. We've got to show solidarity. Tell him, Chrissy! Talk to him."

Chrissy's smile arrived like a surprise kiss as she took her arms from around me and, bowing at the waist, backed away with quick-footed dance steps. Then, placing her forefinger under her chin, she pursed her lips, winked, spread her arms wide, and broke into song.

> *I heared a lot of stories and I reckon they are true*
> *about how girls are put upon by men.*
> *I know I mustn't fall into the pit.*
> *But when I'm with a feller I forgit.*
> *I'm just a girl who can't say no.*
> *I'm in a terrible fix.*
> *I always say "Come on, let's go,"*
> *Just when I oughta say "Nix."*

She sashayed into my arms and gave me a sweet peck on the cheek before spinning away, and, with a pretend-cowgirl assurance, tossed her head as she looked back over her shoulder, adding, "I think Tim's right. I think we should not say 'Nix.'"

Tim applauded.

Then, as usual, we all looked over to Doug for the final word.

And Doug, grinning at us (Chrissy's playfulness had clearly affected him), leaned back on the grass, lifted up his left knee, pulled it in toward his chin with one hand, and stretched. He let us wait a minute. Then, changing knees and hands, he stretched again and spoke up with that nasal high-pitched certainty of his, "Okay. I'm in. We can't simply hide out on our hilltop. Time to join the real world. Time to take a few risks. And, Tim, this is a benefit for Miles? Right?"

Chrissy beamed happily at me. "Oh, it'll be so much fun," she said, dancing around me, taking my hands in hers. "So we're all going, say 'yes darling we're going,' say it, say it."

I didn't say it, but as Tim laughed and then shoved me in the chest, shadow boxing as he backed away, I knew he'd won.

"But I have to work until nine," I protested, still trying to resist. "It'll already be started."

"Chrissy can come with us," Tim shouted, and, joining in with Chrissy's mood, danced over and wrapped his sweaty arms around the two of us. Then turning on his best toothy grin, he tilted his head back, laughed, and then added, "Eddie, stop worrying. We'll save you the center seat in the front row."

I closed the library's Art and Music Department early that night and drove out to the Miles College football stadium. The night air was chilly, and I was a little overdressed, coming from work. As I entered the colored neighborhoods, I kept telling myself that this *was* a benefit for Miles. But I suspected it was also to raise money for the sit-in protesters who'd been arrested. I wondered if the police would be there, undercover cops secretly photographing white people?

Passing through the gates, I began to hurry, hoping I could spot Chrissy and Tim and Doug quickly. There was a full harvest moon, but dark clouds kept rushing across the sky, obscuring the moonlight, bringing a sudden darkness followed by a kind of spotlight brightness. I lit up a cigarette, inhaled, and coughed.

Smiling dark faces of strangers, bright white teeth.

I walked amongst them, a stranger in a strange culture I knew nothing about. *Where was I going?* Lost in the huge crowd, I kept stumbling over the loose plugs of turf from their torn-up football field. I weaved through the crowds in a hurry, moving inexorably toward the center stage. The concert seemed to be between sets. Instruments were being tuned, loudspeakers squawking.

There was no stadium, no bleachers. It was just a flat grass and gravel field with goal posts and tall floodlights attached to the back of a makeshift stage overcrowded with officials and performers. Bright purples and greens and long slinky gowns of silver sequins moved about under the stage lights. Pushing through a knot of people, I finally noticed several rows of metal chairs with a few seated white people. People were milling around waiting for the next set to begin, talking, joking, and laughing.

Then, just as the moon went behind the clouds, I spotted Chrissy standing near the front row, lit up by the stage lights. I began moving in and around knots of black people who were smoking, drinking and hanging out away from the stage, not even trying for the good seats, the rows of metal chairs around the makeshift stage. Avoiding the stares that followed me in the humid semidarkness, I stepped between people, murmuring, "Excuse me." I kept on moving through this huge gathering—no white people—not stopping, just keeping my eyes on the stage straight ahead, stepping sideways, never meeting the surprised eyes. But then suddenly a large, heavy black man reeking of alcohol seemed to appear out of thin air as he reared up in front of me. Tall, maybe six-seven. Out of nowhere. And we collided. But, in our size and weight disparity, he barely noticed me as he pushed through the crowd, in a hurry to get somewhere else while I was sent reeling, stumbling sideways, almost falling to the ground, until I crashed into a group of young men who had their backs to me. Just at that moment the dark clouds, rushing by overhead, separated, and in their absence the moon came out like a spotlight. I regained my balance, but I was suddenly encircled, and more people seemed to be gathering around me. As I looked from one face to another, I had to fight down an impulse to run away. I felt no warmth coming from any of them. Their alien eyes stared at me, encircling me with a strange kind of emptiness, a blackness surrounded by a milky white sclera.

I raised my empty hands and offered a sincere but an inadequate apology.

"Excuse me, uh, someone bumped into me."

I looked behind me.

The big man who had bumped into me was nowhere in sight.

For a long moment nobody spoke. I was sweating profusely.

I casually feinted like I might just amble on and walk around them, but one of them, a guy wearing a hooded sweatshirt, stepped in front of me, blocking my way.

I didn't know what to say or what to do.

I backed up a few steps, thinking maybe I could just turn around and go back the way I'd come, but I doubted it.

Abruptly the young man in the dark gray, hooded sweatshirt threw back his hood and spoke with an educated New York accent.

"What's up, man? Got a cigarette?"

He put out his hand, palm up.

I pulled out my pack of Kools and shook one out for him. But then they all came forward and asked for a cigarette.

They were playing with me.

Grins were all around now, but still nobody was talking. Finally, Hooded Sweatshirt showed off his big, white buckteeth and laughed self-consciously, before continuing.

"Okay now, the next question is…" he paused, let his question hang in the air, his threatening tone mixing with a mischievous grin.

"Have you got a light?"

I quickly stepped forward and lit their cigarettes, carefully, one at a time, my hands shaking.

The strong smell of mentholated tobacco filled the air around us.

"Where are you from?" he asked, conversationally, exhaling smoke, like we were friends suddenly.

"From here. From Birmingham."

"No kidding," he said.

He seemed surprised and interested, as if there were a conversation he wanted to have with me, but then, as if by some hidden agreement between them, they all turned and started away, their animated, laugh-filled conversation filling the warm night air around me.

As the moon once again was obscured behind the fast-moving clouds, I dropped my cigarette on the field and ground it out with my shoe.

And then, in the darkness, occurring in rapid succession, there were loud explosions and shouts of alarm.

Gunshots? Were those gunshots?

An awful noise rose up around us. It sounded like wood being strained to the breaking point, and then there was an explosion, followed by a crescendo of sounds of things breaking and snapping.

A woman screamed. There was a loud popping, and suddenly the whole football field was plunged into darkness.

As if the air had been sucked from my lungs, I stood still in the pitch-blackness, unable to take a breath, my mind whirling in the chaos of men shouting and women screaming.

"It's a bomb!" someone nearby cried out.

Angry, unintelligible voices gathered in volume, rose up like a wave.

"It's the Klan!"

Then the moon came scudding out from behind dark clouds.

I stood in its spotlight as a crowd tightened in a knot around me.

Unable to move, I stared into the faces of strange black men and women. They extended outwards as far as I could see, legions of them.

I opened my mouth, but no words came out.

Then a loud, clear, calming voice of authority came over a loudspeaker.

"There was no bomb. I repeat. There was no bomb. Do not panic.

Part of the stage collapsed. We had too many people on the stage. No one was hurt. I repeat. There was no bomb."

Then the lights came back on.

This was a concert.

There was no bomb.

The Klan was not here.

The loudspeaker again: "We have power. Everything is still on schedule. As soon as we clear the stage area we will begin the second set. Please, everybody move back. We need to clear more people off the stage."

Voices. Everyone began talking at once.

An uncomfortable laughter.

A loosening of the circle around me.

Finally, the sweet voice of someone sounding like Lena Horne started singing, "We Shall O-ver C-um-m." Several mellow male voices joined in with overlapping threads of "o-ver come some day-aa."

Hooded Sweatshirt came over, shrugged his shoulders, stared at me, lifted both hands in a sorry-but-shit-happens gesture, grinned and walked away. He had business elsewhere.

I stood by myself, alone, ignored. People walked by. No eye contact.

I saw Doug, Tim, and Chrissy standing together in the distance. They waved. I waved back.

Nothing had happened.

Everything was as it should be.

[7]

Nineteen sixty-two opened in Birmingham with a bang. Three churches were dynamited between 9 and 10 p.m. on January 16. It seemed the amateur hour all the way. Damage was minimal at all three... "We know that the Negroes did it," Bull Connor was saying. The proof was that the two cops who happened to be in their car seventy-five yards from one explosion spied a black teenager running from the scene.[4]

Crestview College stands isolated on a hilltop, boxed in on three sides by low-rent housing projects, with the football stadium, Legion Field, and colored neighborhoods only a few blocks away. If you were to head north away from the campus, however, you would soon discover rural Alabama farmland, pine forests, and weathered barns tilted as if blown askew by a heavy wind. But once you turn left off the highway at the top of the hill and pass through the wrought-iron gates and enter the campus, there are fields of green grass, tennis courts, flowering pathways, and well-dressed students in slacks and button-down shirts strolling across the open Quad at the heart of the college. Beyond the Quad, past the planetarium down the hill, and just beyond a stand of tall weeping willows begin the compact brick structures of married student housing. Here, in Apartment 2C, overlooking the parking lot and the weeping willows in the distance, at the end of our junior year, Chrissy and I threw a going-away party for Sarah and Allan, who were soon to graduate, and as a coming-out party for Doug, who had agreed under Tim's insistence to join us "sinners" and "allow alcohol to pass his lips." Doug was ready to celebrate, Tim informed us, because, after a year of working out together, Doug could now do ten chin-ups in a row.

"Think about it," Tim had explained to us all. "Doug's never tasted liquor, not even beer, never made it with a girl, and never smoked a cigarette."

Sarah had dressed for our party in a Mexican smock cut low, with embroidered rock roses accentuating her breasts. Her blonde hair was arrayed in tiers of curls, showing off her fine neck and red mouth. Ten years older than the rest of us, she was a bright chimera, inviting and untouchable. As she moved through the party talking to each person, one on one, Allan watched her through thick wire-rimmed glasses, his brown hair grown long and flowing. He laughed mischievously as she chatted across the room while he pulled at his beard and took long sips from his gin and tonic.

Tim, bright eyes gleaming, suddenly poked his curly black head into our living room and whispered to me, "Hey, Eddie, thanks for having this party, but I'm putting together some plans for later on, for Doug. Maybe you and Chrissy could join us for a midnight swim? Huh? I know, not your cup of tea, but think about it. It'll be fun. Just a few more details to work out. I need to talk to some ladies. I'll be back before you know it." And he was gone.

Then, a few minutes later, Doug in a blue, button-down shirt, stronger and taller in his new thin, muscular frame, finger-combed his fine hair out of his eyes and strode through the doorway saying, "Somebody fix me a drink. I plan to get as drunk as a lord."

Everybody laughed as he plopped down in our beanbag chair, one foot solidly placed on the floor while the other dangled loosely over his knee and kicked at the air in sharp angular movements. His brown penny-loafer dangled half off at the end of his foot. His hair, freshly washed, again hung down in his face, almost to the tip of his nose. He looked like a towheaded kid facing his first real adventure after leaving the farm.

Allan, chewing at his beard, already a little tipsy, mixed Doug a drink, a vodka screwdriver, and carried it over to him using the album cover of Beethoven's Second Symphony as a serving tray. After Doug took his drink, Allan removed the record from its jacket, set it on the spindle.

"This symphony doesn't get enough attention; let's give it a whirl," Allan chuckled to the room as he watched Doug take his first sip.

Doug smiled and lifted his drink to the room.

Allan twisted his beard thoughtfully as he reciprocated, holding up his own drink to commemorate the occasion. Then he grinned impishly and started declaiming in a loud voice, "I am not Prince Hamlet, nor was meant to be... I am deferential, glad to be of use, politic, cautious, and meticulous, full of high sentence, but a bit obtuse, at times, indeed, almost ridiculous, almost, at times, the Fool."

Having gained everyone's attention, Allan threw back his head and laughed loudly in a high-pitched, almost feminine cackle. Then the record dropped and strains of Beethoven filled the room. Allan was clearly in a strange mood, perhaps because he and Sarah were not happy with each other. A few minutes earlier Sarah had shoved him into the living room and closed and locked the bedroom door because she and Chrissy wanted privacy. The two of them had become embroiled in an intense, "personal" conversation, a serious tête-à-tête.

I stared at the still-closed door, but I did not interfere. Chrissy was already tipsy, and I thought that maybe Sarah would slow her down. Sarah was careful. She never overindulged or drank too much.

On the kitchen table behind me there was a self-serve bar of paper cups, ice buckets, cut lemons, potato chips, onion dip, vodka, rum, tequila, gin, Old Crow, Jack Daniel's, and Cutty Sark.

Our neighbors were in for it.

I walked outside onto the cement patio where I had set up a card table of condiments, two hibachis for burgers and sausages, several kegs of beer, and a giant ice-filled garbage can of fresh oysters that Tim somehow had managed to appropriate on a quick trip to New Orleans.

Odors of rich mesquite-flavored meat permeated our section of the project.

As I stood cooking behind the grill on the patio, I greeted guests, flipped burgers, sipped a gin and tonic, and watched as plumes of smoke, caught in the cross-draft of our apartment hallway, drifted out into the evening sky to disappear in the orange glow of a huge full moon, brighter than any streetlight. Several bats darted above the horizon, gorging on insects. Outside, tree frogs and crickets punctuated the night as they lifted their mating cries above the distant sounds of passing cars. Inside, our three-room apartment had lost any resemblance to living quarters and had begun to look more like the party room of a frat house in the midst of a free-for-all. I spoke to everyone coming up the stairs but didn't have time for a real conversation with anyone. Chrissy and I, as hosts, were rarely even able to speak to one another.

The subject on most everybody's mind was Sarah's imminent departure. Everyone would miss her. But then there was this feeling of tension in the air. Allan was acting bizarrely and being hard to talk to; Anita was walking a fine line between praising and yet mocking Sarah's plans for once again leaving her children behind with her mother while she went off to do graduate work in music at the University of Alabama in Tuscaloosa; and we all were making half-hearted promises about staying in touch.

I was not happy with Chrissy. She had started drinking early, had quickly exceeded her limit of three drinks, and was acting strangely: one moment exaggeratedly cheerful, the next dejected to the point of distraction. She was laughing too loudly, hugging too long, engaging in exaggerated, full-bodied embraces. I was a little dismayed and angry at her behavior. But beyond that, I was also a little ticked off about the way Tim seemed to be turning this whole party into an exercise in voyeurism, encouraging everyone to participate in Doug's getting drunk.

So I stayed outside most of the time, drinking, flipping burgers, and thinking about a term paper I was working on. I was fascinated by the philosophical struggle around the concept of cause and effect as presented in the works of David Hume (who argued that there is no permanent "self" and that our concepts of cause and effect are not provable) and Immanuel Kant (who argued that the mind plays an active role in determining our experience and that cause and effect is a necessary, built-in frame of reference for understanding our world). I tentatively planned to title it "You Kant Go Hume Again." As I thought through my ideas, I began hoping this party would end before it got too late. I had a lot of work to catch up on.

However, it was considerably after midnight when I finally decided it was time to bring the party to an end. Lights were low and I had to step over a few people lying about on the floor, semi-comatose. I started by dumping empties into a garbage can I'd brought in from the parking lot. The apartment was beginning to stink from cigarette butts stuffed into half-empty beer cans. The kitchen floor was sticky and needed mopping, but I couldn't find the mop. In the living room, Howard and Pam from the drama circle sat close together, arms around each other, murmuring. Doug was still holding forth in the same chair he had taken when he arrived; but he seemed to slant sideways, his swinging foot describing a sloshy circle. Tim stood unsteadily in front of Doug with his hands surrounding the nearly-empty bottle of Cutty Sark.

"Now, memory!" Tim said. "How's your memory affected? Question: when was *The Origin of Species* published?"

Doug leveled his gaze and spoke in slow words spaced evenly, "In the year of our Lord, eighteen hundred and fifty-nine!" and pushed his empty glass forward to accept a splash of golden liquid poured over the clinking ice cubes.

I went back into the kitchen for a glass of water and stepped into a dark stain of sticky substance in front of the refrigerator. Some clean-up was required. I looked again in the broom closet for the mop and bucket, but it was empty.

Where was the mop?

I decided Chrissy had taken it. Then I noticed the bedroom door was still closed.

After opening it, I stopped and stared—Chrissy was under the covers, in our bed with Allan. He had a naked white arm draped over her bare shoulder. I hesitated in the doorway. Watched them become aware of me one at a time. Allan stiffened, stopped in mid-sentence. Chrissy rose up on her elbows, turned toward me, said, "Oh, dear..." and then pulled the covers over her head.

Anger flushed through me followed almost immediately by a heavy fatigue, and, closing the door, I retreated back into the living room.

With my back to the door, with strains of Beethoven's Ninth Symphony overlaying multiple conversations, I tried to put myself back together. A little dizzy, I stood in our living room. It was filled with smoke. Nothing seemed familiar.

Could everyone just go away?

Finally, I turned back around, faced the door, opened it a second time.

"What's going on? Chrissy? Allan?"

Allan pulled himself to a sitting position, his beard pasted against his face and neck, his thin bare shoulders hugely freckled, his mouth, fish-like, opening and closing silently. He looked at me as if he were going to speak but then collapsed backwards on the bed and closed his eyes. Anita came up behind me, put her hands in the small of my back, pushed me into the room, and closed the door behind us.

Standing close, Anita touched my cheek with her fingertips, and then ran her hand through that shock of her bright black hair.

"Wait a minute...hold on," she said. "Forget about them for a minute... Something happened between Sarah and Chrissy. I'm afraid... well, Sarah ran out of here pretty upset. She...she left. Nobody out there knows anything," she tilted her head indicating the people in the living room. "And they don't know where she's gone. Maybe she went back to her mother's house... She's not at her apartment—I've just come from there—and she's obviously not here."

Speaking over my shoulder, but still watching me, she said, "Chrissy, do you know where Sarah is?" Chrissy mumbled from beneath the covers, "Sarah? I need to talk to Sarah. I need to explain..."

"Sarah's missing. We don't know where she is."

Chrissy poked her head out from under the covers, face wet, mascara smeared, and with a drunken slur asked me plaintively, "Would you go look for her?"

Anita set her drink on the bedside table and said, "I'll go with you."

A strange voice in my head said loudly, "Allan, I don't want to see you here when I get back."

And suddenly Chrissy, in her slip, with the sheet wrapped around her, hand covering her mouth, made a dash for the bathroom. When she opened the door, the mop became visible, propped in a bucket between the toilet and the sink. Chrissy had already thrown up. Somebody else had cleaned it up. From the unattended phonograph in the living room another record dropped, and the climax to Beethoven's Ninth, *An die Freude*, the *Ode to Joy*, exploded in the living room.

The party was over.

The last guests were slinking out the door. I turned off the record player and put all three records back in their folders. To my left, out the living room window, Doug and Tim ambled across the brightly lit parking lot and climbed into a sports coupe convertible—that must have been part of Tim's surprise. Tim backed out quickly, too quickly, and then burned rubber as they took off down the street.

I could hear Chrissy in the bathroom vomiting.

After checking Sarah's locked, dark apartment, Anita and I walked the length of the parking lot and discovered that her car was not there.

What had happened with Sarah? Why had she run off? It wasn't like her to behave that way.

We concluded that Sarah had gone home to her children in Jasper. Standing in the brightly lit parking lot, Anita gave me a long hug. She said, "You better go back. I can make it to the dorm on my own." Then, as she turned to go, she added, whispering, almost as an afterthought, "Just so you know, about Allan and Chrissy, I think they really were only comforting each other."

I watched her disappear in the trees as she headed up the winding path toward the dorms, and then I jogged across the pavement, taking the stairs to our apartment two at a time. Inside, everyone was gone. In the after-party silence and standing in the wreckage of our living room, I could hear the shower running. The bathroom door was open. I went in and got the mop. The shower-glass and mirrors were completely fogged. I couldn't just stand around and wait, so I started on the kitchen floor. Next I picked up the obvious trash and carried the garbage can back down to the pickup area at the back of our building. The full moon was gone. Off in the distance I could hear a breeze rustling in the willow trees. The entire red brick housing complex was dark except for the street lamps over the parking lot and our brightly lit corner apartment. I didn't want to go back inside. I felt like I had a hole in me, like a bomb had exploded inside leaving nothing but rubble and emptiness. I stood in silence next to the hulking black metallic Dempsey Dumpster and waited for some feeling to come back to me. But there was nothing. It was if a wind swirled around and around a funnel of emptiness inside me. I waited for some clear direction to come back to me. None did. Then questions started popping up like bubbles released from some underground pressure: *Why had Sarah left without saying goodbye? What had happened between Sarah and Chrissy? Why had Chrissy gotten so drunk? Why were Allan and Chrissy in bed together? Why was I standing out here alone in the dark?*

Standing quite still, I felt like I was hurtling down some dark road on a pitch-black night without knowing where the next turn might be. So I stood there and waited, a little sick to my stomach, in the darkness, in the shadows beyond the pool of light cast down from our brightly lit windows. My hands were shaking. When I looked up at the Big Dipper, low in the sky, usually a comforting and familiar, friendly presence, even that constellation seemed remote, unrelated. And suddenly I could no longer stand still. I had to move. I had to go back inside.

An owl called out in the night. "Whooo, whooo."

My footsteps echoed eerily on the concrete of the empty hallway. I climbed the stairs, turned out the porch light, and closed our apartment door behind me.

[8]

I was not there, but it must have happened this way.

Tim and Doug smoked cigars, laughed and drank beer as they drove, the top down, the night air moving over them in a slipstream of pre-dawn dust and smoke and fog. Tim drove as the convertible danced nimbly over the ghostly white gravel road that was taking them to a swimming hole on Turkey Creek. Tim had planned this for weeks—an erotic outing with willing ladies. The ladies, Margot and Marianne, with Keith and Kathy, who wanted to join in the fun, led the way in Margot's brand new black Pontiac. Tim and Doug followed in their borrowed pale blue convertible, top down. As Tim gunned the car through the switchbacks, the red taillights of the ladies' big Pontiac were continually lost and then recaptured in the windshield. In the Pontiac, Keith and Kathy collapsed on top of one another in the back seat. Margot drove and Marianne rode shotgun.

Midnight skinny-dipping was only a few miles ahead.

Tim steered the two-seater with one hand as he downshifted with every turn, spewing gravel. Above the false green dawn of the dash lights, as if by magic, they flew through twists and turns, their head-lights carving a tunnel in the dust, the pale road appearing to pour out of the night's blackness directly in front of them.

It was the sudden appearance of the wooden one-way bridge around a sharp turn that caused Margot to brake too hard so that the Pontiac's tires lost their purchase and the car began to slide over the wet planks. The Pontiac careened forward as it skidded off the roadway onto the wooden crossties, the front tires bouncing, the back end sliding as it swung around until the car finally shuddered to an abrupt halt. Facing the wrong way. Completely blocking the bridge.

Tim, coming out of the curve, spotted them too late, braked hard and cut his wheels to avoid slamming head-on into the driver's side of the Pontiac, into Margot as she faced back into Tim's headlights. The front wheels of the convertible spun as they left the slick wood and caught purchase on a crosstie. Then the convertible, as if the tail end were being tilted by some invisible hand, slowly shifted, lifted up over the bridge's railing, tipped sideways, and then smashed through the guardrail, turning over in slow motion and landing lopsided, driver side down, wheels, passenger side taillights up in the air. Then the car, now blocking the fast-running current of Turkey Creek, began, slowly, to twist, to give in to gravity and the swirling waters that rushed up against the car's side, splashing over the hood and flooding the interior with water.

Doug was trapped in the front seat. Tim was thrown clear.

Climbing to his feet amidst the tangle of vines, he wiped at the wet on his face. Blood. He was bleeding from a deep gash on his forehead. *Had he been unconscious?* He stood up, almost passed out. Looked around. At first he didn't know where he was. Then he saw the car, the headlights—one eerily lighted the creek bed and the other the picnic grounds across the bridge. He waded, waist deep, into the creek, and, fighting against the downstream push of the current, maneuvered around until he could try the door. It didn't budge.

Keith and the girls were out of the Pontiac. Margot looked down, sobbing, shaking, and fell to her knees. The creek rushed loudly under them. The convertible's headlights were dimming. Keith and the other two girls crossed the bridge. Someone began throwing up.

The car was tilted up on its side, upside down, wheels up in the air. The driver's side was under water, but the passenger side was raised up, seemingly held up by the water rushing in against the car. Tim could not tell whether Doug was conscious or not. He was hanging sideways, unmoving, held in place by the crumpled and twisted dashboard. His head dangled. His legs looked trapped. Suddenly the car shifted in the stream. Tim grabbed hold of the window frame, bent his knees, tried to lift. The pain in his side was immense. He let go. The car had not budged. Tim was afraid gravity and the creek would pull the car over and down, taking Doug's head under water. Turkey Creek, swollen from a recent rain, was crashing loudly against the car. But Doug's head and shoulders were still above water. Tim thought he heard Doug murmuring something, maybe groaning, but the noise from the creek striking the car was deafening. Tim tried pulling at Doug, but that didn't work. He leaned towards him, listened as Doug groaned miserably. He had to do something. Fast.

Tim hurt everywhere at once; his left hand seemed not to be able to close; his left shoulder throbbed incessantly; he had trouble getting his breath. He thought he had broken some ribs. He looked up at Margot on the bridge. No help there. He tried to push the car. He couldn't budge it. He tried shouting for help, but no one moved. He could see Keith and Kathy wandering about by the picnic tables. Keith was throwing up. They didn't seem to understand. Tim tried for a pulse in Doug's neck. He thought he felt it.

Oh God, don't die.

He had to do something. A decision had to be made, a choice he would revisit for the rest of his life. The Pontiac's engine still idled up on the bridge. *How far away was that last service station? A phone? A lighted house they had passed?*

"Margot, come here. We have to keep his head out of the water."

She came down and waded in, sobbing. Incoherent.

"Just keep his head up. Do you understand?"

She nodded.

"I'm going for help."

Urgency filled him as he struggled out of the stream, the water holding him back, then up the slippery bank, and into the car. Finally somehow, tires screaming, rubber burning, slipping, sliding, he fought the wheel and forced the car backwards, off the crossties, off the bridge, onto the gravel road. Then, finally, giving in to his need to hurry, he stepped down hard and floored the accelerator.

The night forest flew by as dust and gravel spewed behind him. Hard-shelled insects smashed and smeared against the windshield. On several turns he almost lost control, fishtailing so badly the car was off the road and into the brush, but he never slowed down. Each time the car found its way back onto the road, and Tim continued to gun it, gripping the wheel with his one good hand, his feet squishing inside his shoes, his wet pants sticking to the leather interior. He wiped at the wet running down the left side of his face. In the dark he remembered he had to keep taking the right forks until finally he turned onto the paved highway and pressed the accelerator all the way to the floor. Tim willed the car to go faster and faster until suddenly he saw the lights of a farmhouse and cut into the driveway, taking out the mailbox on the way. He slid to a stop at the farmhouse's front steps. Climbing from the car, his hip hurting, fighting for breath, he hobbled up the wooden steps and began banging on the door. Lights came on. Footsteps.

It was all taking too long: the old woman in her night robe placing the call on the antique phone to the county sheriff; Tim explaining; waiting for the patrol car to come as the old woman lit several kerosene lanterns to augment the overhead bare light bulb; the infuriating slowness of the heavyset sheriff; explaining again; begging the sheriff to stop talking, to follow him, to help; leading the sheriff's car back through the switchbacks, its red lights swirling, its siren wailing in the dark; and all the while an urgency building inside him that was fighting against a fatigue that kept coming in waves like a need to sleep, like a need to lie down inside that strange feeling that time was slowing down, that everything outside him was moving in slow motion.

As soon as they pulled up, he knew it was all over. The car was completely upside down. Margot was sitting on the bridge, head in hands, not moving.

Tim got out in the dark and leaned heavily against the car's open door, its headlights framing the swirling waters and the upside down convertible. He couldn't move. The sheriff looked over at Tim but didn't say anything and then slowly waded out into the stream and put his big flashlight under water. Stood there with his back to Tim, bent over, for a long while.

Finally he rose up shaking his head and turned with a strange force of inevitability about him, his big belly dripping wet, and he began slowly wading back to Tim who stood, trapped, unable to move, the red lights of the sheriff's car still swirling around them, his knees weak, holding onto the door, not understanding the sheriff's question.

"Why didn't you use the car jacks?" he asked.

"What?"

"You had two of them, one in the Pontiac, one in the convertible. Why didn't you use the two jacks to keep the car off him?"

Tim felt himself falling, but he didn't care. Slowly, it occurred to him that he was letting go of the car door; he was sliding downward. He felt himself going away. He didn't care. Someone was asking him a question. He didn't know the answer. He was letting go of the door.

He let go.

[9]

The bathroom door opened and Chrissy came out scrubbed clean, wet hair combed straight back, in a white robe. A warm mist and the smell of shampoo followed her into the room. The mop still stood in its bucket, leaning against the back of the toilet. Outside our window an owl called and another answered. The rest of the apartment complex slept. From the open windows, insistent moths threw themselves against our screens. As she came out I shifted to the far side of the bed and, sitting up, pulled my bare knees up under my chin. Chrissy walked across the room, head down, hands pulling and twisting at long wet strands of her hair.

I made an effort to be calm, "Okay. I'm listening. Just tell me the truth. What is going on?"

"Eddie, it's not what you think...we didn't... We only held each other."

I heard myself saying, "I don't believe you. I don't...*believe* you!"

She came forward, crawled across the bed, reached out, touched me; and suddenly an electric shock convulsed my body as my legs kicked out and sent her sliding across the bed and, shockingly, arms outstretched, into empty space.

Chrissy hit the floor hard and suddenly I was terrified. I leaped to my knees and saw her curled up on the floor pulling her robe around her, sobbing. I jumped down and knelt beside her on the hard tile floor, "I'm sorry. Chrissy, I'm so sorry..."

Carefully, we helped each other off the floor.

We were almost to the bed when the phone began to ring.

"It's past four in the morning," I said. "Who do you think is calling us at this hour? Allan? Do you think it's Allan?"

Chrissy shook her head, "I don't know."

I stood by the bed and let it ring. Four, five, six times.

"Hello?"

It wasn't Allan.

Between breaths, gasping, her voice shaking, Anita spoke one word, stopped and then tried again.

"Eddie... Eddie?"

"What is it, Anita?"

Gathering herself, she spoke slowly her words evenly spaced. She said, "There's been an accident... I don't know how to say this, but... Doug's dead... Tim's in the hospital... I don't know what happened. I'm trying to get in touch with his parents...the police called the school and somehow got the dorms, got me... Do you have their number? It's not in the phone book."

"Hold on. I think we've got it." I turned to Chrissy, "There's been an accident. Do we have Tim's parents' phone number?"

Chrissy, a frightened look on her face, ran after our phone list.

I gave Anita the number.

Anita's voice sounded distant, far away, almost a whisper.

"They wouldn't tell me how Tim's doing; they only wanted me to help them get in touch with his parents... Eddie, I've got to go."

She hung up.

Chrissy was staring, waiting for me to answer the question she had not asked. I walked her back into the bedroom. We sat down together on the side of the bed.

When dawn began creeping over the top of Red Mountain, when Vulcan's statue began to glow in the early morning sun, we were still sitting on our bed holding two unbelievable words between us— *Doug's dead*. I reached over and pulled the blinds closed. The room darkened immediately. It seemed better that way. Then we lay down together, side by side, not speaking, and not sleeping.

In a few hours we would get up, get dressed, and go for a walk on campus. The beauty of the grounds, the warm breeze whispering through the willows, the noise of early morning lawn mowers, the students out jogging on the paths, everything seemed so normal, and yet so completely out of touch with the reality we shared. We held hands, but there was also a distance between us. We were not sure of each other. The news of Doug's death had overwhelmed us like a tidal wave that took us under water and forced us to find our own separate paths to the surface.

When Monday came around, I went about my daily life, found relief in doing what I had to do, attending classes, going to work.

But Chrissy simply shut down.

She cried every day for a week. She stayed in bed and only got up to go out for short walks or to eat an occasional bowl of hot milk over bits of buttered toast. She kept all the blinds pulled. Our apartment stayed dark. Beyond exchanging necessary information, we didn't talk about what had happened that night. We drifted, waiting in a strange limbo, waiting, I guess, for answers to the unasked question: why? We didn't talk about Doug or Tim. It was too big. And I didn't feel we could talk about Allan, or Sarah and Chrissy, or even the little "whys" of what had happened that night. Chrissy wasn't ready, and neither was I. First we had to bury Doug.

At the funeral three days later we stood around in groups, isolated elements from Doug's life, students, friends, family, and church members. No group knew much about the others. I noticed that Sarah and Allan were not present, which was just fine with me. I didn't want to see either of them. Nothing made sense to me. Feeling confused and emotionally spent, I stood on the outskirts of the gathering with Chrissy and Tim and watched Anita, all in black, reach out, trying to comfort Doug's mother, whose head was veiled and bowed as she turned away from Anita's outstretched hands. Anita looked over at us and shrugged. It wasn't working. Doug's family blamed us, his friends. Rumor had it that the family had tried to have Tim arrested after the accident, that a lawsuit claiming willful negligence was being filed. Negligent homicide. *Blame*, I wondered, *how does one assign blame?* The police were waiting for Tim's deposition, but Tim seemed *non compos mentis,* not present, out of it, lost.

He stood beside me, arm in a sling, bandages on his head covering most of his curly black hair, his face slack, his usual, brilliant, pale-blue, bright-eyed look gone, his eyes empty. A few minutes earlier, looking straight ahead, vacantly, he had said, to no one in particular, "My fault. This was all my fault."

Anita had spoken up quickly.

"It was not your fault."

She had then turned to me and said, "We need to keep him away from the family and their lawyers. Eddie, don't let him talk to anyone. I'll be back in a minute."

As I stood there, lightly holding Tim's arm, I thought how Doug's death was going to affect all of us who knew him, but especially Tim, who had been Doug's best friend almost from the start. Doug had created an aura of excitement and possibility. When Doug walked into a room the world seemed better, cleaner, clearer. His confident aura seemed to extend outward around his inner circle of friends, supporting us. And we chosen few who had lived inside that protection of his clarity and understanding, now, for the first time, felt its absence like a sucking vacuum that could not be filled. The world felt like it was losing dimensionality, felt flat, as if we could fall over a precipice at the edge of this newly discovered horizon, death. I remembered his voice, that nasal, high-pitched certainty of his with which he framed every problem, how he had always startled me with his precision of perspective in the midst of amazing and daunting complexity. Without him around I wondered if we would lose that sense he had given us that the world was out there waiting for us to explore, that it was comprehensible if we but tried to figure it out. I knew that Tim had breathed it all in like a man who, for the first time in his life, had fallen in love with something larger than himself. Without Doug around I feared that our group would disintegrate. Doug's intelligence and integrity had held us together. For those of us who had sat at his breakfast table, nothing would ever be the same. I looked over at Tim, at the vacant, panicky look in his eyes. Doug had once said of Tim as he entered our classroom, "Now here's someone with an imagination that can light up the dark."

Just released from the hospital for the funeral, Tim couldn't remember anything about the accident. He stood beside us. Tense. Stiff. He didn't respond to anything we said, yet he seemed trapped, furtive, and unstable. At Anita's urging, we took him away quickly, avoiding Doug's family and the dark suits surrounding them.

In the days and weeks following the funeral Tim stopped going to classes. He showed up on campus on rare occasions, unshaven, looking like he'd slept in his car. He had lost weight. Randomly, like an unwelcome, visiting relation, he would show up at the cafeteria breakfasts, sit down at the table across from us, and stare at us accusingly, as if we had no right to be there talking. On those mornings, no subjects of importance were discussed. No one knew what to say.

Chrissy and I decided to call Tim's parents. They seemed even more in the dark than we were. They wanted to know if we knew what was wrong. They were worried: Could we talk to Tim? He never came home anymore. Where was he staying? What was he doing? Maybe we could convince him he should see a doctor.

"He's not himself since his accident," they said. "He seems so angry all the time now. He has such strange ideas. Maybe he should be hospitalized for his own good."

We couldn't imagine it: Tim, our friend, confined in a mental hospital. We kept waiting for him to snap out of it, to wake up, to come back to just being Tim. But then Tim would come over to see us and talk as if he were speaking to some invisible listener who understood and followed all the innuendoes of a very subtle logic. Perhaps he talked to Doug. But he was not crazy, we thought. He was grief stricken. He needed to be left alone until he could find his way back into his own life.

One day Tim arrived at our house only marginally aware of where he was, of where he had been, of what he had been doing. We found that he had gone to Ensley to see the housing complex of his childhood. That complex had been part of a "white trash" ghetto on the western side of Birmingham. It was being torn down. Only a few concrete structures remained standing. Inside I imagined they were all alike: red wooden floors, cracked linoleum kitchens, gas heaters loosely attached to walls, and small rectangular windows separated by cheap wooden bars.

As soon as Tim appeared at our door I knew he was in serious trouble. He stood erect, elbows at his side, and held his empty hands, palms up, in front of him. His eyes were fixed on some vanishing point behind us. As he walked into the room we noticed the broken skin over his knuckles and the thin, dark rivulets of blood tracking down his fingers.

"Tim, what happened to your hands?" I asked. His eyes wandered around the room, as though he could hear us but could not see us.

"Yes, it hurts, but it hurts good not bad. It's pain that does it. Pain gives you a clearer insight. Pain shows you what's real and what's not. Now I can understand it! Do you? Do you understand it?"

"Tim, are you okay?" I asked. Then he seemed to see us, and he motioned for us to sit down. We sat down. Tim pulled up a chair directly in front of us, and smiled. He seemed to be running a fever. His face, always a ruddy red color, now flushed crimson, and his pale blue eyes glittered, unfocused.

"I saw my father today. I talked to him, but he wouldn't listen. He was trapped inside our old house. I couldn't get him out. I told him, Dad, do you understand why you're *here*? But he didn't. He just stared back at me through the windows of his fucking house. He didn't even know *I* was there with him."

Tim stared at his hands. "I told him, but he wouldn't listen. I said, 'No, you don't know. Why don't you know? Why don't **you** know that nothing else matters. If you know why you're in here then you can do anything. Anything anybody else tells you is a lie. A fucking lie! A trick to make you stay in your place. You don't have to stay here. If you stay here it's because you're weak! If you understand who you are you can break out. You can smash this whole stupid world like a goddamned fucking pane of glass!'"

Tim's eyes were closed when he finished and then his head drooped forward, motionless, as if he were slipping into sleep. We waited for him to look up again. Tears flowed silently down Chrissy's cheeks. She leaned her head on my shoulder and shuddered. Her hands were shaking. I kissed the top of her head, and she turned toward me with a look of concern, for Tim, for all of us, I thought, all of us struggling to make sense of this tragedy. I took both of her hands in mine, and, in a silence of communion, we watched Tim breathe, afraid to rouse him. Several minutes passed until finally I touched his shoulder and asked him again, gently, "Tim, what did you do to your hands?" His head snapped up, and suddenly he was on his feet again glowering down at us.

"I broke all the windows in my father's house!" Abruptly, he turned on his heels and walked out of our apartment, out of school, out of Birmingham, out of the South.

The next time we heard from him he was in California. A postcard of the Golden Gate Bridge arrived, no signature, with one sentence written in loose script, all the letters piled up against each other, leaning backwards, *In Sausalito, on a houseboat, engaged in salvation of the souls of Republicans.*

[10]

Our next year in school began without the constant presence of friends. Doug's death and Tim's disappearance left us feeling isolated. We saw Anita on campus, but she no longer popped by for visits. Allan called up to apologize for what had happened at the party. He said he'd had too much to drink. I told him I believed him, but I still didn't want to see him for a while. So he didn't come around. And that was just fine with me. With Sarah away in graduate school, the rumor was that Allan had gone "on drift," that he had become one of those "stag" males with nothing to do, who showed up at parties without being invited.

At first we were caught up in the necessities of our lives as students, but soon, without close friends, we discovered we were alone with a future that loomed before us like a growing dark cloud on the horizon. Foolishly, I signed up for a heavy class load: Beginning Latin, The Nineteenth Century Novel, a seminar in the theology of Paul Tillich, and Modern French Poetry. Between classes and jobs, I had no free time. But Chrissy did. And then we began to argue.

We argued about who should carry out the garbage, about which of us should go on to graduate school, about which of us should try for editorship of the campus literary magazine, *The Quad*. Then, in the midst of one of our discussions about our future, Chrissy announced that she really didn't know what she wanted, that she needed to get away to have time to think. She decided to go for a weekend visit with Sarah. I agreed and thought we needed some time apart.

Sarah was only forty miles away in Tuscaloosa, in graduate school at the University of Alabama, pursuing an advanced degree in music. Chrissy packed her bags, and I dropped her off at the bus station.

She was gone for two days. When I picked her up late that Sunday evening at the bus station, I found her sitting on a bench, head down, wearing a blue work shirt un-tucked, wine-colored skirt, and tennis sneakers. Her dark hair was carelessly pinned back with large black bobby pins. Her brown eyes avoided mine.

I'd missed her, but she offered me only a rueful, half-hearted smile as I approached. She didn't seem glad to see me at all.

"What's wrong?" I asked.

"Sarah and I stayed up all night talking, and I'm too tired to go into it right now," she said. "Can we just go home?"

So that's what we did. We didn't talk, and I decided I didn't care. Besides, I had a big test to study for.

In her diary Chrissy wrote:

The skin about my eyes is swollen from crying, but the dark black centers of me are open and looking, struggling to see, to recognize what can be seen. Yesterday, in the lighted darkness of a bus station, I saw people talking and laughing as people do in time-killing situations. I liked them. I felt close to them.

I understand what you said about not wanting ever to recreate this relationship with another friend, and I accept it. It is true: each rare time one moves into the sphere of another, the experience, which opens the way to new dimensions of being, is unique and can never be reproduced. I hope the wise part of me will not search the world for another Sarah. I will remember the simple parts, the all-embracing music, the crowds of people in bus stations, and the touch of your neck, your fingers, and your hair.

That following Monday Chrissy didn't go to classes. She said her legs ached, that her skin hurt, that she didn't feel well enough to go. And so for the next few days she stayed in bed.

Then, slowly, like a person suffering from sleeping sickness, she staggered up and attended classes, but she paid little or no attention to her appearance. She wore the same outfit everyday: an oversized shirt she had borrowed from Sarah, that same wine-colored skirt, and her dirty tennis shoes. She began to lose weight. She no longer seemed to wash her beautiful dark hair. She kept it pinned back out of her face, stringy, dull and lusterless, held in place with a white plastic band.

Each morning at 7:30 I headed out to my 8:00 class and left her asleep in bed. Each night when I returned from my job at the library around 10:00 p.m., she was back in bed.

"I just feel this emptiness around me," she said, "I feel so alone."

"I'm here," I said.

"It's not about you," she said, "It's about me. Nothing feels real anymore, none of it, school, classes, you...none of it. I don't feel safe. I don't know who I am to you, to myself, or to anyone else."

By the end of the week I pushed her to see a doctor, a therapist.

She wanted me to leave her alone, but I wouldn't. I kept after her until she made an appointment to see the campus psychologist.

She said she was afraid a therapist would find a label for her "dark reality" and profane it with a name.

I told her she was hiding from herself.

A few weeks later, after several visits to her therapist, she still didn't seem to be getting any better, and she wouldn't talk about what was bothering her. If anything, her moods seemed to darken, as if she harbored some deep-seated anger that she would not or could not talk about with me. I worried she might begin failing some classes. She never seemed to have any homework. I decided I had to talk to Dr. Elizabeth Cantrell, the campus psychologist she was seeing, so I arranged to have some time off from work.

Dr. Cantrell's one-room office was located in the science building. She had agreed to see me in the evening, after a faculty meeting. I waited in front of her locked door as occasional students passed by loaded down with books and papers on their way to an open study hall. Finally Dr. Cantrell arrived looking harried, with briefcase in hand, and wearing a print dress, heavy black shoes, and horn-rimmed glasses. After fiddling around to find the right key, she unlocked the door as she spoke to me over her shoulder, "Are you Eddie?"

I nodded and followed her in.

Behind her desk was one black, painted-over window. She sat down, her over-crowded desk between us, and motioned towards her guest chair, the only object in the room not covered with books and papers.

"I only have a few minutes this evening. I'm sorry, but as it turns out I have to see a patient at the clinic in a short while."

She was soft spoken, a small, middle-aged woman, her graying hair pulled back in a bun. She sat down, arranged a few papers on her desk, picked up a pen, tapped it against her notepad, looked up and smiled.

"So, Eddie, what's on your mind?"

I liked her right away. She felt comfortable, ready to listen.

"You've been seeing Chrissy for a few weeks now, and I was hoping you could help me understand what's going on with her."

She watched me intently for a moment, as if trying to make up her mind about something.

"What do you want to know?" she asked.

"I want to know what's wrong and what I can do to help."

Dr. Cantrell opened a pad of paper, clicked her pen off and on twice, put on her glasses that hung from her neck, wrote something, and then looked over her glasses at me. Her gentle eyes took on a slight edge of hardness as she spoke, tilting her head slightly to one side, as though she needed a better perspective.

"In your opinion, just what do you think has been wrong with Chrissy?"

"Well, she seems depressed. She keeps the apartment dark and doesn't want to get out of bed. She went off to visit a mutual friend at the University of Alabama, in Tuscaloosa, and when she returned, she was just down. And she doesn't seem to be getting better."

Dr. Cantrell made another quick note.

"Has Chrissy ever seemed depressed to you before this episode?" she inquired.

A memory flashed before me of the day she'd gone to visit Anita when I had witnessed her walking alone away from campus, with that desperate look on her face, and I remembered the way she had cinched the belt of her raincoat tightly about her waist, defiantly, in full sunshine, mascara smeared down her face from crying. I didn't want to talk about that. It felt private. Like I'd spied on her.

"Well, yes, but nothing quite like this. I've seen her act depressed and sad, but she always seems to...come out of it. After Doug's death, the funeral and all—I assume you've talked about that?"

She wrote something on her pad of yellow paper, nodded affirmatively, and then pushed her glasses down on her nose and looked at me carefully.

"Do you think Doug's death is behind this episode?"

"No. That was a bad time, but we seemed to get past it okay, but lately things have been going downhill. We've been arguing a lot, and, well, since she's been seeing you she seems closed in on herself, and angry, and she won't talk to me about it."

"Do you think Sarah is somehow a part of this episode?" she asked.

"I don't know. I don't think so, but something's wrong, and I'm worried."

"I understand."

She took more notes, and then said, "In your opinion, Eddie, how well does Chrissy get along with her mother?"

That one took me by surprise. I said, "Not very well, actually."

She leaned forward, pushed her glasses down her nose, and looked at me over the rims. "What do you mean? Can you be more explicit?"

"I think her mother has been with a lot of men since she divorced Chrissy's father. That and the fact that her mother smokes too much and drinks a lot has been a big problem for Chrissy. I also think Chrissy relates more to her grandmother than she does to her mother. She calls her grandmother her *mama*."

"Has she said anything to you about her feelings towards her mother?"

"Well, she told me she used to be afraid to bring her boyfriends home because her mother always flirted with them. Chrissy laughed about it, but she told me her mother once arranged for them to double date, with two men her mother's age, and then her mother spent the whole evening flirting with both of them. But that's about all I know."

"I see. Does Chrissy know about you're coming here?"

I leaned back in my chair, and thought about that one.

Chrissy was not going to be happy.

As if she were anticipating something, Dr. Cantrell took off her glasses, let them dangle on her chest, and leaned back expectantly.

"Uh, no."

"Well, Eddie, I can't really advise you, but I will say that you should talk to Chrissy about our visit this evening. Then if you want, the two of you can come back and we'll talk again, but for now all I can say is that Chrissy needs intensive therapy. She won't admit that she needs any help at all. She walked out on our last meeting. I don't think she's planning to come back. I'm afraid that until she's willing to receive help, no one will be able to do much for her."

With that Dr. Cantrell stood up and offered her hand. I shook it and was surprised at its strength, its firmness.

Our meeting was over.

Chrissy wasn't planning to come back.

Outside it was a gray winter evening.

A stiff northern breeze blew a cold spray in my face as I left the campus and started walking down the darkening, well-worn path to the married student apartments, crunching wet leaves underfoot. I hadn't learned much from Dr. Cantrell, and now I had to tell Chrissy that I'd been to see her doctor. I sprinted the last hundred yards to avoid the wind-driven rain that was beginning to fall in a steady and determined downpour.

I reached our apartment and stepped under the shelter of the roof's overhang just as the bottom dropped out and the heavy rainfall began flooding the concrete, overflowing the gutters of the parking lot. The street lamps were coming on, one by one, lighting the mist and raindrops in an eerie glow.

Chrissy was not home.

Her note read: "Gone for a walk and visit with Anita. Be back soon."

I put my books on the kitchen table and started to open a can of soup. She had gone out for a walk, so maybe she was feeling better. Maybe we could talk this thing through. I lit a cigarette and watched as rivulets of rain streaked down our living room windowpane.

[11]

Chrissy arrived home late. I was sitting at the kitchen table with a French poem I had been translating when she walked in, gave me a quick hello-kiss on the top of my head, and passed on into the bathroom to get out of her wet clothes. A few minutes later she came out in her slip, her hair wet and dripping. She said she and Anita had eaten supper in the cafeteria. She said she had enjoyed walking home in the rain, but that now she was suffering from a headache. She took three aspirin, went into the bedroom, and threw herself across the bed. From my vantage point at the kitchen table I stared at her prostrate form. I suddenly wanted to get up and go lie down on top of her, but I didn't. She lay still, as if she had already fallen asleep, but I knew she was awake.

I closed my book and put away my partially translated poem. It was by Paul Verlaine. One verse from it kept running through my brain,

> Il pleure dans mon coeur
> Comme il pleut sur la ville;
> Quelle est cette langueur
> Qui pénètre mon coeur?

"Well, how did your day go?" I said.

Her muffled voice issued from the bedroom, "I'm too tired to talk. Can't we just go to bed?"

Rising from the table I walked in and stood over her as she lay on the bed, face down. Her white slip accentuated the curves of her hips and thighs. I reached down and caressed her bottom.

"Don't," she said.

I said, "I went to see your doctor tonight."

"What?"

She sat up, twisted toward me, a large wet spot from her tears on her reddened breast. She wiped it away without taking her eyes off my face.

"You did what?"

I sat down beside her on the bed.

"I went to see Dr. Cantrell tonight."

"You had *no right* to do that. Why?"

"I wanted to know what's wrong."

Suddenly, as if spitting her words in my face, she shouted, "What are you trying to do? Destroy me?"

"I want to help you."

"The one person I can confide in and you go trying to pump her for information. What did she tell you?"

Her hands whipped up and brushed her hair out of her face in rapid angry gestures.

"She didn't tell me much, but she did say..."

"Goddamnit, it's my life, my problems! What did she say? I want to know what she told you!"

"Look, Chrissy, it's not just your problem. I live with you. Remember? I have to go through all this shit with you. I can't stand by and do nothing!"

Chrissy went rigid, her hands over her mouth.

"What did she tell you? What did she say? Tell me, damn you, what did the two of you say about what you know nothing about?"

I stood up. Faced her.

"She said you need intensive therapy, that you..."

"She told you that...she had absolutely no right. That bitch. Yes, and now what else did *my* doctor reveal to you? Huh? What else?"

"Oh yeah...she said that you would not admit you needed help, that until you did no one would be able to help you, and that you'd walked out on your last session."

Tears began to flow down her cheeks. She took no notice. She stood up quickly and pushed me aside; picked up her brown leather backpack, pulled out a cigarette, lit it and inhaled deeply. Exhaling a long column of smoke, she turned back, facing me as she wiped the tears from her face, and then she shook her head as if she were shaking off the rain, as if she were suddenly sure of herself.

"She told you that, did she? That bitch. I'm going to get her license taken away. She can't talk about her patients without their permission."

Chrissy stared at me for a long time, and I stared back, mimicking her anger.

"Get away from me, Eddie! Get out of here! I can't stand the sight of you! I don't understand how you could do this to me…you, of all people! Oh God, you make me sick! Get out of here! Get out!"

Suddenly, something simply snapped inside me, and I leaned in close, too close, my face just inches from her face, daring her to hit me, because maybe that's what I wanted her to do, because I wanted to grab her and shake her, because all of a sudden I could not shut off the flow of anger and frustration pouring out of me.

"No!" I shouted. "I have as much right to be here as you do. I don't care what you don't want me to know about you. I'm sick of you. You're disgusting. Just look at yourself. I don't know who you are. You have all these secrets, but I need to tell you something. Either you want to be with me or you don't. And I'm sick and tired of you staying in bed and crying, moaning, groaning. I've got better things to do with my life than spend my every waking moment worrying over you day and night."

I paced back and forth in front of her.

"Look, I love you, and I want what's best for you. You need help. You need to go back to Dr. Cantrell, and if you can't do that then you can just go to hell!"

She gave me a look of disbelief and said, "Now you listen to me, what I don't need is for you to tell me…"

I interrupted her.

"I'm tired of listening to you, Chrissy. We obviously have nothing constructive to say to each other, and I'm not going to listen to you anymore unless you agree to get help or at least tell me what's going on. Who are you? What is your problem?"

We glared at each other. She said nothing.

I turned away from her and started for the door, when suddenly I heard more than felt a sharp tearing sensation as my shirt buttons burst away from my chest, sounding like a series of small paper bags popping as they struck the door. Time seemed to slow down as I turned, not quite understanding the moment of seeing something coming at me, but I instinctively raised my arm and knocked one of her hands away from my face, her red fingernails on her right hand somehow registering as they went by while her left hand raked down my chest in a searing flash of pain. But then, in this slowness of time, as she recovered and started a new swinging motion, I managed to reach out and grab hold of each of her wrists and hold her away from me. We stood there straining, face-to-face. But time suddenly speeded up again as she began pulling and backing away and kicking out at my legs, and we swayed crazily, knocking over a chair covered with clothes. Stumbling backwards, she changed tactics. She tried pulling my hands toward her teeth, and opened her mouth to bite. But then I gave in to her and abruptly stepped forward, pushing toward her even as she pulled, and we fell backwards toward the bed. But we stumbled sideways, missed the bed, and with my foot behind hers, we fell heavily to the floor, me on top.

I raised myself up and quickly pinned her arms with my knees and shouted down into her straining face.

"Chrissy, stop it!"

But she responded by twisting around and sinking her teeth into my leg. I pulled my leg away and slapped her. Hard.

The echo of it reverberated in the room.

Suddenly she was crying, and I was crying, and we were done. Her muscles relaxed, and I stood up. She turned away from me and cried in long gasping sobs.

I helped her up onto the bed.

I wanted to say something, but my throat was too dry, and no words came out. I coughed and managed one solicitous word.

"Chrissy?"

She curled up on the bed, turned away, still refusing to look at me.

I went into the bathroom, wet a washcloth in warm water, and returned. I pressed it against the back of her neck.

Slowly she rolled over and faced me. There was a sleepy softness in her eyes, a surrendering. Her wild eyebrows were in complete disarray, pointing in every direction. Her lips quivered as she mouthed, "I'm sorry. I'll call Dr. Cantrell tomorrow."

Her right cheek was bright pink where I had slapped her. I leaned over and gently kissed her hurt cheek, her lips, and then I smoothed her eyebrows out, my index finger moving in a long slow arc. She simply lay there looking up at me, her eyes red, still tearing, and then she reached up, took my hand, pulled it against her cheek, and closed her eyes.

After a few moments I pulled a blanket over her and left the room to make us some mint tea. When I returned with a cup for each of us she was asleep. Her face was relaxed. I sat down beside her and sipped the tea and watched her sleep. My chest ached and stung from a long reddening scratch.

Slowly, after a while, I became aware of the rain gusting against the bedroom windowpane, and I remembered my try at a translation of Verlaine's verse:

Il pleure dans mon coeur
Comme il pleut sur la ville;
Quelle est cette langueur
Qui pénètre mon coeur?

(There is this weeping in my heart
as it rains on the town;
what is this lethargy
that penetrates my heart?)

[12]

In 1963, Chrissy entered intensive therapy and made two decisions: to learn to play the guitar and to have a baby.

In her diary she wrote:

*The whole concept of future frightens me now. I'd prefer to ignore that Great Question Mark, to look only to this moment, or this day, but sometimes my solipsism is intruded upon. Like tonight when I find myself in the middle of the realization that graduation is approaching. Graduate school is rearing its ugly head. Me in graduate school? Everyone knows I am no scholar! And then, of course, there is the marital situation...complications abound. I love Eddie, but I am afraid I will hurt him in the end, and he doesn't deserve that. I think I should pray earnestly for one of two things: 1) that I have a baby! 2) that I do **not** have a baby!*

Chrissy called me at work just as the library was closing, "Mr. Andersen," she whispered into the phone, "would you care to come over this evening and help me make a baby?"

I did not oppose the idea of having a baby. I suppose I was pleased. Chrissy, who had always chosen to spend her considerable energies in pursuit of her friends, now seemed willing to spend her time baking bread from scratch, arranging flowers for the dining room table, and putting up ruffled curtains. To help out with some bills, she got a job working as a temp typist for the college. She took a renewed interest in her classes. When asked by one of her English professors for an analysis of the history of the novel, she brought it up for discussion just as we were going to bed, and we talked about it late into

the night, about how much she hated the whole analytical, historical perspective. I urged her to try a new approach, to take her own
position and not just replicate what others had said. Then, surprising me with how excited she got, in a burst of creative energy, she
worked for weeks, night and day, on an original piece that took up
the point of view of Tristram Shandy, Laurence Sterne's eighteenth
century, comedic novel, and invented a modern-day, bisexual character, isolated from her culture, unsure of her strengths, who struggled daily, self-consciously aware of her own ordinariness, to find the
courage to face her own identity in spite of the Bible-belt bigotry of
her upper-class parents. Her notions of bisexuality seemed to me
sincere, but fantasy-like and unreal, and possibly dangerous in our
Methodist-affiliated college. Her vision left me somewhat unmoored
by the sheer audacity of its amoral implications about human sexuality, but her conception, I had to agree, was bold, original, and her
language—delivered entirely in italics—was beautifully constructed
as the fictional, stream-of-consciousness confessions of an antebellum Southern belle. But I was worried that such a paper might not
even get graded. She could have gotten an "F" or, worse, been rejected
and reprimanded. The day after she turned it in we were in a state
of panic. But her professor, a notoriously tough grader, not only gave
her a rave review, he also gave her the only "A+" handed out in all of
his classes for that whole year. That was a day of celebration. I was
so proud and so relieved. That was, in a way, redemption. Proof of
her genius.

And each evening after receiving her "A+," on returning home
after work, her smile seemed to fly across the room and land like
a kiss. I wanted to laugh out loud with pleasure at the sight of her
clean and shining face, the new luster in her freshly combed hair.
She had energy and excitement about everything. Like many a well-
loved husband, I felt the full pleasure of my wife's attention. Flower
arrangements appeared on the table. Once again we talked to each
other about our classes, our papers. On weekends we visited my family, helped take care of my baby sister, took turns on the big tire
swing in my parents' back yard. On weeknights, she practiced her

guitar, which now sat on a stand next to our hi-fi like a promise of things to come. She took lessons twice a week, learning how to use a capo and trying ever more complicated finger placements and chord progressions.

Several months sailed by and then she missed her period. We decided she was pregnant and celebrated with a dinner out. We got dressed up, went downtown to Joy Young's restaurant, and ordered her favorite meal, butterfly shrimp over rice.

But that very evening she spotted.

Small drops of blood stained her panties.

There was no rush of the dark red blood, but even so she grew anxious. She lost her appetite. She lost her smile. Then, over the next few weeks, as if the light in the world were dimming, her depressions began to seep back into our bedroom. She stopped going to her guitar lessons. She said she was tired and began to take long naps.

She did the minimum of her schoolwork, but then, like a swimmer fighting against heavy tides, she rallied and took up the guitar again. She fought to master new folk songs and Elizabethan arrangements. There were also the sudden explosions when she cursed, slapped the guitar in frustration, a loud discordant sound echoing in our living room.

But she stuck with it.

◁▶

Sometimes on Sundays we would drop by her mother's house. Evelyn was now living with Bill, her new husband, her fourth. It was a marriage of convenience. I guessed that Evelyn had married him because she needed someone who could help pay the bills.

Bill, a car mechanic, worked hard, kept the front lawn trimmed, and loved to go fishing on weekends. He seemed to keep Evelyn satisfied, never talked out of turn, and usually managed to go to sleep on the living room couch every evening before ten o'clock. He was an easygoing fellow.

Every time Chrissy and I visited them, I was surprised at how well they got along. Bill, leaning back in his lounge chair and smelling of after-shave lotion, his wet black hair slicked back with Bryl-creem, would tell us once again with a big bright smile on his face that he had never hoped to marry such a good-looking woman. And truly he seemed happy to accept his inferior status in their relation-ship as a price he was more than willing to pay. He always deferred to her understanding of how things should be, including fixing her drinks, getting her cigarettes, and retrieving her slippers from the bedroom. Every day, I imagined, Evelyn extracted another down pay-ment on a debt Bill could never repay, and in return she gave him the occasional pleasures of her well-tended body. At the age of forty, Evelyn showed little sign of deterioration. She was a petite, supple woman with hard green eyes, a cute nose, blonde-tinted hair that curled down beside her face in small ringlets, and a quick, superficial smile that barely disguised a tight cruelty in her mouth. Chrissy, big-ger than her mother, dark-haired like her father, brown-eyed, with black unruly eyebrows that would grow together over the bridge of her nose if not continuously plucked, never felt that she lived up to her mother's expectations.

But most of that February of our senior year, on weekends, while I caught up on my studies, my books and philosophy notes spread out over the kitchen table, sipping coffee, smoking cigarettes, Chrissy, her brown eyes glimmering in the winter light, would sit in a straight-backed chair practicing her songs and staring out the window at the rain, the gray sky, and the leafless trees. Struggling, but lovely in her isolation, she could not be approached. She would sit hunched over, wearing brown pedal pushers and a dark purple, short-sleeved pullover, with her hair held back by a wide black ribbon, and no makeup except for bright red lipstick. She'd hold her big acoustic guitar across her knees, and begin struggling with the difficult chord progressions of Joan Baez songs, songs that she started and stopped and started over again, never quite managing the complicated finger placements, her unique voice weaving her own sweet pain into those haunting lyrics—"All my trials Lord / Soon be over."

I began to fear another breakdown, but the months of February and March passed by without incident. Once again she did not menstruate, and there was no more spotting.

She was pregnant.

This time we did not celebrate, but the weather was changing: winter's crisp cold ground was turning spongy and dark under our feet. Chrissy seemed once again to lose her lassitude and to rise up each morning in tune with the promise of spring.

Soon dogwoods all around us were in flower. Their early white blossoms stood out in a spectacular display against the brown remains of another Birmingham winter. Chrissy had done well enough in her classes without expending much effort, and I had made the Dean's List.

Our baby was due in early October.

On May 2, 1963, Virginia Praytor, in spite of her age, climbed high up on the bookstore ladder in order to re-shelve a book. Holding on with one shaky hand, she wiped wisps of graying, reddish-orange hair out of her face, pushed her glasses up on her freckled nose, coughed out loud for attention, and then addressed her sister across the room.

"Anna, did you, by any chance, find time to get those art books for George Appleby—remember the ones we talked about yesterday—are they wrapped and ready for Eddie to deliver?"

Used to speaking to high-school students in her Beginning Latin class, Virginia's voice always carried an irritatingly imperious tone.

Grinning, Anna winked at me. She never took offense at Virginia's manner. She continued to tally the day's receipts and answered without looking up.

"Yes, Virginia."

Then, after a sufficient lapse of time, Anna turned to me with a nod and mock irony in her soft voice. "Eddie, when you've finished unpacking those boxes, would you please take a few minutes and walk Virginia's art books—you'll find a big package already wrapped up and ready to go in the back on the delivery table—over to George

Appleby, our friendly executive at Loveman's, for consideration for his coffee table?"

Anna smiled again, just for me, as if to say, you and I both know that we must forgive her for that ugly behavior and love her for that other inner person we know her to be. Then she added, in a louder voice, as I headed out to the back room, "The address and delivery instructions are in the envelope taped to the back of the package."

<><><>

I quickly walked the few blocks to Loveman's Department Store and dropped the books off with George's receptionist. Then I decided to amble around town for a bit because I felt like it, because winter was over, because it was one of those warm days when Birmingham's gray smog seemed to have dissipated; when a lovely high blue sky had replaced the ugly steel-mill haze that so often gave the city a depressingly low ceiling; and because so many flowers planted in colorful ceramic pots by local store owners were suddenly in bloom.

I was only one block away from Kelly Ingram Park when I turned a corner and encountered a policeman in the middle of the street putting up a traffic barrier. He glanced in my direction, then ignored me, and continued on with his efforts. The sidewalk was also partially blocked, but I could see a crowd of people gathering farther down the street. *Must be a parade of some sort.*

Without even considering that the sidewalk blockade was intended for me, I started around it. My attention was focused farther up the street on the laughter from the crowd in the next intersection. I didn't see him coming. Without warning the policeman's big fleshy mug was in my face, glaring angrily, and suddenly he put his hand squarely in my chest and gave me a shove. I staggered under the stiff-armed force of his hand and stumbled backwards, almost falling to the pavement.

Spinning around I fought to regain my balance, and then I finally straightened up unsteadily to face him.

"This area is off limits by order of Sheriff Bull Connor." He took out his baton, slapped it against his hand.

Staring back in disbelief, I felt my face flush red.

*Why is he so angry? He shoved me! Why **did** he shove me?*

"What's going on here?" I asked, trying to sound calm and unafraid.

"I'm an officer of the law, and the sheriff has proclaimed this area off limits." He spoke with anger, daring me to disagree.

Flushed with the need to rebel, I wanted to shout something, fling some appropriately insulting remarks into that fleshy, overbearing, fat face, but no words came to me. I just stood there staring, saying nothing, beginning to wither under his gaze and thinking I should turn around and go back to work. Then a noisy group of well-dressed young Negroes in dark suits and ties and white shirts, looking as if they were on their way to church, came around the corner off to our left on the other side of the street.

"We got to get over there...we've got to stand with them."

"...believe it!"

"...me too!"

They stopped in front of the barrier and looked over in confusion at the policeman and me.

Then somebody on a bicycle, also wearing a dark suit and tie, flashed through a gap in the uncompleted barrier on that side of the street, and quickly the whole group of them started to move in behind him. Abruptly, the policeman forgot me and rushed over shouting, "Hey, boy, where you think you're going?"

Suddenly, I knew where I was going. Without even thinking about the consequences, I took my chance and sprinted forward toward the crowd in front of me. I felt irrationally elated as I ran. I was filled with so much energy I felt I could run forever, run like I had as a kid when I had been almost caught stealing watermelons from a black farmer who had chased me from his fields. Without daring to look around, I continued to run until I could mix in with a crowd of well-dressed townspeople. Breathlessly, I looked behind me. The policeman was nowhere in sight.

I edged my way up to the front.

Under my starched white shirt sweat trickled down my sides.

I stood on the corner of Seventeenth Street and Fifth Avenue, a section of downtown that formed a transitional area between black and white business interests. My attention was caught by a sign above a run-down establishment across from me that read "Jockey Boy Restaurant" in small, square, black letters above the bigger, scripted, giant red Coca-Cola advertisement. I'd never seen that sign before. Jockey Boy? What was that about? It seemed I'd entered a part of the town with a history I knew nothing about.

Out in the middle of the intersection, police stood alongside firemen in full gear—heavy raincoats, hard hats, black rubber boots— straddling thick fire hoses, joking and laughing, and pointing in the direction of the park.

Then I noticed a line of spectators on Eighteenth Street sitting on the high fortress-like wall that surrounded the downtown post office. Like an Elizabethan audience at an outdoor theater, they were out of the action but had the perfect spot for viewing the scene.

The entrance to the post office was in the middle of the next block, so I jogged down to the entrance way, entered and walked across the grass to climb up over some cement banisters, hoping to keep my work shirt and tan slacks clean. The soot that covered Birmingham's concrete buildings could leave a hard-to-erase stain. At the face of the wall I needed only to take hold of the ledge and pull myself up and onto the smooth surface of the top. Once there, I spread out a hand-kerchief and sat down on it. The rounded concrete felt warm. The wall was dirty and already my shirt was wet and my hands coated with that kind of greasy Birmingham soot that was hard to wipe off. I hoped that when I went back to work I'd be able to sneak in the back door and clean up a bit before the Praytor sisters could see me.

Looking down over the park, I struggled to take in what was going on. Horns were blaring at every intersection. The police and firemen were gathered in front of Jockey Boy Restaurant, off to the lower left of our view. Groups of well-dressed blacks were standing around at the top right corner, at the back of the park, near their church, the Sixteenth Street Baptist Church. The police were setting up barriers along the other two intersections. They were attempting to cordon off the park and control all ingress and egress for the entire park area. At the center of the park black kids and a few small children, dressed in their Sunday best, linked arms with adults and began singing.

We sat on the walled fortifications of the post office, an audience of uninvolved spectators, and, dangling our feet over the side, called out and laughed, some cheering for the firemen, some shouting out encouragement to the kids as they hooted and hollered, put their thumbs in their ears, waggled their fingers, stuck out their tongues, danced a jig, jumped up and down, each of them challenging the white firemen in their helmets and heavy coats to try and spray them with the fire hose.

"Watch him...there he goes...he made it," followed by a mixture of jeers and cheers and applause.

"They'll get the next ones."

"Ouch...that smarts."

"I could do better than that. Knock him down, damnit."

"Your mama's going to have wash that dress, baby."

"At least they're getting cooled down."

In spite of the blockades, hundreds, maybe even thousands, of people were surrounding the park, and more were still arriving, streaming in from all directions, merchants and business people, blacks and whites, in coats and ties, a gathering crowd of young blacks, news trucks, photographers.

Police sirens seem to be blaring from every street corner like a call to action.

Kelly Ingram Park, named after the first sailor to die in World War I, was one square block of trees, bushes, benches, and well-worn dirt paths that wound through shade trees and sparse areas of grass. Off to my right I could see several new groups of young black kids running toward us from the Sixteenth Street Baptist Church. Down in front, off to my left, the Birmingham Fire Department, like an army taking up defensive positions, had lined up its trucks facing the front of the park. The white firemen, arrayed in threes, were controlling several fire hoses. They were holding large nozzles that sprayed streams of water at the young black kids who kept dashing in and out from behind trees, running into the spray, and then running away. The people on the wall, all white—business people, post office workers in uniform, and even a few young women—shouted and laughed at the antics of the black kids, and at the firemen, who seemed too slow to control the direction and flow of the torrent of water gushing from their hoses. Then, as if by some invisible agreement of good will and mass communication, a communion of understanding passed through us, and we, the white people seated on the wall, became a part of the strange game taking place in front of us, and we rooted for and applauded the antics of the underdogs, the black kids. It was live theater. The kids sprinted back and forth, jumped out from behind the trees and bushes, shouted rhythmical catcalls, and challenged the firemen.

"Nany-nany-na-na...you c-a-i-n-'t get me."

Some feinted, then weaved back and forth on their run, somehow managing to dodge the stream of water, making the firemen seem inept at controlling the spray. Others got caught, got sprayed, laughed, and ran away. It was a hot day. Sitting on the wall, sweat running down inside my shirt, I thought that getting wet after one of those runs must have been kind of fun.

The crowd continued to grow larger and stranger. It was becoming chaotic in the street. Water from the hoses and hydrants began to overflow the gutters. The park paths and grasses were drenched and getting slippery. More and more kids made a run for it. Some slipped and fell, and, tumbling over, got pushed backwards by the heavy spray. Some managed to get away untouched.

More laughter.

Calls came from the crowd challenging the kids to make a run. And they did, dodging and weaving, some getting hit, some getting away. Suddenly one young boy in a bright-white, Sunday dress shirt, dashed between the trees like a football tailback heading for the end zone, then went down on one knee and spread his arms out in a fanciful Fred Astaire slide across the wet park grounds. But rudely the spray found him and he tumbled sideways in the mud. There was a moment of suspense, but when he jumped up, all covered in mud, he bowed before he ran back to the shelter of the trees. Loud whistles, cheers, and applause came from the white spectators on the wall.

Then suddenly, like a drop in atmospheric pressure preceding a heavy storm, it all changed.

Bull Connor arrived, followed by a black police van.

The van's doors opened, and police dogs dismounted, their handlers running after them.

"Clear this park," ordered a policeman with a bullhorn. "Anyone who resists will be arrested!"

In the abrupt silence that followed, we listened to the distant, frightening sound of many wailing sirens, of more police cars heading our way. The applause and catcalls along the wall died down like the faltering whistle of steam from a cooling teapot. There was an ominous feeling in the air, a sense that the fun and the good will were over. In ones and twos, people began to climb down from the wall and, looking over their shoulders, slip away. Then came the screeching of tires, the smell of burning rubber, as police cars and a paddy wagon shuddered to a halt, almost running over the fire hoses, which leaked water over the pavement. Then the van doors slammed open and out poured more uniformed police, pulled forward by their police dogs, leaping and lunging at their leashes.

Official-looking, big-bellied white men in dress shirts strode stolidly into the center of the melee where they were quickly joined in conversation by police captains.

It was abundantly clear the street play was over. A new scriptwriter had taken charge of this reality. Violence was on its way.

The fireman changed their hoses from spray nozzles to force-fed monitor guns. The first blast from those water guns ripped bark off the park trees in front of us.

Protests rippled along the wall, followed by low murmurs and whispers. More black children, grade-school kids, flooded into the street. Firemen, bracing themselves, deliberately turned the hoses on them.

Their first blast blew kids off their feet and sent them spinning. Several demonstrators crouched down, linked arms, and tried to hold onto one another. The blast tore them apart. They were screaming and crying. This was no longer fun and games.

"Stop it!" somebody shouted from the wall. "That's not right!"

A car horn from down the street began ceaselessly blowing into the cacophony as an older white man tried to drive his sedan past the police barricades into the massed groups of black children. They were scattering like deer, fleeing and screaming. The police blocked the car's way with a cruiser, pulled the white driver out of his car and cuffed him. He was shouting incoherently.

Helplessly, we watched as a police dog leaped forward and attacked a black man directly below us. He had walked forward toward the police line, eyes down, hands open, palms up, and accepted the assault as if he had prepared himself in advance to offer no resistance. *Like the Christians to the lions.* The stunned policeman jerked on his dog's leash, and the black man's sweater ripped open. The dog was pulled away.

We watched in stifled silence as the man was then cuffed and led away to the paddy wagon. He walked stiffly, unresistingly; then, just before he entered the paddy wagon, he lifted his head toward the sky as if he were checking for some change in the weather, as if he were not really present, had not really been attacked, or arrested, to be charged with "parading without a permit."

People were crying. I heard myself shouting, "Stop it!" but my voice, like the voices of the rest of the audience on the wall, was lost in the chaos. No one could be heard except for the man on the bullhorn. "Clear this area!" he was saying, and he waved his arms in a gesture of dismissal. "If you refuse to disperse you will be arrested!"

A police captain pointed at those of us still sitting on the wall and said something into the ear of another policeman beside him. That policeman looked up at us, nodded, and started in our direction. That had an immediate effect. Word passed quickly along the wall, "They intend to arrest us."

People began climbing and jumping down from the wall. A young woman fell to the concrete, scraped her knees and hands, and then began limping hurriedly away.

I jumped down and ran with them. I wasn't sure I understood what I'd just witnessed, but I knew enough to know that I did not want to be arrested as an outside agitator. I ran all the way back to Smith & Hardwick, rushed in through the back door, which was luckily still unlocked, and went straight to the bathroom.

A few moments later I heard Anna's voice. "Eddie, is that you? Are you all right?"

"I'm okay, Anna. I'll be right out."

"Virginia and I thought we heard the back door open...we didn't know it was unlocked...we just wanted to be sure it was you."

"Yeah...okay...well, it's just me."

I stood in front of the mirror and washed my hands and face with soap and cold water. I was a mess, and I was still sweating. My shirt and pants were stained with Birmingham soot, and though I was still somewhat in shock, I realized that it was almost time for me to leave and go on to my second job at the Art and Music Department at the library. But I stayed on a few moments in that closed, closet-like room with one bare light bulb attached to a long piece of string, drying my face on a pull-down towel, and then staring blankly into the bathroom mirror, still shocked, but thinking furiously. *What was that demonstration all about? What did it mean? Was this part of what Martha Turnipseed was involved in? Was she going to be expelled from college because she had participated in that lunch counter sit-in in downtown Birmingham, at Woolworth's department store?*

"Eddie?"

"I'll be right out, Virginia."

But as I turned out the light in the bathroom and opened the door, what I suddenly remembered was all the homework I had to finish before my eight o'clock class the following morning. If I wasted no time and hurried through the collecting and re-shelving of all the books and record albums the people of Birmingham had returned that day, I'd be able to sneak in a few hours of study time. It just might be enough.

[13]

[In early May, 1963, at a demonstration of black
children at Kelly Ingram Park, Birmingham,
Alabama, *Life* magazine's] *Charles Moore, who
had gotten his training as a Marine combat
photographer, was hit in the ankle with a chunk of
concrete. Even as his ankle swelled, he continued
to click his camera. In the background of his
crowd shots was the Carver Theater's marquee
advertising the war picture* Damn the Defiant.

*The dogs and fire hoses dominated the evening
news...*[5]

May 1, 1963

I don't remember what the flyer said, but it was probably something like "Support the Sit-ins. Support Martha Turnipseed. Stand
up and be counted. Join in the discussion with a visiting scholar from
Harvard and local students from Miles College."

I do remember thinking: *What could it hurt?*

It was nearing dusk when I left the green lawns on the hilltop
and drove through the gates in my faded blue Plymouth. I turned
left at the light toward downtown Birmingham and the A. G. Gaston
Motel. An open discussion about Birmingham's "troubles" was scheduled for seven o'clock. I had never attended one before. To remain
inconspicuous I planned to be a little late and park my car close to

the public library a few blocks away. I wanted to find out more, but I didn't want the visibility or the danger that came with being identified with the "outside agitators." I turned on the car radio almost by reflex, and suddenly I was transfixed by the lyrics to a song—a really different kind of song, not a lovesick country western heartache, or even a sappy sentimental complaint, but a song that seemed to have something to say. It was being sung by the scratchiest, most insistent voice I'd ever heard. "The answer, my friend, is blowin' in the wind." I had to pull my car over to the side of the road and listen.

At the end of the song I turned off the irritating voice of the announcer and rolled my window down. I had pulled over in a run-down neighborhood just beyond Legion Field, the city's football stadium, across from several unpainted wooden houses that seemed to strain sideways, as if they were resisting a stiff wind. The houses stood in various stages of disrepair, perched up on brick legs with nothing underneath but dirt and cast-off furniture. Across the street from my car, two groups of black men in overalls stood talking in front of a neighborhood grocery store, drinking beer followed by a bottle of something they passed around, probably a whiskey chaser, all wrapped up in a brown paper bag. Their faint voices drifted softly in the warm evening air. Down the street the dogs were barking, and in the distance a siren was wailing, all of it drifting in through my open window with the dirty brown haze of Birmingham's steel-mill smog, all of it just "blowin' in the wind."

As I sat there I remembered a conversation I'd overheard between two pretty young sophomores.

"So, you didn't know?"

"Know what?"

"Well, she's been going out with a *Negro* man, a student from Miles."

"Really. What do you think?"

"I don't know… I've been asking myself over and over again, 'What's wrong with it?' It just never occurred to me. I wouldn't do it, but… I mean they're just people, right?"

"Yeah..."

"So what's wrong with it?"

Then the two sophomores turned a corner, and I didn't get to hear the answer. But that question was still with me. *What was wrong with it?*

As I sat there, I watched the black men across the street suddenly dip their heads together, wave their hands in the air, and then start tap dancing and singing, their voices harmonizing in a strange counterpoint to all the noise around me. I listened a moment and then slowly pulled back into traffic and continued on toward the A. G. Gaston Motel.

Arthur George Gaston, a black millionaire, had made his fortune as a funeral director. In the South, black funeral directors used their hearses for more than just transportation for the dead. Hearses were also used as ambulances for the sick and the injured. Southern white society refused to provide either ambulance or funeral services for the black community. As a consequence black funeral directors were highly regarded individuals in their communities, and A. G. Gaston was no exception. His downtown motel, though I didn't know about it at the time (and the Klan did), also provided the meeting rooms for strategy discussions for the black ministers of the S.C.L.C. (Southern Christian Leadership Conference).

The A. G. Gaston Motel was located just west of Kelly Ingram Park, close to the Sixteenth Street Baptist Church. As planned, I parked my car near the public library, several blocks away, and walked on that warm May evening to the meeting.

At the front desk, I asked where the meeting was taking place, and without hesitation, a clerk gave me a room number. I opened the door, bent down to avoid notice, and sneaked into a chair at the back of the room. A heated discussion was taking place. A heavy, gray-haired white man, tie undone, in white shoes and a white suit, stood up and called for everyone's attention.

"We have to be careful. This can get out of hand. We have to balance the need to dramatize our position and the publicity we can get from sit-ins against the threat of violence to our people!"

A thin, well-dressed white student, Boston accent, rose, turned around and spoke from his seat in the front of the room, "Agreed, but we need to strike now while we have the attention of the press! We won't have a better opportunity than we have right now. And we're ready! Aren't we?"

He directed his attention to what I took to be a Miles student who nodded and added, "You all just give us the word. We ready!"

"Okay, then," an older black man, a minister, I guessed, spoke quietly and then forcefully, almost shouting out his words as his cadence rose and fell with his points, "I know you're ready, and I'm ready, and God knows our people are ready, but let me tell you something, people, *we are not yet organized!* To make this work we need more time, and we need more white volunteers. As a starter I want to pass out this form and get everybody here to sign it and leave us with your phone numbers and addresses and availability. Are ya'll with us?"

A chorus of agreement sounded throughout the room. I sank down in my chair. As he began moving right to left, passing out the forms to the front row, everyone started talking to each other at once, and I stood up abruptly and made a dash for the door. I was not yet ready to give up my name, and I was not ready to be a white volunteer. I had been in the room less than ten minutes.

Once outside, I walked furtively away from the motel. I didn't see anyone around, and I hoped no one saw me. I was scared.

What I didn't discover until much later was that someone attempted to bomb the A. G. Gaston motel later that very night. Fortunately, no one was hurt.

A few weeks later, we took a step forward.

At the suggestion of one of my philosophy professors, who was teaching a course at Miles College, Chrissy and I agreed to meet with a few black students to discuss the racial "troubles" in Birmingham.

Afterwards, breaking up into small groups to socialize, we got to know one another. And Chrissy and I went for a visit at the home of one of the black students, a pretty young woman who had been accepted for study abroad in England, at Oxford. Her mother, a small dark woman, much darker than her daughter, with granny glasses and glistening, straightened hair, was a music teacher. She served us sweetened iced tea in an immaculately kept living room with white lace doilies spread out on the backs of overstuffed Victorian chairs. Then she asked her daughter to play something for us, a Chopin piece. Her daughter acquiesced, but before she started to play she spun around on her piano stool, gave us a quick, trembly, almost apologetic smile. She cast her eyes down, then back up, and said, so quietly we had to strain to hear her, "For you, I'll play because my beautiful mama ask me to." Then she shrugged, turned serious and began to play. Chrissy and I hadn't quite known what to make of what she'd said. She seemed to be implying that she would have refused to play for us except that her mother asked it of her. She was very respectful, but there was strength in her, a willingness to defy our "white people's expectations." She was not intimidated. She was her own person, not like anyone we'd ever met before. She was somebody with real ambitions. She was self-assured, confident, and impressive.

(On a Sunday morning, September 15, 1963, Klansmen dynamited the Sixteenth Street Baptist Church, murdering four black children: Denise McNair, Carole Robertson, Addie Mae Collins, and Cynthia Wesley.[6])

[14]

In June 1964, we graduated on the green lawn of the Quadrangle. A stage had been set up in front of the administration building. Great platters of fried chicken, iced tea, and potato salad were spread out on shaded picnic tables, awaiting the end of the ceremonies. Chrissy's mother wore a pillbox hat with a black lace summer veil and an elegant Confederate-gray, high-collared jacket. My father sat stiffly next to her, wearing a tie and a pressed white shirt that pulled tight across his belly. My mother, who was having one of her good days in her battle with Parkinson's, sat smiling at me with her hands folded tightly in her lap.

I crossed the stage, accepted my diploma, then turned and waited as Chrissy received hers, one hand over her swollen abdomen, her tasseled cap threatening to come undone, her black robes flowing behind her in the light breeze that exposed her bulging belly. She beamed brightly, thin beads of sweat across her brow. Then, as we walked toward the stairs, listening to the polite public applause, our baby rocking along inside her, she gave me a huge open-mouthed grin and whispered in my ear, *"We did it!"*

That night, after graduation, we stopped by Chrissy's mother's house to have a few drinks and share our excitement. We had made it through four years of college. And now, as we looked forward to graduate school applications, potential job offers, and a baby on the way, we felt like anything was possible. And then we agreed to play a game of Hearts, and Chrissy, a little tipsy after a couple of martinis, started telling her mother about our visit to Miles College to discuss racial issues.

Chrissy was in the middle of exclaiming over our reaction to the mysterious and beautiful young black woman who had played Chopin on the piano for us, when Evelyn interrupted.

"Excuse me," she said loudly, slurring her words.

She put her cards face down on the table. Looking sideways at the two of us over the bridge of her half-lens glasses, she sipped at her third or fourth martini of the evening and absently reached over and placed Bill's glass of beer on a felt-lined silver coaster. Then, after rolling her eyes toward the ceiling as if she were caught up in an abstract consideration, she started circling her forefinger in the air like a witching wand, as if she were seeking a direction. Finally, she brought her hand down and pointed her finger directly at Chrissy.

"I don't understand how you could even think about spending your time helping those niggers!"

Chrissy's hands flew up in sudden gesture of anger and frustration.

"They don't really want to be educated, they just want a handout," her mother continued on in a lecturing tone.

"Mother, you don't understand anything about it!"

"Don't you talk to me that way! I'm your mother! And don't you forget it."

"That was your choice, not mine. You really think you know what's going on, do you? You give them your secondhand clothes and that makes you feel so damned superior."

Evelyn, looking shocked, leaned back as if reassessing the situation. She took aim again at Chrissy's belly with her forefinger, her circling hand. Then she raised the thin-stemmed martini glass to her lips, her hard, green eyes over the edge of her drink and her granny glasses. She did not waver.

"Those people are not like us. You just wait and see. In a month or two you'll understand what I'm talking about...and you'll feel as I do..."

"Mother, you're being ignorant."

"What are you saying? You're so ungrateful..."

Then Evelyn pushed backed from the table and spoke in a sweeping summary judgment, her voice rising, "I gave up everything for you. I could have had a life, but I had you instead..."

Evelyn then looked over at Bill as if she were including him in her general condemnation and said disparagingly, "Yes, and what about you? You, of course, also have nothing to offer."

Bill started to speak, but Evelyn waved him away.

Bill, still in his work coveralls with the blue Ensley Ford emblem on his chest, got up from the table, walked into the living room, and sat down in front of the flickering television. Not pleased, Evelyn watched him go with a drunken look of disgust, but then she turned back to Chrissy.

"At least I always respected *my* parents. I never talked back to my parents the way you talk to me. Sure...okay...you go ahead and believe those communist professors over your own mother, but, you just wait, you're going to find out what it's all about! You'll see."

Evelyn stared pointedly at Chrissy's belly.

Chrissy's hands moved instinctively over her swollen abdomen. Caressing herself protectively, she was not about to give up the argument.

I decided to intervene and stood up, my back to Evelyn.

"Chrissy, come on, let's go. It's time to go home."

She gave me a stony look of indignant refusal, waving me away. Her hands trembled over her belly as she leaned to one side, looked around me, and stubbornly began a verbal assault on her mother's assumption of authority.

"My dear mother, just what am I going to find out—just what do you so smugly think is going to happen? Do you think I'm suddenly going to lose my ability to tell right from wrong, that I'm going to become as closed-minded and bigoted as you are? You really think that having a baby is going to drive me to drink the way it did you? Do you really have the gall to compare me with you, to think I'm going to feel the same way about my child as you did about me?"

Chrissy's last few sentences had been high pitched, almost

shrieks. I could hear tears forming beneath her words; but there was also an insistence there, the insistence of someone who could not turn away from a reality that was suddenly opening up before her.

Evelyn, however, seemed to hear nothing of the danger behind Chrissy's words because she had entered into some murky world of indignation and accusation. She stood up, straightened her shoulders, and again pointed her forefinger at Chrissy, trembling as she spoke.

"I pray that God gives you a damn black baby! Do you hear me? I pray he turns out to hate you the way you hate me. I pray that God will curse you, and He will. He will, damn you, you and your baby!"

The two of them stared at each other for a moment, and then Chrissy got up and rushed toward the front door.

She started coughing and gagging the moment she got outside, before the screen door had closed behind her. I caught up, took her arm, and we fled toward the car. Then just outside the gate and the well-trimmed lawn, Chrissy's head drooped down, she bent forward, and she vomited all over the sidewalk.

Her mother appeared behind us holding her martini out before her. She held the screen door open with her free hand, screaming.

"I mean it! I hope you have to suffer the way I've suffered! Do you hear me? Do you hear me?"

Inside the car Chrissy suddenly lurched forward sobbing and then rocked back against the seat, hands over her ears. "Shut her up," she said. "Somebody please just make her shut up."

As we drove away I saw Evelyn collapse into Bill's arms as he pulled her back inside and shut the door against the flickering light of the television.

The dark enveloped us, and Chrissy continued to cry, her sobs punctuated by shaky intakes of breath and deep sighs. I drove us to the top of Red Mountain, where we stopped and looked down over the distant, sparkling lights of the Magic City. We sat at a lookout point high above Gene Crutcher's bookstore in Five Points South, in silence, holding hands until Chrissy's sobs slowly shifted into simple long, heavy sighs. Then in the dark of our car, with the silver statue of Vulcan rising up behind us, Chrissy seemed to return to herself.

"Why? Oh, why is it this way?"

The week after our graduation we rented an inexpensive house on the outskirts of Birmingham in the community of Ensley, where many of the steel-mill workers lived. I had landed a one-year job that would start in the fall as a high school instructor of College Prep English and Beginning French in Bessemer, Alabama, a twenty-minute drive from our house. In the meantime, I would continue working at Smith & Hardwick's bookstore and at the library. We were going to have our child, save our money, and I would apply for a teaching assistantship for graduate school in philosophy the following year.

Two blocks away from a busy roadway on the south side of Ensley, our new home was a small white house with dysfunctional gutters, peeling paint and a dull, rust-red roof. It sat at the end of a long gravel road, more like an alley, in a neighborhood of deserted and half-torn-down homes. We had no immediate neighbors. A highway would be coming through in a little over a year, but we didn't expect to be there when the bulldozers arrived. In the meantime we were happy with the low rent and weren't at all upset at living in what used to be the servant's quarters of an abandoned mansion.

So, all in one weekend, we moved into our little house and furnished it with cast-off furniture from our relatives. We felt quite pleased with our secret hideaway surrounded by a vibrant forest glen of slender-limbed dogwoods, giant red oaks, and tall pines.

Chrissy wrote in her diary:

As I sit here in our enchanted forest house—for there is a spell sitting lightly on it—I sense the current of joy running deep within our life. My husband, across the warmly lit room with his books and his coffee cup, seems absorbed entirely in his thoughts and unaware of all about him, yet I know that he knows I am near and that he would miss my presence if I were to leave the room. In the lamplight my new, brightly colored house robe is pleasing to see, and when I take my eye from the page of the book before me, I let myself feel the robe's satiny warmth as I run my hand over its blue and green flowers. The words from my book—Isak Dinesen's Winter's Tales—*help spread the mantle of magic over the evening scene. Between us and around us there is music: Vivaldi's stringed* Seasons, *Bach's bright harpsichords—two, three, and then four. The child moves within my body; my hand moves, without thought behind it, to meet the movement. The spring, the living spring!*

[15]

The packed suitcase sat waiting by the door.

Chrissy's labor began on Saturday morning in early October. The contractions brought brief grimaces and then laughter as I took out my watch and started the countdown. The pains were regular, seven minutes apart, but then we were surprised by a short period of bleeding. I called the doctor. He said to bring her to the hospital and check her in.

It was drizzling rain, and it took us twenty minutes to cross Birmingham under Vulcan's green light and find a place in the Saint Vincent Hospital parking lot. Once we were inside, a nurse appeared out of nowhere with a wheelchair and a practiced smile and wheeled Chrissy out of the lobby while I stood at the desk and filled out pages of forms for hospital admission. In the whir of the hospital machinery, I felt lost and irrelevant. But it all went by in a blur. What I remember was how when I walked into her room Chrissy reached out with both arms raised in greeting, and how her big smile twisted almost immediately into a grimace. The pains were getting closer together. I hurried over to stand next to her. A young, redheaded nurse on the opposite side of her bed checked her pulse and said, as she pushed back the curtains and exited the room, "It'll only be a few more hours, if that long."

Chrissy gripped my hand and looked up at me bravely.

"Will you stay with me?"

She squeezed harder and went rigid as another contraction came and went.

"You want me to call anyone?"

"No, I don't want you to leave me. You won't leave me, will you?"

A tiny concern flickered in her eyes.

"You look like a happy hippopotamus under that sheet."

Chrissy smiled and pulled the sheet away.

"A shaved hippopotamus. You want to see?"

I moved around the swollen belly and peered down at her, vulnerable and naked without her hair. I kissed her belly.

"Hey," she quipped, "what are you doing down there? See a baby?"

Chrissy's smile faded into a look of surprise and pain as another contraction hit. It was a short one. She smiled as I moved over to her head, washed her brow with a cold, wet cloth, and accidentally rearranged her dark eyebrows so that they pointed in all directions at once. I almost laughed at the effect, but then she gasped for breath and looked bewildered and frightened.

"Do you want me to get the doctor?" I asked.

Then her body relaxed and peace came to her face.

"No, that was a tough one. Just hold my hand."

But the doctor pushed through the door, moved in front of me, picked up her wrist, and said, "Mr. Andersen, you need to go to the waiting room now."

"Can't I stay?" I asked.

Without even looking at me he said, "Too much blood. I don't even allow third- year medical students in the delivery room. I don't want anyone passing out while I'm delivering a baby!"

Wait a minute.

He put a stethoscope on Chrissy's belly and leaned over to listen.

I wanted to protest, but a nurse walked in, forcing me to back up even more. Then another nurse walked in and stood next to her, blocking my view altogether.

Yeah, okay, I get it.

I left the room.

Unable to sit down, feeling left out, I paced the hallways and wandered around until I found myself, nose pressed against the glass, checking out all the newborn babies in the next room. Finally, a nurse came out and found me and told me that Chrissy was just fine, but that the doctor was going to give her a saddle block to help with the pain.

"This doctor almost always gives them," she added as if she was explaining something to me.

But I had no idea what a saddle block was or what its effects might be.

I walked away and continued wandering the length of the empty, green hallway, feeling awash in the sanitized atmosphere of the hospital, staring at newly born babies, looking into nearly empty waiting rooms with empty brown leather chairs, listening to a phone on a wall ring somewhere in the distance. I wondered how Chrissy's mother was going to react when I called her and gave her the news that she was a grandmother. I didn't think she was ready. The big fight between Chrissy and her mother over our visits with black students on the campus of Miles College had left unresolved, bad feelings between us. An unspoken truce had been established, but neither Chrissy nor her mother had apologized. Somehow we all just put our feelings behind us and continued on with our lives. We, being who we were, good Southerners, simply avoided talking about certain subjects and followed our Southern understanding that *if you don't have anything nice to say, you don't say anything at all...* But tonight, as I stopped before a nurse placing a new baby into its crib, I was sure that a new beginning was at hand, that all problems could be resolved, because this night, a new baby, my new baby, was being born. A new life, waving its arms, kicking its bare feet and wiggling its toes, would soon be looking around in its bright, white room and checking out its surroundings, already beginning to reach out and grasp hold of all that life had to offer.

[16]

"This way please, Mr. Andersen. Your wife is doing just fine. You have a beautiful girl, six pounds and five ounces. If you'll wait over by the glass windows—you know where that is, don't you?"

I nodded.

"Fine. Someone will come out and get you in a few minutes."

When I got to Chrissy's room she was moaning, her face pale, but her mouth quivered into a smile as she turned toward me. She had put on some lipstick, and her hair had been pulled straight back, held in place by one of her black ribbons. Sweat ran down her wide, exposed forehead, her pink cheeks. A wet cloth in her free hand, she wiped her face and then twisted up in obvious pain. Her eyes stared at me with an intensely bright blank look. I took hold of her hand.

"Eddie? Where's Eddie?"

"Here I am, love, I'm right here with you."

She leaned forward and looked at me without recognition.

"Who are you? Where's Eddie?"

We both turned as the door opened, and a heavy-set nurse in a crisp white uniform entered the room.

"She doesn't seem to know who I am. Is she all right?"

The nurse ignored me and looked down at her chart.

"It's time to try to go to the bathroom now, *sweetheart*. Come on now, let's try again, I'm sure we can do it this time."

Moving in between us, the nurse took Chrissy's hand out of mine, then began pulling Chrissy up to a sitting position. A long plastic tube ran from an upside-down bottle hung on a metal pole and ended in the back of Chrissy's hand. They were going to have to take the whole contraption into the bathroom with her. The room was cold and antiseptic smelling.

"She's having some slight discomfort and a little trouble controlling her bladder, but she'll have it back in no time at all, won't you,
sweetheart?"

"The floor's cold," Chrissy said, and fell back against the lowered
metal frame of the bed.

"Come on now, honey, you can make it."

The nurse helped her take small hesitant steps to the bathroom
in the corner of the room. Chrissy groaned with every mincing step.
The door closed behind them and then there was only the white noise
of the air-conditioning unit, which continued blowing cold air into
room.

Chrissy's voice: "I can do it by myself! Leave me alone! Bring me
my baby. I want to see my baby. Please!"

The bathroom door opened and they struggled back to the bed,
one fluttery step at a time. The nurse looked frustrated, ruffled, as
though she were the one who had failed to urinate.

After the nurse had helped Chrissy back in bed and put some
warm blankets over her, she suddenly recognized me. She began talking in long run-on sentences. Her face regained a little color.

"Where have you been? I've been calling for you and asking everyone to find you. They said they couldn't locate you, that you had probably gone home... Oh Eddie, she's so beautiful, oh, oh I never wrote
a poem as beautiful as that baby. It all happened so fast, didn't it...
don't you think she's beautiful? Oh, my back hurts. It really hurts.
But she's so lovely, just popped right out like nothing, a baby, a beautiful baby. Oh, it hurts."

I looked up at the nurse who was still straightening out the bed,
and she answered my unasked question.

"It's the saddle-block. As soon as she can urinate freely, the back-
aches will go away. The doctor gave her a shot so she could rest. I
needed her to urinate once more before she fell asleep."

The nurse looked at me as if that answered every possible question and walked crisply out of the room. When she returned with
the small bundle of our sleeping baby and set her in the crook of her

mama's arm, she said, "You can have her for just a minute now. We still need to clean her up a bit."

Baby Andrea. Little fingers, complete with fingernails, curled into a tiny fist.

Chrissy, with our baby curled in her left arm, grabbed my hand and put it to her hot smiling face; she kissed my fingers. Her energy seemed to come and go in spurts. Excitement quickly followed by pain and then exhaustion.

"Where is everybody? I want to call them. I want to tell them to come see me, see my new baby. I want to have a party. It's time to celebrate."

She sighed, leaned back with a big, yawning smile, and then suddenly seemed to fade as blood drained from her face, and her forehead beaded up with sweat, and she went rigid and moaned with obvious pain.

I took her hand and held on as Andrea started crying.

"You did fine; you were good; our baby is beautiful; you're beautiful. You did just great," I said, trying to reach her.

Chrissy pulled her hand away, tried to arch her back, and then moaned. "Oh, my back…it hurts." Her voice was thick and cottony from the pain and the drugs. But now she was drifting into and out of consciousness. Her head lolled over slowly in my direction. She smiled, but she was not really present. Her eyelids flickered. A nurse rushed back into the room and took the baby away. Chrissy didn't seem to notice. She seemed to be drifting, floating on the surface of her own private sea, only occasionally surfacing from a heavily drugged sleep. I stood up, leaned over next to her warm, glistening face, kissed her sweaty forehead, and then tiptoed out of the room.

I drove away from the hospital that night feeling confused and worried but glad that Chrissy and Andrea were warm and safe. As I shifted gears, our old Plymouth responded smoothly, efficiently. It had almost stopped raining. On that October evening as I weaved through the traffic, alone with my thoughts, with the sound of the car's tires whispering softly over the wet pavement, the world seemed filled with promise. In spite of the saddle block, mother and baby were fine. I had the urge to shout that fact out loud, to make some grand announcement to someone, anyone, and so, without really thinking about it, I turned the car around and headed up Red Mountain. Alone then, in the slow, drizzling rain I climbed up on a stone wall and stood under Vulcan's shadow and stared down at the city spread out before me, the iron ore running red streaks off in the distance, thin wisps of gray smoke drifting up through the rain, and then I shouted out into the blinking red and white lights of the night, "Guess what, Birmingham, I am a father, and her name is Andrea."

◁▶

Late that same evening, without remembering which roads I had taken, I arrived home and was surprised to find the lights were on in my house, and a white Chevrolet sedan was parked in front.

When I opened the door, Allan and Anita jumped up from the couch and rushed over, pounded me on the back and began shaking my hand, offering congratulations, and laughing. I felt confused by their presence, by their ebullience, by their laughter. They laughed so much I began to feel a little left out, like I'd not understood the punch line of their joke.

Allan and I had not quite gotten past all that had happened the evening of Doug's death, but we had maintained a strained and distant relationship. Chrissy and I had put it behind us. I still harbored misgivings about it all, but in my most forgiving moments, I knew that Allan had been deeply in love with Sarah, not Chrissy. And that probably nothing had happened. But on this night, of all nights, in spite of feeling odd about being invaded and about seeing Allan with Anita, I offered them a beer and headed into the kitchen. They followed me and stood in the doorway, laughing.

"Okay, Allan, I give up. What's this all about?"

My question really seemed to set them off. They doubled up over each other in helpless cascading laughter, at some sort of secret joke they shared between themselves. My impatience began to grow.

"All right, you guys. Give it up. What's happening?"

Allan, ever the aesthete, brushed back his shoulder-length hair, adjusted his thick glasses, and tried to recover some composure. He gasped for breath, his eyes bulging and glistening with single tears that rolled down his cheeks into his beard. He waved his hands up and down like a conductor who was keeping track of some musical score, while Anita, whose green blouse hung provocatively off her bare left shoulder, drooped her body over Allan's heavy frame. Anita shook her shock of bright black hair out of her face, choked back the laughter that seemed about to bubble up and spill out of her, and then just looked at me impishly.

Allan, grinning wickedly, spoke up briskly, if a bit breathlessly.

"Well, man, are you ready for this?"

"Look, Allan, I don't have the faintest idea what you're talking about. How can I possibly be ready for anything? Now come on, you two, level with me! What the hell is going on?"

Allan spun around in a circle, improbably nimble in spite of his girth.

Anita, in her silky green blouse belted over tight blue jeans, seemed to be calming down. Running her hands over her hips as if enjoying the feel of the silk, she lifted her face toward mine, green eyes matching her teardrop ear rings, nipples showing, no bra, grinning, barely avoiding another bout of laughter, and spoke up. "Go on, Allan, explain it to him."

Allan stepped forward like an actor in an improvisational stage performance, bowed, and then spoke up, his voice forcing a serious note over his bottled laughter.

"Okay, Eddie, what we have brought to share with you tonight is some fine, some super fine…marijuana, some Mary Jane. Some dope. Some boo to celebrate with. Chrissy called Anita and told her we should come and find you. And, guess what, Anita called Tim. He's back in town, staying with his parents."

Allan took a breath and then continued with an afterthought. "We tried going over to see her, but they wouldn't let us in. So we came over here."

I backed up a couple of steps and looked at my friends a little more carefully. *Everything seemed to be happening too fast. I didn't feel ready for a party. It didn't feel right. In fact, I felt a little angry that Chrissy had even called them.* I looked to Anita for reassurance, but Anita arched her back, raised her dark eyebrows, turned her head like a *Vogue* model looking into infinity, and then began giggling again. They were acting weird. *What was going on?* And then it dawned on me. It was the marijuana! But I didn't really quite believe them. I thought of the comic book pictures I'd seen of dope addicts washed up on the shores of hopelessness and wasting away in a dark alley. Is that why they were acting so bizarrely?

Alarm bells were going off in my head, but in spite of my fear, I slowed down enough to think. These were friends of mine. *I knew them;* they weren't *pushers.* But maybe they were just putting me on.

"You guys are too much! Okay, show me your super-fine dope, your boo, and then explain to me where you got it."

Allan turned to Anita.

"He doesn't believe us, he doesn't know about it! He doesn't know…he's suspicious…"

More laughter before Anita spun around in another circle, spoke up impatiently.

"I know…I know…show him…show him…"

Allan whipped out a cellophane bag bursting with some dried, brown and red, grass-like weed. He held it out to me like an offering and gave me a toothy grin.

"Smell it."

It had a musty odor, something like oregano, but not quite.

Allan, readjusting his glasses, moved closer, and then, with a smile and happy, bloodshot eyes, gave me a big bear-hug.

"For you, young father. I bring you gifts from the West. We come to celebrate the birth of your child. You smoke it. You inhale it deeply, and then you will understand the source of our mirth."

I stared at him puzzled.

"Don't worry, it won't do anything but good for you," Allan said in a quiet reassuring voice.

"Is it addictive?" I asked, feeling unsure of myself.

Anita, twirling around again, chimed in, in a singsong voice, "Non-addictive, less harmful than tobacco or alcohol, enlightening and enjoyable. No ill after-effects. What you've heard about this wonderful drug was all lies. Lies. Lots of lies."

She laughed a bell-like laughter, and twirled.

Allan sat down at the kitchen table, rolled a large "number," lit it, handed it over, and then the two of them watched me inhale.

I took two, three big hits.

Nothing. No effect.

Then we passed it around, and Allan demonstrated the best methods of inhaling.

"Take in lots of oxygen with it."

He inhaled with a large hissing sound.

We kept passing it back and forth until they said they were ripped, but I only felt a little dizzy.

"I don't feel a thing. I don't think it's going to work on me."

Allan gave me his superior smile. He rolled another one, and said for me to smoke the entire thing by myself.

I did, but I still didn't feel anything except a little hungry. I remembered I hadn't eaten anything. I got up, walked into the kitchen, and checked the cupboard—nothing there. I checked the refrigerator. Ah yes, I wanted a mayonnaise sandwich.

With the bread spread out on the counter, I dipped the knife into the small jar of Kraft mayonnaise and began spreading it smoothly, oh so smoothly and evenly, over the bread. It seemed to flow in slow motion under the knife like a force-fed magnetic wave of heavy molecules. Then I placed the top on the sandwich and took a bite. Flavors danced across my tongue, sweet and sour mixed together with the cold still lingering from its stay in the refrigerator. Ah! I looked up from my sandwich and discovered that Allan and Anita were watching me intently.

One corner of my sandwich was missing. Mayonnaise was spilling out over the edge of the bread, whitish, viscous—I was witnessing the slow motion fluidity of a strange substance I had always taken for granted. And suddenly the absurdity of eating such a sandwich for supper hit me. *Just a mayonnaise sandwich*, I started to say, but it wasn't just any old mayonnaise sandwich; it was this particular one, in motion, yet still hanging there in front of my face with my arm attached to it.

I cracked up.

Laughter rolled out of me on its own force, shaking me, my arms flailing up and down, watching the mayonnaise fall from my sandwich in slow motion, hitting smack spat on the floor at my feet.

Suddenly I was on the floor beside it, laughing. Then Allan and Anita were on the floor; all three of us were rolling around on the kitchen floor.

Allan was trying to tell me something, but I couldn't hear him, my laughter so loud it hurt. I had to stop. I had to stop! I couldn't breathe and my side ached. I climbed slowly up the kitchen table legs with tears streaming down my face. Allan was still trying to tell me something.

"Did you...say...that...this stuff wasn't...wasn't going...to affect **you**? Is...that...what you said?"

We were out of control again with laughter when suddenly the front door opened and slammed shut, and we stopped laughing.

No one moved or said anything. The house was silent.

Through the open windows we could hear the last songs of summer's crickets and tree frogs.

[17]

Guaranteed his place in history by Birmingham,
Martin Luther King was Time's *1963 Man of the*
Year and the following year's winner of the Nobel
Peace Prize. Compelled to expose King as a "tom
cat with obsessive degenerate sexual urges," [then
FBI Director] J. Edgar Hoover (who had long
lobbied for the Nobel Peace Prize) sent audiotapes
of King's "sex orgies" to the news media (which
ignored them) and to Coretta Scott King, with a
note urging King himself to commit suicide. [7]

The front door slammed shut and it was as if the motion picture of my life had come to a halt, as if I'd been trapped in one frame, an incriminating still shot, the plot stopped mid-action, a piece of evidence against myself, as if I'd been caught out of reality on the night of Andrea's birth.

Paranoia swept over me like insulin shock.

I peeked around the corner into the living room.

Relief flooded through me.

"Tim, my God, you scared us."

Tim was wearing blue jeans, cowboy boots, and a black leather jacket. His wildly curling black hair rose up in ringlets around his large head, made larger by a new jet-black mustache and full-length beard. Looking like he'd just stepped out of a film noir, he stared at me with hypnotic, pale blue eyes, but then, in spite of a big, confident grin, he stumble-walked across the room in a strange unbalanced gait, moving jerkily, but still grinning. Or was it grimacing? At first I thought he was having a joke on us, some sort of imaginative, elaborate ruse, or play-acting, but he didn't break character or laugh. Then he executed a sharp right angle turn, military style, and sat down crossed-legged on the floor in the corner of the living room, and stared at his feet.

Allan and Anita sneaked up behind me like overgrown forest elves, peeked over my shoulders from either side of me in the kitchen doorway, and then the three of us entered the room, exchanging wide marijuana grins in the understanding that there was no obvious crisis here.

Tim slowly scrutinized each of us and sniffed the air. His eyes lit up in a new sparkle, in that delightful, mischievous, switched-on, thousand-watt grin of his, and we were immediately infected, ready for whatever was to come next.

"You...have...more...marijuana?"

It was a request to join us, but he had pronounced each word, each syllable of each ordinary word, as though he had something important to impart. Or was this still a joke of some kind, some new trick, or a staged performance?

Allan, chuckling, winked at me and immediately rolled him a joint and passed it over. After I put the latest Bob Dylan album on the stereo, we all gathered around him in a semicircle, not knowing what to expect.

"When did you get back from California, Tim?" I asked.

Tim tilted his head slightly to one side, looking as if he were trying to see some deeper meaning in my simple question. Then he began answering in that same syllable-paced way of speaking. He talked loudly as Dylan's lyrics began seeping in, "Don't Think Twice, It's All Right," splashing harmonica and blues melodies up against Tim's fixed, syllable-emphasizing monotones. He pronounced each word with an unbearable, freighted emphasis, like boxcars being linked together for some distant journey into uncharted territory.

We listened, stunned into silence.

"I...went...to the hospital...and...I saw Chrissy...she's fine! Very lucky...yes...you're...very...lucky...I told them...I was...her...brother...Andrea...beautiful child, you...are...lucky Eddie...very...lucky."

Tim struck a match and lit the joint Allan had passed him. As he inhaled, it occurred to me for the first time that Tim was more than just not okay. He seemed scary, darkly scary, but also unapproachable. And perhaps over the edge into crazy.

But then, as the sweet pungent odor of pot filled the room once again, hunger struck me, and I couldn't resist. I jumped up and left the room remembering my beer and my mayonnaise sandwich. In the kitchen I started to pick it up off the table, but one large dollop was slipping sideways over the edge of the brown crust. I leaned over and licked it, and my taste buds lit up with a large range of strange sweet-sour sensations. I couldn't tell if I liked them or not. I was puzzling this over when suddenly I noticed Allan standing in the doorway whispering at me. He was pulling at his beard, pushing his glasses up on his nose.

"Eddie, something's seriously wrong with Tim."

"What do you mean?"

"Well, man, he took several big hits from the number I gave him and then, man, he closed his eyes, turned extremely pale, and, well... he seemed just to roll over. His eyes are closed and he won't talk."

"Let me see."

Tim was curled up, lying on his side in a fetal position, arms around legs, head turned to one side. He was not looking good.

My head began to pound, a sharp pain behind my left eye.

"Tim, are you okay? Are you going to be sick?"

He rolled his eyes up at me.

"Do you want someone to take you home?"

There was no response.

Anita moved in beside him, bent down, and began to run her fingers through his hair. Slowly, robot-like, Tim turned towards her and gave her a thin smile. She kneeled down beside him, put her arms around him and pulled him up into a sitting position, like a mother holding a child close against her breasts. Tim responded by smiling up at her and then lifting his arms up to embrace her. Anita, green eyes glowing with concern and affection, pointedly looked over at her purse.

"Allan, Eddie, get my car keys and help me get him into the car. He's stoned and drunk. He's out of it. We'd better get him into a bed."

When we tried to get him on his feet, Tim went limp, but Allan and I managed to link arms under his shoulders and carry-drag him out the door and into the damp night air.

Tim did not help.

Anita held open the car door as we pushed him—like a lumpy duffel bag—into the passenger-side front seat. Tim threw his head back suddenly and then slumped over, one foot in and one foot out.

Anita ran around to the other side and got in. Allan adjusted Tim's body while I bent down and pushed his foot inside. We closed the door and watched Anita's hand smooth Tim's hair back out of his face. Tim smiled at her touch, like a child being tucked in.

"What are you going to do?" I asked.

"I don't know. His parents won't want to see him like this." She smiled ruefully. "Maybe I'll just take him home with me."

Allan and I faced each other in the cool night air with unasked questions until Allan, like the guru imp that he was, gave me his "what-the-hell-let's-enjoy-the-ride" grin, climbed in the back seat, and asked to be dropped off at the nearest bus stop.

Anita started her car, turned it around, and headed back down the alley, its headlights diffusing into the fog and damp night air. Tim's BMW motorcycle sat eerily empty under a pine tree, waiting for its rider.

In the silence of their absence, I waved goodbye to the taillights, listened to the creaking of our pine trees, to the ceaseless cries of crickets and tree frogs.

Then it began to rain again, a light mist and drizzle.

All the lights were on in the house.

I am a father, I thought, *the father of a baby girl...and she will change everything in my life.*

Spreading out my arms to the night sky, I lifted my face into the rain and caught a few drops on my tongue. And then I remembered that Tim had gone up to the hospital to see Chrissy.

What did that mean? Was Tim dangerous? What was wrong with him? And what's Anita doing taking Tim home with her?

Somewhere nearby an owl hooted. Then I heard its wings flap, a muffled eerie sound, the sound of a night predator. I couldn't locate it. I sensed it had come to a landing in a tall pine tree off to my left, close, somewhere in the darkness just behind our house. I thought to call out to it, to see if it would talk to me, "whoo-whoo," but it would not answer. I tried again, "whoo-whoo." No luck. I stood still for a long moment waiting for the owl to change locations, but there was only silence and the drip-dripping of the falling rain. I felt the cold seep in next to my bones and knew I should go back inside. I was getting thoroughly wet. We'd left the front door open. I watched the light spill out of our empty house into the rain and the mist. The yellow porch light dimly lit up the beginning of our gravel alleyway. The rest of our driveway was dark, empty except for the stubborn owl, who wouldn't communicate.

I gave up on the owl and ran for the house, taking the front steps two at a time. As I closed the door I remembered Chrissy lying in her bed in the hospital, her pale face a mixture of excitement, happiness, and pain—"I never wrote a poem so beautiful."

[18]

Chrissy, home from the hospital, went straight to bed and refused to eat. Her back hurt, and headaches drove her to keep the bedroom dark, all curtains closed against the light. Her swollen breasts ached and could not be touched. She could not sleep or breast-feed the baby. We turned to bottles and formula.

The doctor said that Chrissy was having a bad reaction to the saddle block, that she was suffering from a mild case of postpartum depression and that she would be "up and about in no time at all." But one afternoon after coming home from my job at Hueytown High, my briefcase brimming with essays to be corrected, I found Andrea screaming from her crib and Chrissy ensconced in our darkened bedroom with pillows pulled over her head. I knew then that Chrissy was not going "to be up and about in no time at all."

My students would have to wait. I dumped their papers on my desk and took stock of the situation: Andrea had a bright-red diaper rash; Chrissy had burned herself while sterilizing the baby bottles; a tall stack of dirty diapers slumped sideways down over the top of the washer and had spilled onto the floor in a widening stain; a jumble of pots and pans overflowed the sink; and the house reeked with that stale, sickly-sweet smell of spoiled milk and baby poop.

That night we spoke to Mama Barber and Evelyn, and we all agreed that Chrissy's grandmother would come and live with us until Chrissy could get back on her feet.

◁▶

"How's my baby doing?" Mama Barber asked as she entered and, without waiting for a response, dropped her only suitcase on the kitchen floor, pushed her heavy frame forward, and shuffled on toward the bedroom door. At the door she stopped, reached into a shopping bag dangling from her arm and dropped her bedroom slippers on the floor. Winking at me, she bent over and stepped out of her black, square heeled shoes, and, groaning with relief at the removal of each shoe, eased her swollen feet into the well-worn slippers.

"Don't you worry your sweet little head, honey, your Mama's here. Everything's going to be all right." Mama Barber tiptoed into the darkened bedroom and closed the door behind her.

I picked up her suitcase, an old-style leather-strapped affair, and turned back to Bill, who still stood in the open doorway in his auto-repairman's coveralls, smoking his pipe—Evelyn wouldn't let him smoke in their house and therefore, by extension, in ours. Waiting awkwardly to be released from his social responsibilities, he offered me an uncertain smile, then turned toward his Ford pickup parked sideways and waiting in the driveway.

"You want to come in for a cup of coffee?" I offered.

"I guess I better be gettin' on back," he replied.

Bill's smile always gave me the impression that he was stalling because he didn't know what to say. It was as if he had just been told something he didn't understand and needed to think on it for a while.

He took his pipe out of his mouth, looked down at his shiny black shoes, and gave me his good, ready-made explanation as to why he wasn't going to stay.

"She'll be waitin' on me."

Mama Barber's reassuring, sibilant cooing in the middle of the night and her willingness to take care of early morning feedings allowed Chrissy and me finally to get some sleep.

Andrea began gaining weight.

It was November again. Red and brown oak leaves were on the ground, but still a kind of Indian summer hovered around us, bringing a lovely grace to our house. We seemed momentarily blessed, peacefully hidden away at the end of our gravel road, obscured by the surrounding trees: pine, giant red oaks, delicate dogwood, and amber-colored sweet gum.

Mama Barber was joyous and gay, but she was always there, always talking to Andrea or to us, and, at night, always in the room next to ours, listening. Even though Chrissy's back still hurt and her headaches still lingered, she seemed to be recovering. Her breasts were no longer so swollen that they kept her awake at night. But now Chrissy whispered to me that Mama Barber was driving her crazy during the day. She complained that Mama Barber was spoiling Andrea by picking her up the moment she stirred. She said she could no longer abide listening to Mama Barber's incessant ignorant chatter. She said she needed to get out of the house, that she wanted her life back.

Chrissy began going out on long picnics and afternoon jaunts with Anita and Tim.

She wrote in her diary:

*What is this directionless madness? My old explosive energies have burst back on me! Pregnancy was a state of inner-direction, but I—I am essentially an other-directed person. I was safe and rooted when I was with child, but now the dangerous, contingent world thrusts itself on me once again. Perhaps I should pattern my life thus: a baby one year, a lover the next. I offer this capriciously—but then caprice could be the next turn my little adventures will take. I speak of adventure lightly here; I really want to speak about **adventure,** in the absolute; and yet I must deal in the relative. Is my adventure only in relation to my husband and my child, my immediate family? Sometimes I think so; tonight, no. Perhaps it is my part to play many roles. There are at least two faces of Chrissy.*

The rains began again. Then one damp winter's day the highway construction crews showed up in slickers and rain boots with their big yellow backhoes, and they started putting stakes in the ground, tagging trees, and clearing all the wild growth. Before long, with the brush cleared, we could see the pavement at the end of our gravel road, hear the traffic that surrounded us.

Chrissy wrote in her diary:

Pregnancy was a condition of beautiful, purposeful simplicity, but it was not my usual condition. As my energies surge again, the complexities have returned, the conflicts of desires and needs, the questions, the ambiguities, the wonderful plague of sexuality—that power, the very life force in all of us, male and female. I believe that as long as I am capable of caring for my child I cannot fall into utter despair. I can allow myself to explore this Mystery of Self.

Then Anita called and told us that Allan Gregory had been drafted, but that, after basic training, he was going to be stationed in New York as an army trainee learning all about a new field of mathematical computational machines. He'd told her he'd shaved his beard and cut his hair in a buzz cut to save himself the indignity of having the army do it.

On his last day as a civilian, because he had asked us, Chrissy and I left Andrea with Mama Barber and drove him to the downtown Birmingham Greyhound bus station. Then we wandered around the bus station in the rain with the other bundled-up travelers and draftees on their way to boot camp. We didn't have much to say, but he was one of us. We had shared something, and it was hard to let him go. After much hugging and offering of empty promises to keep in touch, Chrissy and I linked arms, backed away, and waved good-bye as he climbed aboard. Chrissy thought he looked like a prisoner about to be hauled off to serve time for a crime he hadn't committed.

On returning home we found Tim's motorcycle in the driveway and Tim in the overly warm kitchen with Mama Barber. The two of them, red-faced, looked up startled as we rushed in out of the rain. Then, with the door still wide open, a blinding flash of lightning struck, followed by a deafening clap of thunder. The house shook, and Chrissy screeched, bending over, putting her hands to her ears.

I closed the door against the storm.

"Devil's takin' to beatin' his wife," Mama Barber shouted out in toothless joy as her body convulsed, her heavy breasts and shoulders and arms jiggling.

Judging by their empties, they had consumed more than a six-pack.

"How's Andrea been?" I asked.

Chrissy started for the baby's room.

"Oh, she's just fine, just fine. No trouble at all. She just taking a nap, her afternoon nap," Mama replied, her voice drifting from laughter to worry as she whistled and gummed her words and began heaving herself up from the table, got her feet moving, and followed after Chrissy.

As soon as they left the kitchen, I addressed Tim.

"I would appreciate it if you wouldn't bring her any alcohol."

Tim stared at me darkly, stood up, and pulled on his black leather jacket.

"Dig it," he said, as if he didn't.

He pointed to a paper bag holding a book and some papers.

"I was just dropping off some stuff for Chrissy...from Anita... Okay, well, I gotta be going."

"Don't you want to wait for the rain to let up?"

"Nah, I like it like this."

As he walked out the door, another clap of thunder rolled across the valley and more lightning lit up the sky.

A few minutes later Chrissy walked into the room.

"Where's Tim?"

"He said he had to go. He left you some stuff from Anita."

I pointed to the bag.

She ran past me, opened the door, stepped out into the rain and shouted his name, but it was too late. The roar of Tim's motorcycle echoed through the open door. And for the first time, it occurred to me that Tim was somehow involved with Anita, and maybe with Chrissy. But as I watched her staring after him in the open door, I put that worry on hold. It scared me, but I didn't really believe it because, maybe like so many uncomfortable truths, I just didn't want to see it.

◁▷

That night, just before sleep, Chrissy rolled over onto one elbow, her breasts bulging out over her loose white slip. She was studying me. And suddenly my worry returned.

"What?"

"Did you know Doug's parents are suing Tim for negligent homicide?"

"No, I didn't know."

"He was served with a notice yesterday."

"Oh, no."

"It's tremendously upsetting for him."

"How's he taking it?"

"He's in trouble, but I think I can help him... Eddie, how would you react if I were to go to bed with Tim? How would you feel about it?"

Her tone of voice had been so casual, I laughed, suddenly awake, suddenly aware of the strange timbre of my voice. I tried to slow my heartbeat, to think of what to say before I said anything.

"I guess I'd be pretty upset. Tim's probably sleeping with Anita. Do you want to be Tim's second mistress?"

Chrissy looked down at me carefully, and suddenly I knew that she was serious. My hands began to shake.

"Eddie, I don't know how to say this... It's a little strange, but Anita told me yesterday that Tim said he wanted both of us. He said he was in love with both of us, that he wanted me to consider what he was offering, and not to take it lightly. He wanted Anita and me to talk it over with each other because he didn't want to come between Anita and me."

I started to interrupt, but I found I hadn't anything to say. Chrissy continued without looking at me. I opened my mouth. No words came out. I closed it. My mind whirled around possibilities I couldn't look at.

"Are you serious?" I heard myself say loudly.

Chrissy put a finger to her lips, nodded in the direction of Andrea's room. Mama Barber was in the next room with her, as we knew, listening.

"Shush... Tim wants us to be open and honest about our needs and our desires, to face our emotions openly, honestly."

"You've got to be kidding me."

"No, he's incredible."

"Are you in love with Tim? This all sounds crazy."

"I...well...I am physically attracted to Tim, and I love Tim *and* Anita. I've known that for some time; I want you to know it too. I don't know what I really want to do yet. I'm afraid...but that's no excuse..."

She looked concerned. She reached over to touch me. I pushed her hand away.

"I want you to know about my feelings...and I want to know what you're feeling."

Her voice seemed so calm, so collected. A panic was rising in me.

"Chrissy, I'm your husband, the father of your child! I love you! I don't understand how you can be saying this..."

Again she offered that irritatingly concerned look. I tried to will myself to be calm.

"But if you ever go to bed with Tim, or anyone else, you had better never let me know about it...because if I find out, well, if I find out...I don't know what I would do, but I do know that it would not be pleasant...for either of us."

Chrissy simply stared at me as if she were trying to take it all in, like a script she was studying, waiting for the next line that hadn't yet been delivered.

"Chrissy, look, I don't know if you are playing with me or not, but we had better get something straight between us, right now!"

Chrissy leaned forward and whispered angrily through clenched teeth, "You have no right whatsoever to dictate to me what I do with my life. I'm honest and open with you. I tell you the truth, and just look at you. Okay, if you don't want the truth, if you can't listen to what I have to tell you, then I won't tell you the truth, I won't share with you what you can't hear. But I want you to remember that you were the one who asked for it to be this way."

"Chrissy, we have a child, we have a relationship with each other and with our child...what you and I do defines that relationship. We are tied to each other through our child. If you have an affair with Tim you will radically alter the way we relate to each other. I am trying to tell you how I feel too, and if you don't listen to me we won't have a relationship, we won't even be together, you and Andrea and I..."

I had been shouting. Andrea's cries suddenly reached us. Chrissy sprang out of bed and rushed into her room. I listened as Chrissy picked her up and tried to calm her down.

Mama Barber had not picked her up. She had passed out from too many beers.

Suddenly I realized why Tim was bringing her beer. He was buying her silence.

I lay there in the middle of our empty bed and pictured Tim in my mind: Tim jumping up on the desk the day the professor fled from the classroom; Tim at Doug's funeral, head bandaged, arm in a sling; Tim, almost catatonic in our living room; Tim curling up in Anita's arms; Tim roaring off in the rain on his motorcycle. I could hear Chrissy now cooing to Andrea in the living room. I could hear the sound of her rocking chair, creaking. I could hear Mama Barber snoring. I could hear my heart pounding.

[19]

[On the same Sunday that four black girls were
murdered by a dynamite bomb set by the Ku Klux
Klan, Virgil Ware, a black boy of thirteen, riding
on the handlebars of his brother James's bicycle,
encountered Larry Joe Sims, sixteen, a white
boy, an Eagle Scout, who was carrying a revolver
and riding on the back of a red motorbike with
Michael Lee Farley. As they passed one another]
Farley told Sims to fire the gun and "scare 'em."
Sims closed his eyes and pulled the trigger.
Two bullets hit Virgil in the chest and cheek,
hurling him into a ditch as the motorbike sped
on. "I've been shot," Virgil said. "No, you ain't,"
[his brother] *James said in disbelief. "Just stop*
tremblin' and you'll be okay."

He wasn't. Instead, Virgil Ware became the
sixth and final black person to be killed in
Birmingham that Sunday.[8]

On a Saturday afternoon, Chrissy and I returned home early from
the shopping center and discovered Mama Barber passed out on the
couch in the living room. I checked the house and found her empties
under the sink in brown paper bags, and behind the bags I discovered
empty Campbell's soup cans containing spit and used tobacco plugs.
It smelled horrible. Chrissy went into a rage accusing her Mama of
drinking and chewing tobacco in secret like white trash, like that

side of her family she never wanted to see again. The people in Mama Barber's family were uneducated, lived in trashy trailer parks, most of them religious fanatics or alcoholics or both. She wanted Mama gone, and I agreed. As I carried Mama Barber's brown bag of empty beer bottles and her make-do tomato soup "spittoons" outside to the garbage can, I thought about how it would be good once again to have the house to ourselves.

On Sunday I told Mama Barber that we really appreciated her help, but that we needed to be on our own now, that it was time for Chrissy and me to take over Andrea's care. We called Evelyn and told her what we had decided, and so Bill drove out the next evening after work, stood in our doorway smoking his pipe, and summing up his feelings on the matter.

"I reckon she done about as much of helpin' ya'll as the Lord wanted her to. She certainly is a good woman. I hope ya'll know that. I reckon you can make it on your own now. We sure will be glad to have her back. Evelyn hates to cook, and there's always dishes to be washed. She all packed and ready to go?"

So we were alone again, but not for long. Chrissy, without a car, at first felt trapped at home on weekdays, alone with Andrea. But then Anita came to her rescue; she had a car. Anita, always a good friend, was now Chrissy's constant companion. But things were changing.

Anita no longer showed up in tennis shoes and sweats. Anita was losing weight and now arrived at our house in sleek outfits with low necklines. She often wore a black-velvet choker, jangling bracelets, and silver hoop earrings. Anita had also let her hair grow out. Long and black, it flowed in a shining waterfall over her shoulders and down her back. Anita often helped out with Andrea and was a regular dinner guest. She had her own apartment across town but a part-time job on campus, and so she often stayed overnight with us. Chrissy and I agreed that she could sleep in Andrea's room and sometimes baby-sit Andrea, giving Chrissy a break, a chance to go shopping alone.

Tim was a sore subject for the three of us, but he was nevertheless an invisible presence we could not ignore. I felt him like a dark spirit stumbling about somewhere out there in the world around us. Over dinner, the three of us talked worriedly about him. Tim and Anita had become lovers. She said that she was afraid for Tim because he seemed always to need to be in control of everything, even the way she dressed, and she wasn't sure how long she could put up with it.

And so it happened one evening that Anita arrived late for dinner, breathless, in high-heeled shoes, and stopped in her tracks in the doorway, mascara smeared. She pushed her black hair out of her pale face, pulled it back behind her ears, and then looked worriedly at Chrissy and me, first one and then the other.

"Tim's getting ready to leave town," she blurted, coming forward and taking hold of my hands, "I've just spent two hours with him… Eddie, he wants to talk to you!"

"Why me?"

"He wouldn't tell me…he just insisted I ask you to come and see him."

She and Chrissy linked arms, backed up, and stared at me.

"Sure," I said, "I'll go see him. When?"

"Now," Anita replied. "He's waiting for you in front of the college theater."

All the way over I kept trying to imagine what was going on with Tim. I still wanted to be his friend in spite of everything. He had taken Doug's death so hard, maybe he was going insane. I felt I needed to find out for myself. And, also, what was going on between him and Chrissy and Anita? Whatever it was, it didn't bode well for any of us. And what did he think of me? Was Tim still my friend? Maybe. Maybe not. I parked the car in the lot and began the walk across the empty campus. Floodlights lit up the brick and cement buildings, the Greek columns. There were no students around. I found him on the hillside above the planetarium. He sat on a bench in shadow, smoking, his cigarette dropping sparks in a constant stream of wind that lifted them out swirling into the dark.

Seeing me, he stood up immediately, began pacing back and forth. Then, as if some starter's gun had gone off, he began hurriedly speaking at me in some stilted form of an actor's speech, his words, in staccato bursts, seeming not so much rehearsed as released.

"Eddie, look, before you say anything... No, let me talk...you see, wait, I've come to the conclusion that I'm a dangerous person..."

"Come on, Tim, the only really dangerous men in the world are the ones who don't know that they're dangerous, like drunks and fanatics."

Tim stopped his pacing, stared wide-eyed, his face a rigid mask. He raised his hands up between us, forefingers of both hands extended stiffly, pointing directly at me. *Maybe he is dangerous*, I thought, suddenly wishing I had not come. Then he bent over and ground his cigarette under his foot.

He seemed to be having some internal struggle for composure and, though losing ground, was still managing a holding action. His movements were stiff and mechanical. He picked up his speech where he had left off, but now he was enunciating each syllable of each word with exaggerated precision, as if he gained control over his words only by means of a focused and concentrated effort.

"As...I...was...saying, I...have come to the conclusion...that I...am a dangerous...person. I believe...I...have hurt people. I...may have hurt...you. I may...hurt you again. I...have hurt people, but I...do not believe I...could kill...anyone...intentionally...but I do not always have control... Sometimes I do, but not all the time...but I am... the person I am becoming...growing stronger every day. Stronger and stronger...and (*His hands covered his face and his head tilted down as he fought to remember something.*) ...oh, yes...I want you... to know (*His hands slowly fell away from his face.*) I care. I want... you...to know that...and to forgive me...if you can...find it in your heart...to forgive...me. Only one thing...is clear...I am leaving. I have to go. Tonight...I had to see...you. I...may not...come back...because it's women. I have to have more women. That's...got to be...the way it is. I...have to...so...I...have to...leave."

His inflated language was clipped, lips pulled back, teeth showing, each phrase bitten off as if he had trouble speaking, as if he couldn't control something that was surging within him. He lurched forward suddenly and took hold of my arm. The immense strength in him hit me with a shock. I tried to pull away, but he held on, his grip tightening.

"Let go, Tim! Tim?"

Tim's eyes went glittery, as he seemed to engage in some inner struggle before finally gaining some control of himself.

"You...had better...go home...Eddie."

Letting go, he turned then and walked away.

I listened for his footsteps as I rubbed my arm, but the wind was too loud.

A kind of inchoate, furious anger swirled around inside me as I fought to make sense of what had just taken place. Tim's arrogance *(was it condescension?)* left a bitter taste as I turned it over in my mind:

Who was I to Tim? What prompted this meeting? What was he trying to tell me? He seemed trapped in a maze of his own making. Did this have something to do with Anita and Chrissy, or was he just slowly slipping into megalomaniacal insanity? Suddenly, I thought I saw him standing under a large weeping willow on the hillside, a dark shadow inside a dark shadow.

I looked closer. He was not there.

I had been summoned and I had been dismissed. I walked back down the path of roughly laid bricks, gravity pulling at me, every step a jarring one.

As I drove back across town, the silver statue of Vulcan rose up gleaming on top of Red Mountain, brightly lit, his green torch glowing, his mercury eyes unblinking, his long shadow on Red Mountain looming ever-present over the city of Birmingham.

[20]

In Saigon...a Buddhist monk set himself on fire
in protest of the suppression of Buddhists by
Vietnam's Catholic government. Malcolm Browne's
photograph of that suicide would join Bill
Hudson's shot of Walter Gadsden...[being attacked
by police dogs in Birmingham] in the finals for the
Pulitzer Prize for photography... [9]

Two days later I found out that Tim had not made it out of Birmingham.

He had gone to his sister's house, and she had talked him into staying on with her for a few days. There, on the outskirts of Birmingham, in his sister's front yard, while she was at work, Tim walked out of her house, leaving the front door open. He stepped over a row of small decorative hedges lining the entrance way and positioned himself, barefoot and bare-chested, in the middle of their front yard. Then he spread his arms wide and turned in a circle, staring up into the bright morning sky, apparently praying.

Across the curbless, tar-black street of this cul-de-sac of suburban homes, small children danced and screamed in a game of Ring Around the Rosy while Tim raised his arms skyward and stood transfixed, unmoving and giving off a low musical tone that reverberated deep in his chest, a sound like humming.

It was only a short while before the neighbors rushed their children indoors and gathered behind their curtains to call one another to talk about the strange half-naked man.

Tim stood staring into the sky for a long time before he lost his balance, staggered around in a circle, and fell down. One of the braver women from the neighborhood ventured outside and, pretending to be picking up her newspaper, checked him out.

There was nothing there in that empty sky. She went back inside, conferred with her neighbors and then called the police.

Tim passed out before the police arrived. Confused and unable to explain himself, he was arrested and taken to the Birmingham City Jail where his parents, after one visit, decided to have him hospitalized.

But there was no space in the hospitals, and the nearest mental institution, forty miles away, could not take him for three days. So it was decided that he would remain in the county jail, in solitary confinement, until space became available at the state's mental hospital in Tuscaloosa.

Tim, we found out later, when he stood outside his sister's house addressing the sky, had been testing the range of his newly discovered power. He knew he could control people, but could he control the weather? To find out, he had walked out into that blinding-white day under an Alabama sun, freshly showered, his dark beard and curly black hair sparkling in the bright morning light, and he had set himself the task of causing enough storm clouds to come together to cover up the sun, to turn the sunny day dark.

His failure had left him in a weakened state, and staring into that bright sky had nearly blinded him. An examining physician had wrapped his eyes in bandages.

Two weeks later Chrissy, Anita, and I visited Tim's parents at their home. We needed to get their permission to see him. His father, James Baker, a small, balding metallurgical engineer, pencil protector in his pocket, sat across the room from us and refused eye contact. Twitching, fiddling with magazines, his eyes blinking behind wire-rimmed glasses, he deferred to Tim's mother, Margaret Baker, who ignored her husband. A large woman with heavy breasts beneath a print dress, she began talking at us non-stop almost from the moment we came through the door.

"Are you from the college? You seem like nice people. I've been so worried... Tim just doesn't seem to have many friends anymore. He used to have lots of friends, but he's just abandoned all his high school buddies. He never brings his college friends over. Can I get you some iced tea?"

She pulled at us, her hands outstretched, touching us, her hair in tight curls about her round face, her sad eyes magnified behind thick glasses, willing us to come in and talk to her.

We all gathered around her coffee table, standing until Mrs. Baker lowered herself into the center of an overstuffed couch. House cats had been at work on the couch's arms, sharpening their claws. Tim's father brought out antique dining room chairs for the three of us, and we sat down apprehensively, facing his parents on the couch. Above them hung a large picture of Jesus wearing a flowing white robe. He smiled benevolently down at us, his cheeks rosy, a halo circling his head, the three crosses of Golgotha rising up behind him in the distance.

After we had each picked up our glass of sweetened iced tea with lemon, Mrs. Baker launched into a monologue.

"Why is this happening to us? Why Tim? Did you know that Tim was the president of the student body in his senior year in high school? He was on the football team and he was voted the student most likely to succeed by his graduating class. I don't know what went wrong."

She sobbed, blew her nose, wiped at her eyes. Mr. Baker stared at his wife disapprovingly a moment, then looked down at his feet. Mrs. Baker talked on.

"He was such a good child...he never gave us a moment's worry... oh, if only it made any sense. I suppose it never does, does it? He always had so many friends in high school... We think he blames himself for Doug's death..."

She paused, looked up at us as if she expected some answer from us, as if she hoped to find some flicker of understanding in our faces.

But then she frowned, and went on talking.

"Maybe…maybe the doctor's right…maybe shock therapy will help… I know some people are against it, but what can you do? His doctor said it was the best thing for cases like Tim's."

Mr. Baker did not speak. He glanced furtively across the coffee table at each of us but refused eye contact. Then, dropping his head, he quietly folded his hands in his lap.

Chrissy and I exchanged worried glances, but Anita, as usual, spoke right up.

"We just want to help. We thought, if you agreed, we'd go down to see him."

Anita reached over and took Mrs. Baker's hand. They held onto one another for a moment, and then Mrs. Baker turned and faced her husband as if settling some unspoken disagreement between them.

Finally Mrs. Baker said "I don't see how it could hurt…" and put her hand to her mouth, sobbed once, gasping for breath as her ample chest heaved, but then she straightened her shoulders, composed herself, turned back to us and smiled as if nothing had taken place.

"Would you like some more tea?"

With written permission from Tim's parents, Chrissy, Anita, and I drove the forty miles down to the Alabama State Mental Hospital to see him. It was a Sunday. We hardly spoke during the trip down. We sat quietly as the car sped down the highway, alone with the white noise of traffic and with our own private concerns, because there was so much unknown about Tim, and so much we couldn't share with one another.

Just off the highway, the state's mental hospital looked like an abandoned, run-down college campus, with Spanish moss hanging from nearby trees. But after we passed through the heavy gates, we were surprised to see a vast expanse of well-tended lawns and a circular drive lined with flowering mimosas and broad-leafed magnolias. We parked in front of four brick buildings set back behind an entranceway of antebellum columns. It was as if we had entered an old movie set worthy of a Walker Percy novel. Beds of roses lined our way as we walked three abreast up a wide sidewalk and staircase, past false-front columns, and into the hospital proper.

Inside, the ambience changed dramatically: metal desks, glass barriers, and institutional-green walls. Our footsteps made sharp-edged echoes on the black and white linoleum floors. Everything around us conspired to leave no doubt that this was a state-run mental hospital, including the unsmiling receptionist who waved us through into a waiting room, where large metal doors opened and closed behind us with an unnerving thud, followed by the click of an automatic lock.

An administrator informed us that because of Tim's delicate recovery situation we would be allowed to see him for fifteen minutes only. Then she led us down a dimly lit hallway and through another heavy steel door, which also locked automatically behind us. She left us to wait in a closet-sized, windowless room, and a few minutes later Tim was led in by a smiling attendant. Black and muscular, he was dressed entirely in white. He helped Tim into a chair, then faced us and spoke quietly, sympathetically.

"I be right outside if y'all need me."

The three of us sat down, a pool of silence spreading out around us. I coughed nervously. A bare light bulb hung from the ceiling and the room smelled of mold.

At our first sight of him, Chrissy and Anita's eyes went wide with shock, their hands covering their mouths, tears suddenly on their faces. Tim was covered with scratches. Abrasions and scabs were everywhere, over his face and hands, even his shaved head. His curly black hair and beard were gone. Even his eyebrows. Gone. Listless, he seemed to stare off into an infinite horizon. I shook my head. Closed my eyes. Opened them again. He was still there.

Tim didn't see *us*, didn't even seem to know we were in the room. Absentmindedly, he picked at a scab.

No one spoke. I felt the urge to turn away, to get up and leave, but I forced myself to sit still. Aware suddenly of the sounds of sobbing from Chrissy and Anita, I handed Chrissy my handkerchief. She blew her nose. Then Anita's voice, small, solicitous, "Tim?"

Nothing. No recognition.

Chrissy leaned over, put her arms around Anita. They sat together, their heads touching.

"Tim, do you know who I am?" I ventured, my voice strangely loud.

He did not respond.

Suddenly fifteen minutes began to feel like an eternity as the four of us sat, not speaking. I began to feel trapped. I wanted to back up, leave, retreat to safer ground.

Slowly, I forced myself back to his face and, as I looked, I felt I was gaining some distance from my first reactions. I knew I couldn't make contact, but maybe I could see the Tim who was sitting here before me. I stared. Who was this person? This was not the Tim I used to know. Where did that Tim go? What happened to him? I thought of Theodore Roethke. *I learn by going where I have to go.* But is that what happened to Tim? Did he go where he had to go or was he forced? The sores on his face and on his hands cried out with the pain that he must have suffered. Where was Tim? Where did he go? Down a rabbit hole? I tried to see into him, through to the Tim I once knew, the boy most likely to succeed, the brilliant Tim whose imagination could light up the whole room. Fearless Tim, who could challenge the authority of professors, the Tim who could do twenty chin-ups without breaking a sweat, the Tim who had stood by Doug, defended him. But the more I stared, the more Tim seemed to slip away. He was not there. Somehow it had all gone wrong. Tim had been in trouble, and not one of us had come forward to save him. I stared at his face, at his empty eyes, a kind of death in them, at the awful scabs, and, as I watched, he picked at one of them, and a drop of blood swelled to the surface. He felt no pain now. Nothing. Tim had gone away. I suddenly realized with embarrassment that I too was crying. I tried to memorize that look on his face, but I kept shying away. I couldn't hold it in focus.

"Eddie." Chrissy was starting for the door supporting Anita who seemed on the point of collapsing. She spoke hurriedly over her shoulder, her voice quivering with barely controlled anger.

"What have they done to him?"

They knocked on the door.

"Eddie, come on. It's time for us to go."

The attendant let them out.

I stayed behind a moment longer with Tim, who stared off into some infinite point on the horizon. He was not aware of me. He was alone in his chair.

"I'm sorry, Tim. We didn't understand," I whispered as I stood up to leave.

Tim picked at a scab on the back of his hand.

What happened, or so we were told, was the following: The Birmingham police had placed Tim in solitary confinement. He didn't belong with the other prisoners, and they didn't know what else to do. No one came to see him. His jailers had put him there and forgotten about him except to push a tray of food under the door and walk away. He had only rudimentary toilet facilities, a toilet bowl, a cup, a sink, and no windows. But he didn't want anything more. Tim didn't want anything from anyone anymore. He was prepared to commune with himself. For the first time in his life there would be no waste. In his windowless cell in the city jail, he sat cross-legged with a cup of his waste and anointed himself. He had covered himself thoroughly, spreading it in a fine, even coat all over his naked body, rubbing it even into his hair, his beard, and his face.

It must have been difficult. Did he have to wet it down? And when it began to dry, and began to stretch him, to pull at his flesh, did he scream? Did he scream for his jailers to set him free? Or did he moan silently to himself, to that self that Doug had loved? It must have been difficult. He was naked and he was covered with excrement. Had he become a holy man in the wilderness? A holy man in the Birmingham City Jail? Or was he just a crazy man? Mad Tim. Crazy Tim. Holy Tim. Saint Tim.

When they came to get him and found him covered in his own shit and had to shave off his hair, even his eyebrows, had to scrub him down with hard bristled brushes, when they were forced to carry him in his sores to the hospital, when they greased his skull and placed the electrodes against his temples, when they emptied his brain of everything except a searing blue electricity, was he still that same Tim? The one once voted most likely to succeed?

As we left, the hospital administrator told us that they hoped for a quick recovery for Tim because he was young, intelligent, and strong.

[21]

[The sometimes-forgotten seventh victim of
September 15, 1963, Birmingham Sunday, was]
Johnnie Robinson, a black sixteen-year-old, [who]
*was shot in the back by Officer Jack Parker as he
ran up a downtown alley after throwing rocks at
a car shoe-polished with such messages as "Negro,
go back to Africa." He was dead on arrival at
University Hospital.* [10]

It was in early in December that Anita informed us that she
had gotten a substitute teaching job at a high school in Vestavia, a
wealthy suburb of Birmingham, and that she was taking up residence
across town in an apartment on the south side of Red Mountain. Her
"free time" was now limited because of her job and her visits with
Tim. It was also in December, a cold wind blowing across the ground,
that the first trucks began arriving to carry away some of the big
felled oaks. Only a few remained standing, barren and lonely, their
naked limbs spread out against gray skies, the ground at their feet
still covered in crisp layers of leaves. But now the bright yellow earthmovers were there, parked at the end of our gravel road, waiting.

I took little notice because I had suddenly found, much to my
surprise, that I was really happy with my high school job teaching
Beginning French and College Prep English Literature. Each morning I left Chrissy and Andrea behind, still in bed, and drove out on
our gravel road, stopped at the intersection, checked for oncoming
traffic, then turned left and sped away. I didn't pay much attention to

all the highway equipment stacking up on each side of the roadway. I was usually looking ahead, eager to get to work early so I could go over my lesson plans before the school officials unlocked the doors and let the students in.

My school, Hueytown High, was located a little over twenty minutes away in Bessemer, a town known as a tough millworker's town. Stories flourished about men who got drunk and fell into a molten stream of steel, caught fire, disappeared, and became part of a beam shipped to Illinois to become a Chicago high-rise.

My first experiences with the unruly classrooms of Hueytown High led me to believe that no one was interested in literature. But then I discovered a few really bright and challenging students who seemed to have been hiding out, blending in, just waiting for someone like me to show up. These few students sat up in class and listened. And talked. They got excited by ideas, by poems and stories, and their excitement got me excited. I changed my syllabus to a more challenging curriculum, and I wouldn't let even my dullest students off the hook. I pressed them to discover what was at stake in what they were reading.

Our classroom discussions became hotbeds of argument that often continued after the bell. Students began to line up at my desk after class. They wanted to talk more about the poems of e. e. cummings and the Jack London stories (mimeographed by me because they weren't in our boring textbook). I stayed late after school helping some with classwork and helping others write their own poems and stories. I brought them new material to read: *A Portrait of the Artist as a Young Man, The Catcher in the Rye,* "To Build a Fire," *1984, Lord of the Flies.* It was as if the spirits of Doug and Tim were in the room with me as my students began challenging each other to stop and think about what they were reading. I asked them to keep a journal about what they thought about after reading a poem or story, and we discussed their reactions. My class was about what *they* thought, not about what the textbook thought. Classroom discussions were exciting. Even my beginning French classes were becoming fun. We laughed and joked in French, and suddenly these young freshmen and sophomores, mostly young girls, began to push me, and I struggled to stay two chapters ahead of them, mastering French irregular verbs as I went. I rose early each morning, excited about the day, and I stayed up late into the night grading papers, trying to engage each one of my students in a dialogue, writing extensive questions in red in the margins. Chrissy and Andrea were usually asleep by the time I hit the bed.

I realize now that Chrissy and I had begun to live in separate worlds. She practiced her guitar, or kept her nose in a book, or sang songs as she rocked Andrea to sleep. Andrea was almost three months old, growing ever so quickly, and she occupied much of Chrissy's day, but still it was not enough, she complained. She was stuck at home with no car, and Anita was no longer around to take her places or help out. Mama Barber was gone. Sarah and Allan were gone. Tim was gone. She was trapped.

And then one day towards the end of December the chainsaws and bulldozers came alive again as the highway construction crews arrived and began taking out the last of the trees.

In her diary Chrissy wrote:

As our leafless trees come down, I wander from room to room, crying, and as I pace the floor I know I cannot stay. Once again my old energies surge within me, telling me to have "the courage to be," as Paul Tillich explained so beautifully.

But I am not free.

How can I be when I know myself to be other than what I am?

Andrea is pink and pearl, and smooth soft-warm fragrance, and she laughs the pure laughter of innocence, cries the real distress of innocence, of needs.

Children are close to absolute emotions. Every feeling of pleasure and pain and all the shadings are complete in their one moment. Andrea is the only light of my days now; she is the only thing in the world I am sure about.

But I, I am in a state of no freedom.

I cannot stay and I cannot go. My mind is a vast desert. I range about in it and find dryness, nothing green and growing.

How can I be so empty?

I ask myself: What is courage? Is it the persistence of hanging on? Or is it the strength to face head-on that desperate last wish to live an honest life?

"No, please don't go," I pleaded with Chrissy, her bags packed, her ticket to New York City in her hand.

She was leaving me.

I had not seen it coming.

I had just come in the door, briefcase in hand, and there she sat, packed bags beside her, dressed up in a new beige suit over a form-fitting sweater in bright brown and yellow checkered squares, complete with pillbox hat and gloves. She was holding the phone in her hand. She had just called a cab.

"Where are you going?" I asked.

She hung up and sat down.

"I'm going to New York."

I collapsed in a chair opposite her, stunned.

"Why? For how long?"

Words came out of my mouth, but just who was this imposter carrying on a conversation so calmly and politely? I seemed to be outside my body.

"What's going on? Do you know someone in New York?" I asked.

Legs crossed, she looked quite sexy in her nylon stockings, and black high-heel shoes. She kicked her foot back and forth, looked away. My mind swirled with contradictions. I wanted to touch her, to kiss her full on the mouth.

"Yes. I've called a friend of Anita's who'll put me up until I can find a job."

I stared at this new person in front of me. Then, leaning back with a sinking feeling, I remembered Tim, his cigarette sparks blowing out into the dark that night at the college, saying *I may have hurt you.*

"Did you sleep with Tim? Is that what this is about?" I blurted.

My voice sounded strange, time distorted, as if this question were reverberating in my head, as if my words were coming back to me from far away, like an echo from someone else's voice.

Placing both feet on the ground, hands in her lap, she straightened her shoulders, smoothed out her skirt, and said, "I hoped we wouldn't have this conversation, but I guess it can't be helped."

"And what about Andrea? What if I'd had an accident, not come home on time; you were going to leave her home alone?"

"Don't be ridiculous. I planned to call you from the airport."

She was all business now. She paused, stood up, walked to the door, checked for her cab, came back to her chair. "I planned to have Andrea down for her nap, write you a note, and then leave before you got here. That didn't work." She began pulling on her beige-colored gloves. "Tim's part of it…"

"Tim's part of it," I interrupted, mimicking her, "What do you mean, Tim's part of it?" I could hear a surge of anger in my voice. "Tim's crazy. He's in an insane asylum!"

She focused on her gloves, smoothing the wrinkles.

"Do you want the truth?" There was anger in her voice.

"Yes, I want the truth."

"I don't want to hurt you, but I guess you need to know, have a right to know… I wasn't going to tell you, but…yes…Tim, Anita, and I were lovers for almost three weeks…"

Holding herself erect, mouth set, she looked straight at me and waited for me to say or do something. But I had nothing to say right then. I just sat down, pulled my briefcase over my knees, and stared at her expectant face.

Time slowed down.

I felt a little dizzy.

"I was the one who broke it off," she continued. "He wanted Anita and me, together, a ménage à trois. But he also wanted more women. We couldn't go along with it. If he had been satisfied with having only us, we might have gone away with him, at least for awhile."

She shook her head, looked away, and murmured as if to herself,

"But that was never ever going to happen."

I was slipping down a long tunnel, the outside world growing farther and farther away. I reached out to touch her knee and knocked my over-stuffed briefcase to the floor. It fell open as it landed, my students' papers spilling out.

Ignoring me, she said, all business again, "I've fixed Andrea's bottles for when she wakes up. They're in the refrigerator. All her diapers are clean and folded on the dryer."

Student papers spread out on the floor, I bent down to pick them up, recognized the handwriting of one of my better students. I stopped. Peered up at Chrissy. For a moment I didn't recognize her. She seemed to be someone else. Someone I'd never met before. Some harder, more determined person. She sat stiffly erect in her new clothes, leaning away from me, looking off into the distance again, eyes fixed, mouth grim.

A horn blared, startling both of us.

Chrissy tugged decisively one final time at her gloves, stood up, took hold of her two bags, and walked out without looking back. I stepped over my briefcase and spilled papers and followed after her, mutely looking down at the Yellow Cab from our porch steps. The young driver, cap at a jaunty angle, held open the back door. Chrissy settled into the cab's interior. The driver closed the door and, glancing quickly up at me before averting his eyes, hurriedly put her bags in the trunk and climbed in behind the wheel.

The engine coughed once, caught, and the cab began to pull away, tires crunching and spewing gravel. I started down the stairs. Chrissy did not turn in my direction.

After standing alone, facing after them a moment, I turned around in a circle, looking at what was there in front of me. Dead and dying trees were pushed together into assembled trash piles for burning. New roadways of dirt wound through our forest, leaving long stretches of exposed bright red clay and upturned roots sheared away and pushed out from the dark soil. Silent, black-smudged bulldozers were parked between the buckets of large backhoes, immobile, waiting for some human force to take them over, bring them back into action, roaring with sound, belching exhaust fumes.

The Yellow Cab turned left and disappeared, Chrissy seated in back, on her way to the airport. It was a Friday evening. I was alone with Andrea, and I didn't know what to do with myself. I had just come home from work. I was standing in front of my house. I had nowhere to go. I had no plans. It was the beginning of the weekend, and I was alone on our gravel road, with dead and dying trees all around me. Chrissy had left me. I was unable to go forward. I was unable to move.

I looked back up the steps to our house. The front door was wide open. A familiar cry emanated from within. Andrea's waking cry. And suddenly I knew what to do. I ran up the stairs two at a time into the house and closed the door.

In her diary Chrissy wrote:

In the long, dark night of the soul of utter aloneness, this darkness cannot be lifted.

Perhaps it could be outlasted.

There may be love in this darkness; it may wait for me, but it cannot reach me here. It knows not me nor itself. I wait and I hang on, but there are no words to scatter this palpable dark.

Nothing dispels it.

Perhaps outside this town there is another world and another life for me. Perhaps that stranger who is myself waits only for me to choose to live in that other possible world. Perhaps she waits in the shadows of my future, waits for me to come to her in another time and place where she may live and not die.

That weekend I rented a trailer, took Andrea to my mother, who agreed to look after her, called the landlord, and canceled the lease. I told him we could no longer live in a construction zone, and then I returned and began packing.

I worked all day without letup until Chrissy's mother, Evelyn, interrupted me with a phone call. Chrissy had called from New

York, she said, but had refused to explain anything. Evelyn said she couldn't understand what had happened. I told her I couldn't talk about it, hung up, and disconnected the phone.

By dusk I had completed loading the trailer, but stuff still filled two rooms. There were the curtains that Chrissy had made, the tables and chairs that friends had given us, the cane couch we rescued from a junk pile but never repaired.

That night I drank a six-pack of beer for supper and, exhausted, fell asleep with the remnants of our life together boxed and stacked in the living room. I dreamed I was back in the U.S. Army, at Fort Jackson, South Carolina. Tim Baker was my C.O. He was giving me instructions about the exercise our squad was about to go on. We were going to simulate a charge on a machine gun nest. He pointed to a machine gun in the distance and warned us that it would be firing live ammo, fifty caliber, five feet over our heads. I had heard about this exercise before, and it was rumored that men had been killed, or at least wounded. I looked up at my C.O. to ask a question, but since Tim and I were supposed to be friends, I realized at once that he wouldn't answer any of my questions. I smiled at him instead to let him know that I understood the situation. But Tim turned away, refusing to acknowledge me, and suddenly we were off, charging up a sandy sparsely covered hillock, straight for the machine gun nest. We ran openly at first, and then they spotted us and opened fire in short warning bursts. Whack, whack, whack-whack-whack! Something whistled beside my ear. My God, they were firing five feet off the ground, not five feet over our heads! I shouted for everyone to hit the dirt! We did, but as I looked back Tim was waving at us frantically to keep going; he was shouting my name, but I couldn't make out what he wanted. The other men started forward again. I stood up, crouching low to the ground, but the sand pulled at my feet. The machine gun was louder, firing sustained bursts, the sand pulling me down...

I woke up, alone, the covers roiled up around me.

There was a pounding on the back door of the house.

I staggered out of bed. The banging continued, and someone was calling my name. The elastic gone in my boxer shorts, I held them up with one hand and opened the door with the other. It was Bill.

"Bill, what is it? What's the matter?"

Without answering my question he walked right past me in his blue denim work clothes, his face set, flushed red, his black hair slicked back with strong-smelling hair tonic. I couldn't figure it out. He didn't stop in the kitchen but continued straight on through to the bedroom. For a moment I just stood there in my bare feet holding my pants up, and then I started after him repeating my question.

"Bill? Bill, what is it?"

We met again in the hallway, but he turned his head away and walked around me. His heavy work shoes echoed in the living room. I looked into our bedroom. The closet door was wide open. Bill had looked in our closet.

"Bill, what the hell is going on?" I shouted as I started after him again just in time to see him exit out the kitchen door. The screen slammed shut. I followed just in time to see him gun his car, spitting gravel, out of our driveway.

I sat down at the kitchen table. The clock read 6:45. All at once it came to me why Bill had come visiting so early in the morning. He had come on a mission for Evelyn, expecting to surprise me in bed with another woman. She had sent him to catch the sinful son-in-law with his pants down, to expose me for the dirty way I had treated her daughter.

I laughed out loud until I could laugh no more, until a weariness covered me in its shadow like a great black bird of prey. I stumbled back to my bed, crawled under the covers, and slept.

[22]

*The bombing of a church, the killing of innocent
children, can take place in any community,
the newspapers assured their readers. But do
atrocities take place in a social vacuum?* [11]

In the late afternoon, having left Andrea with my mother, I walked
naked into the bathroom to shower. No towels. Naked, I wandered
from room to room until I found one in an unsealed cardboard box in
the living room. There were no curtains on the windows and no trees
still standing in the yard. In spite of the late afternoon sun, Alabama
winter was now in evidence everywhere, a dull yellow-brown upon
the land. No green. I stood in front of the window on a bare wooden
floor beside stacks of cardboard boxes and watched Jacob's ladders
of afternoon sunlight play across my belly. I ran my hand down my
arm and sent a rush of golden motes dancing like sparks into the air.
Strange, I thought, *I am alive, the only living being in this house, and
I am radioactive with life.*

Suddenly I knew what I was going to do next. Towel in hand,
I headed back to the bathroom and turned on the tub's overhead
shower. Almost immediately the small room began to fill with steam.
I pulled back the no-longer-transparent plastic shower curtain and
tested the water. It was hot. The window and the mirror over the
sink began to fog over. I climbed in and stood at the back of the tub
and began to scrub myself down with a soapy, rough washcloth. I
rubbed hard enough to make my skin glow red, and then I stepped
into the spray, immersing myself in the heat of it until I could bear it

no longer. I twisted the handles in opposite directions.

The hot water went off. The cold water came up to full volume. A biting, stinging cold rolled over me. I waited until I had adjusted to it, and then I turned the water off, rubbed myself dry with the towel, and got dressed in a red and black checked work shirt, jeans, and my lace-up work boots.

I was ready.

First I added all the soaps and toiletries and the last of the kitchen utensils to my unsealed box and stuffed it into the back seat of the car. Next I gathered up Chrissy's curtains from the floor in full armloads and carried them outside and spread them out in a big circle in a ready-made hole partially filled with branches and debris. Then, after taking out the shower curtain, I dragged our antique dining room table outside and pitched it upside down on the dirt next to the curtains. Standing in the center of the upside-down table, I took hold of each of the legs and pushed on it until it broke free in a splintering of supports. I tossed the legs onto the center of the circle.

But how to attack the tabletop?

I remembered the large sledgehammer our landlord had left in the garage. After retrieving it, I stood beside the table and swung the sledgehammer high over my head and brought it down with a good satisfying smack. The table's expandable metal tracks collapsed. After that, three solid blows and the table splintered into pieces. A few more swings and the walnut boards were destroyed—would never fit into any structure, ever again. I tossed them in. I leaned back and laughed. It felt good, this furniture destruction.

Then I paused for a moment, looked around at the wasteland that was once our lovely forest, and threw back my head and howled three times, a wolf's howl of defiance. From a long distance away came an echo. I listened, laughed out loud, and then I threw the rest of the pieces of the table onto the pile. The dining-room chairs were next.

I worked through the late afternoon into the evening, until it was almost dark and the stack was as tall as I was. Then I disconnected the glass lantern from the base of our kerosene lamp and tossed it on the pile. It shattered. Next, I removed the wick and tossed it on top before pouring the kerosene all around the base of my stack. The curtains soaked it up.

The fire started on one side, then rapidly closed the circle, and began licking its way toward the center, gathering itself into a full-fledged bonfire. I opened a beer, lit up a cigarette, warmed myself in the widening heat of the flames, and watched the sparks rise up toward the stars.

A large fire is blazing, heat and energy and perspiration flowing, more furniture, the fire is growing, more, and in the shadows a lone figure is running and smashing and throwing more; a sledgehammer arcs through the shadows flashing down and smash, a lamp, smash, a chair, a radio smash, tubes smash, bursting, glistening, smash, and the parts glitter as they sail from the shadows into the burning light. Crackling and spitting, the fire is licking up into the air, the fire of the god of cuckolds, Vulcan's fire. The hammer falls. Everything burns.

Part Two

...without wanting to I call out to you,
I reach, knowing you can't be held and
you can't hold me. We are forever you
and I, not we. And that is the hardest
thing I know...

CHRISSY ANDERSEN, *April 4, 1965*

$$[23]$$

December 15, 1964

I am in no-space. I drive to and from work every day, and yet I am not aware of driving. I am only aware of leaving and arriving. I live with my parents, but I do not talk to them. I teach high-school children English Literature and Beginning French. I go where I have to go. Each morning I wake up and play with Andrea, change her diaper, prepare her bottle of formula, carry her around with me, tickling her fancy until Mom comes into the kitchen and takes her from my arms. Time to go back to work. I go back into traffic and forget where I'm going until I get there.

January 19, 1965

I have met a new person, Carina Scott. She is a petite Southern aristocrat, daughter of a rich doctor. She's Anita's new roommate. She and Anita are teaching at the same county school. She has a pointy nose, pale blue eyes, long blonde hair, and a complexion so white she's almost transparent. A revealing deep pink blush seems never far from the surface of her face. Her accent is soft, but thick. She's from Mobile, Alabama, from a home with servants, from an easy life lived close to the Gulf Coast.

Carina is *proper!*

She makes for an amusing contrast to serious Anita, who still visits Tim weekly.

January 25, 1965

Anita's apartment: spare, everything orderly, some tea bags in a box on the cupboard shelf, Vivaldi's *Four Seasons* on the small record player. Then along comes Carina, and it's hooked rugs, elegant crystal vases with dried pussy willow arrangements, flowering cacti, a new stereo, and Dixieland jazz.

On Friday nights, after work, the three of us sit around, talk, and drink Carina's scotch. The subject of Chrissy, by mutual agreement between Anita and me, is off-limits. I know Anita and Chrissy talk on the phone, but that's all I know. "It has to be that way," she told me, "because I can not...I will not take sides...and the only way I can do that is by keeping my conversations with her private. So don't ask me about her because I won't tell you." Carina talks endlessly about her students and the social interactions between teachers and administrators. The flow of her words is soothing, a comforting, soft, white noise.

Then I go home, to my parents' house, and Andrea. Mother seems to have been revitalized by Andrea's presence. Even the shaking seems to have abated somewhat. I watch her cooing over Andrea's crib, a wonderful welcoming smile on her face. It's as if taking care of Andrea has given her a break from her battles with Parkinson's disease. Dad, however, still moves through the house like a hornet trapped inside a window screen, though he seems grudgingly willing to give me space. But it's a small space, a space reserved for a failure that he can't quite comprehend or confront. My brother Bobby is now feeling the full force of his anger, as are the rest of my siblings, but he leaves me alone. And I'm grateful not to have to fight with him.

It was a Friday night. I'd just driven back to my parents' house from an evening with Anita and Carina, a scotch-induced warmth inside me, Bob Dylan's lyric "The Times They Are a-Changin'" rolling around in my head, and there it was in my mother's handwriting, a note, her penciled letters in perfect Palmer-method script, childlike in their large, shaky connectedness, telling me that Chrissy had called and that she wanted me to return her call, no matter the hour.

It was nearly midnight.

I collapsed in Mother's overstuffed easy chair and fingered the note.

Andrea, my parents, my brothers and sisters slept.

In the hallway the floor furnace clicked on as the gas jets lit and its metallic sides began creaking as they warmed. The house was dark except for where I sat, a pool of light spreading down over the mahogany end table onto my mother's gray-blue rug. Across the room, out the window, dark clouds were gathering behind an eerie full moon that lit up our back yard like a spotlight.

I stood up, walked into the kitchen, and looked outside at the big red oak with its large-limbed shadows and at the dangling tire swing my brother Bobby and I had built an age ago. Its heavy rubber form hung motionless in the dark, backlit by moonlight. Fast-running clouds were passing overhead, momentarily obscuring the moon. I remembered how Bobby and I had taken turns, timing our runs beside the swing, jumping on, and letting it sweep us off the ground. And I remembered Chrissy and me, in better days, taking a turn on the swing, when we'd drop by for a visit. For a moment I wanted to go outside and take another turn, to go swinging high up in the night air, but instead I walked away from the kitchen window, sat back down, picked up the telephone, and dialed the number Chrissy had left for me.

"Hello, Operator, I want to place a call to New York City... Yes, that's right, Manhattan..."

(The sound of a phone ringing.)

"Hello..."

"Is Chrissy Andersen there?"

(A male voice.) "Just a minute. I'll get her."

(Sleepy sounding voice, distant.) "Hello, Eddie. How've you been?"

"All right I guess, and you?"

(Loud voices in the background. Long pause. Sounds of a party.)

"I'm fine...how's Andrea?" Chrissy's voice is nasal, raspy, congested.

"She's fine; she's beautiful. She rolled over by herself yesterday."

(Silence.)

"Eddie, I...I miss her! I miss her so much, you don't know... I want her... I want her here with me." (Long hacking coughing spell.

A deep breath.) "She belongs with her mother. Would you, do you think we could work something out?"

"Chrissy, uh...I don't know...are you working? Can you take care of her? I mean, well, Chrissy, how would you take care of her?"

"What are you asking me? I don't understand."

"Do you have any money?"

"I'm not working now, but I will be soon. Eddie, you wouldn't try to keep her from me, would you?"

"No, of course not."

"I have a right to my own child!"

"Chrissy, I couldn't keep her away from you, but, well, I've been in touch with Dr. Cantrell and she said..."

"You what?"

"Wait a minute...listen to me...Chrissy?"

"What is it? What do you want from me?"

"I'm worried about you. Your doctor suggested you find another therapist there."

"Eddie...I don't believe you're doing this to me!"

"I'm not doing anything to you."

"I thought I knew you, but I don't, do I? I don't know you at all!"

"Chrissy, please, believe me...I care about you! And I'm not trying to keep Andrea from you, but this was your choice."

"Damn you!" (Coughing fit, voice cracking) "What are you up to, Eddie?"

"I'm not up to anything. Andrea's my child too...I just want to be sure that you're all right, that you can take care of her. You need to get a job, get an apartment. Then we can talk about what's best for Andrea."

"You're not in charge of my life!"

Pacing around, whispering loudly into the phone, trying not to shout, "Look, Chrissy, you're the one who left us! Remember?"

"Is that your case? Is that the best you can do? For your information I've been to see a psychiatrist here! He said that there's absolutely nothing wrong with me, and I have every right to custody... I haven't done anything wrong. I can take care of my own child!"

"How?"

"Eddie, I want my child! Do you hear me? I want her and you can't keep her from me, I won't let you."

Deep breaths, slow release, eyes fixed on the moonlight and the tire swing in the backyard, "Okay, Chrissy, I hear you. Maybe we can work something out...when you get a job."

"I am getting a job!" (Coughing. A deep breath. A pause.) In the background, the faint sounds of voices, music, a loud jazz saxophone.

"Chrissy, I've missed you...what's it been like? What have you been doing in New York? I mean...how do you spend your days? Who's there with you?"

"Look, I can't talk any more...someone's waiting for the phone. I've got to go."

"Wait a minute..."

"I'll work something out. Good night, Eddie."

"Wait...Chrissy, where are you living?"

"I'm staying with some new friends, but I'll have my own apartment soon. One of the girls who lives here wants to share an apartment with me. We're going looking tomorrow after my job interview."

"Will you send me your address as soon as you find one?"

"Yes, of course...I have to go."

"All right, good night."

"Good night."

After I rang off, I moved about the house in a daze. I didn't know what I'd expected, but there was no reconciliation in her voice. I did not know what to think. I stood at the kitchen sink for a long time in the dark. Outside, our first winter storm was brewing. It was probably going to rain and then freeze over. As I stood there in the warmth and silence of my mother's kitchen, I stared out the window as the big black "O" of my old tire swing began to twist and turn in the wind.

◁▶

January 27, 1965

Tonight I am wide-awake and thinking about you, Tim Baker.

What was it you said—that you *may* have hurt me, that you wanted me to forgive you if I could find it in my heart to do so.

No, I don't forgive you, Tim. You see, I'd like to chalk it all up to your madness, but I can't—even though I know you've suffered, maybe more than the rest of us. I can't forgive you.

But I need to forgive you because I need to forgive Chrissy, and because I know you're suffering, and because I know, just as you took charge in the accident that killed Doug, that you took it upon yourself to try to do something, even if it was wrong.

Yeah, you hurt me, but I don't hate you. I want to, but I can't. We all got hurt. And it's still not over. Not even close.

In some ways, Tim, I envy you. I couldn't look at you in the sanitarium, but now I see how you made visible what was invisible.

Almost three o'clock. Thirty-four test blue books were stacked on my desk and ready for my briefcase. The minute hand of the big wall clock backed up and then clicked forward. Every muscle tensed for the bell and the great surge for the door, but then a grinning embarrassed freshman swam sideways into the room trying to avoid the attention that was focused on her. She handed me a note from the office just as the bell rang and the room erupted into chaos.

The words said: "Your mother wants you to call home."

The note sent a chill through me. My mother would never call me at work unless something was wrong, something that could not wait.

I rushed to the office, weaving my way through the emptying hallways of kids suddenly released from the school.

"Hello, Mom, what's the matter?"

"Eddie, I don't know if anything is wrong, but I thought you ought to know..."

"Ought to know what?"

"Well, uh...did you know that Chrissy was coming back today?"

"No, I didn't. Is she there now?"

"Well...no. She was here...it was quite a surprise to see her. I thought you knew and, well...she wanted to take Andrea over to her mother's house to see her grandmother, Mama Barber, and..."

"And you let her?"

"Well, yes...I, I..."

"Okay, okay, uh, is she at her grandmother's now?"

"That's just it...Chrissy forgot to take Andrea's coat and it's so windy out and since Andrea has a cold, well, I called Evelyn's house and Chrissy wasn't there...They didn't even know she was in town. Oh, Eddie, I know I should have called you first, but I believed her."

My heart racing, my vision narrowing to the desk before me, I forced myself to be calm.

"Okay, Mom, it's okay."

"I didn't think... I just didn't know what to do. She was so natural; we had a cup of coffee together and then she said she wanted to take Andrea over to see her grandmother, and...I couldn't refuse, I couldn't tell her she couldn't take her own child..."

A sudden jolt of energy passed through me like a shot. Something was wrong. She was here, in Birmingham. I could almost feel her presence, a strange sense of her, muffled, as if she were bundled up in sweaters, heavy coats, and scarves. What was she doing in town? What was she up to?

"Did she walk over from her mother's house?"

"No, she had a car. It looked new. Eddie, I don't know where she could be, and it all seems so strange to me now the way she behaved..."

"Look, Mom, I'm leaving work right away. Call her mother's house again and see if Chrissy is there now. If she's not, call her mother at work, and see if she's heard from her. I'll be home as soon as I can."

I leaped into the car and told myself, slow down, take it one step at a time, but my heart wouldn't listen. I started the engine, slammed the car into reverse, backed up, and then began threading my way out of the teachers' parking lot, creeping through knots of students crossing the street as they continued on, laughing, shoving each other, waving at me happily. Everything inside me was moving at one speed, my car at another.

I gripped the steering wheel, edging my way forward, blowing the horn, waving at my students, seeing Chrissy in my mind, thinking, *Yes, I know why you're here. I know why you didn't call me. You've come for Andrea. You've come to take her back to New York.*

Turning onto the highway, I stepped on it. My old Plymouth sedan shuddered and then accelerated. I shifted into high gear. It was going to take me at least forty or fifty minutes to get home.

Maybe she had stopped off at a store for diapers. Maybe she had first gone to see her mother, or perhaps she had arranged a visit with Anita. But Anita was teaching. Her mother was at work.

I ran a red light, changed gears, and pushed my car over the speed limit through the slow-moving traffic of downtown Birmingham. I had to go completely across town, west to east and north to south, across the steel-mill overpasses, over the smoking red rivers of steel mill slag. Pushing my car to new limits, I kept down-shifting, never braking, weaving from one lane to another, hurrying toward Vulcan and Red Mountain, toward the Atlanta highway, and then exited onto the back roads that cut through fields of kudzu to East Lake and my parents' home. Finally, under the distant, looming shadow of the fire tower on the eastern end of Red Mountain, I turned off Eighth Avenue South into my parents' driveway.

I could tell from my mother's grave face that Chrissy was not at her mother's.

I grabbed the phone book and called the airport.

The next and only flight to New York City was scheduled to depart in twenty minutes. The airport was over twenty minutes away.

It took me exactly eighteen.

I parked the car in a loading zone and dashed inside looking for the information desk.

I didn't know which gate.

A line of people blocked my way. I pushed past them.

"The flight to New York, please, this is an emergency, what gate are they leaving from?"

The startled desk clerk eyed me suspiciously, but he looked over his shoulder, checked the lists.

"I think you're too late, but it's Gate 10."

I fled down a long, shining, waxed hallway. People startled, stepped out of my way, and stared; other people flowed past me going in the opposite direction, old men and women, men in business suits arguing and laughing and disappearing in a flash of faces.

Gate 10 was deserted but for a wrinkled old black man emptying the ash cans.

I walked back to the airline's desk.

"I'm sorry, Sir, but our passenger lists are confidential information. I could page the person you're looking for if you think he missed his flight."

"No, no thank you."

I drove back to my parents' house in twenty-five minutes.

I hoped that Chrissy and Andrea would be waiting for me; but I didn't believe it would happen that way. They were gone. I could feel their absence in the way people drove their cars past me; I could feel it in the way the red lights changed to green so I wouldn't have to stop, because there was no reason to hurry; I could feel it in the gray overcast of the winter sky over Birmingham.

They were gone.

I stopped my old Plymouth in my parents' driveway, switched off the ignition, and, as the car engine cooled with metallic clicks, I looked up at my mother who stood inside our house looking back at me. Her hand covered her mouth the way it always did when she was upset, and an image of Andrea floated across my mind: she was lying on my mother's rug, reaching up for my outstretched hands; she was giggling with high-pitched squeals of laughter.

I couldn't bring myself to get out of the car. I didn't feel like I could start moving back into my life. I just wanted to sit still for a while. I stared at my hands on the steering wheel. I had nowhere to go.

My mother did not move.

We waited, a tableau of two, until it occurred to me that my mother was worried about me just as I was worried about Andrea. Or was I worried about myself, trying to live without Andrea? And then, as my mother waited for me, a comforting thought came to me: Andrea didn't know she was missing. She didn't know she was on a plane bound for New York City. She was going where she had to go. Andrea was with her mother.

[24]

The phone rang, and my heart leaped: *Maybe it was Chrissy; maybe she was still here.*

It was Anita.

"Eddie, are you all right?"

"No, I'm not all right, Anita. Do you know what's happened?"

"Yes...Chrissy called me from the airport. Eddie, I'm so sorry."

"Has she gone to New York with my child?"

"Andrea's her child too, Eddie...she's doing what she thinks is best; she was afraid you were planning to keep Andrea..."

"And do you agree, Anita? Do you think she's doing what's best? Did you agree with her enough to help her kidnap my daughter?"

"Eddie...I tried to talk her out of it."

"Well, she's not going to get away with it. I can do just what she's done; I can go to New York and steal her back."

"Eddie, look, I know you're upset, but, listen, Chrissy is going to call you tonight. Just wait and talk to her before you do something you might regret."

"Did Chrissy tell you to say that?"

"I've told you what I thought I ought to tell you, and now I think I'd better hang up."

"Wait a minute...what time did she say she would call?"

"She said she would call you as soon as she could after she got back. Eddie, I'm sorry. I... I didn't want to be the one to call you... I don't know if Chrissy is right. I told her I disagreed with what she was doing, but she's my friend too, you know. You're both my friends, and it hurts me to watch what's happening to you, both of you."

"Sure. Okay. Good-bye, Anita."

That night, throughout dinner, my family left me alone. Dad was working late, and everyone else was quiet, out of respect for me, out of worry for Andrea. During that meal, as I looked across the table at my silent brothers and sisters (even the youngest knew something was wrong), I remembered another time when we were younger and our family was poor, when there was no money for such frivolities as movies, when, because I was the oldest, I was allowed to go. But that was only if I could earn enough money on my own to pay my way. I usually managed to get more than enough by cutting weeds for neighbors. I only needed a quarter for movie, popcorn, Coca-Cola, and candy. But the part I enjoyed most was staying up late into the night—afterwards—telling the movie's story to my brothers and sisters as they sat gathered around my bed asking me to tell them what happened next, and then tell them the best parts again, and then again, until Dad would shout through the wall telling me to shut up.

But that evening, the evening Chrissy took away Andrea, they all sat around the table keeping me company. There wasn't a story to tell because none of us knew where the story might end. But here they were: my long-limbed brother Bobby with his blonde hair hanging in his eyes; little Stevie with his crewcut and ears sticking out; and Katie Anne, wearing a calico dress that didn't quite fit her. Bobby jiggled his knees, seemed ready to break out and run; Stevie pushed his food back and forth on his plate; Katie Anne kept glancing at Andrea's high chair. Me, the big brother. I was the one who was supposed to know what to do, but I didn't know what to do, and I didn't have anything to say to them. I felt I was radioactive with "don't-speak-to-me" signals. And so, after a while, they got up, one at a time, and walked into the living room, leaving me alone. The whole house was suddenly eerily quiet.

When Dad finally came home late and they all went to bed, whispering to each other, the awkwardness was palpable. Bobby came back to the kitchen in his pajamas. He leaned in the doorway, his blonde hair in his eyes, waiting for me to let him come over and say something, but I waved him away. I couldn't talk. Then, as Dad left the bathroom, after turning out the hallway light on his way to bed, I overheard him whisper to my mother in an anger-laden voice, "I think Evelyn's right; he's gone and done something that caused all this. He must've, I tell you. Why else do you think that girl would just up and run away like that?"

"Now, Charlie, hush up; you don't know what's going on," my mother replied in a shaky voice as they disappeared into their bedroom.

Later, the house gone completely silent, my mother quietly re-entered the kitchen in her nightgown and slippers. She put her hand on my shoulder and said, "I know it's hard now, but it'll all work out somehow. Chrissy may be wrong in what she's doing, but I believe she's doing what she thinks is best for Andrea."

I said, "I hope you're right. Don't worry. Go back to bed, Mom."

She squeezed my arm and turned away, her slippers echoing down the hallway.

With the house finally asleep, I made myself some coffee, added milk and sugar, and sat down at the bar in the kitchen next to the black phone that hung on the wall. Sipping the sweet, hot coffee in the dark alone, I waited until midnight and then I called her.

"Hello, is Chrissy Andersen there?"

(Male voice.) "Yeah, I'll get her."

"Hello, this is Chrissy Andersen."

I whispered, "Chrissy, you bitch! Is Andrea okay? Why didn't you call me?"

(Congested, nasal, raspy voice. She still had a cold,) "Eddie, we just got here... I know how you feel..."

Struggling to keep my voice low, I said, "You don't have any idea how I feel. How could you? You obviously don't care how anyone feels about what you've done."

"Eddie, I'm sorry." (Coughs. Clears throat.)

"How could you do it? What were you thinking of?"

"I'm truly sorry, but you didn't leave me any choice."

"What? What are you talking about?"

"Well, I talked to my father and he said…"

"You talked to your father? You haven't talked to your father in years. He abandoned you. Remember?"

"Yeah, so what. He said he'd help me, and he told me that you were going to use Andrea against me! Were you?"

"Chrissy, what are you talking about?"

"He said that you were probably talking to a lawyer. My friends warned me what could happen. I didn't want to hear it, but you *were* threatening me. I talked to a therapist and a lawyer and they both agreed. They said you were probably trying to set up legal grounds to prove I was not a fit mother."

"I was trying to do what? You know that's absurd. Don't you?"

"No, I don't know that's absurd. I don't know what you're capable of. You went to see Dr. Cantrell behind my back…but even if you weren't doing what my friends suggested, I'm not at all convinced you wouldn't have tried to keep Andrea away from me. I'm sorry, Eddie, but I couldn't take that chance."

"I don't believe you… All right, so you don't trust me, and now I really don't have any reason to trust you. Do I?"

"Eddie, I don't know what to tell you."

Suddenly, I knew what I was going to do.

"Chrissy, I'm coming to New York. I want to see you. I need to see you in person."

"I don't want to see you…at least not now."

"Chrissy, I can't come right now. I have a job. I can't just leave. I was thinking about spring vacation. I'll have a few days free. What do you say about spring vacation?"

"Yes, that'll probably work. I'll have to see…"

"Chrissy, I'm trying to understand, but I…I don't understand what's happening. I miss you. I miss Andrea."

"I don't want to take Andrea away from you; I want you to be able to see her."

An irritated female voice in the background: "Chrissy, your baby's crying…"

"Eddie, I have to go now; Andrea's awake." She blew her nose and cleared her throat.

"I understand, but Chrissy...she has a bad cold, please be careful with her, all right?"

"Damn you, Eddie! You think I can't take care of my own child? Well, fuck you!"

"Well, fuck you too! She's as much my child as yours, and I didn't run off and leave her. You did."

In the long pause that followed, laughter could be heard in the background, then muffled voices and Andrea crying.

"Chrissy, what flight did you take out of Birmingham?"

"I took a flight to Chicago with connections to New York. We had a two-hour layover. It took forever. Eddie, really, I have to go now, but please apologize to your mother for me. She deserved better. I just didn't know any other way."

February 12, 1965

Last night I dreamed that Andrea—now a young girl, wearing a blue scarf and a gold hoop of an earring—and I had traveled on foot high into the Andes to visit an old, dying man. He'd spent the best part of his life translating the ideas of another man whose work had come to nothing in the eyes of the world. Upon our arrival the old man sat up and pointed at Andrea, saying, "In her lies the future and the reasons behind all of my life's work." Suddenly a great gray cloud rolled in, covering everything, and I woke up, frightened.

I got up and walked over to her crib, Andrea's empty crib, and thought about our mornings together at breakfast, the way she struggled to control her hands trying to put food in her mouth, about her joy as I spread a warm washcloth over her face, washing her small body in the kitchen sink.

Gone now. A crib with no baby in it.

March 15, 1965: Spring Vacation

On board a midnight flight for New York City, I look out the window as the plane taxis down the runway, turns, hesitates, and, with a great shaking and rush of power, leaves the ground. I lean over to catch the lights of the Magic City, Vulcan, the furnaces, the glowing orange rivulets of iron ore, and then Birmingham passes beneath us.

March 16, 1965

After a brief layover in Atlanta, a sleepless flight to New York City followed by a long bus ride to Manhattan, I walk out into a cold New York morning and find a bright yellow taxi sitting waiting outside the East Terminal bus depot. I lean over and give him the address.

"Third Street between Avenues B and C."

The driver, unshaven, thick Bronx accent, looks me over, then nods his head and says, "Okay. Get in."

I open the back door and climb in, my bags beside me on the back seat, and he speeds away before I get settled. He eyes me in his rear-view mirror.

"I don't usually go to that side of town. I guess it's okay this time of morning. You're my last fare... Where you from? Georgia?"

"No, I'm not. I'm from Birmingham, Alabama. Why do you ask?"

"You planning to be a writer?"

Flattered, I improvise, "I guess you could say I'm going to be a writer."

"Thought so."

"Why do you think so?"

"Lots of Southerners got lots to write about, I guess."

He goes quiet. He doesn't offer any explanation. I don't ask for one.

The tires whisper over the wet pavement.

I stare out the window into a damp, gray morning that reminds me of the cover of Bob Dylan's new album, *The Freewheelin' Bob Dylan*. It's a wet, gray morning in my New York, too, as I watch a man leaning forward into the wind, shoulders hunched against the cold. I hum a line from one of his new tunes, "Don't think twice, it's all right."

In spite of myself I'm excited to be in New York City. Looking at the buildings going up to the sky, listening to the hypnotic susurration of the tires, I fall into a trance of exhaustion, undisturbed in the warmth of the cab until I notice we're turning onto Third Street, slowing down. Looking up, I see Third Street is littered with broken glass. A large overstuffed couch sits in the middle of the block. Abruptly the driver pulls over to the curb.

"Well, this is your address, you've arrived, the underbelly of Sin City, just waiting for you," he says as he turns around and gives me a phony grin.

Climbing out of the cab into a bitter wind, I lean back in and ask how much.

"Five bucks," he replies without looking, writing something on a pad on the dashboard.

Already, I miss the warmth of the taxi. I check my wallet, my pockets. I have ten twenties, a five, and forty-one cents—a quarter, a nickel, a dime, and a penny. It occurs to me that I need to tip. How much? The wind is whipping at my pant legs. Without calculating I hand him the five-dollar bill and the forty-one cents, take up my bags, and start across the street. I am head down against the wind, almost across the narrow street, a bag in each hand when I hear him shout.

"Hey, you! Writer!"

I turn around in time to see him step back from the taxi, cock his arm, and throw the change at my head.

"You going to need this more than me, asshole!"

I duck as the coins fly past and hit the pavement behind me with small emptying pings.

Baffled, I watch as he speeds away, leaving behind a gray vapor stream of exhaust, leaving me standing alone next to the abandoned couch in the middle of the road. I button up my coat against the cold.

"I guess my tip was too small," I offer to no one in particular and pick up the dime and nickel. The penny and quarter are nowhere in sight.

Across the street sits Chrissy's three-story apartment building. She's inside with my six-month-old child. It's stark gray with an iron fire escape, nestled cheek-to-jowl with a brick building painted black on its front, displaying a neon bar sign at street level, Slug's, with musical notes and a martini glass tipped sideways. Empty garbage cans line the street, most of them on their sides. The wind pushes some newspapers about. It's a little after 5:30 in the morning.

Okay, I tell myself, *so this is Chrissy's new neighborhood.*

Bags in hand and staring up at her street number, I start around an obstacle course of mangled, gray garbage cans lining the sidewalk and almost stumble over a man's leg. An old man. Asleep, and wearing nothing more than a light-tan summer suit. *I almost stepped on him.* The smell of urine rises up powerfully. His bald head rests on a paper bag filled with newspapers. His grizzled face is an inch away from chunks of pink, dried vomit. I lean closer. He's wearing a partially unbuttoned white shirt, thin black tie, and his deeply stained dress pants are undone, unzipped, pulled down over his hips. No belt. His wrinkled and torn gray-brown boxer shorts are also stained and open at the front, revealing his withered, wrinkled penis. Two broken, brown shoes are abandoned beside him, without strings. The man's feet are bare.

He's been robbed, I think. *Someone's even taken his shoes and socks.*

I stand up straight, look around. A newspaper flaps against a garbage can. *Call the police when you get inside,* I tell myself. Then, acutely aware of the weight of the bags in my hands, I step over him and start up the stairs.

Chrissy's apartment is on the first landing. I put down my bags. *Can this really be the right apartment?* The hallway reeks. One dim light bulb reveals moldy, flaking walls, and a dimly lit apartment door at the far end of the hallway. The floor is old tongue and groove oak, black with age and soot.

I knock on her door and wait, beginning to shiver from the draft coming up the stairs.

Wearing an old quilted bathrobe that I always hated, her hair pinned back in big bobby pins, her cheeks flushed, she bends over as she backs up and begins coughing, deeply, loudly, as if she's about to throw up. Trying not to stare, I pick up my bags and push past her into the room.

The warm air of the apartment brings with it another terrible odor. I put down my bags and turn to help her shut the door, but Chrissy, still coughing, says, "Let me do it. It's tricky if you don't know how."

A solid iron bar runs from a hinge in the door through a metal ring and connects to a socket in a heavy metal brace that is bolted to the floor. Chrissy closes the door and swings the heavy bar solidly into place; it clicks shut in a catch at the top center of the door.

"Well, that door seems burglar-proof," I offer.

"Put your bags anywhere," she says and turns away.

Still shocked at the sight of her, at the strange repulsion I feel, I look away and begin hunting for a spot to put my bags. But finding no place that seems right, I slide them against a wall and take off my coat just in time to watch Chrissy throw off her robe and, wearing only a white bra and panties, climb back into her bed, a single-bed mattress on the floor, and pull the covers up around her.

"Are you all right? Where's Andrea?"

She lights a cigarette, brushes her dark hair back with her free hand, and begins coughing as she talks, spewing smoke.

"She's asleep right here. We're both sick."

She points with her cigarette at a small wooden box seemingly stuffed with clothes. The sickening odor seems to be coming from there; it's the odor of vomit and spoiled milk.

I bend over Andrea, pull back her baby blanket. Her face is flushed. She is congested in her breathing but asleep, head at one end of the box, her feet flush against the other. It's an orange crate. Her bedding is damp, her blanket stiff. I put my hand on her forehead. She's burning up.

Turning around, I discover Chrissy is watching me intently, and, before I can speak, she begins coughing violently.

"Is she...are you running a fever?" I ask, thinking, *slow down, take one thing at a time.* "Have you called a doctor yet?"

"No." She looks at her cigarette. "We're out of money. I'm expecting a check from my father any day now..."

"Where's your phone?"

"Over there." She points at a wall phone next to the stove. "But the service has been shut off."

"Okay. What's the doctor's number? What's his name? Where's the nearest phone?"

The nearest phone turns out to be in an all-night drug store around the corner, one block away.

"Yes, it's an emergency," I tell the doctor's answering service.

I have to wait in the phone booth for him to call me back.

He doesn't want to come. Chrissy owes him money. Can we pay him sixty dollars, in cash, at the door, before he enters the apartment?

I assure him I can.

He agrees to come over right away, before going to his office.

I walk back slowly. The streets are still empty, cold. My footsteps echo off the concrete. Snatches of another Bob Dylan lyric come to me, "It's all right, Ma, I'm only bleeding…"

I have started back up the steps to her apartment before I realize something. The old man. He's gone. I'd forgotten all about him. I walk back down to where I'd last seen him. The dried vomit is still there. *I didn't just imagine him,* I tell myself. The shoes are gone too. Relief. The old man has actually gotten up and walked away.

Chrissy's apartment is one long room divided into two parts by a bookcase and counter-top. The floor is slanted toward the front door at an angle of several degrees; if anything round is dropped it will roll to a stop at the front door. Her bathtub serves as a multi-purpose table when it's covered by a thin metallic top, white and enameled with red trim. The W.C. is indeed a closet and sits across the room from the tub, with hot water pipes running down on either side of the toilet. When I sit down, I find my knees pressing against the closed door. If I shift to the right or the left, I scorch my bare legs on hot pipes. These same pipes serve as the major source of heat for the apartment so the door is usually left ajar. There is only one window in the apartment. It opens onto the adjoining brick building, barely four feet away.

I unpack the baby clothes that my mother bought for Andrea and show them to Chrissy. For the first time since I've arrived she perks up and smiles, reaches out for the frilly dresses. Then there's a knock on the door. It's Dr. Epstein. I move the bar, open the door, and help him into the room before he can change his mind. Immediately, I open my wallet and hold out his sixty dollars.

He stands still, dignified, pushes his glasses down on his nose and quietly checks out the room, then looks me over, my hand extended with his money. He has long sideburns and a funny looking black hat.

"You husband?" he asks in a thick German accent.

He's wearing a long, expensive-looking black coat with a fur collar.

I nod yes, still holding out the three twenties in my hand. He smiles finally, nods, and takes the money. I take his hat and coat and put them on a chair.

"In neighborhood like this, *ja,* one can never tell if one is going to be paid or robbed."

I try to beam reassurance at him.

He opens his black bag, takes out a stethoscope, and bends over Andrea.

Chrissy lies back looking at the ceiling, coughs and waits.

We don't look at one another.

After he finishes with Andrea and Chrissy, he stands up, snaps his bag shut, and offers me an apologetic smile full of good-natured warmth.

"Just a little bronchitis, I tink. Also, they both little dehydrated. I give them strong dose of antibiotics. They both sleep soon. Give them lots of water."

He dashes off some prescriptions to be filled and pulls on his heavy black coat. We are to bring "baby and mama" to his office in a few days.

"Good for you to call me, *ja,* good for you to be here," he concludes, walking out the door.

◁▷

After I return with filled prescriptions, Chrissy fixes Andrea a bottle. Andrea has grown; her hair is golden, curly; she has fat rosy cheeks; and now she can hold the bottle by herself, with hands and feet. I realize all this with dismay. She's changed so much in just under three months, and I've missed it all. Disconsolate, I sit down beside a small end table under the window and watch Chrissy with Andrea, mother and baby. Chrissy, hair pulled straight back under those ugly black bobby pins, turns toward me as she bends over to tuck Andrea in. A small, welcoming smile of recognition plays over her face. It's really the first time since I arrived that she's seemed glad to see me. She stands up, stretches, bends at the waist, her hands kneading her back, and then comes over to sit across from me. She really looks different. Her hair is cut short in the back but long on the sides and the front, and now she parts it down the middle. I try not to stare, but I don't like it; it gives her a masculine look. Also, she's gotten heavier, thick around her waist.

"Thank you for getting the doctor and the medicine," she begins as she looks directly at me for the first time since I've arrived. "How's everything in Birmingham?"

"About the same...and you, what have you been doing?"

She lights up a cigarette, begins coughing immediately, puts it out, looks up at me, grins familiarly. "I need to quit smoking...well, I've been meeting lots of interesting people. I do a lot of reading, and I've applied at the welfare office for a job as social worker. I think I'll get it. The turnover is really high, and all you need is a college degree."

She's distant. Her smile has gone away. I sip at a glass of water and wait.

"Eddie, we need to clear something up... I asked a friend if you could stay with him while you were here."

I look around the room.

"You don't want me to stay with you?"

"No, not now. I'm exhausted, I need to sleep, and I don't know how I feel about your being here."

"I could sleep on the floor…"

Suddenly, sweeping her head back, gesturing angrily with her cigarette at the dirty clothes and dishes on the floor next to her mattress: "No! There's no space here, and I don't want to be cramped up in this small apartment with you and Andrea driving me out of my mind…"

Standing up, I turn away from her and stare at the brick wall of the apartment next door.

"Okay… All right, sure, what's his name?"

"Gary Yuri. I know you'll like him. He's a poet and a friend. A neighbor. And he's been very good to me. He's helping me find a job… Oh, oh, what time is it?"

"Nearly ten o'clock."

"Oh, no. He was expecting you before nine."

Gary's apartment is located on the first landing of an adjacent building. I knock loudly. No answer. I knock again and shout his name.

"Who's there?"

"Eddie Andersen!"

"Who?"

The door opens slightly, chain lock in place, then a head appears in the opening. Big head, bloodshot, bulging eyes, unshaven face, hollow cheeks.

"Chrissy's husband!" I say, a little disconcerted at the designation "husband."

He closes the door, unlocks the chain, opens the door and walks away, shouting over his shoulder, "Come on in…been expecting you."

His apartment is large and painted completely in black and dark blue except for one wall where the plaster has been recently ripped away to reveal the brick beneath.

Gary's attending to the coffeepot on the stove, talking away; I'm still standing in the hallway, bag in hand. He steps out briefly wearing only boxer shorts, droopy T-shirt, and a pair of dark socks. He speaks in rapid bursts.

"Have a seat. Make yourself at home," he passes by me on his way down a short hallway to what must be his bedroom.

Two steps in, I discover I'm standing in the entrance way to a large living room which faces onto the kitchen on my left, and then I see that down a hallway straight ahead is, first, the bathroom, and then, a few steps beyond that, a bedroom. The bedroom and the bathroom are the only two rooms with doors. It's very dark and quite warm inside his apartment. The living room is littered with beer and whisky bottles and cigarette butts. I drop my bags on the floor next to his black leather couch.

Suddenly Gary bursts back into the room fully dressed.

"Have some java?" He heads for the bathroom.

"Sure. Can I help?"

From the bathroom he shouts, "Yeah, that'd be great. Coffee, stove, and everything you need is somewhere in the kitchen. You'll have to hunt around some for a cup. I always do. Gonna clean up the mess someday, but not today."

There's a coffeepot on top of the stove percolating, dishes in the sink, and some liquid soap on a cabinet shelf. But before I can wash and rinse out a cup, I have to clean off some plates that are in the way and dump some garbage into an overflowing trash container under the sink. But then, while my back is turned, the front door suddenly opens and slams shut. Puzzled I turn around. No one has come in.

Gary is still in the bathroom, whistling.

The living room is empty.

Someone must have just left the apartment...

I pour myself a cup of coffee, but I can't find any milk in the refrigerator, only beer and unwrapped, green, moldering cheese.

No sugar bowl in sight.

A few minutes later Gary enters the kitchen, clean-shaven and smiling. Sticking out his hand he beams at me. "Hi. I'm Gary, as you know by now; glad to meet you, Ed."

He gestures toward the front door.

"Sorry about that, but she's married to a very suspicious, husband-type fellow and didn't want to meet anyone at this time of the morning. Man, that coffee smells good."

He pours himself a cup before it finishes perking, winks at me, and begins slurping it down, black and hot.

"Let's see now, only an hour late for work."

"You have to go to work on a Saturday?"

He laughs.

"Yeah, some goddamned officious assholes are checking up on me, and I need to make sure a few things are done right."

His laugh is infectious.

"I used to work for the Welfare Department, almost ten years, but now I'm a contract social worker, and I've got a special appointment with a client of mine to help her fill out some new 'Information Request' forms—we call people who are so down and out they have to live on welfare our 'clients.' I'm my clients' advocate. I protect 'em from the system, at least that's how I see it. I don't think my bosses agree with me. Their intent is to deny benefits whenever possible. I don't let 'em, so they keep checking up on me. But, hell, I'm smarter than they are, and they'll never figure out what I'm up to. I know the game and this bureaucracy like the back of my hand. So let 'em check up on me."

He throws an ugly, polka-dot tie around his neck, knots it, and grins. His bulging eyes are so bloodshot it's hard not to stare.

"I'm not your typical revolutionary." He sips some more coffee and pulls on a leather jacket he takes off a chair. "I work within the system, and for what it's worth, it pays the bills until I can sell my novel."

"What's your novel about?"

"An exposé of the welfare system, naturally."

He fishes around in his coat pockets and comes up with a key to his apartment.

"I was going to leave this with Chrissy if I left before you got here. Almost forgot to give it to you."

He pauses at the door, looks down, laughs with self-deprecation, explains, "Don't have any grub in the pantry. If you get hungry you'll have to try the deli down the street. Pretty good food and not too expensive."

◁▷

It's warm and dark in Gary's apartment. As soon as the door closes and the bar slips into place I realize that I'm exhausted. I turn off the blue flame under the coffee pot and lie down on Gary's overstuffed leather couch. A cockroach scurries across the carpet. It's the last thing I notice before I fall asleep.

When I wake, at first I don't know what time it is or where I am, and the room is pitch black. There is a strange moldy smell in the air. I have to use the bathroom. I get up, fumble around with a lamp, but, unable to turn it on, I give up and stumble toward Gary's bathroom. There's a light switch next to the door. I flip it on and am amazed at the decrepitude. Gary's bathroom is coming apart. The plaster ceiling is drooping, close to falling; black paint is peeling away in long strips down the wall; and there is crumbly mold and mildew everywhere. The bathtub is shrouded in a soap-stained, corroded, black polyethylene shower curtain. The tub's porcelain is cracked and broken, covered with rust. I use the toilet, wash my face and hands in a sink that's pulling away from the wall, and return to the living room.

Rounding the corner I realize that a soft lamp has been turned on and that the low sound of jazz is floating across the floor. Then, as the sweet pungent odor of marijuana fills my nostrils, I notice Gary, sitting on the floor next to the stereo leaning back against the wall, a lit joint in his hand, his tie loose at his neck.

How long has he been there? I wonder. *Was he here before I went to the bathroom?*

"Sit down, Ed, have some beer and a drag of this... You look like you need it."

He passes me a quart bottle of Ballantine Ale with one hand and a marijuana cigarette with the other. I accept both, take a large pull from each, and sit down on the floor across from him.

"It's really good stuff. Just got it today," he adds.

I mumble my thanks, passing back the beer and the joint.

He leans forward, arm draped over an antique scarlet-red ottoman, head back, looking wasted, his long thinning hair spilling down into his face. In the reflected light I study him. His cheeks are sunken. His eyes push out from their sockets, big sad eyes that look like they've seen more than their fair share of suffering. He has a large dome of a skull and a short chin. I guess his age at about thirty, but his face is heavy with wrinkles.

"Tough day," he says dully. "One of my clients got beat up by her old man; her kids are freaked out; Department's trying to cut her benefits..." And then he shifts gears suddenly, his voice cheerful, rising, "Well, Ed, how are you and Chrissy making out over there?"

"I don't know, Gary. I really don't know. She's a strange girl."

"Now that's where you're wrong, Ed. Chrissy is no longer a girl. She's a woman, a strong, fine person. But she is primarily a woman, if you know what I mean. You have to relate to that fact above all the others."

The grass is beginning to take effect.

Is he making it with Chrissy? I wonder.

The music hits a new gear; a trumpet takes off. It moves like the echo of a wind down an empty New York street. Makes me think of the drunk I stepped over that very morning.

I let myself go on drift until Gary brings me back.

"Ed, I'm going to be off to Fire Island tomorrow; if you and Chrissy want to use my pad you're welcome to it. I know her place is a little small."

"Thanks, Gary, maybe we will. I don't know what the plan is."

"Okay, well look, man, I have to get up before dawn tomorrow so make yourself at home. And remember what I said...treat her like a woman. Make her feel like a woman, 'cause if you don't someone else will. Maybe I'll see you again before you leave, and we can sit down and rap, okay?" He stands up, ready to leave the room.

"Sure, Gary, and thanks again for the use of your apartment." Then, for no reason at all, I hear myself say, "It's been a tough day for me too."

Gary turns back toward me with a puzzled look, lifts his head as if he's trying to decide something, then locks onto me for a moment with his hypnotic eyes. He seems to decide something, shrugs, takes one more drag, and hands over the beer and the joint.

"A man's first duty," he offers, "is to himself." He leans over, transfixing me with an unwavering gaze. "Look, Chrissy is my friend, but I'll tell you something. A man has to be free before he can meet a woman on an equal basis. He has to *not* give himself to her, has to keep something back for himself, because a woman always has the advantage. Mothers. Lovers. Friends. Women create the world we men live in—make no mistake about it—and, in the end, a woman can either leave you or die on you, and you can't ever trust 'em *not* to do one or the other. So you have to be willing to walk away, have to keep your soul, stay your own man, or you're fucked."

Like a character out of a Beat novel, he looks down at me with his sad eyes, arches his back, stretches out his skinny frame, and then walks off, weaving his way toward his bedroom. He's had too much to drink.

Suddenly I am alone, sitting crossed-legged on Gary's floor, the couch at my back, the dark walls closing in around me. I take another hit from Gary's joint, inhale deeply, and let myself go back on drift as the music begins a reprise of the earlier trumpet riff.

I look across the room at my unpacked bags and review the events of this day: the drunk on the sidewalk; the angry cab driver throwing my change at me; Chrissy and Andrea next door in that foul-smelling, tilted room of an apartment; Gary's filthy black bathroom; Gary's hypnotic eyes.

Maybe he's right, I think, *maybe I need to court her all over again, as a woman, and maybe I need to create some kind of emotional distance between us. But how? "A man may smile and smile and yet be a villain." Perhaps I can learn how to smile and pretend that what she's doing is okay with me, but, without a doubt, I have to* not *ask her to come back with me.*

Then, for the first time, I realize that in fact I had thought that I would ask her to come back with me, and that I know now that she won't.

Can I be all right about this? I ask myself. *Can I* not *ask her? Can I go back to Birmingham without my wife and my daughter? Can I just be here for a few days, visit, help out, and leave?*

The record ends and the room is plunged into a silence that crowds around me, a silence of resolution, mine, alone: to go back without her, without Andrea.

There is a terrible knot in my stomach. I hear myself sigh deeply as Gary goes into the bathroom. The sound of his pissing fills the apartment. When he comes out he asks if I'm okay. I say I am and he goes back to bed.

I know what I'm doing, I tell myself as I turn off the lights. *I will smile; I will help out for a few days; I will make myself indispensable; and then I will go back to Birmingham, alone.*

[25]

March 23, 1965

I am sleepwalking.

I have returned from New York, returned to work, returned to a life that is not my own. I do not care where I'm going; I pay no attention to where I've been. I put one foot in front of the other. I go where I have to go.

April 6, 1965

I wake up and the world is still with me, my brothers and sisters, my mother, my father, the Magic City of Birmingham, the State of Alabama, and the South.

My grandmother once told me that when I left her house I was no longer just one more person in the world. I was the representative of my family, and hers, and that whatever I did or said was a reflection on her, on my family, and on my culture. But I am no longer content to be one more piece in this puzzle of what I represent. I am not happy to be a representative of my culture. I want to be seen as just myself, as an individual making his own way in this world...

But who am I? I am a student of philosophy. If I am accepted, I will try graduate school at N.Y.U. in philosophy. Also, I am a teacher of beginning French and College Prep English.

What excites me?

My students excite me. They ask me amazing questions. Last week my College Prep English class petitioned me to allow their class to spend more time discussing two of the books I had recommended for extra credit: *1984* and *Lord of the Flies*. I put them off. I told them: the last week of school, if the whole class agrees to read the books and, if they are able finish the text ahead of time, then we will open the floor for discussion of any of the books assigned for extra credit. After much debate, the majority of the class agrees. Now, as I begin to think about how open these class discussions could become, how relevant these texts are to some of their lives, and how repressive this little town of Bessemer really is, I'm a little worried. But I'm also a little pleased.

April 10, 1965

I have been seeing a lot of Anita and Carina. We get together once or twice a week, usually on Fridays, for supper. We take turns, rotating the responsibility for the meals. We reveal who we are by our choices. Anita, not much for domesticity, pushes frozen packages of Jolly Green Giant vegetables, especially lima beans, and sometimes spinach, and frozen chicken breasts in a cream sauce. Carina and I make fun of her insistence on lima beans, but we adjust. Carina's Gulf Coast specialty is Red Snapper Almondine and green beans, and I, having found a good recipe, have learned to cook up a mean spaghetti sauce with lots of garlic and Italian herbs.

But our evenings, though friendly and pleasant, are strangely formal, each of us locked up in our own private misgivings about what can be talked about. Anita refuses to talk about her visits with Tim. Petite and coy, Carina seems jauntily determined to keep us away from dangerous subjects such as politics and religion. She talks about her students and her obstructionist school principal. And I, the perfect guest, usually go along with our unspoken agreements.

We are all too polite.

I miss Chrissy, her search for truth, her unwillingness to accept the easy way out. She would never sit still for these polite, social conversations. But then again, maybe this social formality is brought about because Carina is not part of our shared history, and her presence, her difference, forces us into a false atmosphere of small talk. Or maybe it's because Anita is Chrissy's close friend, and she stifles our after-dinner talks out of a fear that there is some betrayal brewing. Because Carina and I flirt with one another. Or maybe it's simply because I am a married man having dinner parties with two close female friends who are not quite sure what to do with me.

April 13, 1965

I spoke to Chrissy on the phone last night. She misses me, she says, and then asks if I miss her. Our conversation was short and littered with maybes, but her voice had a life of its own within my body. It stays with me. I think of her learning to play her guitar, playing those same chords over and over while she sits on the front steps of our forest cottage, pregnant, waiting for me to return from work.

But do I miss this new Chrissy? Does she really miss me? And what about Andrea? Every time I think of Andrea, the thought of her arrives with an electric jolt of worry and misgivings because I am not there with them. Now Andrea can hold her bottle with one hand, Chrissy tells me. I remember how she curled her small fingers and toes around her bottle as she lifted it, dripping, to her mouth. Will she even know me when I next see her?

April 20, 1965

I have come to see Birmingham not as a place but as a state of mind, as a public perspective. How did we become what we are? Perhaps the politeness we Southerners insist on is actually disguised repression. Everywhere I look there is this insistence on sameness, on allowing no divergent views. I listen to the news about the troubles brought on by the "outside agitators," and the phrase itself seems to implicate us all in a conspiracy of "true believers." This belief in segregation infects us like an airborne disease. I never questioned it, never thought about it, never understood it.

Now I feel as if I have been lied to.

I begin to think we Southerners do not question our beliefs because we live in the heart of the Bible belt, and we have been told what to think by our Baptist and Methodist ministers, who, as God's spokesmen, are the policemen of public opinion. But they have failed us. The majority has preached from the place of privilege about heaven and hell. They have *politely* protected the status quo. They have protected the powerful and said nothing about the KKK and the four dead little girls.

April 27, 1965

Sewanee Banks, age sixteen, who sits in the first row of French class and stares up at me with mesmerizing, shy, deer-brown eyes, rushed breathlessly into my office to talk to me. Usually, she approaches me with an alarming, innocent coquettishness that always puts me on my guard, but today she was very upset; her usually bright eyes avoided mine as she shook her head from side to side in a quick nervousness that mussed her bouncy, newly coiffed curls.

I sat on the edge of my desk, looked straight into her swollen face, and waited for her to say something. My first thought was that some boy had been mean to her. Almost immediately, I felt a tinge of anger on her behalf.

"Sewanee? What's the matter?"

She turned her big brown eyes on me and suddenly blurted, "Mr. Andersen, I don't care what everybody's saying about you! I just want you to know there's at least one person in this town who appreciates you."

Then she turned and fled from the empty classroom.

Do I disturb the universe?

Is something amiss?

May 1, 1965

Oh, Carina. Just who are you? You are not from Birmingham. There is no iron rust in your blood. You are from money, from Mobile, from mansions, from freshwater lagoons, and from the white sugary beaches of the Gulf Coast. The Gulf runs blue in your veins. You hold yourself aloof, floating in that rare atmosphere of Southern aristocracy. You offer me Chivas Regal over ice in a crystal glass. You lift your head high and show off your cool white throat.

May 5, 1965

Last night I slept with Carina in a bright, glorious flame of bodies ignited by need.

Anita spent the night with her mother.

Carina and I were alone.

She prepared cheese fondue, wearing only running shorts, a man's blue shirt, no bra. We sat across from each other on her expensive hooked rug, dipped our bread in the hot cheese, ate fresh oysters, drank scotch, and smoked grass.

I teased her about her aristocratic tastes, told her she was too polite, too reserved, too formal.

"You don't know me," she laughed as she stood up, leaned over and shoved me backwards. But I grabbed her wrists as I was falling backwards and pulled her down with me. We began wrestling, rolling over and over on the floor until we rocked up against her couch, and I pinned her.

Then holding her wrists to the floor, I sat on her, leaned close, and we allowed our lips to meet, exploring, touching with tongues.

Slowly, breaking away from our kiss, I pulled back but held onto her wrists and watched as she struggled to break away, watched as she stopped struggling, as her eyes glazed over with seriousness and her breasts seemed to rise toward me. And then she looked into me and became frantic, her head moving side to side.

I let her go. She rose quickly to her knees, and began taking off her shirt. I pulled off my shirt. Then she untied my shoes, took off my socks, reached up, unbuckled my belt, slowly pulled my pants down, my jockey shorts, until I stood naked before her. Then she leaned over, pressed her face against me, and took me into her mouth. I stood transfixed, watching her face, until she pulled away, fell backwards, and I followed her down until my body was stretched out over hers, our naked skin just barely touching, the whole length of us, and I held myself above her, suspended in time and space, in the dark pool of her welcoming eyes, until I could stand it no longer. An inch at a time I let my body descend then and slipped into her slowly but so easily it came over me with a shock—*so this is how it's supposed to be, so wet...*

When her slender legs lifted and closed around me with acceptance, my body jerked with an unforeseen pleasure, almost overwhelming, at the feeling of being inside her. Again, my hands on the rug beside her face, I raised myself up on my arms and looked down, watched as she opened her eyes wide, searching mine, time slowing down, and we allowed ourselves to feel the penetration, the joining together in the wet, white heat of her center.

We remained like that for a long time, unmoving, locked in sensation, in the waves of her heat, until she stretched her white bare arms out toward my face and pulled me towards her, her throat, her small turned-up breasts flushing to a deep roseate pink. She took my head between her hands, but still I resisted, and we stayed like statues until her mouth parted, her eyes rolled backwards, and I collapsed into her body, into her sweat, into that wonderful wet heat and the movement of her hips, my mouth on hers, our bodies locked in rhythm together until, vaguely aware of her guttural sounds as they transmuted into sighs in my ear, I realized that we had reached orgasm simultaneously.

Afterwards we dressed and became strangely distant, poured ourselves some more scotch, and sat down to talk.

I told her that she was wonderful, that our lovemaking was like nothing I had ever experienced in my life, but that now I needed to tell her about Chrissy, my estranged wife, and my seven-month-old child, Andrea. I told her that I had agreed, in one month's time, to go back to New York City to be near them, and that maybe I was leaving Birmingham for good.

She smiled, lit a cigarette with long cool fingers, and replied, "You know you don't have to worry about me. Don't you? I knew you were married. I'm a big girl, and I am not out to get you."

When we parted, we hugged, we folded our fingers together, and we kissed each other on the cheek. The smell of her perfumed hair followed me out the door.

Outside her apartment, the smell of honeysuckle and star jasmine was in the air. I leaped into my car, waved to her small form standing in the doorway, and headed for the highway. A few blocks away I looked left and the sight of Vulcan's impressive backside surprised me. Lit up by spotlights, his sandal-clad feet and sturdy silver legs rose high above me, straight up into the night, tall and erect, and his muscular right arm was raised above Red Mountain, his green light glowing.

May 24, 1965

The school principal called me into his office after my last class on Friday. (He used to be a football coach before he became principal. Tall and heavyset, he talks down to his teachers as though they were members of his team.)

He said, "Mr. Andersen, I have a problem, which, in this case, means you have a problem. But I believe there's an agreeable solution for both our problems. My problem is that I don't want to fire you with only two weeks of school remaining, and your problem is, as I'm sure you'll agree, that you don't want to lose the three months of your summer pay. So I think it's up to the two of us to come to an agreement that will solve both our problems."

"What's this about?" I stammered.

"Let's just say you've stirred up a hornet's nest. I know that was not your intention, but that's what's happened. So, I had to take time out of my busy schedule to meet with some of the upset parents of your students. Believe me when I tell you they were pretty angry with you. But I've calmed them down, and they've agreed to let me handle this situation my way."

"Why wasn't I included?"

"That's not any of your concern. I've talked them out of any further action against you. You just need to be grateful. All you have to do is turn in your grades, pack up your bags, and leave this school today."

"But why? What have I done?"

"It's not about what you've done; it's about what you were planning to do in the last week of classes."

"For my College Prep classes for graduating seniors?"

"Mr. Andersen..."

"What's wrong with discussing George Orwell's concept of personal freedom and totalitarian governments? Or the relevance of literature to..."

"Let me assure you that we are not about to discuss any of this at this time. I have acted in everyone's best interests, especially in your best interests, as I'm sure you will agree."

"But what do I tell my students?"

"I have already cancelled all your classes. Your students are no longer your concern. The parents are content, and you're done. Just turn in your grades. You will not be asked to return next year."

"So that's it for me, then?"

"Yes, that's it."

My first thought was that I should fight this arrangement, but then I thought better of it. I looked at my principal, and I knew I'd lose that fight. They would win in the end. My principal had indeed solved his problem. I did not have the heart for a fight. Besides, this way my students would get out of their classes early (that'd make *them* happy), and I would get to keep my three months' summer pay, which I truly could not afford to lose.

May 25, 1965

One sad note. Although most of my seniors did seem just as happy to be getting out of classes early, one of my students, or so I was told, was forced to stand by in tears and watch while her father tore the pages out of the two novels I'd assigned her, *1984* and *Lord of the Flies*, tossing the pages into a fire in their living room fireplace.

May 26, 1965

Last night Carina and I sneaked out and left Anita behind fixing dinner. Anita suspects or knows something has happened. She gave me an exasperated look as we went out the door, ostensibly to buy French bread and dessert. That look was directed entirely at me. It said: "You know you are not fooling anyone; and you are making a big mistake."

I offered her my best, friendliest grin, and shrugged her off.

The moment my car door closed, before I could get the keys in the ignition, Carina said, "I hate you," and threw herself into my arms, kissed me passionately, and then whispered, "You're a rat, but I'll miss you."

On returning from the grocery, we almost made love in the car, but then Anita turned on the porch light, and we pulled apart, straightened out clothes, and put back on our social "small talk" personas.

I think about her now and I want to make love to her again. I want to lie down inside her small compact frame and forget New York. She is everything that Chrissy is not. She is petite, has delicate, easily bruised flesh, a white, blue-veined body with small uneven breasts. Carina's body has a well at its center. Chrissy was never so.

But there is more to Chrissy than body. When I am with Chrissy I feel...engaged, involved, real. There is no such thing as "small talk" with Chrissy. She is always pushing for the truth, for the hidden meaning in every situation, because she's always daring to try to live up to the adventure of life. She's awake, and she's never content to go to sleep because the social occasion seems to call for it. Chrissy raises my expectations about my own life; she makes me want something more from myself. Chrissy makes Carina seem empty-headed and shallow.

Oh, this is all nonsense! I don't know what I'm talking about.

Yes, I have a wife and a child, but can I get over my lovemaking with Carina? I replay it in my mind, again and again. She is so surprising. I shall miss her body heat, that touch of her skin against mine, and that scent of perfume in her soft, silky hair.

May 28, 1965

Carina, why am I leaving you?

I have ongoing flashbacks of our lovemaking, a visceral bodily force that leaves me empty-headed and astonished.

I don't understand how you can make everything so wonderfully simple for me. How can you make love to me and then give me up so easily?

Does everything you say mean just the opposite? Why *did* you give yourself to me? What did you want from me? Only an evening of passion? Was it easier because I am married?

You said that I didn't know you. Maybe I don't.

This is my first affair.

Affair? What does that mean? To let the body have what it wants to have. To love without regard for consequences because you know there is an end to it?

Carina, you said, "If you were devoted only to me I should be deliriously happy, but you aren't. So I must let you go. Toodle-oo." And then you laughed.

I hated that laugh.

So, I guess it's true, from the start: you kept me honest because you did not require the lies.

I would have lied to you. Maybe I did lie to you. I told you I loved you that night after making love.

Did I lie?

May 30, 1965

Tonight, at age twenty-three, I am leaving Birmingham. I have just boarded the plane for New York City.

Now, strangely, my body pulses with energy. I am asking nothing of myself for the time being. I don't know how Chrissy will receive me. I am leaving behind that feeling of never being able to say what you think that comes with being a citizen of Birmingham, but I am also leaving behind my friends, my brothers and sisters, my family.

And I am leaving you behind, Carina. Am I making a mistake?

Looking out the window of the plane, I see it has started to rain. There is a red haze of blinking lights smeared across my window-pane. Someone in front of me is humming and tapping out the tune of an old English ballad, "Barbara Allen." Several young girls are laughing. A clinking of glassware echoes in the galley. A rattling of the shifting metallic frame, of its plastic overhead compartments, and the plane's powerful engines roar loudly into life.

I lean back into my seat, close my eyes, and try to imagine Chrissy and Andrea and me living together in the East Village of New York City, but instead I am treated to a vision of Carina, naked, lying on her back on the floor, staring openly into my eyes that moment just before I entered her.

[26]

A note pinned to her front door reads: "Eddie, I had to go to work. Andrea is at babysitter's. Gary is expecting you. Chrissy."

It's a little after eleven and morning traffic blares and echoes up the stairs as I exit once again onto Third Street, dragging my duffel bag behind me. The sun is out and there are no drunks on the landing. People are rushing to and fro. As the smell of grease and exhaust fumes hits me, I am strangely exuberant. The sharp-edged noise of the people and traffic of the East Village fills me with energy. Tossing my duffel bag over one shoulder, I walk past Slug's Jazz Club—inside the plate glass windows I can just make out a stage, sawdust on the floor, and tables covered with upside-down chairs—then I charge up the next set of stairs to Gary's apartment and bang on the door.

Nothing happens. I try again, louder, longer.

Finally Gary's gray, unshaven face appears in the gloom behind the chain of his partly opened door. He gazes at me without recognition. His bug-eyes surprise me again with their prominent road map of red ink.

"Hey, Gary, it's me, Eddie Andersen."

I grin and we stare at one another until he recognizes me, and his face lights up with a smile.

"Eddie, you bastard! Come on in. How's it going with you, man?"

"I'm doing pretty well."

I drop my duffel bag next to his couch and look around. Gary's apartment has not changed. It is still a dark and gloomy place, same stained, overstuffed couch, same stereo.

"Gary, you look like you had a long night."

"I did, man, I really did. Want some coffee?"

"I can take care of myself. Why don't you just go back to bed."

He starts off to his bedroom, but then he pauses to tell me something.

"Oh yeah, Chrissy wants you to meet her at some uptown address after she gets off work at three. I scribbled it down. It's there by the telephone under the key. Can you make it out?"

I can, and he disappears around the corner, asleep on his feet.

I too have been up all night, but I'm not sleepy. I put on a pot of coffee hoping Gary will come back and join me, but he doesn't. So, after my second cup, I'm ready to go exploring, to check out my new neighborhood, the Lower East Side of Manhattan. After washing up in Gary's dingy, moldy bathroom, I pull out my map of Manhattan, take the key and address, and head back down the stairs.

Out on my own, with no plan, I walk slowly from block to block, and watch, taking it all in: a concrete world; curbs; sidewalks; fenced-in trees barely holding their own against the smog; scraps of garbage, trash, and abandoned furniture spilling onto narrow streets lined with parked cars and double-parked delivery vans; storefronts and apartment buildings separated by fire escapes. Between parked cars, a melon-bellied old man in a frayed red sweater and unbuttoned overcoat, dark pork pie hat, stands peeing, staring upwards, unfocused, while his white-and-black-spotted dog squats beside him, haunches aquiver, at the end of a red leash, muzzle to the sky, in a dreamy-eyed expression. In an alley, bent, corrugated garbage cans lie on their sides, chained to wrought-iron gates; pigeons fly suddenly out of a stairwell that leads to a below-ground apartment. People are queued up outside of bakeries, delis, fruit stands—men in dark coats, funny black hats, and long sideburns; blacks in muscle shirts and leather jackets; and young Puerto Ricans in red bandanas, speaking rapid-fire Spanish.

It's a warm day, not a cloud in the sky.

"Mira! Mira! Cuidado!"

Suddenly, stepping out between delivery trucks, crossing the street, I am surprised to find myself in the middle of a game of stickball. I sense more than see or hear that someone has gotten a good hit, and then a Puerto Rican kid I hadn't noticed before crashes into me. Instinctively, I reach down and try to take hold of him to keep him from falling, but he jerks away from my grasp, and without losing his balance, leaps backwards and spins around sideways in mid-air, comes to rest in a fighting stance.

He screams, "Keep-you-hands-off-me-you-mutha-fucka-white-face!" He backs cautiously and then runs past me down the street. Stunned, I watch him go. He's young, maybe ten years old.

The game stops. The boys all turn and stare.

I hurry on. They follow me with their eyes until I turn down a side street. I can hear their fading voices behind me. They have returned to their game.

A few blocks later I come to a little park on Ninth Street and Avenue B. There's a sign that says this is Tompkins Square Park. I go in and settle down on a patch of grass next to a sandbox where a group of black and Puerto Rican mothers are sitting around in a circle, rocking prams and tickling babies. The women are all wearing big silver earrings, long dark skirts, brightly colored shawls. I lie back in the grass and surreptitiously watch them talk, rock their prams, tend to their babies. Chrissy and Andrea float into my mind and I wonder if they come to this park. In the warmth of the sun, I drift off into a light sleep punctuated by the sounds of traffic. There is a soft ululation of mothers' comforting conversational voices, their good-hearted laughter and camaraderie.

I wake to the sound of a dog barking and growling. My throat is dry, my undershirt dank with sweat.

The park has changed hands while I slept. Stubble-faced old men in baggy clothes, with canes and thick glasses, have replaced the mothers and babies.

Next to me, on a bench built into the park's path, a skinny old man in a stained Salvation Army jacket appears to be offering his dog a drink from a pint whiskey bottle. The dog, hunched down and stiff legged, is trying to pull away, but the old man continues to drag him forward by a thin rope that is tied to his collar and to the old man's belt. The dog is a small, dirty-white, clipped poodle. He growls, straining at his leash. A small blonde Kewpie doll dangles naked from his collar by a purple ribbon. The old man pulls the dog closer, plays at offering him a drink, then clumsily slaps his muzzle and pushes him away. Each time, as the dog gets within reach, he wags his tail, tries to lick the old man's hand, but the old man holds the whiskey bottle in the dog's face, tilts it as if to pour him some of the whiskey before he jerks it back, clubs the dog with his hand, and shoves him roughly away. Then the grizzled old man tosses his head back and laughs at the sky. The dog growls low in his throat, backing up until his rope leash tied to the old man's pants is taut again, then he wags his stub of a tail and whines. Once again the old man begins to reel him in; the dog's stiff front legs slip in the loose gravel, the naked Kewpie doll dragging. As he pulls on the rope the old man croons to the dog in a high falsetto. "Com'on to me, poochie, I'll let ya hav' som'."

And as the cycle begins again, I get up. I'm ready to go.

The old man looks over at me and laughs loudly, "You wan' som'?" He waves his whiskey bottle at me.

I shake my head, no, and walk quickly out of the park, checking my watch. It's almost two o'clock, time to think about my meeting with Chrissy.

I have to take a crosstown bus. That's not a problem; I have a map and bus schedules, but I don't feel quite sure of myself. I feel shaky, a little fearful. It feels like I'm in a dream, as if I've started down a strange path in unfamiliar woods, and I've forgotten to mark my way.

After catching one bus and then transferring to another, I realize I am going to be a little early for my meeting with Chrissy, but I decide that it'd be good to get there before she does so that I can observe her without being seen, so that I can watch her walk, catch her body language, her sense of herself in the city.

What if we've changed? What if we no longer have any affection for one another? What if we no longer belong in each other's world? What if I don't love her anymore?

The bus lets me off in front of a bar on the corner where we are to meet. I enter, order a beer, and take a window seat. Well-dressed customers mingle, laugh, drink, chat. The atmosphere is upscale, impersonal, sterile, a place for early afternoon drinkers. I sip and wait.

What will she say? What should I say?

Three o'clock comes and goes. No Chrissy.

Where is she?

Finally I leave the bar, walk over to the street corner, and begin looking in all directions, making myself as obvious as possible, hoping she will see me.

The traffic light changes again, and again a crowd of people hurries in my direction. Searching for her face, I watch them come toward me. People I don't know smile and walk on by. One casually dressed woman in tennis sneakers keeps smiling at me. I turn back to her.

It's Chrissy.

She's cut off more of her hair. It's a dusky, dark color, lusterless, really short, and jagged across the front of her forehead. It gives her a hard, masculine look. Her dark eyebrows have grown together over her wide nose. She's wearing her wrap-around, wine-colored skirt, bright white tennis sneakers. She stops in front of me, smiles behind rose-tinted sunglasses, a really big smile.

I retreat a step or two. She comes forward.

"Chrissy?"

We are on the sidewalk at a busy street corner, not touching, but friendly. Crowds of people surge around us. The light changes.

"Eddie, so you are here. It's so good to see you..."

"Wow, Chrissy, it's you. I didn't recognize you...let's have a drink! What do you say?"

In the noise and the dim light of the bar Chrissy takes off her dark glasses and runs her hand through her short hair. Her face is puffy, no lipstick. Two people get up from their stools at the bar. We take their seats and order whiskey sours, her favorite drink.

We toast each other and sip them.

The bar is filling up.

Chrissy sniffs loudly, wipes her nose with tissue paper she takes from a big leather purse. She looks harassed, tired. Sitting on the bar stool, big black purse in her lap, wearing an unflattering white cotton blouse, she leans toward me and speaks over the noise, "I don't really want to be here in this bar. Can we just go?"

I nod in agreement, and we leave the bar without finishing our drinks, walk several blocks pushing our way through masses of pedestrians before finally catching a bus and settling into our seats. The bus is not crowded.

Chrissy talks as we ride.

I listen, but I don't seem able to focus. She talks rapidly about her job at the welfare office and how she feels like she's making a difference; about the hopeless state of her clients who have no advocates except the welfare workers who defend them against the government's bureaucracy. Her words keep floating by me and I keep nodding, and some part of me is hearing her, but some other part keeps disappearing, fading out, giving over to a kind of emptiness that simply absorbs, that listens to the other conversations around us, that watches taxis sail by in slow motion, that remembers Carina and watches her small hand lift away strands of perfumed hair while waving goodbye with that breezy Gulf Coast in her eyes.

"Eddie...this is our stop."

Suddenly, without warning, she takes my hand and we dash to the front of the bus and exit onto another sidewalk crowded with pedestrians.

With the transforming rapidity of bright sunlight breaking through a heavy summer storm, everything feels changed, and we are walking side by side, weaving in and out of the foot traffic on Fourteenth Street, heading east past subway stops, camera shops, pizzerias, delis, drugstores, check-cashing establishments.

Chrissy and I are not strangers. We found each other once before. We can do it again.

In the noise of cars, cabs, and buses, in the sounds of jackhammers ripping up the street, in the midst of conversations and the accents of all the people weaving around us, Chrissy seems to read my thoughts and reaches out and takes my hand, and I surrender it. Suddenly, I feel I will be able to swim in the tidal forces of this world surrounding us, because, at her touch, at the interlocking of our fingers, I remember her.

She's smiling again, and I'm happy to be here walking down Fourteenth Street together. I remember the Chrissy I saw on our first date, the excited Chrissy still flushed from her starring role in *Oklahoma,* the Chrissy who was always trying to live the honest life, who was always challenging me to keep up with her. And suddenly it dawns on me that I am once again following her lead, and that this time she has led us to New York City to try to start over in a new life.

I stop to look at her. She stops and waits for me say something. I desperately want everything to work out for us, but I don't say anything, so we just stand still looking into each other's eyes. We are a stationary bubble of two, stopped in a moment of time, and people flow around us, going elsewhere, until, without warning, I put my arms around her, pull her off balance into a hug. As her warm body suddenly presses in next to mine, I close my eyes, take a deep breath, sigh, and then whisper into her neck, "Don't worry. It's going to be all right."

[27]

Our first evening together we have Chinese takeout. But no conversation. We feel like strangers to one another. It's awkward. But then, after putting the dishes away and carrying out the trash, I begin warming a bottle for Andrea. And Chrissy, down on her knees beside the mattress on the floor, looks up from changing Andrea's diaper, and there is some small exchange of understanding that passes between us. We need each other. Taking the diaper pin out of her mouth, looking like a penitent in her plain white cotton slip, she pushes her hair out of her face, smiles, and says, "It feels good to have you here... I don't think I should be alone anymore."

Testing the milk's temperature against my wrist, I smile back at her, and I want to go to her, hug her, but I don't. I don't know what to say to this new Chrissy. There is an air of distance about her, but also a strange vulnerability. I remember her pregnant, sitting on the stairs of our cottage in Birmingham, her dark hair pulled back by a black ribbon, bending over a guitar that rested on her big belly instead of her knees, looking back at me ruefully, her swollen fingers failing to find the right frets of a difficult chord.

"I think it's just about perfect," I say and hand her the bottle.

Chrissy accepts the bottle, then tests it on her own wrist, and smiles, and I smile, and together we watch Andrea take the bottle of warm formula in her tiny fat fingers and curl her feet up around it and begin sucking. *Such a tiny little thing in such a big strange world.* I can barely believe I'm here, hovering over her, squatting, reaching down and fingering the curls of my golden-haired daughter.

Before I know it, it's bedtime, because Chrissy has to be at work at seven and Andrea has to be dropped off at the babysitter's at

6:30. So I turn out the lights, take off my clothes, and feel my way in the unfamiliar dark to the mattress on the floor. I lie down beside Chrissy. Almost immediately Manhattan's June evening air settles down over us like a warm blanket. No need for covers. Andrea sucks on her bottle on Chrissy's side of the mattress. After my eyes adjust to the dark, I turn over and find Chrissy looking back at me. A trickle of sweat runs down my side. We do not speak. Our legs do not touch. Rising up on one elbow, I put my hand out, caress her warm cheek, then wet one finger and smooth out her wild eyebrows. Her eyes search mine. Her mouth opens. No words come out.

I leave my arm resting lightly across her breast for a moment, then my hand moves down the length of her, her cotton slip damp to the touch, and I lean over her, hesitate in the heat that rises up off her body, and start to kiss her. Abruptly she pushes me away, her hand against my chest.

"Wait," she whispers.

I pull back a little, my weight now balanced on my arms.

She looks over toward Andrea, then continues to whisper softly, "I need to tell you something."

"What?"

Her hand remains steady against my chest as she turns back to face me, "I...I've had an infection."

"You what?"

I imagine Chrissy, naked, slipping into a bed with another man.

I pull away and sit up in the bed.

Her hand hangs in midair a moment, then drops.

She speaks softly, "It's okay. I've been taking antibiotics for almost two weeks now, and I don't think I'm infectious any more."

"What kind of infection?" The word "crabs" comes to mind—little, nasty, nearly invisible, parasitic creatures crawling about in pubic hair.

She turns her head into her pillow, murmurs something I can't make out, then she sits up beside me and takes my hand.

"Eddie, I understand. If you're worried about it, don't make love to me. We can wait. We don't have to make love tonight."

A disease, yes, she's had a disease; she's gone to bed with other men, but it's all over now; she's taken her medication. There's a risk, yes, but we need to connect. I need to connect. She's watching me now; she's waiting for me to decide. She's leaving it up to me. I don't know what to say.

"It's okay. I'm not worried."

She falls back, raises both arms toward me, and I roll forward over her, bury my face in her neck, in the familiar smell of her skin, and she reaches down between us, takes hold of my growing erection, and guides me in. I close my eyes and push myself into her in spite of the friction, push against her because I want a connection, push until suddenly, without warning, an almost-angry impulse comes over me and I push harder and deeper into her heat, push against the burning friction, and suddenly a wild possessive urge comes over me and I really want to take her, to fuck her. But then she seems to fall away passively, and I am aware of how her fingers are fidgeting, moving restlessly on my back, and for a brief instant, out of the dark, Carina swims forward over us and dives elegantly beneath a wave of ocean water, and my hips are rising and falling, everything easier now in our heat and in the liquid sweat flowing off our bellies, and I am moving toward some irresistible distant place, and I can feel this wonderful need building inside me, and then I seem to be rising up in the air above the two of us entwined in our sheets, the two of us below me in a shadow-filled, one-room apartment, copulating on the floor, the sheets all askew, with Andrea in her wooden crate beside us, until abruptly my whole body shudders in orgasm, and I collapse down over her, empty and spent.

After a few moments I roll off her, and we lie side-by-side, not talking. Chrissy drifts off into sleep almost immediately, her soft breaths marking time in a slow, regular sibilance. In the dark I listen to the soft call of a saxophone and the answering scattery play of drums from Slug's echoing up the walls of our stairwell, and I feel a light breeze blow in under the door, double-locked, with its steel bar wedged into the floor. Out in the hallway the sound of a door opening, hinges creaking. People pass by, talking, laughing. Andrea whimpers and then coughs in her sleep.

Using some of the money I've saved from teaching, Chrissy and I rent a large, two-room apartment on Eleventh Street between Avenues B and C. Eleventh Street is more of a community—no bars or liquor stores. A young couple from Tennessee stops on the front stairs. They hold the door open for us. They explain in their soft Southern accents that they have also just recently moved in. Rod, in jeans and penny loafers, is a graduate student in English at N.Y.U. Linda, tall and thin, a strawberry blonde, holds onto his elbow, moves about with lots of nervous energy. She's looking for work. They are on their way, they say, to visit the N.Y.U. campus just off Washington Square Park.

Our two-room apartment is one flight up, with high ceilings, ornate cornices, and a big bathroom with a tub. It feels quite spacious after our one-room affair on Third Street. One of the rooms, we decide, will serve as bedroom, nursery, and study for me, and the other will act as a combination living room, dining room, and kitchen. Our spacious bathroom has white walls, new black-and-white tile on the floor, a huge antique claw-footed tub, and an overhead shower with plastic curtains showing a map of the world. The kitchen, built in an alcove, we separate from the living room with a makeshift table—its legs constructed from cement blocks, its top an old plywood door. A red and white checked tablecloth hides what's underneath. There are two windows at the back end of our "living room." They look down on a square patio garden surrounded on all sides by adjoining high-rise apartments. This garden, though seemingly abandoned and cluttered with garbage and urban junk, is a welcome surprise of green amidst a world of concrete gray. We will have our own secret garden, once we clean it up a bit.

In June we receive two letters: one, on blue and pink flowery stationery, is from Mobile, with no return address, from Carina, and the other is from Birmingham, from Anita. I open them both before Chrissy comes home from work. I've told her about Carina, about our friendship but not about the affair. I still don't understand what happened between Carina and me, and I'm not prepared to talk about it.

Carina says she got our address from my mother. She and her brother are going to France. They have several hours of layover in New York. She wonders if I can find time to see her and adds that she will understand if I don't make it. She provides the date, the arrival time, the gate number. She leaves no phone number. She signs it, "Yours, Carina."

Anita's letter is really just a quick note. She asks if we can put her up for a week. She says she wants to "shake the iron dust out of her hair" and forget all about teaching literature to high school students. Her letter is on legal-size yellow notepad paper. Her note seems lost against the blank lines of the empty page, but her signature is large, filled with flourishes.

I leave both letters on the kitchen table for Chrissy and take off. I'm on my way to my first excursion across town to register for my summer classes at N.Y.U. I have been accepted for graduate study in philosophy. Chrissy will continue working for the welfare department, and we have found, in our Tennessee neighbor, Linda Grammer, a willing babysitter. She says she loves kids, has "just enormous amounts of time" on her hands, and doesn't know what to do with herself. Rod and Linda say they haven't yet made friends with anyone in New York except us.

And before we know it, Linda, a high-school graduate and part-time temp secretary, is showing up at our door with cookies and inviting herself in for a bit of conversation. Rod is seldom around, and Linda seems at loose ends. One afternoon, after an early morning conversation, just before I have to leave for school, as she's going out the door, she flashes her green eyes at me and blurts, "I just love being here in New York, don't you? Nobody knows a thing about anybody else—everybody's just as friendly and as anonymous as people can be."

She pauses in the doorway, chews at her fingernails and looks up at the ceiling.

"We were going to have a baby, but I lost it. We're going to try again when Rod gets his degree and can support us. Catch you later."

As I watch her hurry away, before I close the door, remembering her bright fresh-faced glow and her smiling eyes, it occurs to me that her marriage to Rod will not survive New York. Already the education gap between Linda and her graduate student husband is a problem. When they are together Rod condescends to her, seems not to value anything she has to say. It's a shame, I think, closing and locking the door behind me and hurrying down the steps to move out into the foot traffic on Eleventh Street. But at least it's not my problem. My problem is that I have to get across town to N.Y.U.'s bookstore at Washington Square and order the books for my early morning class, Phenomenology of Jean-Paul Sartre.

It's Saturday, late morning, almost time for me to leave for the airport to see Carina. I've just come back from the deli with our breakfast, and the two letters lie open on the table above a row of unpaid bills. The bills are arranged in alphabetical order, in neatly organized stacks of hers, mine, and ours. We split our living expenses, and I pay for my graduate school classes.

I've brought us orange juice, coffee, bagels, and knishes for break-fast. Chrissy is still in her slip. I get out some plates, sit down across from her, and put her food within arm's reach, but away from the bills. She has not spoken a word.

"Chrissy? What is it?" I ask quietly.

Even though she's shielding her face, I see that she's been crying. Her nose is running. She wipes at it with some tissue.

"What is it?" I try again.

Her voice soft but steady, she says, staring down at the bills, "The night you arrived I told you I had a disease..."

There is a long pause as Chrissy looks around and across the room at Andrea's fold-up playpen, at Andrea taking her nap sur-rounded by teething rings and colorful toys.

"Yeah?"

"Well, the man who gave me that disease may have given me something else... I haven't had my period this month. I should have had it a week ago... Eddie, I'm...I'm afraid. I may be pregnant!"

Questions begin multiplying in my head; they rush through me carrying images of faces I can't quite make out. For a moment my eyesight plays tricks on me as morning sunlight plays against our living-room wall producing something like the quick shadows of dancing marionettes flying across our darkened room.

Suddenly she turns and lifts her tear-stained face toward me, openly vulnerable, and grimly says, "This is not okay. I made a mistake."

Then, as if she has just come to a sudden conclusion, she continues, "It's my fault. I want you to understand something...no matter what...this is not your problem."

Dejected, she sits before me, her face in her hands.

"Chrissy, slow down. You don't know for sure that you're pregnant. You're only a week late; right?"

She doesn't answer.

I continue, leaning toward her.

"And besides, even if you are, we're not in Alabama. We can do something about it. We're not helpless, and I'm sure Gary can help us."

She stares at me. A few tears trickle down her face, but she is not crying—a quick intake of breath, nothing more.

"Look, it was a mistake, and there is no way I will go forward with it... I don't want *his* child. If it's there inside me, attaching itself to me, I'll have it ripped out. One way or another. I don't want it! I'd rather die."

I reach across the table, but she pulls back.

She will not let me touch her.

She gets up, walks determinedly toward the bedroom, and says dismissively, "Leave me alone, Eddie. Go meet your friend at the airport."

Quietly, she closes the door behind her.

◁▶

Out in the brilliant morning light, on my way out to the airport, looking out the window of the bus, I find myself staring into the vista of a huge cemetery with thousands upon thousands of white crosses. I can't stop thinking about Chrissy's possible pregnancy and her declaration that she'd rather die than have *his* baby. I sit and look outward as the bright sunshine sparkles over this cemetery, and the bus rolls on and on, and I don't care if we ever get anywhere. I just want to ride forever in this warm bus, let the monotonous white crosses flow by, and I want to stop thinking about this new turn of events, but I don't—because I know there is so much more and I know she won't talk about it. Why? What's behind her anger? Why is it so big and scary? Is it Gary she's been fooling around with? No. She's still friendly with him. But what is it then that's driving her? I think it's because she's done something she's ashamed of, that has scared her. I don't know what that is, but I do know that she is prepared to take whatever risks it takes to end this pregnancy, if she *is* pregnant.

At the TWA terminal, I walk around for fifteen or twenty minutes before someone taps me on the shoulder and points to a bench and a small girl with a big smile on her face.

It's Carina.

Puzzled, I turn back to the guy who has tapped me on the shoulder. He could only be Carina's brother, such a clean, aristocratic presence. He's wearing a navy-blue blazer with gold buttons; he parts his hair down the middle, Gatsby style, and he's sizing me up: taking in my casual, short-sleeved shirt, blue jeans, and tennis shoes. His blue eyes give me a cold feeling. He seems as if he's about to make me an unpleasant proposition, but then he spins around on his heel, in a military about-face, and walks away.

I don't know whether to laugh or be insulted.

As I walk across the floor toward Carina, I see why I didn't recognize her. She has cut off her beautiful blonde hair. It's been styled in a close pixie cut, with one curl coming down over her forehead. She looks like she's thirteen.

I move over a sea of polished tile, my sneakers squeaking, past people in a hurry, listening to announcements of flight arrivals and departures. She does not stand, and so, in the strange antiseptic anonymity of an airport thoroughfare, I kneel down beside her.

"Hey, you, remember me?"

She sits, shoulders scrunched, as if she's trying to make herself even smaller than she is. She looks like a character out of a musical, just off a stage scene on a ship, the *H.M.S. Pinafore* maybe. She's wearing a dark-blue sailor suit with tie, white silky ruffles poking out from under the jacket's sleeves, red lipstick, heavy rouge, and a lot of makeup over a couple of tiny red zits on her chin.

She offers her hand, looks up, grins, speaks softly in that ever-so-familiar Southern voice of hers, "Yes, I do remember you."

On one knee, I hold her hand a moment before she takes it back.

"I gather that was your brother... He wasn't exactly polite."

"I'm sorry..." She looks down at her feet, twists a Kleenex in her small hands, then stares over my shoulder where her brother had been standing.

"Hey, Carina, this is me. Remember? Don't be sorry. Just tell me what's going on! Are you really off to Paris?"

She pulls her shoulders back and sits up straight, but her hands flutter nervously in her lap like small birds striking against a windowpane. Then she stands, gathers up an oversized white purse, and hooks it on her arm.

"Quick, before he comes back."

Looking back in the direction her brother has gone, she takes hold of my hand and leads me in the opposite direction.

"Eddie, I told my family about us..."

She stops. Faces me.

"My brother hates you. He didn't know you were coming. He said he would give us just ten minutes."

"Why? What do you mean?"

Walking rapidly, her heels clicking on the polished floor, I let her lead me around a corner past a series of shops with people standing in line to buy food, and then she slows down.

"Let me explain," she whispers, her voice careful, serious, each distinct word pitched just for me. "I thought I was pregnant."

My voice too loud, "When? While I was still in Birmingham?"

A finger to her lips, shushing me, she nods, yes.

"Why didn't you tell me?" I whisper back.

"Would it have made any difference?" She looks up, very direct. The question hangs in the air.

"I don't know...but I would like to have had the chance to know..."

Abruptly, Carina leans in towards me, puts her head on my chest, says softly, in an almost inaudible voice, her warm breath on my neck, the sweet smell of her filling me with memories, "Stop talking and kiss me."

In spite of myself I look back for her brother.

He's nowhere in sight.

Taking both of her hands in mine, I pull her arms around me. She looks so young in her pixie haircut and strange sailor outfit. I want to feel about her the way I did back in Birmingham, but she seems so different, young, not the sophisticated Carina I knew. But then, as I stand there hugging her, intoxicated by the smell of the perfume in her hair, that same perfume she wore back in Birmingham, I just don't care why things are the way they are. I bend down, lift her up off the ground, my hands locked around her bottom, and kiss her, a long hungry kiss. And then I spin her around and around in a circle till I'm dizzy. Businessmen with briefcases, students with backpacks, people running with their luggage, men and women, anonymous people, all stream around us, smile conspiratorially, and then she takes my head into her hands, pulls me toward her for a more meaningful, good-bye type of kiss.

I place her gently back on the floor.

Her lipstick is smeared.

We straighten our clothes, turn, and join the flow of traffic back toward her waiting brother.

He is pacing impatiently by the bench, waiting for us. The three of us sit down together, her brother between us.

He says to me, "I think you should go now."

I look around him and ask Carina if she wants me to leave.

Carina, hands fluttering, Kleenex in one hand, a long blue vein standing out clearly on her forehead, asks her brother to please go buy her a Coke, to give us a few more minutes.

Her brother gives me another cold look of disgust and rises up in his good blue blazer, his firm jaw set, his hair plastered down with Vitalis hair tonic. Then he straightens his jacket and explains to us both that he will not be gone long and takes off at a brisk stride. There is a Coke machine just around the corner.

"Carina, please, what did you tell them?"

"I didn't have any choice. I was scared. I was alone. I thought I was pregnant. My mother guessed. She just barged into my room and demanded to know if it was you, and I...I told her everything. She went with me to our family doctor."

"Did you have an abortion?"

"No! Never! I would never have an abortion! That's murder! No, it turned out I wasn't pregnant at all."

I don't know if I believe her. I wait for her to say more.

"I said I wasn't after you! Remember? I wouldn't try to hold you with a baby, even if I was pregnant!"

"Are you telling me the truth, Carina?"

She nods as her brother returns with her Coke.

"Eddie, I think he's right. You should go."

We are all three standing.

"Carina, will you write me from France?"

Her brother glares at her. She looks down, says simply, "Good-bye, Eddie."

"Good-bye, Carina."

But I do not go. I'm waiting for something more, some release.

Then her brother speaks up, mockingly, and sarcastically dismisses me.

"Good-bye, Eddie."

Still I do not go. I stand there, ignoring her brother, until finally, Carina walks around her brother and raises her arms, kisses me on the cheek, whispers, "Go now. Let it be. *Que sera, sera.*"

At Fourteenth Street, I get off the subway, walk into a liquor store and buy a large bottle of Mountain Red claret, the cheap wine that Chrissy and I used to buy back in Birmingham.

With the wine in a brown paper bag, I wrap my hand around the neck of the bottle and break into a run at the next intersection, and then I keep on running. Past the delis on Fourteenth Street, past the camera shops, past the slow-moving crowds of people getting off a bus, past the beautiful lamp shop next to the old Avenue B theater, past the fire escapes and garbage cans, running faster and faster, running back to my wife and child.

Three days later Chrissy has her period.

[28]

A knock on the door, and there Anita stands, bags in hand. She is much changed since I last saw her. She has let her black hair grow long; she tosses her head, and her hair flows over her shoulders and tumbles down her back. Her body appears shapely and slender under her green silk dress. She greets me with her winning smile, but it seems forced, not spontaneous; her green eyes gaze openly at me, then shy away. For an awkward moment we just stand there before she puts down her bags and we hug politely. I am surprised at the changes in her appearance, but I am even more surprised at the formality of her bearing.

Is she judging me? Have she and Carina been talking?

"Come in...come in." I pick up her bags and step aside. She smiles and sweeps into the room. Anita and Chrissy have not seen each other for almost a year, so the moment she walks in the door Chrissy shrieks, jumps up from the kitchen table and rushes to her with open arms.

This transformation also takes me by surprise. I put Anita's bags behind the couch and watch the two of them interact. Anita still seems circumspect, unsure of herself, but Chrissy seems oblivious, hugging her, touching her, pulling her into an embrace. They sit down on the couch. Chrissy holds onto Anita's hand and exclaims, "Oh, just let me look at you. It's been such a long time."

Anita looks over in my direction as if she's embarrassed by so much attention, but Chrissy doesn't notice. The whole of her attention is on Anita, touching Anita's face, her arm, her hair.

As I pull up a chair to join in, I feel awkward. The intensity of Chrissy's attention seems overwrought, out of place. She appears to have forgotten that I am in the room, and Anita seems what? Unfriendly? Distant?

"So, Anita," I try, inserting myself, "did you have a good flight?"

Chrissy looks back at me as if she were surprised to find me there.

Anita, obviously uncomfortable, pulls away from Chrissy, leans back in the couch and speaks evenly, politely, guest to host, "Yes. Fine. Uneventful. I got to read John Fowles's novel, *The Collector*. Have you read it?"

I hadn't.

Chrissy sits back in the couch, studies her hands impatiently.

"It's about a man who kidnaps the woman he loves. He adores her, but he keeps her locked up, thinks he owns her...it's an unsettling book... I won't tell you how it ends."

Late that evening, after we've played with Andrea and put her down for the night, Gary shows up, unexpectedly coming to my rescue with a joint, his lovely MaryJane, or, as he pronounces it, his "marriagejuana." He lights up and passes it to me. I inhale and then offer the jay first to Chrissy and then to Anita. They reject it. Anita seems to retreat into herself before the full force of Gary's personality. She says she's very tired. Chrissy says she's not in the mood either and runs her hands through her short hair, yawns, and looks at me expectantly. But I ignore her because I *am* in the mood; I am desperate for an escape. I take another hit and pass the joint back to Gary.

It's called "Acapulco Gold," Gary says, but Chrissy and Anita are not interested in the agricultural heritage of this plant. They make excuses and quietly retreat into our bedroom to talk. I can hear their voices, and I try not to listen, but I keep hearing Tim's name.

Gary and I pass the joint back and forth a few times and then Gary speaks up, "Hey man, I got to go uptown. You want to come along for the walk?"

"Yeah, let's get out of here," I reply, picking up my coat, shouting to Chrissy and Anita that we are going out for a walk, inviting them to come along.

They decline.

I'm stoned. The bustling cool night air of New York City bursts over me with noise and energy as we walk—the cabs, the people, and the neon lights flashing on Fourteenth Street. We drop down into a subway entrance and board a train. We are heading for Times Square. I want to people-watch, catch the sights: the junkies, the businessmen, the streetwalkers in black stockings; to visit this special place where there is always a cross section of the human race on display.

We stand in the lead subway car and I can feel the rush of speed as the train shakes, as the long tunnel continues to swallow us, as sparks fly up in the dark underground passageways. Holding onto overhead straps, we are thrown about, first one way and then the other, as the train twists and turns on its way toward Forty-second Street.

Gary turns to me, bumping up against the subway driver's door, and casually asks me, "What is it, Ed, old man? You and Chrissy having problems again?"

I try to gauge Gary's willingness to listen to my problems against my worry that he and Chrissy were lovers, and that he is involved with our struggles for his own reasons. But I am too stoned to care, and besides, for no really good reason, I trust this man. I believe he is a *mensch,* a truth teller. I decide to talk.

"I don't know what it is, Gary, but Chrissy and I are so far apart I find it hard to believe we really manage to live together."

He looks at me thoughtfully, his bloodshot eyes bulging out from his gray, weathered face.

"Ed, I'll tell you, old man, you're going about this whole thing the wrong way. I know that it's an easy thing to say, but take it from me, you shouldn't get hung up on trying to control the people you love. You have to let 'em have their own lives."

The subway screeches to a stop. There is a churning of passengers coming and going, and then we jerk forward again.

"Gary, I don't know, sometimes it feels like I don't really know her anymore. We used to talk about our 'shared reality.' Now I'm not so sure we have one."

[221]

He leans in towards me, bending at the waist, gets right in my face, his eyes impossible to ignore. "Okay, listen man, this is a lesson I learned the hard way. If you put everything you have inside somebody else, then they control you, and what happens to them happens to you."

The train lurches. We pull apart. He straightens up and continues.

"My dad died when I was a kid. My mother brought me up…all by herself. I loved her! She was my whole world until I was fourteen. And then, suddenly, for no reason at all that I knew anything about, she died. And I couldn't take it. I flipped out."

The subway screeches around a corner. Sparks fly in the dark tunnel. I wait for him to continue.

"I spent some time in an orphanage and learned how to be alone. But then when I was twenty-one, after I was out on my own, I got married. We had a real thing going for three months, and then suddenly one day, on her way home from the grocery, a seventy-year-old lady ran a red light: no more wife, no more life! I flipped out again. I was a long time coming back. Woke up one day in New Orleans and started over. Even spent a few years in ministerial studies at Tulane. Became an itinerant Baptist preacher for a few years. Now I'm here on this subway with you."

Holding on to an overhead rail, he put one hand on my shoulder.

"Do you understand what I'm saying?"

I nod, but I'm not sure what he's saying.

"And it doesn't have to be death that does it to you, you know… life can do it to you, too. I'm not telling you all of this just to tell you my sob story, man."

He grins. I nod again.

"I'm just trying to tell you that every human being is a trap baited with the scent of false security…there ain't no such thing as security, man, there's only traps and delusions and dreams of getting out of being alone."

Suddenly, he straightens up and laughs, a laugh that shakes him as the train snakes its way through the subway tunnel. People ignore us. He stops laughing, wipes his face, and becomes serious again,

"Look, the best dream a man can have is a woman."

The train is slowing down. People are standing up. He continues on as we head for the doors, "But don't trust 'em, man. Love 'em, give 'em all you can, but don't trust 'em...they'll die on you one way or another. It's always that way...least it's always been that way for me."

Forty-second Street. It's midnight, but people are everywhere, jostling for position, hurrying to get where they're going, shoving, pressing up against me as we exit into the night. We navigate past flashing neon lights and skirt the vomit on the sidewalk, taking in the spare-change trumpet player in an empty alcove who plays Dixieland jazz to the beat of blaring car horns. We shake our heads, no, to a barker who steps out from a doorway, wearing tuxedo and top hat, and invites us to buy tickets for an Arthur Miller play. Across the street neon lights are announcing: "Mongo Santa Maria, live and in person." Alcohol, crowded bars, blondes, beaded and bejeweled black women swaying, bumping, grinding on a stage partially visible from the sidewalk. Gary chooses one of the bars and we go in. The bartender waves to Gary and we cross over. They chat and Gary buys us drinks, scotch on the rocks. All the tables are taken. Then a large, blonde-wigged, black woman walks in, pushes her way through the crowd, and steps between Gary and me. She leans back on her elbows and says throatily, "Hello, boys."

Gary grins at me, laughs, hugs her, and begins chatting her up in a surprising, brisk black dialect I can barely follow. Stunned, I watch as he talks with his hands and moves suggestively with the rhythms of the room. On a stage off to our left through the smoke-filled room, I see bongo drummers beating out a Latin beat and Spanish dancers swirling around in brilliantly colored costumes, tapping their feet. The bartender refills my drink as Gary finishes his tête-à-tête, and his friend pushes herself away from the bar and sashays back into the crowd.

Gary bends close to my ear, says he knows her from work, and then adds apologetically, "Sorry, Ed old man, but you and I need to split up now. I have a deal I need to conclude with my friend." He nods at his black lady "friend" in her skintight gold-sequined dress and shiny red high-heeled shoes, who gathers herself, and begins to strut her stuff back in our direction, with a fire-engine red smile on her lips. On her way over, she's caught by someone who reaches out and takes hold of her arm. She hesitates. Her associates seem to be trying to talk her out of leaving. She throws her head back, laughs, and pulls away.

Did Gary know she'd be here? Was she waiting for him? Are they lovers? Is this a drug deal? Or are they just friends?

Surprised at being abandoned, but keeping my disappointment to myself, I offer up a toast.

"Bonne nuit et bonne chance."

We click glasses and I down my drink.

We grip hands in a sturdy connection, and, a little relieved at not being included in Gary's "deal," I take off. But then, as I'm pushing through the crowd for the door, I feel a strange elation about having come here, at having seen Gary with his friend, seen them interact. It's exciting, maybe just because she's black and he's white and because they aren't afraid to be seen with each other, because this is New York City, not Birmingham, Alabama, because here it's okay for a white man and a black woman to be together. No one will kill them for it. In a sudden feeling of being released from my Southern upbringing, I laugh out loud into the bar noise.

"Thank you, New York."

Outside it's raining, a summer's fine mist, a drizzling rain. Then there is the lovely sound of tires whispering over the wet pavement. No one seems to mind the rain, least of all me. We walk about in it, cooling off, we, the after-midnight crowd. Under the street lamps, in the fumes of the traffic, the rain holds an electric rainbow.

Arriving home, I find Anita lying on the couch, under covers but staring at the ceiling. The door to the bedroom is closed. I start to speak but change my mind because Anita refuses to look at me.

In the bedroom Chrissy is also awake, but she doesn't turn over to greet me when I enter the room. I sit on the bed and lean over her.

She's crying, sobbing quietly, covers pulled over her face.

"Chrissy? What is it?"

Her breathing is slow and deep. I put one hand on her shoulder and start to pull her over to face me. Sleepily, she tries to push my hand off her shoulder.

"Chrissy? Talk to me, damnit!"

Angrily, I pull her towards me. There is no resistance and she falls over, her right arm and hand flopping.

"Chrissy?"

Her voice sleepy, her words slurred, she murmurs, "Leave me alone...please...just leave me alone."

"Chrissy. Please talk to me. What's going on?"

Chrissy's arms and hands are loose, rubbery. Something is wrong. She's going back to sleep. Is she drunk?

Moving closer, I lift her head onto my lap. Her fine hair is matted with sweat. Is she sick? I smooth out her eyebrows.

"Chrissy, wake up! What's wrong? Chrissy?"

Eyes closed, talking to someone else, she says, "It's all right... I love you...but you don't love me, do you? I've always loved you, Anita... Why, why can't we? It isn't wrong, I tell you...you can, yes, you can...yes...no, don't leave... No... Please... Don't leave..."

Shaking her, I shout at her, "Chrissy! It's me, Eddie!"

Her eyes flash open, wide. She seems to recognize me.

"Eddie, send her away... I can't see her again, please, I can't, please, I don't want to... I can't. Please." Her voice trails off. Her eyes roll back into her head. She is asleep.

I place Chrissy's sleeping head on the pillow and stand by our bed, my head spinning. I don't know what to do. Andrea is fretting. I go over to her crib, put her bottle in her mouth, and tuck her blanket in around her. She takes her bottle in both hands, sucks on it contentedly. I tiptoe out, close the door, and head back into the living room.

Anita is sitting up on the couch. She's crying. Her legs are pulled up under her. Her head is down against her knees.

"Anita, what happened? What's wrong with Chrissy? She's acting really strange. I can't wake her."

She doesn't look up, murmurs, "I don't know. We had a few beers."
The bathroom door is open.

There is a small bottle of sleeping pills on the sink counter; the cap is in the sink. I fish out the cap. I can't remember whether it was full or not. How many has she taken? I count the number of pills still left in the bottle, and then estimate how many are missing. She has taken three or four, five at most. I envision her dropping the cap, shaking them out into her hand without counting. The directions say that adults can take two in eight hours and should not exceed four in twenty-four hours.

In the mirror I look at my face and see a familiar stranger looking back, blue eyes, blonde hair, big ears. He is nice enough looking, an intelligent face, I think, but does he know what's going on? Is Chrissy in love with Anita? Or is it all a figment of a dream? A bad dream.

I dump out two more sleeping pills, put the pills back in the medicine cabinet, and go back to Anita in the living room.

Anita looks up at me defensively, with her arms around her legs, knees under her chin.

I ask, holding out the sleeping pills, "Anita, don't you want to take a few of these sleeping pills? Chrissy just took about five! She'll be out for a while."

Anita turns her head sideways on her knees and looks at me suspiciously through strands of her hair. "No, I don't want any sleeping pills."

She lifts her head, tosses her long hair over one shoulder in an automatic gesture.

"I'm not staying. I'm leaving here tonight."

"Why?" I ask, my voice asking a different question, one I knew she would not answer.

Straightening her back, she resolutely places both feet on the floor and pulls her hair back using both hands, sighs, and answers, "Will you call a cab for me? I've got to get out of here."

"What's going on between you and Chrissy?"

"I rejected her...and... I need to get out of here."

"There's no place to go this time of night."

"I'm sure the cab driver can find a decent hotel for me."

"Come on, Anita, she...well, it might be better for her to have to face you, and for the three of us to work this out in the morning."

"Oh, no. I don't want any part of it. Not anymore. Eddie, I know what I'm doing, and I don't think it will do either of us any good for me to stay here. I've already overstayed my welcome."

"Well, wait a minute... Anita, talk to me, what happened?"

"No. This is between you and Chrissy. I am not involved...this is not my problem."

Anita swings her legs off the couch, shakes her head in that old, confident manner of hers, with that old, secretive Anita smile of self-knowledge, and stands up. "I'll say this much. I'm leaving because *I* have to go...for my sake...and maybe for hers, too. If I stay...well, I can't take that responsibility. I'm going because it's over and before there's any possibility of its ever beginning again. Call me a cab, Eddie, please."

I call her a cab.

Then I fix us some hot tea. We sip it while we wait. It's almost two in the morning.

"Anita...what can I say?"

"Nothing. Don't say anything. Say good-bye and let me go."

"Yes, maybe you're right. But, Anita, what do you think, does she... does she love *me*? You don't have to answer if you don't want to."

A knock on the door, and a male voice calls out, "Somebody in there call a taxi?"

Anita begins gathering up her things, "One minute, please."

She picks up her bags. "Eddie, I can't answer your question...you know that. Just love her, take care of her. She needs you now more than ever."

I open the door, and the taxi driver takes Anita's bags.

On the stairs Anita hesitates, turns, and says, "Eddie, she does love you, but she loves other people, too... It's not an easy thing to be loved by Chrissy. What she offers is everything she has, and she's always willing to risk it all, absolutely. She never holds anything back for herself. Eddie, I'm afraid for her... I know it's not right to leave you like this, and I know you will, but, Eddie, please take care of her."

I listen at the door until the taxi drives off. Later, in the bathroom, I put the sleeping pills back, and then I watch as the man in the mirror brushes his teeth.

[29]

The next day, Sunday, Chrissy refuses to get out of bed. She says, "Leave me alone. I'm so tired. Let me sleep." So I take Andrea for a walk over to Tompkins Square Park. Andrea loves the park, the excitement of the outdoors, the sand pile and the other children. The warm day brings the mothers out, Puerto Rican, black, Jewish, Spanish, all with different accents. We all move slowly because we are tuned-in to our children, channeling our understanding of the world through their eyes. Everything is interesting: a leaf; a children's bucket on its side, half-filled with sand; a bright white shovel; a red balloon floating just off the ground. I kneel down beside Andrea and point: there, a yellow-headed finch hops about in the grass, and over there a red ground squirrel skitters across the path and disappears down a hole in a tree. Andrea wants to go after the squirrel. I watch her struggle with her sense of balance. This is a new thing. She's struggling against feet that don't quite cooperate. Stretching her arms out for balance, she rises to her full height and tries to take a step, but then she wobbles and sits down suddenly on her bottom. Surprised, she looks up at me for reassurance. I laugh. She's bottom heavy. She laughs. She's spotted a black starling looking for food, its head cocked, its yellow eye tracking her movements.

Sunday evening, with much coaxing, I get Chrissy to eat some chicken noodle soup. She sits in her slip, wearing sunglasses and house slippers, nods, answers my queries with one-syllable responses. After a few bites, she sleepwalks back to bed.

Monday morning, surprising me, Chrissy gets up when the alarm goes off. I am not sure what to expect, but our morning routine holds. I change Andrea and get her ready for the babysitter while Chrissy showers and dresses. Running late, as usual, we barely have time to speak. But, except for a lack of energy in her movements, she seems almost back to normal. Then, standing in the doorway, as I hand Andrea over to her, in that moment of transition before our paths fork, before our usual perfunctory kiss, and before even speaking the words I intended to say, I see her stop working on her checklist of what has to be accomplished next. And then she smiles, making an effort in spite of the trembling that could have led to tears, and I see how she is asking me with her eyes to be with her, asking me to know that she is struggling to be here in this world, with me, and not someplace else. And time slows down, and the only thing that matters is the glow in her eyes, and we are together again, not needing to talk, not needing to explain about the hurt and the pain, not needing to worry about the vast emptiness in the world just beyond our doorstep, and she leans into me and presses her body next to mine, her face buried in my neck, and whispers, "Thank you for being here. I feel so alone."

Graduate school classes are beginning. I only have two, Introduction to Symbolic Logic and the Sartre class. They are time consuming, with rewriting lecture notes and lots of homework, but my teachers excite me, and I am committed to doing well. Chrissy and I move through our nights and days with a kind of easy, friendly warmth. I go across town to N.Y.U. She goes to work at the state welfare office and drops Andrea off at our weekday babysitter. There are no fights, no discussions, and no lovemaking. There is a peaceful coexistence. We are very careful with each other. It's as if she has been on a long trip overseas, and having just returned, is trying to get over a persistent fatigue from jet lag. We live together, yet we are not together. I bide my time, waiting, but we have misplaced the map of our way back to one another. We share our evenings: reading, eating, sleeping, cleaning the apartment, paying the bills, and changing diapers. I am beginning to clear the debris from our secret garden outside the apartment, but it's a bigger job than I thought. I give an hour or two a week to it, but I don't seem to be making a lot of progress.

It is Wednesday morning, "hump day," and Chrissy, dressed for work, is sitting on the couch with Andrea on the floor before her, strapped in her baby rocker. I walk past them before I notice that there's something wrong with Chrissy. Has she fallen asleep with her eyes open? Is she in some sort of hypnotic state? I kneel down directly in front of her. She doesn't seem to see me. *Is she thinking about her work?*

Chrissy told me about one of her welfare cases where she found a ten-month-old child who had cigarette burns on her legs and stomach. She had to be there when the authorities took the screaming baby away from the distraught mother, and she's been pretty upset ever since. I take hold of one of her hands and begin to rub it. Her eyes flicker, then seem to find a focus somewhere over my head.

"Chrissy? How do you feel?"

Her eyes move across my face as if they haven't quite found me.

"Chrissy?"

"I can't move." Her voice is an off-key mixture of fear and resignation.

"What can't you move?" I am not sure she's hearing me. I have an impulse to take hold of her shoulders and shake her, but I don't.

"Sweetie, what can't you move?"

Strangely calm, as if she's talking to herself, she whispers, "I can't move my head. There's no pain... I just can't move it. A few minutes ago I couldn't move at all...now it's just my neck; I can't turn my head..."

"Easy now, take it easy. Maybe it's going away..."

"No, it isn't...it isn't going away..."

"Should I call a doctor?"

An internal struggle resolving itself in her eyes, she replies, "I don't know, but I can't move... I really can't move," a tinge of panic in her voice.

I call the N.Y.U. Downtown Hospital.

"What kind of emergency?" they want to know.

"I think my wife has fallen and injured her neck," I lie.

We arrive just behind a bearded old man in a black suit and purple skullcap, a victim of a robbery. He has a gunshot wound. So we have to wait, but finally, after forty-five minutes, they come and get Chrissy and lead her away. She walks stiffly, allowing herself to be led. The nurses give me puzzled looks. I sit in the waiting room until the doctor on call comes over and tells me he can find nothing physically wrong. The x-rays were all normal. He's given her a tranquilizer. He says she seems to be recovering and wants to know if she's experienced any recent traumas. I tell him, "No." He is quite friendly, tells me the drugs will make her sleepy, and then says he's made an appointment for her to see a psychiatrist next month. He says we should go home, but that she should not return to work for a while, that she should get some rest.

It's morning, and Chrissy sleeps. I called and cancelled the baby-sitter, but Linda, our neighbor from Tennessee, says she'll watch Andrea for me. I tell her that Chrissy has strained some muscles and needs to rest. Chrissy seems unable or unwilling to pick up the threads of her life. She barely leaves the bedroom. Last night she twisted and turned in a restless sleep, crying out, "Mama!" and "No, no, no..." After speaking with Linda, I return to the darkened room and find Chrissy curled under the twisted sheets, knees pulled up in fetal position. I tiptoe past the bed to get my wallet off the dresser and hear her whispering, "I want my mama... I'm so afraid." In the dim light I sit down beside her on the bed. She seems drugged, more asleep than awake. Perhaps she's dreaming. I take her hand and ask her, "Chrissy, it's me, Eddie. What can I do?"

Hair matted over her forehead, eyes red, she turns her face into the pillow and murmurs wearily, "Nothing...nothing anyone can do... I'm so tired, just let me sleep."

Linda, in a seductive voice and exaggerated Southern accent, says, as she walks me to the door, "Now, you just go on to your class, honey, and don't worry about a thing." A cigarette dangles from her mouth. Her blonde hair in curlers, she pushes her glasses up onto the bridge of her nose, leans over, and bats her eyes in a mock Marilyn Monroe gesture. I feel my face flush red as Linda laughs and continues her joke, "You take care now, you hear?" She's wearing tight blue jeans that accentuate her long thin frame, and on top, one of her husband's white dress shirts, partially unbuttoned, sleeves rolled to her elbows, no bra.

Trying for a noncommittal friendliness, I laugh appreciatively, say, "Thanks, Linda, I appreciate your help, I really do."

She offers me a complicated look that leaves me confused, then becomes businesslike, and says, "I need to do some shopping today. Do you think it'll be all right if I take Andrea with me?"

"Sure, I don't see why not. Just let Chrissy know when you'll be back, and again, many thanks for your help."

Halfway through my Sartre class, discussing his play, *Les Mains Sales* (Dirty Hands), suddenly I think, *something is wrong*. And then, in spite of myself, I can't stop worrying. I can't concentrate on what anybody is saying. My skin feels strange. I have a slight nausea. It feels like I've had too many cups of coffee on an empty stomach. I gather up my books and sneak out. Outside, crossing McDougal Street, I hail a taxi. There is a terrible urgency inside me. I sit on the edge of my seat all the way across town.

But once in the apartment everything appears normal. I feel stupid. Nothing seems out of place. The apartment is quiet, the door to our bedroom closed. I put my books down, walk into the bathroom to wash my face and hands, flip on the light switch and, as my arm and hand are extending over the sink, reaching for the faucet, I stop, unable to take in what I'm seeing. At first it makes no sense. I stand before the sink, one arm outstretched, and stare...and then, in a returning wave of nausea, I see it for what it is.

Blood—red, dried blood on the counter, wet blood in the sink, blood on the towels, blood dripping down over the side of the tub. It's all over the floor. I'm standing in it. There is an empty bottle of sleeping pills lying on its side, covered in blood. It's on the mirror, smeared. It's on my hands; I turn around; it's on the light switch. It's on my pants.

Where is it coming from?

I start backing out of the bathroom; everything seems to move in slow motion, nothing making sense, the soundless apartment suddenly dark and dimming until I feel my stuck left foot lifting out of the blood, and there is a sucking popping sound as the blood releases its grip on my shoe, and suddenly time snaps back into place, and I can hear my own voice echoing in the emptiness around me. "Chrissy? Chrissy, where are you? Chrissy?"

Something is blocking our bedroom door from the inside.

I slam my shoulder into it, knocking a chair over.

Chrissy is lying in a pool of viscous, congealing blood. Her white slip is brown-stained, red-stained. The sheets are wet with her blood. *How can there be so much blood?*

Chrissy's face is splotchy, skin pale gray, and lips white. Her head lolls on her neck, rolls side to side. She is still alive.

How can she have spilt so much blood?

As if I am seeing myself from above, I watch my hands on her shoulders. I am shaking her, lifting her up from the bed, letting go, watching her fall backwards, her eyes open, her body limp. Her head bounces, and then I am ripping away the stiffening, bloodied sheets, pulling her towards me, shouting into her face, "Chrissy, what have you done? Wake up!"

Head turning, eyes coming into focus, slowly opening, eyelids fluttering, and then finally her soft eyes find mine, rest there, smiling. She is so calm. She seems happy to see me, looks at me as if nothing is wrong, offers me a warm, glad-you-came-to-see-me hello. A happy surprise on her face, she smiles with dry lips, tongue touching the whitish cracks around the edges of her mouth. She tries to talk, but there is only a soft, dry, coughing sound. She licks her dry lips, tries again. I listen carefully as she manages a low rasping stream of disconnected words.

"Eddie...don't...worry. Oh, don't be upset with me, you seem so... upset...don't be upset...it's all right...this is okay...the way it is... didn't expect you so...soon...but it's okay...going to be okay..."

I let her go. She falls back and closes her eyes.

There is a rage inside me furiously pacing back and forth like an animal, a furious irrational rage. My eyes are not focusing. There is a sound like an ocean wave blowing in and out through the mouth of a cave. My stomach is churning with the need to throw up. I fight it down, and then I realize that my lip is bleeding. As I wipe away my own blood I begin to shout.

"Get up. Get out of this bed! Now! Get out or I'll drag you out. Now. Right now!"

I seize her limp arms and jerk her up into a sitting position. Her head snaps back and then she seems to collapse into my arms. She looks up at me, concerned, looks as if she is trying to understand. She raises one hand as if to ward off a blow, and I see for the first time the wide, jagged slash across her wrist, the congealed blood next to the yellow meat of her flesh spilling out, the whitish bone revealed, the pale pink insides of her flesh. I gag as I stare at that gash across her wrist, and then I lift her out of the bed, both of us stumbling, almost falling to the floor. And all the while I irrationally want to hurt her, hurt the Chrissy that hurt this Chrissy. I want to punish her, pummel her, but that Chrissy is not this Chrissy.

Fighting to lift her dead weight out of the bed, I take hold of her arms and force her to stand up. Then, struggling to hold her erect, her feet dragging over the floor, we stagger through the door. Her legs move, but will not hold her. Somehow, finally, we make it out of the bedroom into the living room. I lower her onto the couch.

"Try to sit here. Please, hold on. Where are your clothes? Never mind. We don't have time for clothes. I'll get you some water and then I'm calling the hospital and an ambulance."

I get her a glass of water and return. I prop her up, put the glass to her lips, and spill water over both of us. Her body suddenly starts sliding down off the couch. I pull her up against me, and I can see she is trying to stand, and I get one arm under her arm and lift her suddenly to her feet.

"Eddie...please, you're hurting me, please get my clothes, at least get my coat. I can't go out like this. Eddie..." she pleads.

I'm still furious. I don't care about how she looks. I don't care about the damn coat. I just want to get her to a hospital.

"Please, Eddie, please let me get dressed, please, at least...my coat, please..."

I try sitting her down in the chair again. She seems more alert.

"How many sleeping pills did you take?" I ask, thinking of questions I will need to answer.

"I don't know...whatever was in the bottle," she murmurs.

The door to our apartment opens, and Linda walks in with Andrea on her hip, a bag of groceries on her other side. She stares open-mouthed, but says nothing.

"Linda, can you keep Andrea?"

Linda mutely nods her head in agreement.

"There's blood everywhere... She's slashed her wrists. I have to get her to a hospital fast. Can you call us an ambulance? Tell them it's an emergency. Then call the N.Y.U. Downtown Hospital. Tell them we're coming. I'll get her dressed."

I sit beside Chrissy in her hospital bed. An I.V. drips fluid into her right arm. Both arms are strapped down. Thick white bandages cover her wrists. Eyes closed, her head twists from side to side. "Linda is with Andrea," I tell her, knowing she can't hear me. I watch her slip in and out of consciousness. The doctor told me that she lost a lot of blood before her veins collapsed. That's what saved her. She cut all the way to the bone. No halfway measures in her attempt. Her hair is pushed back revealing her wide forehead, her widow's peak. Her face is still starkly pale beneath her wild, dark eyebrows. The doctor said that she'd be okay, but that she sawed through several nerves and will lose some feeling in her left hand. But she's alive. I can't get myself to think beyond that. I can't imagine a world without her in it.

[30]

Out the hospital window the world is gray, overcast. In the distance, between buildings, sunlight is leaking away, disappearing behind dark clouds over the western horizon... Chrissy is heavily sedated. It is dark when I start to leave the hospital. She has not severed anything major. The thin razor blade cut deeply, but was apparently too slippery, too hard to hold. The doctor tells me she is lucky, that she will recover from the loss of blood because she is young and strong.

As I walk through swinging doors into a hallway of brightly lit, polished linoleum, the bustling activity of nurses conversing with doctors in white coats startles me, and suddenly I remember Tim. Tim, the one whom everyone had voted most likely to succeed. The last time I'd seen him, I'd been with Chrissy and Anita, all of us in shock as he sat before us, staring straight ahead, eyes unfocused, his body rigid. His face, even his ears, had been covered with a disturbing patchwork of new skin and scabs. Helpless, we'd walked away from him, left him there with his white-coated attendant at the Tuskegee Mental Hospital in Tuscaloosa, Alabama.

What happened? Where did we go wrong?

Out on the pavement, everyone is busy, busy. I walk by. They do not look up. They do not see me.

Under the streetlights, the red, yellow, and green traffic lights, with the subway noises and the ground shaking beneath my feet, I stop and look at my reflection in the storefront windows, and I hear Bob Dylan's voice blasting forth on a boom box, "like a rolling stone." The sound of his nasal voice grows louder, coming toward me, and then it fades away, disappearing in the ubiquitous traffic.

I walk all the way back without noticing which streets I am taking, and then I am surprised to find myself standing alone in front of our apartment, and I have no memory of the passage of time, of how I got to where I am, or even of how long I have been standing there.

I run up the stairs.

Inside Linda is waiting. Andrea is asleep beside her on the couch.

"How is she, Eddie?" Linda whispers as she stands. Lifting one finger to her lips, she turns, looks back down at sleeping Andrea, thumb in mouth.

"Chrissy is going to be all right," I tell her. "Tomorrow they're going to move her to the mental ward. I don't know how long she'll have to be there..."

I move forward past Linda, sink down on the couch beside Andrea and gently comb back her golden curls from her face with my fingertips. It's a warm night. She's red faced. I watch the rise and fall of Andrea's rosy cheeks as she sucks on her thumb. After some time has passed, I ask, "How's Andrea been?"

Linda, standing over us, smiles down at Andrea, protectively, maternally.

"She's been upset all day. She knows something's wrong. But she's an angel. She just went to sleep." Then, as an afterthought she adds, "Oh, Rod said to tell you that he'd be here with me but that he couldn't cut his class tonight. He's giving a presentation, and they always go out afterwards for a drink. He said to let him know if you want him to notify anyone or do anything for you at school."

"Oh, school... I don't think so..."

"Hey now, let's put Andrea in her bed and see if we can't get some food down you...you look like you need it."

She gathers up Andrea in a bundle of pink blankets and leaves the room. I stand up, fight off a dizzy spell, and notice for the first time that Linda has cleaned the whole apartment. Dishes are washed and stacked. She has mopped the floor. In the bathroom, only a few brown telltale stains remain on the tile grout next to the tub. I tiptoe from the bathroom into the bedroom. Linda is finishing tucking in Andrea. By the dim night-light I notice that Linda has turned over the mattress, put on fresh sheets. There are no visible bloodstains.

I walk over beside Linda, place one hand on her shoulder. She is propping Andrea's bottle up on a pillow. She stands up, leans back stretching and digs her fingers in next to her spine. I bend down and kiss Andrea, and Linda slips her arm around my waist and leans heavily against me. When I straighten, she doesn't let go, but hugs me tightly. As we close the door and tiptoe into the living room, I say, "Linda, I can't thank you enough for what you've done."

She grins, pushes her glasses up on her nose, runs both hands through her strawberry blonde hair, and says, "Yes, you can. Just say 'Thanks, Linda.' That's all. Then forget about it. I'm just glad to be of help."

I give her a big, long hug and drink deeply from the warmth of her soft body, her willingness to be hugged.

"Would you like a drink while I fix you some food? I brought over some Jack Daniel's. The best whiskey you can buy. Made and bottled in my own hometown."

I agree, and a few seconds later we are sipping from large jelly glasses filled with bourbon and Coke over ice. As we chat I notice she's changed her clothes since this morning. Now she's wearing blue-jean cutoffs with frayed edges and an oversized man's blue work shirt. Her shoulder-length blonde hair frames her freckled face with tendrils that curl down over her eyes. She keeps brushing them aside with one finger as we talk; she's wearing bright red lipstick. We stand uncomfortably across from one another. She stirs her drink with one finger and then sucks on it.

"This drink strong enough for you?" she asks in a waitress-like Tennessee drawl. I grin and nod in agreement. I watch as she straightens the tablecloth, lays out a plate and silverware, takes first some pickles and then a tuna fish sandwich out of the refrigerator. It is wrapped in wax paper. She seems strangely upbeat, a little brittle but warm and cheerful, softly offering me her wanting-to-please smile of welcome. Pickles in one hand and sandwiches in the other, she walks toward me, unconsciously swaying. I notice that she's not wearing a bra, that her long thin body seems barely contained by the front zipper on her tight-fitting cutoff jeans. The cloth strains outwards towards her hips, and two small mounds bulge outward where her thighs join just below the zipper. She looks up and I quickly turn away, say, "Let's sit a minute."

As we collapse together on the overstuffed couch, she starts talking about how Rod is doing great in school, about their adjustments to living in New York City, and about how they don't get out very much. The sweet Coke tinged with the strong bourbon goes down quickly. I ask her for another. She's quick to please. Jumps up, fills the glass with ice, pours us another tall one. After that we have yet another. And then we forget the food, and Linda rubs the back of my neck with one strong hand, and I feel myself letting go. I close my eyes and let the whiskey have its way with me, let myself drift on the warm currents of the sensations flowing down from the base of my skull, let myself disappear into Linda's fingertips moving down my neck to the sore spots in my lower back. Vaguely, I hear her place her drink on the table, stand up, and move over in front of me, her hands on my shoulders, kneading. She bends down over me, her perfumed hair tickling my face, her voice warm and whispering, "Take off your shirt; lie down; turn over... I'll give you a back rub."

I lift my shirt off over my head, drop it on the floor, roll over, and sink, fall into the gray velvet fabric of the couch.

Linda bends over me; her strong hands push my shoulders into the forgiving springs of the couch; and then she pulls her hands down toward my waist, her strong fingers sliding over me, her thumbs digging in on each side of my spine.

"How does that feel?"

I moan in pleasure, "That's wonderful," and think of how the word is made up of *wonder* and *full* and how perfectly apt the word is.

She whispers close to my ear, "Slide forward... I'm going sit on your legs for a better position...if that's all right..."

I moan again, "Yes. It's all right."

Linda straddles me, sitting partially on my ass, partly on my legs. She pulls her legs in next to mine and begins rhythmically moving her hands up, gripping my neck, and then sliding them down my back as her thumbs push in against my spine, until finally, in the completion of each long stroke, she grips my hip bones and pulls my bottom up against her front, and with each pull she pushes her pelvis in against my buttocks, until we are moving together in a dance, breathing together, moaning together, wet with each other's sweat, and I am moving with her, under her, joined in with her in this dance with her wonderful fingers and hands and pelvis until she falls over me exhausted, and I can feel her breathing, her soft breasts against my back, and her hands are sliding down under us. I lift my hips; let her unbuckle my belt, unzip my slacks, take my swollen cock in her fingers, and squeeze. There is no resistance in me. I surrender myself into the warmth of her strong hand. We stay put. I am content. But after a long moment of unmoving intimacy, she lets go of me, and I roll over on my back to face her.

She sits up over me, flushed cheeks, tendrils of blonde hair in her face, wonderful caring eyes, drops one shoulder and removes her unbuttoned shirt. She tosses it aside. Shakily, she stands up over me on the couch. Never takes her eyes from mine. Pulls her pants down over her hips. Steps out of them. Slides her black panties down. Kicks them away. Bends down and pulls my pants off over my feet. Drops them on the floor. Slowly kneels, then sits down on my thighs, and focuses on my penis rising straight up before her. She reaches out. Her long fingers close around it. She bends over and licks it, and then takes it into the heat of her mouth. We are flowing together in the same river, touching, tasting each other, and then she is rising up over me. She lifts her hips and then settles herself down over me, slowly dipping me into the pool of her wet heat, until my pelvis is pressed against hers, and we are coupled together, rocking back and forth, and the couch is singing with us, and the springs are groaning with us, now, now, now, now now.

We lie still. Sweat drips. Our bodies are stuck. A thick glue seems to hold us together. After a while, she presses her head against my chest and whispers, "You were so upset... Is it okay?"

"It's okay."

"I'm not sorry. Are you?" she asks.

"No. I'm not sorry," I say.

"But are you all right?"

"Yes, but…"

"I just wanted it to happen…"

"I don't know what or who I am."

"Shush now."

"I'm so tired."

Caressing my cheek, she says, "It's okay."

I take hold of her hand; lift myself up on one elbow.

"Can you let yourself out? I have to go to sleep now."

She pushes herself off me, stands, then gathering up her clothes starts for the bathroom. The door is closed. She hesitates a moment and then rushes forward. The door closes behind her. I pull on my pants and then curl up on the couch. There is no way I will sleep on that bloodied mattress tonight. Linda returns, dressed. She spreads a blanket over me.

"Thank you," I say.

She bends down, lightly kisses my cheek.

"Just call if you need me to watch Andrea tomorrow."

[31]

The mental ward is clean, antiseptic, but the windows are barred. Chrissy has a private room. They have given her Thorazine—chlorpromazine—common side effects: drowsiness, psychomotor retardation, skin disorders, sometimes liver dysfunction and jaundice, sometimes masked face rigidity and drooling, sometimes tremors: exact influence on behavior unknown, dependent on chemical balance in certain brain areas. The nurse informs me I can see her for only a few minutes. Afterwards I am to see her doctor and clear any further visits through him.

Chrissy's room is dark. Heavy brown curtains cover the windows. She is lying on her bed dressed in a hospital gown. There are thick bandages surrounding her wrists. Her arms are stretched out beside her body, palms up, bandages up.

She is not asleep, but her eyes are unfocused. I pull my chair closer to her bed. Her head rolls toward me. The rest of her body does not move; her arms lie still. I am not sure she knows who I am.

"Mama? I want my mama. You're not my mama. I don't have a mama. No mama. No mother for me. Please. Please I want *my* mama. Mama, Mama..."

"Chrissy, do you want me to call your mother? I can call her tonight, and I'm sure she'll come to see you tomorrow."

Chrissy stares at me, but she does not move. She says, "I don't have a mother. Do you hear me? I never had a mother. I want one, but I never had one. That's why I want one. That's the way it is. No mother for me. I'm alone you see. There's no one but me."

Her head is twisting back and forth in nervous agitation, arms unmoving, and perspiration breaking out on her forehead. I reach over to touch her. I try to calm her down, "Chrissy... Chrissy, it's me, Eddie. I'm here, I'm here beside you."

It doesn't help.

I try again, "Chrissy, would you like me to call your mother? Do you want her here?"

Her eyes go wild, head rolling back and forth, her tongue licking at her dry, chapped lips. Suddenly her whole face collapses into a look of despair as she begins crying and then shouting, "No! Get out! Leave me alone! I don't want to see you... Get out. Get out!"

A nurse suddenly appears beside me and leads me out of the room. She shuts the door behind us. "There's nothing you can do." She takes my arm and begins gently pulling me down the hallway, but after a few steps I stop, pull my arm away. Chrissy is still moaning. I can hear her muffled voice through the heavy door. My hands are shaking. As if I'm falling down a tunnel, my vision narrowing, I stagger back against the wall and listen to Chrissy scream, and images fly through me like freight cars from a runaway train: *Chrissy's mouth opening as her head tilts back and her body rises up against the restraints, neck cords bulging, and Linda rises up over me, naked, her mouth parted in passion.* I stand with a nurse outside her door in the hallway, not moving, but vibrating, yet I am utterly alone. Chrissy is strapped down in her room, her arms held flat by her side, a large mound of white bandages covering her upturned wrists. I am trapped in my own head with my own betrayals and my own adultery. Several patients in hospital green walk down the hallway, eye me furtively. They cannot see into my head. They do not know who I am. I wrap my arms around myself and slide down the wall while Chrissy screams.

Finally another nurse rushes into Chrissy's room carrying a hypodermic on a tray. A few minutes later Chrissy stops. Her room goes silent. I climb to my feet and allow my nurse to escort me down a long hallway of locked rooms. *Is there one for me?* A large door blocks our exit. It's a one-way door with a small window of unbreakable glass. Anyone can enter, but no one can get out without a key. My nurse unlocks the door. I exit and it closes behind me. With the solid sound of heavy metal falling into place, the lock's bolt slides home. I have escaped. I walk quickly away through a set of swinging doors toward a nurse's station. There is a beefy, pot-bellied security guard in uniform outside the door. He sits with one hip perched on a stool. We nod and then look away.

I don't want this to be happening. I want her back. I want my life back. I don't want to be walking away. I don't want to be leaving her here. With each step down this antiseptic hallway I know I am leaving my life behind me. This is not supposed to be happening. It's wrong. It's all wrong.

I cross over to the hospital's administration building. Chrissy's doctor is on the first floor. His office is dimly lit. Walnut desk, high-backed chair, old medical books are lined up on shelves behind him. He is tall, handsome, and black. His dark eyes seem to swim behind his glasses in a milky brown liquid, impenetrable, distant.

"Mr. uh...Andersen? Have a seat, won't you? I'll be with you in just a few minutes."

His faint Jamaican accent surprises me, but I don't want to talk to him. I don't want to make the effort to talk to him. Chrissy's mother floats into my mind, her mouth set hard in her hatred against even the suggestion of integration in Alabama. I remember the ugliness of the anger on her face that night when she and Chrissy fought about it. I imagine her shock should she ever find out that Chrissy's doctor is black.

Dr. Williams sits behind his large desk filling out papers. He seems serene, so confident behind his desk, wearing his white coat. He is wearing a multi-colored tie displaying pictures of underwater fauna. *Symbolism?* Finally, he closes his manila folder, takes off his glasses, leans back in his dark-leather chair and faces me with the air of a very busy, very tired man.

"Mr. Andersen, I only have a few minutes, but I have to ask you a couple of questions, and I need to let you know what we are doing for your wife."

Why we? Why not I? The royal we?

"Okay," I hear myself say.

"As you can see from your visit today, your wife shouldn't have any visitors for awhile. I hope you agree."

I don't agree. I ask, "For how long, Dr. Williams?"

"That depends on Chrissy. A few days. Perhaps a week. Maybe more. It depends on how *she* feels about it. Right now it is my conviction that she should not see anyone until she asks to see them."

I am listening to my own unsteady voice talking, telling this stranger, "I wasn't sure she knew who I was. She asked for her mother, but then she said she didn't have a mother."

He's careful with me. "Yes, I understand. She is still adapting to her level of medication. She will adjust in a few days. It takes time. We must allow Chrissy to set her own pace. When she wants to see you, I'm sure she'll ask for you."

Is this condescension? Does he think I am to blame?

"All right, Doctor, but you will call me as soon as she asks for me?"

"Yes, most certainly. Now, has Chrissy ever had an episode like this before?"

A vague memory of seeing Chrissy, on campus, inconsolable, sobbing.

"No."

"Has she ever seen a psychologist or psychiatrist?"

"Yes."

Time slows down; I find myself coming awake as if I've sleep-walked into wakefulness. I arrive into a moment of consciousness with no memory of where I have been, how I got there, or quite how to proceed. I take Andrea to the babysitter but do not remember preparing her diaper bag. Yet it is all there in my hand. Exactly as it should be. Someone must have done it. It must have been me. I call the welfare office. They ask me questions. I hear my voice tell them that Chrissy has been in an automobile accident. I am making up lies without thinking. I am telling her boss that I don't know when she'll be released. My voice tells them they should mail her last paycheck to her home address. I go to my classes and then, as if all my worst nightmares were coming true, I discover I am unprepared for the class discussion. I wander around in Greenwich Village. I sit in a piano bar in the afternoon, in a dim, smoke-filled room, until it's time to pick up Andrea. After I put Andrea to bed, I stay up late, smoke some of Gary's grass, listen to the new Bob Dylan album, *The Times They Are a-Changin'*.

The next morning I wake and discover Linda in my bed, a nymph with soft blonde hair and a refugee smile, and a naked, warm, rosy body. Holding my erect penis in her hand, she kisses me and tells me not to worry. Rod has scheduled early morning classes. She rolls over on top of me, sits up, and says, "I'll make love to him in the evening if he wants me. I'll make love to you in the morning after he's gone."

The phone call from Dr. Williams's office doesn't come for five days. When it finally does come, I take Chrissy a black notebook of blank pages, a pen and pencil set, a drawing pad, colored pencils, and a single red rose in a crystal vase surrounded by green fern and white baby's breath. I knock on her door as I enter. She's sitting up in bed. The bandages on her wrists are much smaller, white tape over narrow cotton pads. As I look, she turns her wrists in against her body. I look up; feel caught; embarrassed. She looks away. She has put on lipstick, pulled her hair straight back with a purple ribbon.

"I have a roommate now," she says, indicating a second bed in the room, "but she went down the hall so we could be alone."

I put the rose on the table beside her.

"That's lovely," she says in a small voice.

I spread out the rest of my presents on her bed. "I brought these in case you felt like writing or drawing."

She doesn't touch them. Her wrists are still clamped to her sides. She says, "How's Andrea? I've missed her so much... I can't see her now. Not the way I am. But I miss her dreadfully. Funny, isn't it? I want to see her, but I don't want to see her. I'm not ready, I guess."

The curtains are pulled back from the barred windows, and sunlight is suddenly bright as it breaks through a cloud. A breeze stirs the curtains. Light fills the room.

"Chrissy, you look great. Andrea's fine. Linda's helping out...she... takes care of Andrea for me a lot...well, she's been a big help."

"Yes, I'm sure she has."

She lifts her head, picks up the book and spins through the blank pages. She keeps her wrists turned down, away from prying eyes.

"Do want me to bring you something to read? A novel?"

"No. Not right now."

"How do you like your doctor?"

She perks up, speaks forcefully.

"I like him...he's very popular on the ward. I think I'm in love with him. I've never been close to a black man before."

Why is she saying this? Did she hear something in my voice about Linda?

"What do you mean?"

More confident now, bravely, she stretches out one bandaged hand, takes mine and raises it slowly to her cheek, says, "Eddie, I've thought a lot about you and me."

She turns and faces me.

"Dr. Williams and I spend a lot of time talking about us. I've gone over our whole life together with him. Yesterday, after I'd finished talking to him, he said, 'It hasn't been a very good marriage, has it?'"

She pauses, watches me closely, then continues, "His question shocked me; it even made me angry. I didn't see how he could say that, but I've thought about it a lot since then."

Stunned, I take hold of her hand, interlace my fingers with hers, careful of her bandaged wrists.

"What did you say to him?"

"I told him that it might not make any sense to anyone else, but that he was wrong to characterize it that way. I told him you had stuck by me in spite of all the bad things that happened, most of them not your fault. I told him about all the things that went wrong with Doug, and Tim, and Anita, and Sarah, the people I've loved..."

She squeezes my hand, looks as if she's going to cry, but doesn't.

"And I told him about my infidelities, but I didn't talk about what it means when you share what we've shared together, you and I. We had a baby together."

She looks down at her wrists, shakes her head, lets go of my hand, and pulls away. She looks out the window and speaks as if talking to herself.

"Sure there were bad times, but there were some good times. I can't pretend to be somebody I'm not. I have to have a life that's worth living... I can't just go on pretending, but there were some good times..."

"Yes, of course there were, of course."

Turning back, she seems suddenly to remember that I'm in the room with her. She looks confused. Her focus wanders. She's quiet, but then, picking up the thread of our conversation, she seems to be herself again.

"Eddie, think about it...it's...well, we have been through hell, you and I, but not because we didn't like one another. I mean we are who we are. Perhaps we should never have married, but we've tried to live a real life. We tried to live by our own rules, not ones made up by politicians and preachers. Maybe we didn't always know what we were doing, but we weren't afraid to try and find out what was real and what wasn't...like my mother. Everybody lies, but we tried to know the difference...even when it hurt. Our relationship can't be defined so simply as 'it was good,' or 'it was bad.' We found each other, and we got married. It's what happened. We didn't go to sleep, and I don't accept standards that don't apply."

She lets go of my hand and looks at me expectantly. I'm not sure where she's going with this. I nod affirmatively.

She continues, "There are things I didn't talk about. I didn't tell him about Anita's last visit, but I talked at length about Tim and Anita and me. And about Allan and Sarah and me. And I told him about my mother's affairs... But the one thing I don't like about my doctor is how he wants to put everything into a box so he can wrap it up and give it back like it's his gift to you."

She stops and waits for me to say something.

I think about Doug, and then about Tim and Anita and Sarah, Chrissy's lovers? And suddenly I am grateful for Linda's affection, grateful for the flashbacks that are here with me even as we speak. My secret.

I don't say anything.

"Eddie, do you still love me?"

Her voice brings me back into the room, to this strong-willed woman, the mother of my child, who even now is trying her best to figure things out, who will not accept the easy explanations of her doctor.

Linda disappears.

"Chrissy, I love you. Sometimes I think I've hated you too, but... well, what is a good or bad marriage? I don't know what that is, but that sounds like somebody else's idea, somebody back in Alabama. It's not about us. All I know is that I have come to New York to be with you because when I'm alone without you, I don't know who I am, I don't know what I'm doing when you're not with me."

"Eddie... It's not fair. You can't ask that of me... I am not sure I can be your wife anymore. I am more and less than what you think of me."

She looks down at her wrists. Tears begin welling up in her eyes.

We both look out through the barred windows.

"Chrissy, are you still taking Thorazine?"

"Yes, every four hours. They're going to take me off it slowly, starting in a few days."

"Does that mean they're thinking about letting you out soon?"

Sudden strength in her voice, "No, I don't want to leave. I don't want to leave until I know...until I don't want to stay here any longer."

A knocking at the door, and it's Chrissy's roommate, frail-looking, thin, long brown hair, big eyes in an oval face. She stands, one foot on top of another, playing with strands of her ponytail. She puts them in her mouth with her left hand, holds up a deck of playing cards in her other hand, says, "Chrissy, would you and your husband like to play some bridge with us?"

I see white jagged scars on her thin wrist as she holds up the deck of cards.

As we follow Chrissy's roommate to the card table, I remember Chrissy saying that when she was a teenager and visiting her father, he'd taught her to play bridge. And each time she made a mistake, her father would stop the game and place one finger in the middle of her forehead, and hold it there for a long time, saying nothing, just staring at her, testing her, not letting her knock it away, until it drove her crazy, and then he would lecture her about paying attention because bridge was an important game to master, because important people would base their opinion of her on how well she played bridge.

I take Andrea to Central Park. She walks unsteadily in the grass, pulls flowers, smiles at everyone. We are father and daughter in the park—her chubby pink fingers grasping her shovel, her fat forearms, a crease for a wrist. I back away from her for a moment, pretend I am not the father. Andrea's just some little child playing in the park, a child who has no father or mother; she doesn't realize she's abandoned; she plays securely, unaware of the city surrounding the park, unaware of the absence of her mother and father, unaware of all the people who live in hospitals, who live behind bars.

She sits down, opens one hand on a crushed flower; she wants to show it to someone; she crawls around in a circle searching for someone; she calls out "DaDa, DaDa." No one answers. The sheltering sky opens over her. She rises, stands unevenly against the universe; she is not afraid; she sits down again; her legs bend at the knees and she is on the ground. She drops her prize. Forgets it. There was no one to show it to. It lost its value. I sweep down on her, pick her up and swing her around. There is something solid to the universe after all. There is a little girl, squealing with delight, who is being thrown into the sky. There is a father who catches her, who cuddles her in his protective arms.

Chrissy's black book diary entry.
It is a stark and frightening fact that nobody but me knows what

it is to be me. The bright lights that have exploded in my head and the heavy hurt that I carry in my breast—they're mine. They belong to my aloneness, to that dreadful, awesome gift of myself, to that thing I cannot give away and can't really even share.

These words I write now do not show me to you who read them.

These words are my cover-up, don't you see? I can't let you see me. But in spite of myself, without wanting to, I call out to you, I reach, knowing you can't be held and you can't hold me. We are forever you and I, not we. And that's the hardest thing I know.

"Do you have an appointment?"

"Yes."

"Your name please?"

"Eddie Andersen."

"Just have a seat. Dr. Williams will be right with you."

Old copies of magazines, *Life, Parents, Reader's Digest*, hard-backed chairs, and smooth-topped coffee tables.

Inside his office, tall, self-assured Dr. Williams stands, extends his manicured fingers, then sits and opens the case history file on his desk. He pushes his glasses up on his wide nose and reads. He tells me he wants to include his study of Chrissy in a statistical study he's working on in conjunction with Vanderbilt University Hospital. Is that okay?

I agree and ask, "Dr. Williams, can you give a prognosis?"

Raised eyebrows. "Prognosis?" He closes the file. "No, Mr. Andersen, I don't think so."

"Can you tell me what you think is the problem? You must be able to tell me something…"

He picks up the file, looks through it, puts it down again.

"Can you at least tell me how long she will have to stay here in the hospital?"

After a long moment, he answers in careful, mellifluous tones. "I don't think it would be of any value to try and label your wife's problem, Mr. Andersen, but I can tell you that I do believe it would be most beneficial to get your wife back into the outside world as soon as possible. I have two reasons for thinking so. In the first place, this hospital is not designed to handle patients over a long period of time. Here we handle short-term situations, with emphasis on outpatient care. If a case requires long-term care we prefer to reassign patients elsewhere. Secondly, I don't think your wife requires long-term care. So, I want to put her on an outpatient basis beginning next week."

He leans back in his chair, his framed medical diplomas on the wall behind him.

"But, Dr. Williams, Chrissy doesn't believe that she's ready to leave the hospital just yet…are you sure she's ready?"

Coming forward in his leather chair, he picks up a fountain pen from his desk, unscrews the top, screws it back on again. Then twirling it in brown fingers highlighted by pink, manicured nails, he looks at me as if he's prepared now to explain something to a slow student. He says, "Mr. Andersen, most of our patients come here because the outside world is too upsetting, too complicated for them in one way or another. Here we build up a buffer zone for them. We protect them from the outside world. They have no responsibilities here. They have plenty of activities and someone on whom they can unload all their anxieties. Most patients begin to build up a dependency on this buffer zone and the protection it provides them from the outside world. Here they are safe; they don't have to cope. And that's as it should be for a while. But we don't want to encourage our patients to live in a hospital. We want to encourage them to live in the real world, outside, learning to cope under their own resources."

He waits for me to respond. But I have nothing to say. He shows me his busy face, and continues on hurriedly. "I know Chrissy doesn't wish to leave just yet, Mr. Andersen, but I do think she should be strongly encouraged to do so. We will let her adjust to the idea slowly, with walks, with attendants at first, and then by herself. I think she'll come around once she realizes that we will be here for her to see on a regular outpatient basis."

"Dr. Williams, uh…you don't think she will try again…to kill herself?"

"Frankly, no, I don't think so. If a person is truly determined to commit suicide then, of course, there's nothing any of us can do. But in my opinion Chrissy has learned a lesson, and I think she knows now there are easier solutions. Suicide is not exactly the easiest way out, and most suicides really kill themselves accidentally because that was not what they really wanted. Well, Chrissy is quite an intelligent girl, and I'm sure she understands herself a bit better now."

He gives me a manufactured, congratulatory smile. "But you must be prepared to keep an eye on her and try to keep her spirits up. Do you think you can manage that?"

I am not sure of anything, but I nod agreement.

"I know that it's been hard on you, Mr. Andersen, but I think she is making progress, and things will go well for her."

Walking home past Saint Mark's church, past policemen on horseback, past the canopied shops and restaurants, past the Greeks, Italians, Arabs, blacks, everyone in a hurry in the afternoon sun. The sweet smell and sounds of the street: sweat, hot tar, the jackhammer's black dust, construction and deconstruction. Everywhere. The city changes even as I walk by. A kind of violent impermanence. Change or be trampled underfoot. There is no permanent truth. Chrissy is not the Chrissy I thought I knew, if ever I knew her. Do I even like her? Why am I here? Where am I going? I don't know what to do. If I leave her will she survive? And what about Andrea? I walk slowly. I'm not ready. I have to pick up Andrea soon. Can I leave Andrea with Chrissy and get an apartment on my own? Can I afford to live here on my own? Can we work out an arrangement? Like Sartre and Simone de Beauvoir? Can I learn to go where I have to go? Tomorrow the hospital will release her into my care.

Chrissy's black book diary entry.

A glimpse of Mystery: that love must break through barriers of need and can and does. And though we are encased in our need and near suffocation for the lack of the pure love of the free spirit, there is this wholly other God, which cannot be denied, which is Truth.

Truth is a controversial term. I suggest that Truth is that which we sometimes glimpse and long for, but into which we cannot look fully because we are creatures of the cold dark. We have crawled out of Plato's cave, upward, and we seek our completion in the warm light. But we cannot survive except in the shadow of Mystery.

Oh, if only we could leave Truth behind, then perhaps we could wrap ourselves in the mantle of Mystery, we could put out this chill, and we could walk unafraid upon the land...

[32]

*Rarely are we met with a challenge...to the values
and the purposes and the meaning of our beloved
Nation. The issue of equal rights for American
Negroes is such an issue...the command of the
Constitution is plain. It is wrong—deadly wrong—
to deny any of your fellow Americans the right to
vote in this country.*

**President Lyndon B. Johnson speaking
before Congress after the passage of
the 1965 Voting Rights Act.** [12]

Saturday afternoon, after putting Andrea down for a nap, I'm about to open my books when there's a knock at the door. It's Linda and Rod, over for a quick visit. I offer them drinks and pour myself a Coke. Rod wants Jack Daniel's over ice. Linda takes hers mixed with Coke. Rod sighs wearily as he loudly sips his drink and takes a seat on the sofa, ignoring me. He stares after Linda, who appears to be ignoring him as she walks primly over to the table, gives me a significant look, raises her eyebrows, proprietarily gathers up some of my dirty dishes, and begins washing and stacking them in the drainer next to the sink.

"Where's Andrea?" she asks over her shoulder.

"Napping," I say. "She didn't sleep well last night. She's got a diaper rash." Rod fidgets uncomfortably as Linda placidly does my dishes. She whistles a popular Beatles' tune, "I Want to Hold Your Hand." He picks up a magazine, thumbs through it, puts it down.

He's been having a hard time with graduate school. His grades are not up to par. His scholarship might be in jeopardy. If he loses it, they'll have to move back to Tennessee.

"What are you guys up to?" I ask Rod as I stand and begin straightening the room, picking up some of Andrea's toys, reorganizing our books and magazines, trying not to act as awkward as I feel.

"Oh, I don't know, I'm trying to take a break..." Rod pauses, but then Linda cuts him off. "Yeah, right." She moves in between us, swirling and clinking the ice in her drink, and perches herself on the arm of the sofa. Looking down at her own tight blue jeans and high-heeled, ankle-high, lace-up black boots, she says, with faux sweetness, "Oh, he's with me today. You see, we're on our way to do some shopping, and I thought since we were out we should drop by to say hi and see if you needed help with Andrea tomorrow. We're going out to shop for curtains for our kitchen, and maybe buy some new dishware, and besides, since Rod's taking a break from his books, he can afford to spend some time with his pretty little abandoned wifey, and so maybe we'll even take in a movie."

Rod leans back, crosses one leg over his knee, and swings his penny loafer back and forth. He sighs and mutters under his breath, "Oh, shut up, Linda! Sometimes you're so bourgeois..."

Linda laughs. Turns. Looks at me in mock shock. She stares down at her curly haired husband. "Yeah. Okay, so I don't care if I'm not as educated as you are. So what? Who pays the bills? Who's been paying them for the last four years? Yeah, me!" She points a finger at herself.

Rod runs his fingers through his thick hair and sighs audibly, almost a nasal gurgle, as if to say, well, what can you do with her anyway. He stands, downs his drink, and says, "I think we'd better go. Sorry about all this."

I stand also, "Hey, no problem."

We walk to the door, stand waiting. Linda is back at the sink, rinsing out Rod's glass. "You ready to go?" he asks her.

Linda puts Rod's glass away in the dish drainer, picks up her drink, and ignores us. She swirls her finger in her drink, pushing the ice around in small circles, then puts it in her mouth and sucks noisily. She looks up, says peevishly, "Aw, go back home. You don't want to go shopping with me. Besides, I want to talk to Eddie about Andrea. Let me finish my drink. I'll be along in a minute or two. I'll go shopping by myself tomorrow."

Rod remains standing. He pleads with her, "Linda, come on."

I try to be invisible.

Linda refuses to give in. "Go! I said I'd be along in a minute."

Rod shrugs his shoulders and walks out.

I close the door behind him.

Linda strolls over, plops down and stretches out on the couch. Then she rolls over onto one elbow and says, "Honestly, I don't know what I'm going to do with him. I think I should leave him. He's such a baby sometimes."

I remain standing, leaning my back against the door as I tell her, "Linda, I'm planning to take Andrea with me tomorrow. I want Chrissy to see her as soon as she walks out of that hospital door."

Linda sits up quickly. She gives me a fierce look and asks, "Is it over between us? Just like that?"

I come over and kneel down before her.

Looking hurt she says, "I knew that when Chrissy came home it'd have to change between us, but..." She holds out her hands, palms up. I take them in mine. She continues, "Yes, I guess it is, isn't it? Over, I mean. But...all right, I knew...but Rod doesn't talk to me. He ignores me until he wants sex... I don't think he even likes me."

I sit down beside her. "Linda, that awful night when you came over and took charge... I was going over the edge. You not only helped out, you saved me. You pulled me back into my body, into *my* life. I don't know what I would have done without you. I'll never forget what you did. But we didn't make any promises. We just let ourselves love and be loved. Didn't we?"

"I know. I just thought, maybe..."

One tear runs down her cheek.

"Linda, please..."

She stands up, her back to me. "I guess I'd better go. Rod's waiting for me. I was mean to him. I'll make it all better." She pushes her hair back with both hands and then wraps her arms around her body. "Yes, well, I guess it's okay. Isn't it? I mean we can still be friends, can't we?"

I put my arms around her warm body, whisper, "Of course, we're friends. I count on it. Look at me. Are we friends?"

She spins around quickly with a bright smile and says cheerfully, "I think I'll dye my hair."

Chrissy's first day out in the open, I take her to Tompkins Square Park. The small bandages on her wrists are barely noticeable. She says that there's a chill in the air. She wears a bright yellow sweater and a plaid skirt with brown and yellow squares. It's an overcast day. There is a feeling of early autumn in the park. Andrea makes noises in the sandbox beside us, filling, emptying, and refilling her bright red bucket with cement-colored sand. Chrissy is very careful with Andrea, who has become shy around her. Andrea reaches out for me, squirms when Chrissy picks her up, but she doesn't cry. Chrissy, for her part, seems content to take what she can get. She hugs Andrea, kisses her on the neck, and puts her back down.

Chrissy floats back and forth in the playground swing, her arms around the chains, her hands in her lap. A breeze plays in her hair. We do not talk. Words feel dangerous. We are simply present for each other. She smiles, light and gentle as she swings by. I back up quickly, step behind her, and give a small push on her bottom. Time has slowed down. She leans back in the swing, feet in the air. I stand aside, watch her climb into the sky. It's like she's floating. She leans back with a small grin, a playful sparkle in her eyes. She is swinging back and forth, all yellow and brown, floating. As I look up into the gray sky at the trees lining the street across from us, a big wind kicks up, and a bright yellow leaf floats by overhead, twisting and turning like a kite without a string. Andrea begins to cry. The wind has blown sand into her eyes.

Chrissy's mother is on the phone. I say, "Evelyn, Chrissy has been in the hospital, but she's home now. Yes, she's all right. Yes, she was there for a little over a week. Well, she tried to kill herself. Yes, it's true. She slashed her wrists. Yes, really, but she's all right now. She's fine. Yes, sure, by all means, fly up this weekend for a short visit."

Bill calls from the terminal. They're here.

Chrissy is nervous. I have never seen her like this before. She and her mother never discuss anything; they always fight. She pulls at her hair, chews her nails; her fingertips are red, raw, and so sore she can't touch anything without wincing. She looks at me with puzzlement, as if to ask, "What's happening to me?"

After the hellos, after we open the door and Bill and Evelyn enter our apartment, emotionally it's like a change in the weather, like a high-pressure system has moved in, surrounding us, stifling our ability to talk, and building slowly into a silence that extends outward around Evelyn and Chrissy. They stand face to face in the center of the room, not speaking.

Bill is wearing his Sunday best, a dark-blue suit, a black string tie, and a white shirt that pinches his neck.

Ever the stylish one, Evelyn is wearing small, crescent-shaped gold earrings with green stones in the bottom curve. Her hair, recently cut, is now streaked with blonde and brown waves—she's still a stunningly pretty woman.

Chrissy, pale, bones too visible in her thin face, wears tennis shoes; a wrap-around, wine-colored skirt; and a white, long-sleeved blouse with a bow. Her dark, unplucked eyebrows cross over the bridge of her nose like iron filings caught in a magnet. She walks into the center of the room, stops, and stands before her perfectly coiffed mother like a poor relative or supplicant. But, as their eyes meet, there is a fierceness in the of two them that stretches into a long silence. Neither greets the other, and the room grows eerily quiet.

No one speaks. Then Chrissy extends her arms toward her mother and slowly turns her hands over, palms up, exposing her wrists. The bandages only partially cover the jagged, angry, red scars that disappear beneath the thin strips of gauze and white tape. Evelyn stares, open-mouthed, and then her gloved hand goes to her face as she starts to cry, turning away from Chrissy toward Bill. He takes her in his arms.

"Oh God," Evelyn murmurs into Bill's shoulder, "My baby, oh my baby...how could you do this to yourself?"

Andrea begins to fret and cry out from the bedroom. Chrissy drops her arms to her sides. Evelyn remains with her back to Chrissy, burrowing into Bill's shoulder, reaching for a white handkerchief from her handbag, sobbing and sniffling. Chrissy stares after her mother, then walks into the bedroom. The door closes with a bang.

Bill and Evelyn sit down. Evelyn sobs bitterly, to no one in particular, "How could she? It's a sin, for God's sake."

Bill and I look awkwardly at one another, and then, after a long silence, he says, "Weather ain't been much good for fishin' this summer, too hot, but I go out every Sunday, after church service, catch one or two ever so often, crappie or bass occasionally. I clean 'em at the river and cook 'em up when I get home. She likes 'em fresh. They's good eatin.'

There are no more confrontations. Bill and Evelyn leave New York City the following day. They do not call from their hotel to say good-bye, and for three days after they leave Chrissy won't get out of bed except to go to the bathroom. I worry that she's increased her daily dose of Thorazine.

On the fourth day I make a plan. A plan to force her to get up. I fix her some coffee and toast and bring it to her bed. I sit by her side and shake her, but she ignores me. Then I pull her up to a sitting position. She goes limp. She says, "Leave me alone." I lift up her head and try to make her drink some coffee. She knocks it out of my hand. It spills all over the bed. In my frustration I begin screaming at her, shaking her, "You don't care, do you? You don't give a good goddamn about me or Andrea!"

Her eyes come open. She looks at me, but she doesn't speak.

"You don't care about anyone but yourself, do you? You're not interested in how much of a pain in the ass you've become."

Her eyes now seem to snap into focus as she shoves her hair out of her face, says, "Yes, I care about you, and I care about Andrea."

"But not really. Just look at yourself. You haven't even put on clothes for three days. For three fucking days, and I'm fed up with you!"

She comes up on one elbow. She's angry. She says, "Well, get out then. Leave me. I never asked you to take care of me. You're not my keeper. Get out. Go back to Birmingham. That's where you belong. Get out, get out, get ooout!"

I lean down into her face, crowding her, "No way, baby."

She pushes at my face, my chest. I push back. She glares furiously and spits as she speaks, "What do you mean, 'no way, baby.' Listen to you, you fuck-head. Get out of my life. I don't need you. Do you think, *do you really think* you can be my keeper... You don't understand anything...there is no way you could ride the wild horse of my emotions."

"I can try if you give me a chance..."

"What a laugh. You're a nice guy, but you don't get it. Haven't you figured it out yet? You're in love with a lesbian! I'm damned no matter which way I turn."

She looked up at me, speaking softly, almost choking on her words, a tear running down her cheek, "What I want...I can't have."

Then pulling herself together with a defiant gesture she wiped away her tear.

"But you know what: unlike some, I haven't lied to myself about what I am!"

"But I love you...we can make it work. I know you care for me," I tell her.

"Eddie, get over it. I don't desire you. I don't even like for you to touch me. I'm in love with Anita, but she won't have me. We were lovers, but she can't deal with it. She's afraid. When push comes to shove, she's like everybody else. She tries to avoid even looking at what it means to be in love with another woman. She can't face it. Go away, Eddie. Just go away."

Backing up now, staring down at her, holding myself still, her words echoing in some reverberating sound chamber in my head, *a lesbian*, but managing to slow myself down, breathe evenly.

What is she saying? Is this real? Is everything I believed about us simply self-delusion? Or is she trying to protect me?

Trying not to react, trying to stay calm even though I see my hands are shaking, trying to get my equilibrium back, I say, "No...I'm not going to leave you, not now, not like this. You're right, I am not your keeper, and I never should have tried to be, but I love you, and I'm not going to leave you. Maybe I'm wrong, but I think I know you better than you think I do. And you can go if you want. You can leave. You did it once before. But you have to get out of this fucking bed in order to leave. So if you want to go, go. Get up, get dressed, and go. I'll give you half of our money. Go, go on; it's your decision..."

She just glares at me.

"Okay, so you think you're a lesbian. Okay, I get it. And I am not your keeper. So next time, if you want to kill yourself then go ahead and kill yourself! I won't try to stop you. Once was enough for me. It's up to you what you do with your life..."

I think I have thought it through. I feel like I've entered into some dark labyrinth in order to find her and lead her back to safety, but she won't go. I think I have to challenge her to come with me. I think, even as my words are bouncing off the walls with my challenge, that I have understood what's going on, and that I know what I am doing. She needs to know that she's a free agent.

She's sitting up now. She's breathing hard, but her eyes are fixed on mine, and she's listening. She raises a hand as if she's about to protest.

"Chrissy, wait. Let me say something."

Her hand comes down.

"We can't go on like this. I can't do it anymore. There has to be an end to it...you have to try, you have to want to try...and if you don't want to try, then there's nothing I can do about it. It's over."

She pulls back and looks up at me, and suddenly, like magic, she's all there, the old strong Chrissy who is not afraid of anything. Even though we are both still breathing hard, she is looking around as if she's just awakened and is not sure where she is.

She offers me a wry smile, says, "Okay. It's a deal."

As I reach over to pick up the empty coffee cup, I turn back because I feel strange, because I know without looking that she's watching me, and I'm watching her. We can see into each other. It's as if we are tuned into one another, like matched tuning forks, vibrating, alive, without sound, with some inner certainty of feeling that crosses over into a shared reality, or maybe simply into that realm that we sometimes call love. But we both know, in some strange way, that there is no bullshit, no struggling for understanding, and no fighting to force one perspective over another. There is only this willingness to surrender to whatever is required of us, to be present, not out of courage, but out of a sudden, immediate willingness to be with one another, and to go wherever we have to go, at least at this moment, together.

"Don't bother with that. I'll take care of it." She grins, "Sorry about the coffee. Can I have another?"

There is no more fighting. There is only this clear understanding of our agreement with each other. But, in spite of myself, as days go by, her words keep returning: "I don't desire you. I don't even like for you to touch me. I'm a lesbian. You don't get it."

And, truth be told, I don't get it. I think she's just had an affair, and that she'll get over it. But I don't know how to go forward. We are married, but perhaps we should not be married. So time passes, and I wait. We both wait. Days pass, and it's clear, in spite of our new understanding, that she and I are a part of each other. But doubts creep in. Just how are we connected? Should we separate now or should we stay together?

And what about Andrea?

Our conversations about our future plans are careful, too careful, and always inconclusive. Chrissy wanders about the apartment as if she is unsure of her bearings. She grows quiet, and I can feel her slipping.

It's as if she's pulling on some inner thread in quiet desperation, a thread that has grown taut. And the far end of it remains wedged beneath some invisible impediment that's down a dark tunnel she cannot or will not enter. I fear for her, and I fear for me. I fear that the thread will break.

We talk about her "depressions," about her abrupt mood swings. She and I sit up late, almost until dawn, night after night, talking about this inner maze of hers. We draw maps of ways out, of dangerous tunnels we cannot enter. We say she cannot go back to her welfare job; it's too debilitating. We say she might try graduate school. We say we should try therapy with someone we can trust. We don't talk about her mother; we don't talk about Sarah, or Anita or Doug or Tim; we don't talk about Birmingham; we don't talk about her wrists. Each night, exhausted, we seem to reach an agreement on a plan, on how to go forward, but then morning comes, and the way out has not been found.

"I can't do it," she says. "I just can't."

We are exhausted. I have an overwhelming need to sleep.

But then one morning somehow the cycle is broken. At first I don't believe it. I'm suspicious, even when she reaches out and touches me as we pass in the bathroom, an exchange of goodwill, of warmth in hands, of the softness of bare shoulders. I stop, turn around, and as she brushes her teeth, bent over the sink, I allow myself the chance to place my hand below her bra on the small of her bare back. She looks up, gives me a frothy white grin in the mirror before rinsing away the toothpaste. She tells me that she wants to keep Andrea home for the day. She wants to take her to the park, to spend some quality time with her while I'm at class.

At home, early that evening, I pick up an essay on categorical imperatives, about how Kant bases all morality on reason and how what's morally right for one must be morally right for all, not because of some objective reality but because it's how our brains work, how we think. The text is a dense translation from the German. I stop reading. Across the room, Chrissy is laughing out loud as she tosses Andrea into the air before snuggling her up in her arms and loudly kissing her belly and neck. I drop my book into my lap, and I lean back, close my eyes, and listen to our new recording of Edith Piaf belting out, *"Non, je ne regrette rien."*

◁▶

Something has changed, but I don't know what. There is a new clear-eyed deliberateness to her. She is not herself, but she is no longer absent-minded or distracted. She is back in charge of herself. There is sadness about her, but there is also firmness. She goes about the apartment ordering things, washing dishes, arranging towels, and putting everything in its place. She sits down, picks up her guitar, strums a chord or two, and then puts it back in its black case in the hall closet.

"Chrissy?"

She walks over to me. Her eyes are sad. She runs her hand through my hair, looks off into the distance.

"Yeah?"

"Are you all right?"

She gestures toward the book in front of me, *Phenomenology of Perception.*

"How's it going?"

"Okay. We're supposed to be discussing Merleau-Ponty next week. I have a long way to go to catch up."

She backs away into the hallway. I can't see her face.

"I'd like to go out for a walk," she says. "I need some time for myself...if that's all right with you?"

It's a small challenge. I understand. We have an agreement. We are still very careful with each other.

"All right, but don't stay long...it looks like rain, and it's going to be dark soon."

"Don't worry about me. I can go out for a walk, for God's sake."

"But I will worry about you."

"You study...I can go out of the apartment without ruining your day, can't I?"

"Okay...just..."

"Just what?"

"Oh, nothing. Just have a good walk."

She leaves the room and returns a few minutes later wearing her bright-yellow wool sweater, her brown and yellow plaid skirt, and tennis shoes.

"Take an umbrella," I say.

"I like the rain. I don't want an umbrella."

As she goes out the door, I joke, "If I don't hear from you in an hour, I'm going to call the police."

She frowns. Using two fingers she lifts her mouth at the edges and gives me a smiley clown's face. Then she waves good-bye.

The moment the door closes behind her, I lose my ability to concentrate. The silence of our empty apartment closes in on me. For almost an hour I fight to understand what I'm reading, but as soon as I read a paragraph, I realize I don't remember or understand what I just read.

Something is wrong.

I begin to watch the clock. Another thirty minutes crawl by. It's time for Andrea to wake up, but she sleeps on. I begin pacing the floor; I go into Andrea's room, watch her sleep, and return to the living room. I pace beside the telephone.

Should I call the police?

This is how it must have been:

It's just past rush hour, and the fast traffic of East River Drive flows on at the speed limit. The East River is gray. Lowering black clouds drift over the water. The air is filled with the smell of ozone and the oncoming rain. In the distance, thunder. The sound of a lumbering tugboat drifts over the darkening night. Now a few drops begin to fall, wetting the pavement. At first it's only isolated wet spots, but then headlights are turned on, and then the sound of car wheels dominates as the cars begin spitting streams of water into the air.

The few pedestrians on the sidewalk scurry toward shelter. Some put up umbrellas. But one pedestrian, a female, does not hurry. She has managed to climb over the guardrail and stands delicately on the roadway, close to the flow of traffic. She lifts her head and lets the rain fall over her face, soak her hair, drip down her throat. She pays no attention to the occasional Doppler effect of blaring horns. The frightened faces of drivers fly by and disappear into the dark. She lifts her arms, totters, but gets her balance. Her right foot now rests against the railing. She faces forward, focusing on the speed of an oncoming car. And now she pushes off, like a diver, headfirst into the flow of traffic.

◁▶

I walk back into our bedroom, look around, and then I see it: her black book diary on the table beside the bed. I flip through the pages to the last entry. There is no date.

One should be able to live with some small degree of self-sufficiency, with order and beauty. I cannot. Not if I am allowed only this selfless love that is required of me.

I am what I am. I cannot change it. I have lost control of my life. I can no longer deny it. I'm nothing. What I want I can't have; what I want to be, I can't be; and so I have nothing. I am nothing.

Am I a mother? No.

Am I a wife? No.

There is no love left over if I cannot be what I am. So, there is no value to my life.

◁▶

The phone is ringing, but someone is coming up the stairs. I ignore the phone and rush for the stairs. On opening the door I see a man standing at a neighbor's apartment at the end of the hallway.

He eyes me suspiciously before entering. The phone is still ringing. The hallway is empty. No one is coming up the stairs.

"Hello?"

"Is this Mr. Andersen? Mr. Eddie Andersen?"

"Yes, yes, this is he."

"Mr. Andersen, this is Dr. Samuels's secretary. He has asked me to call you. He would like to see you as soon as possible in his office. Can you come right over?"

Dr. Samuels is the head of the philosophy department. I have never met him personally. I don't know what he can possibly want with me.

"Uh, look, can't it wait... What's it about?"

There is a long pause. "Mr. Andersen, uh, Dr. Samuels didn't say, but I believe it's some kind of emergency concerning your wife."

"Okay, okay. I'll be right over. Thank you for calling... I'll be there as soon as I can make it."

An emergency! Maybe she's all right...

I call Linda.

"Can you come over?"

Down the empty stairs three steps at a time, holding onto the walls, bouncing through the door into the dark street. Pedestrians back up, out of my way, stare after me. Sprinting down the street. Finally flagging down a cab. And then, after arriving and running into the building, I realize I am out of breath. I slow to a walk as I locate the office down a long hallway filled with students standing around chatting before their evening class.

Dr. Samuels approaches me in slow motion in a wrinkled suit, silver-gray hair flowing back from his forehead. His outstretched arm closes around me. Inside his office there is an empty brown leather chair behind his desk. There is a stuffed owl on a perch in the corner. It rises up in my vision like a living thing. I force myself to look away at the mahogany desk with its side table, littered with blue books and papers. They are chaotically stacked. The slightest shift will send them tumbling. The world has gone silent, I realize. I can't hear anything. I reach out to steady myself, but there is this problem with the stack of blue books. They're tipping over in slow motion. I watch as my hand, of its own accord, reaches out and steadies them. But then, as soon as I touch them, like a train arriving in the station, sound tumbles back into the world, the loud conversations of students in the hallways, the shouting and the laughter. Dr. Samuels is speaking to me. I think he's offering me a chair. I can almost hear his words. His face and mouth seem to blur out as he speaks. *Wait, I want to say, wait,* but everything just keeps moving past me as I struggle to catch up. There is this strange delay in my brain. It's as if words come out of his mouth, and then I hear them a few seconds later. Then, suddenly, he closes the door with a bang, and everything comes back together.

"Mr. Andersen, Eddie, Ed, I don't know quite how to say this...the police called me a short time ago...they found your I.D. card on your wife...your wife was in an accident..."

Oh, an accident, only an accident.

"She was hit by a car... Ed, your wife...is dead."

DEAD! What did he say? Okay now, stand up straight. Be clear.

"Dead?"

"Yes, Ed, I can tell you...it was instantaneous...there wasn't any suffering..."

Didn't suffer? No suffering?

I lean against the desk. As I watch the blue books spill onto the floor, I am surprised to learn that I don't care. I just watch them fall because for unknown reasons, the strength in my legs is going out of me and I have to hold on or I will fall.

I stare down at the books. Neither of us moves to pick them up. I want to know... I want someone to tell me what to do. I look up at Dr. Samuels as if to ask him, but I can't say anything.

"...leave them alone. I'll pick them up later. Do you need a few minutes...yes...okay then...a few minutes...I'll be just outside the door."

Where are my tears? Dead. This room, so cluttered, all those blue

books on the floor, focus, think, remember, dead. Chrissy, is it true?
Are you dead?

Dr. Samuels is still standing in the doorway. He says, "Ed, the police are asking if you can come down to identify your wife's body... can you? If you're not ready, I..."

We are in a small chamber of a clean white room with a table in the center. She's on that table. I am dizzy. The room spins, settles, stops on a narrow metal table with a green sheet covering what's underneath.

Is it you? Chrissy, are you in here with us?

The room is brilliantly lit, white walls, white floor, metal table, green sheet. We are closing around it. Dr. Samuels moves forward with a policeman to stand quietly beside me. No one speaks. Then there is the sound of heels clicking on the hard linoleum and a thin, balding man in white steps in front of us, one hand extended to the top of the sheet. He waits, looking at me as if expecting me to say something. I nod, okay. He peels back the green sheet, and steps away.

"Yes, that's my wife...Chrissy," I say, and then everyone backs away, leaving me alone. I step forward. I'm suddenly not sure she's dead. I lean closer, wait for her to sit up. Her hair is wet and pushed straight back away from her face, which is gray. There is a dull pink gaping hole on the left side of her forehead. It's a deep, dark hole. Her eyebrows lie straight, left side joining with right over the bridge of her nose. Her arms are folded across her yellow sweater.

Chrissy? Is that you, Chrissy?

"Could you remove the sheet?" I hear myself asking.

"I'm sorry, Mr. Andersen, but...her legs...well, it's not a pretty sight, we had to break them in several places in order to straighten them out... I'm sorry, but..."

Her legs...they had to break them...to straighten them...her legs...

I remember her soft thighs, her rounded calves. I think of them broken beneath this green sheet, and suddenly my knees give way, and someone is holding me up.

And I think that they think that I'm overcome with grief. But it's just my body. It's always the body, living its own life, the body doing its own thing, trying to take care of me. These people think they see me, but they don't. They interpret my feelings from the way my body is acting. My body is behaving for them; tricking them; giving them all the right impressions. It looks like I'm about to pass out, but I'm not. I'm not just my body. And Chrissy is not just her body. That was not Chrissy over there. She wasn't there. She was no longer with that body. She was gone... Where did she go?

Must call someone. Must find a phone...

"May I use your...telephone? I'll make it collect."

My voice is so distant, like hearing someone else speaking with my voice...

"Yes, of course, right this way."

"Bill, this is Eddie... I'm calling you because...I need to...because there's been an accident. Chrissy is no longer...she's dead... She was hit by a car."

"Good God, boy, you've got to be kidding me, do you know what you're saying?"

"You'll have to tell Evelyn... I can't talk any longer..."

"Wait a minute, boy, you've got to tell me more than that!"

I hang up. My hands are shaking.

"Eddie?" I hear my mother's soft small voice.

"Mother, Mother, listen, I can't talk very much. There's been an accident... Chrissy is...dead."

"Oh no, Eddie, are you all right? Is Andrea?"

"Yes, mother...we're both fine." Tears are streaming down my face. I wipe them away and realize I am losing control of my voice.

"Mother, I can't talk any more."

"All right, Eddie, we'll be up on the first plane. We'll be there just as soon as we can make it. You take care of yourself. We're coming."

"Yes, all right...good-bye, Mother."

As I hang up, Dr. Samuels walks up. He hands me a piece of paper.

"I thought you'd want to see this. The police brought it over...it's addressed to you."

He looks away as I take it from him.

It's a note from Chrissy:

Eddie, it's no use.

Je suis non-recouvrable.

I recognize it. It's from one of Sartre's plays, *Les Mains Sales* (Dirty Hands), about a freedom fighter who cannot deny the choices he's made and acted upon which have all gone wrong, who knows he's doomed, ruined, and unsalvageable.

"But what about me?" I cry out loud, ignoring the strange look on Dr. Samuels's face. "What about Andrea?"

Dr. Samuels stares at me, but he doesn't ask me anything. He just reaches out, takes the note from my hand. He says, solemnly, "The police say they need to keep this for awhile. I don't think they'll need to ask you about it." Dr. Samuels's face seems to waver in the fluorescent light. The glassed-in room seems suddenly filled with twisting reflections. He doesn't feel real, this silver-haired man, this man with the stuffed owl.

Dr. Samuels asks if I want him to come up with me. I tell him no, and I get out of the car. It pulls away. Outside our apartment there is a bent Schaefer's beer can in the gutter, reflecting the light from the streetlamp. I step over it and stand in front of our apartment building, staring at the old ironwork of the ornate railing, at the worn concrete steps, at the row of brass mailboxes beside our front door. Off to one side of our building there are black counterweights dangling from the fire escape. People walk past me. They're speaking in Spanish. A car's horn blares in the distance. A siren wails. Everything is the same, outside. But I stand here, and no one can see the new hole in me. I am containing it, this completely empty space that was once filled with her life. I am keeping it open, but contained. I know it will close soon enough, but for now it is all that remains of her, this hole in me, this wound, this place where she once lived...

[33]

[In Birmingham, Alabama, in a major step
forward to attempt to redress grievances, a new
program is established for the Black Community
as the City Government agrees to take advantage
of] *Project Head Start,* [which was] *launched as
an eight-week summer program by the Office of
Economic Opportunity in 1965...to help break the
cycle of poverty by providing preschool children
of low-income families with a comprehensive
program to meet their emotional, social, health,
nutritional, and psychological needs.*[13]

In Birmingham part of the world is gone, but it's business as usual. The funeral arrangements have been made, and Chrissy's body has arrived at a local mortuary for viewing. It's late afternoon. I sit in my parents' house and receive guests, friends, family, cousins, aunts, and uncles. My many relatives come from far and wide to pay their respects. Some I haven't seen in years. Some have even traveled down from Tennessee. They arrive with small children and home-baked goods: fried chicken, black-eyed peas, turnip greens with ham hocks, fried okra, corn bread, apple pie, peach cobbler. They enter through the back door, drop off their offerings, and solemnly whisper to my mother before approaching me in the living room. They take my hand in theirs and offer their condolences. Then we suffer the overheated house and a Sunday afternoon together and drink my mother's iced tea with a twist of lemon. My relatives talk softly amongst themselves. They gather in a semicircle around Andrea, who sits in my lap, subdued and quiet, as if she knows something is amiss, all of us uncomfortably perched on my mother's French Provincial furniture—recently fitted with clear plastic covers—our bare skin sticking whenever it comes in contact with plastic.

The sun is going down and the heat of the day dissipating when my mother answers the telephone in the kitchen, her voice formal, official. I hear her say, "Yes, I understand, I'll tell him. Of course, just as soon as he can."

She calls me into the kitchen.

"Eddie, they want you to come down to the funeral home. There are people waiting to see Chrissy, but they won't let anyone in until you see her first."

"Tell them to go ahead. It doesn't matter to me."

She looks at me sadly, a nervous tic in her hand as it curls in front of her mouth, her Parkinson's beginning to take its toll. Her head shakes, and her mouth trembles as she speaks.

"Eddie...people have come a long way. You have to go. It's expected. They're waiting for you."

"No, Mother, I don't have to go, and I don't want to go...all those people standing around saying stupid stuff. I'm not going."

A few minutes later, back in the living room, I can hear my father and mother arguing in the kitchen. One of my aunts, my favorite, my mother's oldest sister, the oldest of eleven, the aunt everyone calls Elise, sits down next to me. Elise is a nurse. She always speaks her mind. "Eddie, I think you ought to reconsider. I know you don't want to go, but I also know you don't want to cause trouble. Those people are trying to be considerate. You should understand that and act accordingly. Besides, I know you don't mean to, but you're making this into your mother's problem."

Right then my father enters the room, which suddenly goes quiet, and he stands there facing me, his big belly straining the buttons of a starched white shirt, his tie untied, his face a deeper red than his usual out-of-doors tan. He gives me that look, his blue eyes narrowed, his teeth set, rigid, chin jutting out, and I know this look well, I know trouble is coming. But for a moment longer my mother, always the peacemaker, stops him. She pulls on his big arm, distracting him. As he turns toward her, Elise gives me her significant I-told-you-so look, and so I stand up before he can get started and declare, "All right, I'll go. Where are the car keys?"

My father, condescension in his face, flips them to me, turns away, and two of my first cousins, teenagers, Linda and Joan, resume their suspended conversation about boys as I walk by them into the dining room, past the bowls of potato salad, the fried chicken, the home-made biscuits, and into the kitchen where Mootsie and Roseanne, two more of my mother's sisters, are whispering, and then I try my escape out of the house through the back door when my mother calls out to me.

"Eddie, wait a minute."

With my hand on the screen door, I watch my two aunts leave the room. They are leaving us alone for a private conversation. I surmise that I have been the subject of a tête-à-tête. My mother, looking concerned and exasperated, comes close, puts a shaky hand on my shoulder. But before she can speak, I sense what she's about to say, and I try to head her off.

"Mother, I'm okay the way I am."

Her voice steady, she says, "Eddie, you can't go dressed like that."

She points at my loafers, no socks, and my dirty blue jeans.

"I've ironed you a shirt and pants."

I am about to protest when the worried faces of my brother Bobby and my sister, Katie Anne, appear on either side of my mother, probably recruited by my aunts, and I decide it's not worth the upset to fight.

"Okay," I say and push past them to go change my clothes.

Back in the spare bedroom, I stand before the dressing room mirror in the small space between the baby crib and an old mahogany four-poster bed with my partially unpacked suitcases spread open behind me, the bright-blue diaper bag on the floor, and my dirty clothes draped over the only chair. It occurs to me that this funeral is not about Chrissy, or Andrea, or me. My thoughts are as scattered as my clothes. Evelyn is taking over. And my mother and father are her willing accomplices. Since I refuse to go over and see Evelyn, she has been organizing through my mother. I keep trying to hold onto my own private connection to Chrissy, but it keeps slipping away.

Glancing in the mirror I realize I haven't shaved in a week. I hardly recognize myself. Then thinking back over the last few days I sense a plan. I can feel Evelyn's hand in all of this. She'll have talked to the minister and set up the plan for how the funeral will go. Probably she wants to be the center of the show, put her grief on display: *My beautiful daughter is dead. Pity me.* And yes, she'll want to hide the suicide, the sin of it, the stain on the family. But I simply don't have it in me to fight her about it. No one will tell the truth. It will all be buried with Chrissy. Evelyn is so worried about what people will think about her suicide, but no one even knows about her struggle with being a lesbian. No one but me, and I'm not talking. Homosexuality is worse than suicide as far as our families are concerned. How honest can I be?

In the mirror, the unshaven face that stares back at me seems cynical, tired, and detached. My cheekbones stand out against this new growth of beard. I feel better behind it, but there is still this heavy lethargy that hangs over me like a fog. I don't know what I'm doing. I'm just standing still while events continue to swirl around me. Even my beard growth is something that is happening while I watch...

So after I have put on my black (mother-polished) shoes, clean and pressed slacks, and a shirt still smelling of a hot iron and starch, I stop at the back door and face my mother. She's standing next to the sink, having just finished washing dishes, and is now pouring boiling water from a kettle onto tea bags at the bottom of a large ceramic crock. Beads of moisture gather on her forehead as she pours out the steaming hot water. The tea's aroma mixes unpleasantly with the odor of dish-washing liquid, lemon-fresh Joy, coming from the white suds in the sink. I watch and wait while she adds two cups of sugar to the darkening liquid. She stirs it in with a long wooden spoon, and the Lipton tea bags, strings still attached to their paper tags, rise to the top and circle on the surface. She wipes at her forehead with the back of her hand and then looks me over, a forgotten, red and white checked dish towel dangling from her fingers. I know my mother loves me and that all she wants is for everything to be okay, but I can't help feeling bitter about how all this social formality seems to obscure what has happened, how it makes it impossible to let the sorrow in. I feel like a betrayal is underway, and I am part of it.

"Now are you satisfied?" I say in spite of myself, knowing I'm being obstinate, and knowing that I can't stop myself because everything is wrong, and I am not going to do anything about it; because I am not who I thought I was, because here, in the midst of my family, I am a stranger. Even to myself.

"Eddie, Evelyn called several times to talk to you about this funeral, but you haven't even called her back. You never used to be like this. And you still haven't shaved."

Her lips tremble and her hand shakes.

"Mother, I've talked to Evelyn. She just wants everything her way, and I don't want to fight with her. The more I talk to her the angrier I get. She can have the funeral her way. I don't care."

I turn away from her because I can't answer her unasked questions about why I am behaving so badly, and I walk out into the warm night letting the screen door slam shut behind me. My mother follows me outside, stands in the yellow porch light, hand at her mouth, and waves silently as I climb into the family Buick and back out of the driveway.

Ten minutes later, as I pull into the funeral home parking lot, I see Johnnie Mack, another first cousin, Elise's son, waving to me. He shuffles over. Johnnie Mack will never completely recover from all the football injuries he sustained as a slow-footed, six-foot-four, rollout quarterback. He stands now and waits as I finish parking, shifting from one foot to the other, looking uncomfortable in the heat in his ill-fitting suit and tie. He's a little overweight, I notice as I step out of the car; his belly is beginning to hang down over his belt buckle.

He has still not adjusted his image to fit his new job as an insurance salesman. His gray seersucker suit is wet at the armpits and he looks like he'd prefer running a quarterback sneak, never his favorite play, to being here in a suit and tie. His mother, my aunt Elise, has insisted he come. Johnnie Mack and I have not spent much time together, at least not since the two of us were kids and played tackle football in Woodside Park across the alley from his mother's house.

I get out and we greet each other awkwardly.

"Eddie, I've never had to face what you're...going through...I don't know what to say..." His voice trails off; he's embarrassed by what he's heard about Chrissy; so he looks away over my shoulder toward Red Mountain. I am the center of a scandal, the talk of the family, the man whose wife ran away and committed suicide. Everyone wants to console me, but no one can think of what to say. I follow his look, thinking to find Vulcan somewhere in the distance, but the trees are too dense. There's nothing to see.

To break the silence I say, "They're waiting for me inside." And we walk, without saying more, across the fresh black tar of the parking lot of this new church-oriented funeral home. A huge illuminated cross rises above the apex of the A-frame roof. Inside, on one side of the room, I recognize more of my relatives, Bud and Rebecca, Joe and Jewel; and then on the other side, some of Chrissy's relatives. They all stand up as I come through the massive front door. Immediately in front of me, a black, plastic sign on a small pedestal before an entrance way spells out "ANDERSEN" in block letters.

Through an inner open doorway, a church-red carpet leads down a long aisle to a copper-colored coffin, three immense, backlit, gold-plated crosses rising up behind it. Deciding to get this over with as soon as possible, I stride through the open doors down the aisle, stop, and peer into the coffin. And it's only then, when it's too late, as I look down into the coffin and see her there, that I understand something about why I did not want to come. I did not want to see her like this. But now I cannot look away, and I stand before her transfixed, staring down at this objectified, doll-like version of my wife...

In a long-sleeved green dress, arms folded across her body, she is surrounded and supported by satiny, cream-colored folds. She is visible only from the waist up. Her sleeves cover her arms, which are crossed so the scars on her wrists won't show. On her left temple there is a striking discoloration over the spot where the hole was. Her cheeks are painted rosy pink and powdered. Her hair has been coiffed stiffly bouffant, and she looks like a wax museum version of a debutante, at a coming-out party, except for girlish bangs combed over her forehead, concealing her wound.

This is not Chrissy.

Only the wild eyebrows remind me of her. They still assert themselves. Tiny stubborn black sticks stand straight up in the makeup, refusing to lie down. Her mouth is fixed in a curious crooked smile. I think they must have had to break her jaw...

"She's so beautiful, it looks just like she's asleep."

One of Chrissy's relatives, an older woman dressed in black, with a heavy sagging face, gives me an earnest smile as she moves in beside me. I back away surprised, stunned. She says, "If you didn't know you'd never guess."

I hurry back up the aisle, rudely pushing past my relatives, who are all trying to make eye contact. I can't. I rush by them without stopping and, once outside, break into a jog until I reach my father's Buick. Sweat runs down inside my starched white shirt. The night air is thick with the ubiquitous smell of honeysuckle. I stand immobile, unmoving. Time slows down. I remember Chrissy crossing the street in New York City, in her wine-colored skirt and white tennis sneakers; she steps lightly in slow motion, then stops and turns toward me, a smile of recognition playing over her features, the pedestrian traffic spilling around her.

For a long moment I don't know where I am. Nothing looks familiar, but I don't care. I don't want to go anywhere. I don't want to do anything. I'd like to go to sleep, but I just stand there in the funeral home parking lot, a slow breeze blowing on the back of my neck, and just then Johnnie Mack, both arms extended, bursts through the funeral home doors, spilling light. Before he can turn in my direction, I jump into my father's car and speed out of the parking lot.

Inside the hermetically sealed Buick, in the smell of leather and the soft purring sound of a new car with A/C on, I drive the highway across town, past the smoking furnaces, and then turn left, up Red Mountain, until I am high above the city and can park at a lover's spot, a turnout overlooking the city lights of Birmingham. Occasional traffic winds its way up the dark mountain behind me, headlights flashing briefly in my mirror. I have no idea why I have come here, but I cannot yet go home. The feeling of Chrissy is still around me. I don't want to let her go. I think of all those people standing over her coffin. I want to keep her to myself for a while longer.

The lights of Birmingham are spread out below me. Across the valley the furnaces are alive, glowing. Thin streams of burning red slag wind like snakes along the ground. Somewhere the big buckets of melted iron ore are being poured into molds, and a flame leaps up high into the air and then disappears. I sit and stare and remember Chrissy's words:

> *Oh, the poetry of us,*
> *the music of us,*
> *the painting sight of us,*
> *the eye of us.*

Chrissy was the eye of us.

And then I realize that my body is shaking because I am crying. Not because she's dead. Not because she chose to die. But because without her I feel so invisible. Because I don't know where to go from here. I don't know what I'm doing. Because Chrissy saw me and now she's gone. Because without her I am so alone.

It is a long time before I can bring myself to turn the key in the ignition, but as the Buick's engine comes to life, as the headlights find the road ahead, I know I must go back to whatever's next.

◁▶

An hour later, back at my parents' house, Dr. Bingham, Evelyn's pastor, our neighborhood Methodist minister, who has waited for me, now stands and extends his hand. He's a large man with a soft grip, his gray-streaked hair slicked back with a strong-smelling hair tonic. The living room is empty of relatives.

"Eddie, your mother tells me that you were brought up in the Methodist Church…"

There is accusation in his tone of voice: why haven't you been in church, why don't I ever see you there?

"Yes, that's true. At least I attended Sunday school for a time, when I was a child."

He smiles, pulls up the pant legs of his brown suit, settles back into an easy chair, the plastic covers crinkling audibly, and puts on a pair of black-rimmed glasses. My mother has retreated into one of the back bedrooms with Andrea. Once again, I feel Evelyn's hand in a plan, and I suddenly realize that it is no accident that the two of us are now alone in the living room.

"Well…perhaps I'd better explain why I've come to see you tonight," he says, then waits for me to talk, but I have nothing to say.

"Well, your mother-in-law, Evelyn, as you may know, is a member of my church and she's asked me to conduct the services tomorrow. She's made her thoughts known to me, and so it's my responsibility to respond positively to her requests. But since I didn't really know Chrissy, though I've spoken with her mother about Chrissy at great length, I'd like to find out a few more things from you."

He pauses again, waits, but finding nothing forthcoming, continues.

"Well. Okay, then. There are many things to be decided regarding tomorrow's service that I'm sure you would like to have a say-so about, and I would like the service to correspond with your wishes too. For example, do you desire an open or a closed casket service?"

I watch him take out a small, three-ringed, black notebook and spread it out on his lap, one page covered with careful Palmer Method script. Then, as he unscrews the top of his fountain pen, the vision of Chrissy's broken body in the funeral home, in her satiny casket, returns with an accompanying ugly thought of how someone has tried to make her look like a wax doll, and suddenly it comes to me that this falsifying image is a complete betrayal of her life, a cover-up of who she was. And sure, no one wants to see the broken bones and blood of people who really do struggle to try to live out an honest existence, but do we have to completely lie to ourselves?

"Closed," I tell him.

Dr. Bingham looks surprised but unperturbed, and he writes my answer down slowly, in neat circular letters, followed by a question mark.

"Also, there is the question of the type of service. I myself prefer short simple ceremonies." He's now all business.

I nod in agreement. He takes a note.

"But then there is the problem of her suicide… I assume we all agree that we don't want it mentioned…after talking with her mother I am sure that Chrissy was in such a state that she did not know what she was doing on a conscious level. I am quite sure that she could not conceivably be held responsible for her act, not in my eyes, not by our church community, and not in the eyes of our Lord and Savior, Jesus Christ Almighty."

He looks up for my approval.

"What?" I ask, slowly trying to digest what he's just said.

He continues on with his list as if he hasn't heard me. "Also, are there any special Biblical passages you would like to request?"

He removes his glasses and rubs the bridge of his nose as he waits.

I lean forward, trying to prepare myself to speak calmly.

"Dr. Bingham, I want to thank you for coming tonight. I appreciate it, I really do, and I do want to make some requests concerning tomorrow. But first I need to tell you that Chrissy and I, for some time now, have rejected the religious presumptions of the Methodist church, and we do not accept your beliefs about sin or guilt or God."

I wait for him now, but he does not speak. He leans back into the crinkling sound of the plastic cover of his chair and studies me, holding his glasses up and twirling them in his left hand. So I continue.

"I want you to understand that I would prefer to have no religious service at all, but now…well, since there is going to be one, I would like to provide you with two poems. I'd like you read these two poems and let that be it. I would prefer that you *not* preach a sermon about my wife's death. And I don't want your forgiveness for my wife's suicide, and I don't want you to ask for God's forgiveness either."

Dr. Bingham sits facing me, the tip end of his glasses in his mouth, and concern clouding his face. Sweat trickles over his forehead. In an automatic gesture he pulls out a white handkerchief and wipes his brow. He looks down at the floor, thinking.

"I'm trying to give you what you said you wanted: to know something more about my wife and me. And at the same time I'm trying to tell you, if it matters, how I want the service to be. I apologize if I've offended you."

He looks up, smiles too quickly, and lifts his hands in a practiced gesture of honesty and sincerity.

"Eddie, I'm not offended... I'm only puzzled, and a little confused by what you've just told me. Perhaps you can explain something to me?"

"Of course, if I can..."

"How do you face...no, how are you going to face...this death, Chrissy's death, alone? Without the comfort of knowing that God is with you? Without knowing that there is a plan for all of us, for you? Don't you know that God is always present, that He is waiting for you to come to Him? I know you are feeling this tragedy deeply... But maybe you can explain to me how it is that you are not completely crushed by your grief. Because, without God, without Jesus Christ, we are all of us alone, and we face a universe empty of any promise of life after death, a world empty of any eternal significance. I know for myself that I could not do it. I can only face this world because I have the assurance of everlasting life and the forgiveness and the help of God. Without the grace of God, without His promise of eternal life through Jesus Christ, I would be lost."

"I don't know where to go from here, but I do know that 'eternal life' doesn't mean anything to me and..."

Andrea begins crying and my mother goes into her room whispering, "Shush, shush, honey. Don't you cry; everything's going to be all right."

I hesitate, wait to make sure Andrea is okay, then conclude, "Your belief may comfort you, but for me it's just a pretense."

"I see," he says, "but surely you must believe there's some reason for our existence, some basic ground of being that gives life meaning… Otherwise, when things went wrong we would all kill ourselves, wouldn't we?"

As he puts his forearms on his knees and stares across at me, I start to say, *And maybe more of us would if we had Chrissy's courage*, but then, as I look at his attentive face, I realize he's not listening. He's arguing. And suddenly, I'm exhausted. I want to go to sleep. I don't want to talk anymore. I close my eyes for a moment, and in the silence I feel as if some unidentified and amorphous being is singing to me, but not really, but still it's like someone somewhere from far away is whispering in my ear. Or maybe it's only a memory from my childhood and, if I can focus on it, I can identify it.

Dr. Bingham is starting to talk again, but only a part of me is paying attention. The rest of me is trying to remember a feeling or listen to a sound somewhere inside me, something from my childhood, something like that time when I sat alone beside the Black Warrior River after a rainstorm when the water was singing, swollen with dead branches and leafy debris, or when I stood still and listened to the sound of an ocean wave as it slid in at high tide, as it began settling, sifting downward with that hissing sibilance as it washed away my sand castle. But I can't find it or even identify it and instead, I continue to look toward Dr. Bingham as if I'm listening. And then Dr. Bingham is standing up and shaking my hand, and we are bidding each other good-bye, and I can stumble into the bedroom and sleep.

On an unusually warm, sun-filled day near the end of January, the long line of cars comes to a stop on a grassy hillock overlooking a mound of wet, iron-rich earth. It's rained recently, but now the sun is out. The slick dirt is piled up behind the steep, shadowed emptiness of a waiting grave, hers. As I stand alone in my too-warm wool suit, I remember the morning's ceremony at the funeral home. Dr. Bingham had tried to read one of the two poems I had given him, "And Death Shall Have No Dominion," but his low-key, apologetic approach to the poem fought against Dylan Thomas's insistent rhythms, and it was an embarrassing failure. So then he turned to the Bible and promised the assembly of relatives that Chrissy was now taken back into the fold and forgiven for her sins, and that she was with God, in a better place, and that she was even now looking down on us all from heaven.

In the overheated alcove, as I listened to the preacher drone on, and to Evelyn, seated in front of me, blowing her nose and weeping uncontrollably, I stared up at the light streaming in through a stained-glass rendering of a beautified, long-haired Jesus, hands clasped in prayer, and I wanted to scream for it all to just stop. But I didn't. I sat still. I bowed my head and gave in to propriety and tried to remember the real Chrissy, her poetry, and her willingness to give of herself, all of herself, if she loved you. Yes, it was true—she broke the rules. And she had paid the price. And, as Nietzsche once warned, she'd lost the thread. She'd not been able to find her way out of the labyrinth—she couldn't live if she couldn't be the person she'd tried to be.

As I climb out of the car, holding my handkerchief up to my leaking nose, I step into red mud before I can move under the green canopy that will shield us from the sun. From there I see people gathering along the edge of the chert-red road that leads up to the grave site on the hill: relatives, old and young, hers and mine, and some friends from college in suits and dark dresses. They all walk single file, heads down, toward the grave site.

Mama Barber is not here. Inconsolable in her grief, she wouldn't get dressed or even come out of her room. My aunt Elise is babysitting Andrea. Allan is not here. He left me a phone message saying that he couldn't get away, couldn't get any leave from the U.S. Army. Then I see Sarah standing far back on the road. In high heels, she seems nervous about the soft wet grass in front of her. She takes the arm of—not Allan, but—a tall, handsome stranger, her husband-to-be, I guess, and steps across the curb, balanced on her toes. Head down, wearing a black hat and a form-fitting dress, her long, blonde hair flows out behind her in a light breeze. It occurs to me that maybe Sarah has finally found that man who could take control of her life.

From my side of the open grave, I watch as Evelyn and Bill move toward the folding metal chairs under the green canopy, and, even through her black veil, I can see that Evelyn is emotionally devastated. She seems barely able to walk. Bill, holding her up, bends over as he helps her into a chair. His shiny black hair slicked straight back, he looks over and gives me a darting look through clenched teeth of barely suppressed anger. *It suddenly comes to me that Bill is angry because he believes that I am somehow responsible for Chrissy's death and, therefore, Evelyn's pain.* They are seated away from my family, at the opposite end of the front row. My mother, her shaking hand holding a white handkerchief to her mouth, sits with my red-faced father under the canopy; my younger brothers and sisters, heads down, sit quietly all in a row next to him. My skinny brother, Bobby, seventeen and already taller than Dad, looks up, trying to catch my eye, but I turn my head away. I don't want to be comforted. I prefer Bill's anger.

The graveside service is mercifully quick. Dr. Bingham reads the Twenty-third Psalm. And suddenly, the coffin is being lowered on felt straps into the ground. I watch as it slips down into the clay with a heavy muted thud. And then the workers are shoveling red clay dirt into the grave. I walk to the edge, twist my wedding ring off, and let it drop. It hits the coffin with a bright ringing sound and then spins briefly in the sunlight before landing silently in the dirt. With the next shovel-load it disappears.

It's over. People are talking quietly and crying and moving back to their cars. The funeral director folds the chairs and stacks them and carries them to a waiting truck.

Feeling as lost and alone as Dr. Bingham said I would, I start to walk away when I see Tim. I'd heard that Tim might be released from the mental hospital for the funeral. His arm appears to be in a sling. High up on the green, grassy hillside across the road, his face hidden by the blinding sun and looking like he's posing for a movie, Tim stands rigidly straight, not moving. He stares directly down at me as if he's willing me to hear some secret message he's intent on sending. We do not wave. I don't want to hear him, see him, or talk to him. We just stare at each other until a big, burly, black hospital attendant in a white coat comes up beside him and takes hold of his arm.

"Eddie..."

Anita is standing beside me. One hand shielding her eyes from the sun, she too is looking up the hill where Tim is conversing with his white-coated attendant.

"Did you help bring Tim?"

Turning back to me, she lifts, then tosses her hair over her shoulder and nods her head affirmatively. "We came together."

"Anita, I don't know what to do." I stammer, and then stop.

Her voice is almost inaudible, her lips barely moving as she leans close and says, "Let her go, Eddie, let her go. She was always willing to make the hard choice...wherever it led her. The rest of us weren't. There was nothing you could have done. Let her have her peace..."

She touches my shoulder with a shaky hand, offering sympathy. For a moment we just look at each other. We had both loved Chrissy; I knew that. And, sometimes, we had competed to stay within the intense beam of her attention. But now we are together in our loss even though there are no tears from either of us. And no hugs. Then she turns away and begins walking up the hill where Tim is waiting with his attendant. I watch her go up the grassy knoll, bent over, head down, and turned in on herself, her long black hair falling to her waist. And suddenly I feel intensely, utterly, alone.

I sleep all day. Every day. My mother tells me that Allan has called me from where he is stationed, in New York, that he wants me to call him back. I don't. Anita doesn't call. Tim remains in the asylum. Doug is dead. Chrissy is dead. Sometimes I wake up to a sleeping house just before dawn and eat leftovers from the refrigerator before returning to bed. I climb back in and gratefully draw the heavy covers up over my head, close my eyes, and find sleep waiting for me like a lover who wraps me up in her heavy arms and carries me dreamlessly away.

Sometimes noises slip into my consciousness like comforting reassurances of life being lived out there somewhere, outside my sleep-world: Andrea's cries followed by the sound of my mother's slippers; garbage cans being dragged down the driveway for their weekly pick-up; high winds and rain beating sideways against a window pane; water rattling down the outside drain; the big red oak in our back yard moaning, creaking under the weight of the wind.

Sleep is where I live. Sometimes when I wake I can barely walk around, or eat, or go to the bathroom. My eyes keep closing, and I begin drifting, wanting to go back to my oblivion, to my sleep-world. But sometimes I wake and drive the family car into downtown Birmingham, past Vulcan, past the steel mills. I park in front of Smith & Hardwick bookstore, look in and remember the Praytor sisters shelving books, Virginia—thin, freckled face, red hair tied back in a messy bun—up on a ladder shouting down at Anna who smiles and checks her inventory list. I'd like to go in and help out again, but the store is dark. So I walk the empty streets, traveling in a large circle past the post office, past Kelly Ingram Park where the riots took place, past the Sixteenth Street Baptist Church where the four little girls were murdered, past the A. G. Gaston motel, and return by way of the Birmingham Public Library. Along the way I stop and look for ghosts, but the streets are empty, and so I return home, eyes already closing, ready for sleep.

For six weeks I sleep, but then I begin to dream. It is the same dream. I have it over and over again. I dream I am out in a field in a foreign country, maybe France. I have come in the spring, happy and filled with joy. I am light hearted and gay for no particular reason, the best of reasons. But then the flowers and the shining, iridescent, blue-green river and the smiling, friendly country people begin to seem strange. Worrisomely so. Until I see a warm beauty of a young girl who laughs delightedly upon meeting me. She knows my name. She dances around me, teasing me. She wears wildflowers in her hair, red, like painted daisies, and her hair smells like freshly cut hay. But still there's something wrong. The landscape is confusing, the river troubling. There's some danger I am not seeing. I turn to this beauty standing before me and ask her, "How do you know my name?" She tries to tease me out of asking. She tells me that I don't need to know. Laughs. I reach out. Take hold of her hand. But she pulls away. She backs up and will not let me get close to her again. Then she turns and runs away. I chase after her until I catch her. But now she's wearing a veil, and I can't see her face. She pulls back, looks as if she's afraid of me. She speaks my name loudly, "Eddie." She says that I must let her go, and then she begins twisting and turning, pulling harder, and shouting that I will be sorry if I do not let go of her. And then, suddenly, I know who she is. This is Chrissy. She's not dead after all. Somehow she managed to fake the whole thing. Somehow she simply ran away. How did she do it? I want to shake the answers out of her. How could she possibly have gotten so many people to go along with this ruse? And whose body was that in the coffin? I pull her close to examine her face. But she begins to faint, falling backwards, her whole body going limp, and I cannot hold her up. As soon as I let go of her, I see there's something else wrong. This girl, whether she's Chrissy or not, is dying right before my eyes, and the country people are gathering around me in a circle. They're angry. I try to protest that I didn't do anything wrong, but I can see they don't believe me. I look down at the girl on the ground, and I know that this really is Chrissy. There's a gaping black hole in her forehead. She's wearing the same yellow sweater, and it's covered with the dark brown stain of her blood. And her legs are mangled, twisted backwards and broken.

I wake up in a sweat.

The same dream comes to me night after night until it finally occurs to me that I can no longer escape into my sleep-world.

She won't let me.

Epilogue

March 15, 1966

Last night over dinner I told my family that I had decided to take a job with Head Start. After I explained what that meant, my father went red in the face, called me "a traitor to my race," and added, "If you're going to be teaching niggers how to take jobs away from whites, then you'd better start looking for someplace else to live." My mother stared helplessly as my father and I glared at each other across the table, and then she began to cry. She dropped her napkin over her food and left the table. My five younger brothers and sisters sat in shocked silence as I told him, okay, if that's what he wanted, I would move out as soon as I could find a place for Andrea and me.

Later on that evening, the house ominously quiet, my mother came to my room in her nightgown and slippers, sat on the edge of my bed, and said, "If this is what you really want to do, then do it. I'll help you with Andrea. I just want you to do what's right for you."

She held my hand in hers; she was shaking.

June, 1966

My first day of real classes, with the door to my classroom closed, I stand to one side and peek out at the parents walking their children across the hardscrabble yard. Polished black shoes, print dresses. Dressed for work. Some bend down and hug their kids; others just push them through the gate where a swirling force of six-year-olds is gathering inside the chain link fence guarding the entrance way. There is a tiny bit of grass on one side of the sidewalk next to the broken water fountain. As the kids run and play across the beaten-down landscape, as I think how I came to be standing where I am, a Zen poem comes to mind, "Barn's burnt down—Now I can see the moon."

I have been told I am the only white male in the state of Alabama working as a teacher for Head Start. I don't know if it's true or not, but I have seen no other males, white or black. Certainly there have been none in our teachers' meetings. Bending over, I look through a cracked window pane of the door and watch as the kids, in a strange overlay of perspectives, seem to leap across time and space, moving from one side of the crack to the other. As I watch, in a trick of shifting images, I see my own watery reflection in the glass. I now have a full beard. It grew while I slept, and when I awoke there was a new me, a thin, bearded stranger. And here he is before me. Now as I look, I feel as if the kids and I belong together in this cracked image, in this transparency of glass. We are being given a new start...

The school bell rings. Time for classes to begin. Behind me are twelve small desks. I have arranged them in a semicircle around my chair. Behind their desks are tables covered with our new wooden alphabet and animal puzzles, with coloring books and crayons, with brightly colored ABC books for beginning readers. This is a summer-school program designed to prepare underprivileged children for first grade, which will begin in September. All of my children are black, most of them desperately poor and without a father in the home. None of the children has been to preschool or kindergarten. All are, or soon will be, six years old and come from the nearby communities south of the airport.

I open the door and walk out to gather in my twelve kids. I travelled by train to Howard University in Washington, D.C., and took classes in preparation for this day, and, for several weeks prior to this day, I walked the neighborhood, talked to parents, and tried to convince them that Head Start was a good deal, that their kids would benefit.

On a sweltering hot morning, coffee in one hand, handouts in the other, my white shirt already wet under the armpits, I found myself stepping inside the screen door of a one-bedroom, military-style barracks apartment. After my eyes had adjusted to the dark of the room, I noticed wrappers from fast-food restaurants and the strong smell of barbecue sauce and ammonia, and then the beautiful momma, maybe twenty-two years old, who'd invited me in. She was wearing nothing but a white slip, her brown skin almost glowing in the morning heat. She stood up straight behind an ironing board. In the dim light of the room I could see the back door was open for the breeze. She looked me over and then returned to her ironing, pressing the hot iron onto her dress. I waited for her to look up. Her nearly naked body moved in rhythm with her strokes as the point of her iron pressed into the pleated material. She stopped, looked at me, and stuck one long brown finger in her mouth, drew it slowly out, and then touched it to the surface of the hot iron. It sizzled. Then she gave me a full, warm, and generous smile, eyes sparkling, teeth showing. Her hair was piled up on her head in rollers.

"I gotsa get myself ready for work," she apologized and cast her eyes down in a confident coquettish grin, and then asked me if I was Robert Mitchum's son. The movie star.

I told her: No, I was a Head Start teacher, and I wanted to talk to her about her son.

She put down her iron. "Well, you look just like him."

I decided it was my beard.

She then asked me if I'd like to have a beer with her.

I told her I'd better not.

She turned back to her ironing and asked, "Well, what wuz it you wanted from me?"

I could tell she still thought I was Robert Mitchum's son, or somebody from Hollywood, so I decided to take advantage of that and told her I was here to tell her about the Head Start school starting in the summer, how it was going to be free, what a good deal it was going to be for her son, and how schooling and childcare for the summer wouldn't cost her a dime.

I handed her one of my pamphlets.

She looked it over as if she didn't quite believe me and said, "Well, how long can you keep him for?"

As I explained Head Start's hours, I found myself wondering about her complete trust in me, in what I was saying about the program, and in what I was promising to do for her son.

Could I live up to my promises?

Afterwards, with her signature on my parental agreement form (no father in the home), as I walked away from her house into the bright sunlight, the sidewalk already hot enough to fry an egg, she came out from behind her screen door and said, "You welcome to come back and see me sometime," and I knew I had a smile on my face that would last all day.

And now as my kids enter the room, I am ready. I start trying to match up faces with names. But they rush by me too fast, fluttering, noisy as a flock of skittish geese coming down for a landing. They won't stay still. Scattering around each other. Roaming the room. Climbing over desks. Sitting down under tables. Pushing and shoving, laughing and shouting. They seem to have no idea what is expected of them. And don't care. One little boy with a bandaged knee, name tag reading "Brandon," grabs for a little girl's pigtail. But before he can get hold and yank down, she turns around, her pleated skirt twirling, and without any hesitation, slugs him. And then Brandon laughs. Shoves her back. She's almost a head taller than he is, so, no fool, he runs away. She chases after him as he dodges behind other, bigger boys.

I shout for order, but it doesn't have any effect. I shout louder.

They turn towards me suspiciously, begin to settle down.

Quietly, with a low voice, I ask them to take their seats.

Some take a seat. A few continue roving around the classroom, opening boxes of crayons, thumbing through our stacks of storybooks, picking up alphabet puzzles, turning them upside down, laughing as the pieces fall out.

I go over, close the door.

Suddenly, in the closed room they stop talking and look at me. The room grows quiet.

"Please take your seats," I say again, softly.

Sudden minor chaos as a game of musical chairs ensues as they search for a seat.

After they sort out just who is to sit where, I go over and write my name on the chalkboard and then turn to face them.

Elaborate sets of pigtails adorn the girls' heads. The boys have close haircuts, freshly ironed shirts and big, wide, toothy grins. They all stare up. Big wide eyes. Suppressed excitement.

This is what I wanted. I know I can't go back to graduate school. I can't imagine trying to study. But this I can do. I can be here amongst these children. I can give them, however meager it might turn out to be, a chance, a head start.

I say, "My name is Mr. Andersen."

One hand starts up hesitantly in the front row. This boy is exceptionally good looking and has a great smile, even though he has more white teeth than his mouth seems capable of containing. His name tag says that his name is Dwight. His grin lights up the room as he looks back and forth from me to his classmates. Then, rising up in his desk onto his knees, looking back and forth between his buddies and me, he gains energy and confidence and begins waving one arm around in an exaggerated circle.

"Yes, what is it, Dwight? Do you have a question?"

The class goes suddenly silent.

Dwight crashes back down in his chair, faces me, and asks his question.

"Mr. Andersen...is you white?"

ENDNOTES

1. Excerpt from the author's poem, "Birmingham," which first appeared in the chapbook, *All Pieces of a Legacy,* published by the Berkeley Poets Workshop & Press, Berkeley, California, 1975.
2. *Carry Me Home: Birmingham, Alabama: The Climactic Battle of the Civil Rights Revolution,* author: Diane McWhorter, pp. 141, 151, Simon & Shuster, 2001.
3. Ibid., p. 203
4. Ibid., p. 259
5. Ibid., pp. 371, 373
6. *New York Times,* May 18, 2000. See article for pictures and story of indictment. C.E.
7. *Carry Me Home: Birmingham, Alabama, The Climactic Battle of the Civil Rights Revolution,* author: Diane McWhorter, pp. 571, Simon & Shuster, 2001.
8. *Time,* September 22, 2003, from an article by Tim Padgett and Frank Sikora titled "The Legacy of Virgil Ware."
9. *Carry Me Home: Birmingham, Alabama: The Climactic Battle of the Civil Rights Revolution,* author: Diane McWhorter, p. 465, Simon & Shuster, 2001.
10. Ibid., p. 531
11. *A Time To Speak,* author: Charles Morgan, Jr., pp. 166–167, Holt, Rinehart, and Winston, 1964.
12. http://www.historylearningsite.co.uk/1965_voting_rights_act.htm.
13. http://www.acf.hhs.gov/programs/hsb/about/history.htm.

Acknowledgments

I would like to thank the following:

The early readers of the manuscript who offered valuable critiques and encouraged me to go forward—my friends Kim Culbertson, Peter Sagebiel, Belden and Yashi Johnson, Judy Crowe, Eleanore Despina, Diane Perea, Steve Haimovitz, Art and Sue Duey, Karla Arens; my son Nathan Entrekin; and my wife, poet Gail Rudd Entrekin.

My editor, Kit Duane, whose encouragement and good suggestions were invaluable.

Diane McWhorter whose fine work, *Carry Me Home: Birmingham, Alabama: The Climactic Battle of the Civil Rights Revolution,* is a must read for anyone who cares to understand that period. Charles Morgan, whose *A Time To Speak* helped me, a young man living through that time, understand some of what went wrong in Birmingham. And Paul Hemphill for his *Leaving Birmingham* and Glenn T. Eskew for his *But for Birmingham,* which I read as background preparation for this book.

Photo by Steve Haimovitz

ABOUT THE AUTHOR

Born and raised in the Bible belt, in Birmingham, Alabama, Charles Entrekin has lived in Northern California for more than thirty years. Author of several collections of poetry, including *Casting for the Cutthroat*, and for two decades managing editor of the Berkeley Poets Workshop & Press, he is currently managing editor of Hip Pocket Press. *Red Mountain: Birmingham, Alabama, 1965*, is his first novel.